About the Author

Stuart Tidman was born in Coventry, England, in 1972 and grew up north of the city within the shadow of the M6 motorway. In 1995, he graduated from Coventry University, but is still yet to practice his qualification, as he couldn't be bothered to enter the real world and find a proper, real occupation. He has two sons from a previous marriage, and currently resides in the West Midlands with his fiancée and two pet cats. In his spare time, he gains increasing grey hair, bitten fingernails and high blood pressure watching Coventry City FC try to perform 'Association Football'.

The Nicholas Duncan Mysteries:
Everyday

Stuart Tidman

The Nicholas Duncan Mysteries
Everyday

Olympia Publishers
London

www.olympiapublishers.com
OLYMPIA PAPERBACK EDITION

A CIP catalogue record for this title is
available from the British Library.

ISBN: 978-1-80074-321-2

This is a work of fiction.
Names, characters, places and incidents originate from the writer's
imagination. Any resemblance to actual persons, living or dead, is
purely coincidental.

First Published in 2022

Olympia Publishers
Tallis House
2 Tallis Street
London
EC4Y 0AB

Printed in Great Britain

Dedication

For Caine and Jeff

This book is also dedicated to the memory of WPC Mandy Rayner of the Hertfordshire Constabulary. She was the first British female police officer — and to date still the youngest — to perish in the line of duty. Mandy died in October 1982 on board a police patrol car, hit by another vehicle driven by a drunk driver. She was eighteen years old, having been a constable for only five weeks.

Acknowledgements

Thank you to my fiancée, Debbie, for encouraging me to turn several tatty, coffee-stained notebooks into a readable story, rather than allowing it to waste away into the ether.

INTRODUCTION

Hello, and thank you for taking the time to read my work. If you'll indulge me for a few moments, I'd like to explain some of what you are about to read. This fictional story is set in a real part of British history, some fifty years ago. The language, attitudes and opinions expressed by some of the characters some readers will find uncomfortable and are thankfully out of touch with Society in the 21st Century. Having grown up through the 1970s myself, I know them to be true and reasonably accurate, but I have *'watered them down'* compared to what life was actually like.

Everyone should be free to live the life they wish, free from prejudice and derision. No one should have to face hostility over their race, gender, religion, sexual orientation, disability, nationality — anything. I have close friends and members of my own family, who in 1973 would have had infinitely more difficult everyday lives than in 2022 due to something back then that was considered *'not normal'*.

Compared to my main character, I'm a heterosexual, a non-smoker, happy to potter along with my hum-drum existence with little hassle and zero conflict. Nicholas Duncan has a level of confidence I would love to possess, an unquivering determination I dream to aspire to. Yes, part of him is me — we share the same sense of justice and protecting those who can't help themselves.

Hopefully you'll be back for the next instalment!
Stuart Tidman April 2022

PROLOGUE
TUESDAY APRIL 17th 1973

"How much further, Mark?" Yvonne Keogh tittered as the Riley Kestrel edged its way into the darkness.

"Not too far, sweetheart."

Mark West smiled at the leggy auburn-haired young woman in the passenger seat, winking at her. Yvonne beamed back at her date, leaning towards him and taking his left hand. Mark looked back at her and couldn't help but return her smile. With his hand now in the warm embrace of the breath-takingly stunning Yvonne, her fingers slowly beginning to entwine between his own, it was near impossible to change gear. Mark though didn't mind one bit. He gasped inwardly at the delicious sensation her touch caused, intense electricity racing across his skin which darted straight up his arm.

He never considered such an amazing looking woman would be this interested in him. He'd been filled with such a consuming level of anticipation leading up to the date, he struggled to think of little else. Mark had wanted to take Yvonne on a date since he'd first set eyes on her, perched behind the reception desk in the front office. He was staggered when she reciprocated his advances a couple of weeks earlier. Managing to borrow the car from his older brother, was the icing on the cake — especially as Chris had only bought the Riley three months earlier. Yvonne seemed way too classy to be hanging off the back of his motorbike — his faithful Royal Enfield Interceptor — although at the back of his mind lingered an image of her in full leather catsuit a la Suzi Quatro. The image had piqued on more than one occasion within his fantasies. His favourite day-dream was of undoing the full-length zip on the catsuit, and running his hands inside…

Mark had also decided to wear the Avon aftershave he'd received as a gift from Auntie Paula last Christmas. Chris had advised him it would work like a charm, despite Mark's reservations about the fragrance making him smell like a girl. So far, Chris had been absolutely right.

He had a hunch Yvonne was keen on him too from the moment she had first set eyes on him. As his parked his bike in full view of reception, peeling off his leathers and helmet, Mark had wanted his exhibition to become the highlight of every morning for her. He imagined her waiting for the sudden roar of his bike as it exploded into the car park, waiting for him to come to a stop right in front of her, watching him climb off the machine and begin his dismounting ritual. He deliberately went through his 'show' as slowly as possible knowing she was watching, having caught her giving him her undivided attention on several occasions. With his near neck length hair in a centre parting, he did bare more than a passing resemblance to American singer David Cassidy. Rather than being a 'handsome' man, Mark was more 'beautiful' — as was Mr Cassidy.

The engine note of the Riley, dropped to tick over, as Mark depressed the clutch pedal and coasted along. Through the near darkness, he could still make out the tips of Yvonne's immaculately manicured fingernails peeping out from between his chunky digits. As they passed under another street light, he gazed at her again. *"You look gorgeous,"* he couldn't help but think. He drank in every detail he could absorb — the pair of slight blemishes in her tight-fitting top where her nipples were, how she was barely capable of crossing her long, slender legs due to her skirt being so fitted around her curvaceous hips, the way her long hair was styled around her face, and above all how her excellently applied cosmetics made her eyes something he wanted to fall into and remain for some time, and as for her lips... The size of his smile was clearly giving away what he was contemplating in no uncertain terms, as Yvonne giggled.

Quickly returning his attention to their direction of travel, Mark flicked the car's headlights onto full beam as all street lighting had now ceased, being on a back lane near the edge of the city. At once, the road in front was brighter. The slight downhill gradient of the lane assisting their travel forwards, allowing the car to roll along.

"Just a little further — there's a private spot along here where we shouldn't be disturbed."

Mark cooed softly, still staggered his advances were being so well received. Yvonne continued to titter softly.

"Where are you taking me, Mark West?"

He had been the consummate gentleman all evening, if a tad cheeky in an inoffensive, but saucy way proving he wasn't completely a boy scout. It was clear to him Yvonne liked that — a confident guy who could treat a lady right, but had that exciting, somewhat naughty glint in his eye as well.

"Just a quiet place I know, where we can be on our own."

He tried his utmost to sound as confident as possible, hoping his nerves weren't showing.

"I like the sound of that."

15

Yvonne whispered into his ear, squeezing his hand tighter.

Now finding his left leg beginning to shake at the strain of keeping the clutch pedal down, Mark fortuitously managed to knock the gear stick into neutral with his thumb, releasing the clutch completely but covering the brake with his right foot. *"That's better,"* Mark reflected, *"Don't want her to think I'm shaking with nerves."*

Then, much to his surprise, Yvonne let go of his left hand and placed it on his inner thigh. From nowhere, Mark felt an incredible sensation inside. Something began to build from deep within his core, that gained intensity and started to fill his whole being with wonder. Alongside this sense of euphoria, a physical aspect began. A steadily growing bulge in his trousers emerged, the excitement of what may lay ahead getting the better of him. He fidgeted in his seat, trying his utmost to disguise the rapidly increasing erection. The awkwardness of his active member inside his tight clothing was offset against the glorious feeling it gave. *"She's bound to notice,"* he mused to himself, and perhaps she had. Stroking his inner thigh, Yvonne's hand ran up his leg till it fleetingly brushed the tip of his member. Using all the self-control he could muster, Mark somehow prevented himself from exploding on the spot, but could do nothing about his bulge growing further.

The car drifted effortlessly along, past a near deserted gas works into a secluded back lane. The headlights of the car illuminated a small recess in the hedge, a cutting used as a passing place for bigger vehicles. It was cut deep enough into the undergrowth so the car could be hidden from view. Completely unexpectedly, the same bright headlights made out a shape in the road. Braking abruptly, Mark brought the car to such a sudden stop, Yvonne could do no other than take her gaze away from her beau and onto the mysterious item in front of them.

"What is it, Mark?"

"I'm not sure. Maybe someone has ran over a dog or a badger and failed to stop."

Mark quickly applied the handbrake, and stepped out of the car.

Walking slowly over to the unknown object, he glanced nervously over his shoulder back at Yvonne watching from the safety of the car. Crouching, he gingerly reached out. Touching it lightly, he moved as though in a trance. Abruptly, the young man recoiled. Leaping upright in an instant, he sprinted back to the car for all his worth as though the devil himself was chasing him.

"What was it? What's the matter, Mark?"

Yvonne began to equal the distress shown on her date's face as he jumped back behind the wheel. Mark's expression had contorted into horror, all colour had drained from his face. Any prospect of anything illicit that night was now the furthest thing from his mind.

"It's a Paki — a young woman — about the same age as you!"

He tried to gulp, but his throat was now drier than he'd even known.

"I think she's dead! We need to call the police!"

Heaving a few times, he did his utmost to control the acidic taste in the back of his mouth. Swallowing hard several times again, he hoped the nausea would dissipate.

"There's a public telephone in the Bantam pub, just back inside Hen Lane."

Mounting the opposite verge in his haste — he'd explain

17

the clods of earth and undergrowth now affixed to the front bumper to his brother another time — Mark turned the car around on the narrow lane. Moving at a speed the car was never intended for, he shot straight to the pub. Coming to an emergency stop outside the main doors, the car left the next two months wear of rubber off the tyres as skid marks. Leaping out of the car and running into the pub, Yvonne dashed after Mark for comfort as the reality of the situation began to sink home, but he was already at the bar on the payphone, dialling *'999'*.

CHAPTER ONE
TUESDAY APRIL 17th 1973

A wooden door, well painted in sky blue gloss. The paint several coats thick, having been applied with loving attention to detail repeatedly many times over many years. Many decades, in fact. In the background, a large football crowd were chanting, singing, then groaning in unison, as an opportunity was missed by the home team. A man's fist, protruding from a quality cloth grey sleeve knocked at the sky-blue door several times. There was no response. He tried again, this time with added vigour.

"All right, all right — hold your horses! Where's the sodding fire?" A muffled, elderly male voice shouted from inside.

After a prolonged rattle of keys, a stubborn lock reluctantly slid across. The sky-blue painted door creaked open to reveal an elderly man in his mid-sixties, shabbily dressed, wearing a flat cap that really needed disposing of and replacing. Before he got chance to say another word, a police warrant card, was thrust into his face, causing him to recoil slightly.

"Detective Sergeant Nicholas Duncan, Warwickshire Police. And this is Detective Constable Joan Cavanagh."
The man attired impeccably sharp, gestured in the direction of an appealing long-haired brunette, standing behind him. The

dark brown near black colour of the woman's hair was offset by her near porcelain white skin and deep blue jewel-like eyes. Complimenting her natural appearance, she was dressed as equally as fashionably as her colleague. Duncan noticed the old man perform a double take upon initially setting eyes on the constable — he had witnessed this several times before over the last year or so he had worked with her, many people remarking upon her likeness to the actress Lesley Anne Down.

"Police? Why don't you just go around to the Main Stand and blag your way in there, like the rest of your mates?"

Nick pondered if the elderly man could ask a question with any more disdain.

"I need to find a colleague — he's inside. Pardon me."

The detective pushed his way through the narrow doorway before the older man had chance to invite him through, with the attractive brunette following closely in his wake.

"That's what they all say! The match is nearly over, anyhow!"

Moving into the ground, the crowd continued chanting and bemoaning the state of the eyesight of the referee, the detectives were faced with a substantial flight of concrete stairs heading upwards. The stairs appeared to head right up to the heavens, high into the sky which was not inky black interspersed with the silver pin-pricks of stars, but was an unnaturally artificial deep purple caused by the match day night-time lighting. Joan gazed upwards at the floodlight pylon they passed — the harsh temporary lighting was even confusing birds that had nested in the stanchion. They fluttered here and there, baffled whether it was sunrise or sunset. Duncan made his way briskly up the stairs, his slate grey overcoat billowing out and flapping behind like a cape.

20

Halfway up he stopped, glanced over his shoulder back down at his Constable.

"Come on, Joan!"

As quickly as she could, she trotted up the stairs after him. Catching their breath at the top, they were now confronted by a wall of people, swaying and moving like waves breaking on the shore.

"Whereabouts will he be, like?"

Cavanagh raised her voice to be heard over the noise of the assembled mass, which had the desired effect as Duncan heard the constable, but could see her thick Scouse accent was turning several heads in the crowd.

"Underneath the scoreboard, if my memory serves me correctly."

Duncan semi-shouted in her direction, with which he promptly evaporated amidst the throng as it swallowed him whole. Losing sight as to where Joan was, he paused. It was rather overwhelming — a wall of bodies swaying this way and that, moving as though it was one living entity. A split second later, a gap appeared. The detective had just enough clearance to get his head and shoulders out of the melee. Forcing himself between two large men, he saw the Scouse Constable, somewhat taken back.

"Joan — this way — don't dawdle!"

He grabbed her hand pulling her into the scrum.

"I bet this takes you back to undertaking matchday duties at Anfield and Goodison Park."

The two detectives continued to barge and force their way through the densely packed bodies.

"Aren't you a Sky Blues supporter, Sarge? After all, didn't you say you grew up here."

"Oh, no — not at all. Football doesn't interest me. Motor racing is my thing."

Bumping and bouncing off countless others, people around them formed unexpected walls as though a particularly fiendish maze had developed sentience and was trying its utmost to entrap them. Briefly, Cavanagh caught a glimpse of the Highfield Road pitch, brilliantly lit up like a championship snooker table, the green grass more than resembling the lush baize. Joan began to pause, watching the action on the field of play, the home side under the cosh as the visiting team in their all-scarlet kit pinned them back.

"Isn't that Pete Cormack and Kevin Keegan?"

Nick glanced back at his colleague. Cavanagh was now standing right on tip toes, craning her neck as much as possible. He could clearly see she was becoming engrossed in the match, speaking out loud without fully realising what she was saying. A tall skinny man within earshot obviously had.

"Yeah! They've been ripping us apart all night! Flaming Scousers!"

The sergeant grinned broadly at hearing what had just been said to the face of a native Merseysider. The tall man grinned sheepishly, no doubt realising the same. Joan glared back, about to retort when Duncan pulled her along once again.

"What about yourself? Are you an Everton supporter?"

Nick knew this would get her heckles up further. The way the whole of her face lit up at seeing her home town team in action showed exactly where her allegiances lay. Duncan glanced at the constable over his shoulder with a cheeky glint in his eye, still holding her hand towing her through the crowd.

"Everton my arse!"

Cavanagh replied with as much venom as she could muster, which he found all the more amusing as she cursed in the slight two-tone style her native accent caused.

"Liverpool are my team. Me Arl Fella used to take me to Anfield to see them play when I was little like, standing on the Kop. You never said they were here tonight?"

The brunette spun her head around towards the pitch again, now bouncing up and down on the spot between much taller people to try to gain a glimpse of play.

Duncan quickly noticed Joan was suddenly very distracted — alarmed, appalled and disgusted, all at the same time. Rapidly she let go of Nick's hand, turning on her heels, and confronted two chunky men behind her grinning ear-to-ear. Whipping her warrant card out, she pushed it into their smug, fat faces.

"Do that again you Gobshites, and I'll have you arrested, taken down the cells, and I'll stamp on your bollocks 'till they burst!"

The two men, shocked at the reaction from not just a woman, but a Woman Detective Constable too, attempted to melt into the crowd. Occupied with more pressing matters, Cavanagh put her warrant card away and caught up with Duncan.

"Some folk would pay good money for what you just announced to the world, there.

Joan glared at Nick fiercely, not finding his comment remotely amusing in the slightest. Nor the daft smirk rapidly spreading across his face, Nick surmised.

"Guv!"

The sergeant shouted forwards entering a less densely packed area, seeing the person he was looking for — a man in his late fifties, attired in a smart overcoat and trilby hat — his senior officer, Detective Inspector Albert Edwards.

The older man was a long-established and much respected police detective, his face clearly showing he'd seen the distasteful side of life on more occasions than what was palatable. Others would say his facial appearance had 'character' or appeared 'lived in'. Nick compared the inspector's face to an over-used leather chamois that someone was sentimentally attached to and could not bring themselves to throw away. Duncan had immense respect for his superior, Edwards having been part of the sergeant's life for many years. As a younger man, the inspector had been shown the ropes within the then Coventry Police, by a certain Robert Duncan — his future Sergeant's father when he was demobbed from the Royal Marines some twenty-seven years earlier. Immediately, Nick experienced a flashback from his past.

The sound of the key being thrust into the lock and turned echoed along the parquet floored hallway. This was not lost on Nick and his older brother Alex. They knew Dad was home. Alex leapt up from his Meccano crane kit and ran for the door. Busy trying to complete a jigsaw of Muffin the Mule, Nick did the same. The chase was on — he had to beat his older sibling to the door and greet Dad first. He leapt to his feet and ran for all his worth.

"Dad! Dad's home!"

Alex cried excitedly at the top of his voice, so the whole house was aware. The two young boys raced into the hall, Nick eager to keep up. He struggled for grip on the smooth, polished wooden floor, his sock covered feet slipping here and there as he attempted to accelerate.

"Alex! Wait for me!"

As siblings do, Nick even at his tender years knew his brother heard him, but ignored the request. The younger Duncan knew Alex had already decided he was going to greet Dad first at the door.

"Alexander! Nicholas! What have I told you both about running through the house?"

Their mother's voice fell on deaf ears, as the brothers could clearly see through the frosted glass of the front door two large shapes dressed in dark blue.

The door gently opened, revealing two tall men dressed in the deep, dark blue uniform of the police, one with sergeant stripes on his sleeves. The single-breasted tunics were immaculate, with shiny silver buttons, their own personal numbers on their collar right under the chin. The outfit was completed with the infamous helmet. The Brunswick Star which resided on the front of the custodian helmet, rather than being shiny like the buttons on the tunic was still 'blacked out' and dull from the War a few short years earlier. It required the onlooker to get quite close to the officer wearing the headgear to read *'Coventry Police'* upon the helmet plate.

"How are my little soldiers?"

Sergeant Robert Duncan asked his offspring gleefully, taking his helmet off and stooping to embrace the two boys. The two little lads jumped into their father's arms, all three of them hugged each other warmly. Quick as a flash, Alex took his father's helmet and placed it upon his small, child head — it virtually dropping down to his shoulders, he had to hold it up with one hand over his eyes to in order to see. He raced off back into the house to show his mother.

Nick watched his brother tear away back into the room from where they had come. The little boy spun around to his father looking glum, feeling really sorry for himself. He wanted to wear Dad's helmet, but there was no chance of that now — Alex would never relinquish it. Bob rubbed his younger son's head, soothingly.

"Next time, Nick — you'll be first next time."

Bob wandered off into the back room, chuckling, where Alex was being quite vocal as he pretended to be the best policeman ever. Nick stared up at the tall man who had arrived at the house with his father.

The man crouched down, removed his own helmet and smiled at the little boy.

"Hello Nick — I'm Albert."

He reached forwards, placing his own helmet onto the boy's head. Instantly, Nick's face lit up with unexpected joy, as he smiled broadly while trying to lift the helmet high enough in order to peer from underneath.

"Thanks Mister!"

The constable can't help but laugh.

"Call me Albert!"

Without warning, the sound of an animated football ground filled the hall way, causing both Nick and Albert to look into the house.

The sergeant returned to present day with a snap as the Sky Blue faithful urged their side on. The inspector's attention was solely focused on the game panning out in front of him, completely oblivious to all and sundry around him. That was until he all of a sudden became aware two of his detectives were approaching.

"Nick! What the hell are you doing here?"

Distracted, Edwards tried to re-focus on the match, just as the entire crowd groaned in unison vehemently in huge disappointment at yet another missed chance. Edwards remonstrated further at the top of his voice.

"Fuck me, Stein! My grandmother could've scored from there wearing carpet slippers!"

Cavanagh hopelessly tried to stifle her laughter at the inspector's outburst, receiving a disapproving look.

"And you can button it, Cilla Black."

Between giggles, Joan tried to apologise.

"Aye, Sir. Sorry Guv."

"And as for you Nick, fancy bringing a woman to a match! That's really jinxed it!"

Coughing to regain his composure and cover his own mirth, Duncan began. *"Ahem! Guv, uniform have found the body of an Asian adult female near Foleshill Gas Works. They've already sealed off the scene. The chief Inspector wants you to be C.I.M."*

Realising the gravity of Nick's words, Edwards' face changed instantaneously.

"I'll be right with you after this. There're only a few minutes left. Stay if you like, or I'll meet you outside."

Once again, the crowd become loudly animated, with some of the people around them more resembling the audience ringside at a prize boxing bout, urging the two fighters on.

"We'll wait in the car Guv, if it's all the same."

Duncan turned to head back towards the exit.

"Are City playing well, Guv?," Cavanagh asked.

"They're trying, but Liverpool are just too good for them." Edwards grumpily replied in a clipped tone.

"I'd love to see City beat Bill Shankly's side."

"What's the score?"

"2–1 to Liverpool. They're good. Really good. They should win the League and UEFA Cup this season."

The inspector answered painfully, in a manner those listening would believe he was enduring severe toothache.

"Sound!" Cavanagh began to crack a huge grin, at Edwards despondent comments.

"Come on, Joan."

Duncan urged the constable to follow him, tugging at her sleeve. Cavanagh sighed heavily, following Nick back into the crowd.

The same sky blue painted wooden door as before opened abruptly, spilling the two detectives back onto Swan Lane. Duncan strode out into the road itself, not bothering with the pavement, beginning to search through his pockets as he headed towards a row of parked cars. Joan had to walk near double-time to keep up with the long gait of her taller superior.

"We could've stayed to the end of the match, Sarge."

Duncan pulled his right hand from his pocket, to reveal an immaculate packet of Park Drive cigarettes. In one smooth action, he slid open the left side of the packet only to find it empty. Sighing in disappointment, he promptly opened the right side, revealing six cigarettes. Cooing in approval, he selected one and placed it between his lips.

"Stay till the end? And watch you arrest anyone who dare brush against your backside?"

Nick couldn't help but grin, trying to stifle a laugh as well. Karma nearly bit him back straight away, as he only just managed to stop himself from dropping his cigarette.

"It's no laughing matter, Nick. What makes it acceptable

for a woman to be treated that way?"

The way Cavanagh spoke, obviously a nerve had clearly been struck. Or was she just that feisty? Duncan deduced maybe a bit of both.

"Joan, I whole-heartedly agree. Just promise me you'll never transfer to the Met in London. You'll break all records for arrests just on your first morning commuting to work on the Tube!"

The scouser pulled a face at the sergeant, but he was too lost searching his pockets for his lighter to notice.

Approaching the parked cars, Duncan stopped next to the driver's door of the first one outside the Mercer's Arms — a bronze Series II Alvis TD21. The luxurious motor was in impeccable condition, gleaming seductively in the half-light generated by the nearby floodlights of the football stadium.

Nick had owned the car for a couple of years now, the Alvis holding a special place in his heart due to him inheriting it from his mother's older brother, his Uncle Eddie. Duncan had even kept the car's given name which his uncle had bestowed upon it — Alice — named after his aunt. Every time he set eyes on the car, he recalled travelling with his uncle to the Alvis factory to collect it brand new ten years previous.

"Well Mr Lawson, if you'd like to sign there, there and there, we're all done."

The salesman urged Edward Lawson to complete his part of the paperwork. The gentleman in his mid-sixties, dressed extremely dapper and suave, picked up said paperwork slowly and mulled over it one final time. Nick watched his uncle, and could see he was trying with all his worth to prevent the huge smirk he was desperate to show

appearing on his face. He adored the way Uncle Eddie dressed, always attired in the most stylish clothes. On his own modest income, he endeavoured to dress in a similar manner.

"Just a moment, young man. A gentleman cannot rush these things." Eddie gave his nephew a cheeky smirk and winked.

The salesman shuffled in his seat, eager to look approachable and friendly. However, his polite composure and poise were clearly wearing severely thin with this customer. Nick thought his uncle would test the patience of a saint, as he was so fastidious over every detail of his new car it wasn't amusing any longer. He felt sorry for the salesman, Paul Dickinson. *"Thank God I don't have to serve Uncle Eddie,"* Duncan contemplated.

After a brief silence, Eddie announced *"Yes, everything seems to be in order,"* taking a fountain pen from his inside pocket and began to sign the documents — but stopped abruptly.

"The price stated here — 3,968 guineas, 7 shillings and three-pence?"

Paul's gaze conveyed how perplexed he was. *"Yes, Sir — that's the price as quoted with the additional extras you requested prior to manufacture."*

Eddie rubbed his clean-shaven chin, mulling this over as he read the sale document and his order instructions once again.

"I tell you what young man. Knock off the loose change, and we have a deal."

Nick didn't know where to look, and was trying his best not to laugh out loud at the cheek of his uncle. Paul was dumbfounded for a few moments at this. It took a while for him to regain his composure.

"*Well... er... I think we might be able to do something, Mr Lawson.*" Not wishing to lose a high value sale at the final hurdle, the salesman clammered for something to say.

"*Excellent!*"

Eddie promptly crossed out the shillings and pence part of the price on the document, and signed it. Pleased this long, drawn-out process was over, the much-relieved Mr Dickinson took the paperwork and hastily placed it in a drawer of his desk.

"*Shall we go take a peek at what you're taking home?*" Paul began to rise from his seat, and gestured to the desk. In front of them were three keys attached to a brand-new black leather key fob, printed on which was a red inverted triangle. Embossed in gold within the triangle was the manufacturer's name — Alvis. Nick reached forward and took the keys, handing them to his uncle. "*Yours, I believe.*" This time, the elder gentleman now allowed himself to smile as he held the keys.

Eddie and Nick followed the salesman from his office, through a labyrinth of corridors, and outside onto the small, tight car park mainly used by senior management and directors, or — as in this case — highbrow customers collecting their pride and joy. Traffic busily made its way past in both directions to and from the city along the main arterial 'A' road, the Holyhead Road where the Alvis works were based. Nick couldn't take his eyes off his uncle. The elder gentleman stood in a trance, absorbing every detail of the car in front of him — a brand new Series II TD21, finished in bronze with chrome wire wheels. The Alvis shone in the early spring sunshine, not an imperfection to be seen. Eddie began to wander around the car, gently running his fingertips along its sleek flanks, across the bonnet to the chrome grill.

"As you can see, Sir, the car is exactly as to your instructions."

The salesman pandered with as much smarm as he could muster. Eddie walked around the car again, keys in hand, eventually stopping at the driver's door, pausing.

"Nicholas, could you do me a favour please?"

"Of course, Uncle."

Nick spoke, but was unsure of what Eddie had in mind. The older man beckoned him forwards. Eddie reached out a clenched fist — holding something, Duncan instinctively placed his own hand underneath. Eddie opened his hand and dropped the keys to the new car into his nephew's. Nick stared open mouthed at the keys in his hand. Uncle Eddie had only just bought the car, and was giving him the privilege to drive it first! He began to smile broadly, the grin spreading rapidly across his face.

"Really, Uncle Eddie? You want me to drive it first?"

Nick couldn't believe it. He stood there open-mouthed.

"It?" Eddie exclaimed with disgust. *"Please — treat this lady with some respect! Nick, this is Alice — Alice, this is Nick."*

The suave gentleman strolled around to the passenger side of the car as he finished speaking. *"Alice..."* Nick uttered from behind his smirk. He stared across the roof of Alice at his uncle, only to find Joan Cavanagh standing there.

Joan was briefly checking the condition of her make up in her reflection on the bodywork, it having been polished to such a high sheen, a man could have his morning shave with ease in the mirror-like surface. Delving into his pockets again, Nick eventually found his keys, but still no lighter. Letting himself into the car, Nick pushed the cigarette lighter into the console, while slotting the ignition key into its barrel and turned it clockwise. With a pronounced roar, the straight-six engine erupted into life, before quietened to a barely audible purr of an overfed contented cat. Alongside this, the in-car eight track player started, piercing the quiet in the car with Gene Vincent's hit song *'Blue Jean Bop'* mid-way through.

"Can't we listen to something else, like? You were making my ears bleed singing 'Be Bop-A-Lula' on the way over." Joan protested in her usual sarcastic, sense of humour. *"In fact, I think you should seriously consider going on 'Opportunity Knocks' as a new form of torture!"* In cod public announcer voice, she added, *"Play this to your kids to keep them away from the fire!"*

Without waiting for Nick to reply, the constable switched off the 8 track, and flicked on the car radio. Crackling through the static could be heard Glam-rocker Alvin Stardust with his latest release *'My Coo-Ca-Choo'*.

"Now he's got potential."

Duncan approved of the modern tune, tapping the steering wheel in time to the beat.

With a loud *'clack'*, the cigarette lighter handle popped back out of the console. Duncan swiftly lit his cigarette still gripped between his lips. He exhaled bluey-grey smoke from his nose, taking the cigarette from his mouth with his right hand. The Park Drive tasted good, giving him focus on what may lay ahead that evening. Cavanagh entered into a bout of lame amateur dramatics, beginning to feign a cough. She waved her hand side-to-side to clear any smoke away from herself.

"I know it's your car, Sarge but can't you at least open a window?"

Hearing his Constable's words, Duncan elaborately and deliberately took a theatrically long draw on his tobacco, looking at his passenger out of the corner of his eye, exhaling more bluey grey fog from his nostrils.

"If you don't mind."

Begrudgingly, Nick rolled down the window on the driver's door, hung his right hand out of the car and exhaled the remaining contents of his lungs into the cold night air.

"Ta, Sarge."

"Anything to oblige."

Equally as sarcastic, Duncan retorted with a forced sick grin.

"I don't envy any guy who may enter into a relationship with, Joan. You're soooooo demanding!"

Not waiting for a response from his colleague, Duncan switched the radio off. Silence filled the car heavily as the music was cut short. Reaching for the lower centre console, Duncan lifted what appeared to be a telephone handset receiver. Placing it to the left side of his face, he flicked a switch on the dashboard, using his right hand still with burning cigarette between his fingers. Cavanagh frowned at the cigarette in close proximity to her once again.

"Mike One, this is Mike Zulu Two, over."

After some initial static, a female voice speaking in a thick

Black Country accent was heard.

"Go ahead, Sarge, over."

"I've located D.I Edwards, proceeding to crime scene, over."

"Understood Mike Zulu Two. Mike Zulu Three already in attendance at scene. Will inform him Mike Victor Two and yourself enroute. Mike One Out."

Nick flicked the same switch into the opposite position with a loud *'click'*, returning the receiver back to the console.

"Fantastic! He's already there!"

Duncan cursed through gritted teeth.

"Detective Sergeant Sebastian St John?"

"Yes! That Scottish arse — "

His words are cut short as suddenly the huge doors on the side of the stadium burst open, allowing thousands of supporters to spill out onto the corner of Swan Lane and Thackall Street. Some darted across the road, making a bee-line for the pub. As the mass of bodies swarmed past on both, the sergeant was forced to bring his right hand back inside complete with cigarette, still smouldering. Sensing his Constable's disapproval and her stare burning into the side of his head as equal as the cigarette itself being pushed into his temple, he began to extinguish the burning tobacco in the ash tray in an over exaggerated manner.

"Sorry."

Abruptly, the passenger door of the Alvis opened.

"Get in the back, Madam — age before beauty!"

Edwards declared matter of factly. Reluctantly, the Liverpudlian stepped out of the car, then climbed into the back. Unexpectedly Joan stumbled, slightly catching herself on the bottom frame edge of the folded seat.

"Oh, for Fuck's Sake! This sodding old car of yours! I've just laddered my tights!"

"I'm forever reminding you to be more careful, young lady." Edwards folded the seat back into position, removed his hat and climbed into the car alongside Duncan.

"Right — off to the crime scene!"

The sergeant put the car into gear moving away smoothly, performing a 'U' turn with a dexterity that defied the cumbersome size and nature of the luxurious motor. This was no mean feat — as Nick needed to avoid the mass of bodies heading away from the stadium in the road. They edged forwards gingerly at walking pace.

"Is this old bucket fitted with a siren, Nick?"

"Yes, Guv. And less of the 'old' — Alice has barely reached her tenth birthday."

"Ya Wha? Alice?" A female Scouse voice giggled from the backseat. *"This barge has a name!"*

Ignoring the constable's outburst, the Guv'nor growled.

"Then may I suggest we sodding well use said siren, or we'll be here all pissing night!"

"Good idea, Sir!"

While Duncan spoke in a forced upper-crust British accent, reminiscent of the Pathe News announcers in the cinemas, he reached towards the console and flicked a switch, whereby a two-tone Police siren screamed out into the road ahead. *"You've got to admit, Nick — it's like a stately home in here."* Edwards pointed at the veneered walnut dashboard, hand-sewn leather trimmings, and clock that would not have seemed out of place in Kensington Palace.

"I could've sworn when I climbed inside, I could hear that clock tick over the sound of the engine! I haven't the privilege

of that in my Riley!"

Once again, Cavanagh tried not to laugh at the Guv'nor's comments, but found her fidgeting on the beige leather upholstered back seat made low squeaking sounds that resembled uncontrollable flatulence. This just fuelled her mirth further. Like Moses parting the Red Sea, the siren and discreet flashing blue lights hidden in the car's fog lights cleared the crowd. Duncan blipped the accelerator, to which the large car leapt forward like the proverbial scolded cat and set off at pace into the night.

"She's a stately home that can lift her skirt and run, Guv."

Minutes later, the bronze Alvis came to a halt in front of a Police cordon, having traversed across the city at a speed only the Warwickshire Fire Brigade would normally entertain in a built-up area when on a 'shout'.

"Do you think you're in an episode of 'The Persuaders' or something, Nick?" Edwards mocked his Sergeant. *"Your father always said you were a bit tasty behind the wheel, but bloody hell!"*

Duncan couldn't help but give his Inspector a sheepish glance, mouthing silently the words, *"Sorry Guv."*

"I take it back, like" Cavanagh added, releasing her grip on the top of the two seats in front of her, where she had hung on for all her worth. *"Alice isn't antwacky at all — she can fly!"*

The Inspector grunted in disapproval.

Approaching the cordon on foot, the three detectives were stopped by two uniform constables standing next to their Ford Escort panda car, it's flashing blue lights causing a strange strobe effect on the nearby buildings and undergrowth. Further down the country lane, the only real lighting offered was unintentionally provided from the nearby gas works, which caused more shadows than it prevented.

"Sorry folks — Police incident — the road is closed at the moment," the WPC on the cordon informed them.

"I sodding well hope so!"

Edwards produced his warrant card. The PC on the cordon shined his torch onto it, both he and the WPC read its details. They both quickly looked up at the senior detective and smiled nervously.

"Apologies, Sir." The PC quickly back pedalled.

"And these two are with me — my Sergeant and Constable." The Inspector gestured towards Duncan and Cavanagh.

"Very good, Sir."

Walking along in the near total darkness, the three detectives could see activity ahead of them. Numerous hand-held torches, and a couple of temporary battery powered lights poorly illuminated a shape on the roadside. Edwards marched towards the scene, the speed of his lumbering stride such Duncan could just about keep up, let alone Cavanagh. The Scouse detective stopped dead in her tracks, crouched and rubbed the calf on her left leg. Duncan paused too, noticing his colleague had halted.

"Are you all right?"

"I think that ancient old bucket of yours has not only torn my tights, but maimed me too!" Cavanagh barked at her superior, rubbing a graze on her leg several inches long.

"You could always ride in the boot next time."

"Piss Off!"

"Come along, children. Both of you — take as many notes

as possible. Nick — find Sebastian and establish what he's already gleaned."

"Yes, Guv," both younger detectives reply in unison.

Approaching the crime scene, several people were around a body lying in the gutter. One of them, a dark brown-haired man wearing an ill-fitting cheap brown suit, slowly stood up from crouching, beginning to scribble intently into his notebook. With a double take, he swiftly became aware of his three colleagues approaching, slid his notebook into the inside pocket of his jacket, and trotted straight towards the inspector.

"Guv! Good to see yer! How did City get on?"

St John greeted Edwards, attempting to be charming but came across more as smarmy, even speaking in his Glaswegian lilt. He glanced in the direction of Nick and Joan, looking down his nose. *"Typical,"* Duncan said to himself. *"Always trying to kiss arse".* Nick felt it needled his opposite number he had been promoted to sergeant three and a half years ago, just shy of his thirtieth birthday. St John, recently having become forty-two, did not receive his own promotion until he was in his mid-thirties. But at times it felt as though there was more to his ill-feeling towards him. The more worrying situation for Duncan was Sebastian had somehow learned about his life outside work. The repercussions of that were unthinkable

"Cut to the chase, Sebastian — what have we got?"

The inspector did not pander to the Scotsman's smugness.

"A Paki female — cuss be Indian — early twenties. Been strangled — a bit gruesome dis — wi' someas hands."

St John recited matter of factly from his hastily retrieved notebook, with unpleasant glee in his voice.

"Someone strangled her with their bare hands?"

Cavanagh exclaimed in disbelief, putting her hand to her mouth. Nick could see his colleague in the corner of his eye, seeing her say those words before she had realised.

"Aye, appears so. Definitely nae hit an' run as uniform fust fort. Marks left around her neck, but nae other injuries on initial inspection to say otherwise. Dissnae appear to be ane sexual assault."

Edwards and Duncan nodded as they listened, absorbing the details as quickly as they could.

"Cuss be a Tom?"

"Unlikely Sebastian."

The Guv'nor shook his head in disagreement.

"A young Asian female who's a prostitute? Not impossible but highly unlikely. Liaise with Nick please — I'm going to have a look around. Are SOCO on the way?"

Producing a small torch and switching it on, the inspector paused, waiting for an answer from the Scotsman.

"Enroute from Leek Wootton as wa speak, Guv — due ane minute. We're making preliminary notes an' preserving da scene fa their arrival. Da landshark team wa be here a' first light, to sweep da scene again fa anything wa missed. Plus, da drains wa need t' be checked too."

Edwards nodded in approval and strode onwards into the darkness, the beam of light from his torch turning this way and that, reminiscent of an errant lighthouse.

"Are yous still hanging onda da Guv'nor's shirt tails, Golden Bollocks?"

St John sneered at Duncan.

"Sticks and stones, Sebastian. Besides, I'd have expected you'd have more to be concerned about being a Jock!"

St John glared back at Duncan, seething.

"Sarge, is there anything else we need to know?"

Cavanagh quickly interjected addressing St John, attempting to defuse the growing hostility between the two sergeants.

"Wa need t' establish if aneone nearby noticed or saw anethin'. There's da Bantam pub a' bottom o' Hen Lane, a working men's club close by, plus a nearby scrap yard anna Gas Works. Plenty o' places t' begin."

St John began to cool down as he spoke.

"Well, uniform can undertake most of that. Plus, there's a fish and chip shop and pub up the road back towards Foleshill we passed on the way here. It'll be a good idea to organise that please, Sebastian."

Nick partially interrupted, becoming more professional.

"Let's take a look around, Joan."

The two detectives wandered in the direction of the partially lit crime scene, approaching slowly. They passed uniformed constables, searching the gutters and hedgerow as best as they could with hand-held torches in the darkness. Their progress slightly hindered by the cold night air causing infrequent clouds of warm breath to fog their torch beams. Cavanagh reached into her handbag and found her own compact torch, switching it on to illuminate the road in front of them.

As they walked closer to the scene, Duncan quickly produced a torch of his own from his coat pocket, and pointed it straight at the tarmac. Within the beam of light, a substance on the road had a sheen like the feathers on a magpie's back. Nick recognised immediately a trail of oil. Their splatter pattern had been formed at a steady, consistent rate trailing off along the tarmac. Duncan shone the torch back up the road to where they wandered come from. The spots of oil continued back towards the cordon in the same, steady pattern, still fresh.

"What's that on the road?"

Joan started to ponder out loud, as Duncan crouched down and dipped the fingertips into the substance. The sergeant slid the thick, dark coloured liquid between his finger and thumb, rubbing them together and smelt it.

"It's some sort of oil. Quite thick too. Not necessarily engine lubricant. Unless it's in dire need of changing, hence why it's all gungy."

"What makes you so certain, like?"

"You don't think Alice remains in such fine fettle by sheer luck alone, do you? I'm not immune from getting my hands dirty with a spanner when the need arises."

Duncan focused the beam of his torch towards where the unfortunate girl was lying. The spots of oil continued in that direction as well.

"Didn't St John say there's a scrap yard nearby? Something being towed there could've caused this."

"Possibly..."

The sergeant was not convinced. Standing up briskly, he cast the torch beam onto the splatter marks and followed them. They continued towards the deceased girl, forming a small puddle before moving off again away from the scene.

"I'd say our perpetrator has an oil leak on their vehicle, and I'd even be as bold to add its engine is in dire need of a service. This oil is filthy. However, it could be from the gearbox or rear axle from the scent of it."

Shining her torch onto her superior officer as he spoke, the detective began to wipe his fingers repeatedly on his handkerchief. After a few over-exuberant rubs, Nick found to his dismay some of the oil would not budge, leaving a rather unappealing stain on his skin, plus he'd most likely permanently stained the high-quality white cloth of the hanky. Unaware Edwards was close by and listening, the inspector's voice boomed out of the darkness.

"Just check these oil spots don't go straight to the scrap yard, as Cilla Black just surmised. Their wagon might've paused along here to allow traffic through — it's hardly as wide as a normal road."

The inspector stepped into the torch beams of his junior officers, before turning his own torch on.

"Of course, Guv."

Joan chirped up, snatching the torch out of Duncan's hand and following the trail of oil marks with a torch in each hand. Nick walked speedily after the Liverpudlian, briefly looking at the girl lying in the road, under the torch light from his colleagues. *"Quite pretty,"* he regarded to himself, *"What an absolute shame, whole life ahead of her."*

Eventually, he caught up with the constable a few yards after where the crime scene was.

"We don't know which direction the vehicle came to the scene from, do we?"

"May I?"

Without waiting for a reply, he reached inside the young constable's handbag.

"Oi! What are you after?"

After a brief rummage, Duncan removed a bottle of baby pink nail varnish. Unscrewing the lid, he began to pour the liquid as droplets while walking backwards.

"Nick! That stuff isn't cheap!"

Taking several paces backwards, the sergeant spun around

on the spot, and repeated the process in the opposite direction.

"If you carefully observe the pattern formed from the nail varnish, you'll see the drops form a certain shape when they hit the ground. Thus, revealing the direction of travel of the source."

Joan threw the beams of the torches upon the nail varnish splatter. Low and behold the drips did form a trace, splashing on the tarmac in a pattern that showed direction of travel of the origin.

"If you wanted to be really clever, it would be possible to work out the speed of the source from how close — or far apart — the drips are."

Duncan immediately knew the constable was losing interest, as he heard her sigh quite distinctly. He refrained from chuckling, as he guessed she was miffed her cosmetics were now being used in basic forensic analysis.

The Sergeant pointed at the closer together spots near the body of the girl, and how they spread further apart after, heading towards a nearby junction. The two detectives jogged towards the other cordon, passing through. The oil drips did not veer off to the right, so the vehicle wasn't heading for the nearby scrap yard nor the gas works entrance. As they walked on, their torch beams picking up the shiny spot-marks on the road continuing through another junction, under a train bridge and past the Bantam public house. The detectives found themselves on a residential street now under the gloomy street lighting from pre-war kerbside lamp-posts. Joan just managed to pull her superior back onto the footpath as a car appeared unexpectedly at speed, blasting its horn at them wandering in the carriageway. Nick gave the constable a sheepish glance, flicking his eyebrows upwards in gratitude. Absent-mindedly, he'd forgotten completely they were wandering around in the middle of the road.

A few hundred yards later, they came to a crossroads controlled by traffic lights. A small puddle of oil was here also, near the stop line. Joan peered into the distance along Holbrook Lane, towards the city centre.

"They must've waited at a red light, Sarge."

"Hmmm... very law abiding."

From here, the trail bore left — but inexplicably vanished a few short yards later. It was completely gone. Joan glanced at her colleague, most agitated.

"Where did it go?"

"Look!"

Duncan pointed down the street, at what he could see moving away from them at walking pace.

"The City Engineers finest!"

Further along the street passing a nearby British Leyland car dealership, was a council road sweeper scrubbing the gutter and left side of the road clean.

Upon walking back to the crime scene, they found the police doctor, Jocelyn Tyler had arrived along with three SOCO vehicles. Walking past the side door of a van being used as the incident unit, St John exited with two polystyrene cups of hot, steaming 'brown', and trotted towards Inspector Edwards. He flashed a disapproving look over his shoulder in Duncan's direction. Nick blew him a kiss in return. St John's demeanour, already dour, quickly darkened further.

"Yes, early to mid-twenties I'd say."

The Doctor informed the Inspector, the two of them crouched over the poor unfortunate girl lying in the gutter.

"On initial inspection, cause of death appears to be

strangulation, due to the bruising that's beginning to appear around her neck."

The Jamaican medic pointed at the areas of the girl's neck where dark patches were forming on the skin. SOCO officers continued to circulate around, taking photographs and measurements. Duncan noticed St John appeared to over enjoy all of this, liaising with SOCO beyond what was necessary, as though desperate to score 'brownie points'. Sebastian was a good copper, but flapped too much in his day-to-day work, in Nick's opinion. Plus, seemed too determined to appear better than Duncan to his peers. Nick found it amusing, and a little flattering — the older, more experienced Sergeant found him such a threat.

"Any idea of time of death, yet?"

"Not yet, Albert — I can hopefully calculate that once we get her back to Walsgrave and begin the post mortem. Beautiful girl — her life was just starting."

"The initial alarm was raised by a courting couple around 8.30pm, so we can confidently say before that. Any signs of sexual assault or being raped?"

"I can't say for sure here, will know for certain at the post mortem, but on initial inspection I'd say 'No'."

The Doctor gently rearranged the dead woman's clothes as a mark of respect, redressing her.

Hearing the Inspector and Doctor's words, Duncan scribbled into his own note book balanced on his knee, while holding his torch in his other hand to assist Dr Tyler. Nick noticed something in the gutter partially obscured under the poor girl's coat. Crouching, the sergeant carefully moved the edge of her coat with his silver cased ball point pen to reveal a cigarette butt. The dog end had a brown filter on the end with a gold stripe around. Nick gestured to a SOCO officer he knew well.

"Frank, take a few pics of this, please."

An officer came forward carrying a Leica M1 camera with flash attached. Just as Frank approached, Nick noticed something more — there was a scorch mark upon the girl's coat. Either she had been laid virtually on top of the still smouldering cigarette, or it had been discarded carelessly and rolled into her, slowly extinguishing. Several photos were taken from different angles, after which using a cloth from his kit, Frank collected the discarded cigarette.

"Marlboro Longhorn 100. See the Marlboro lettering just about legible on what's left of the cigarette above the filter?"

Duncan and Edwards leaned forwards and peered at the stub, seeing what the crime scene officer was referring to.

"Marlboro? Rather expensive and exclusive fags to be smoked in Coventry, don't you think?"

"I'd say." Nick agreed with his superior. *"Marlboro have recently began sponsoring some of the Formula One teams the last few years, so might explain why an American brand is becoming popular".*

Edwards listened to his Sergeant, as a logical air washed over his face. He nodded slightly, carefully pushed his trilby to the rear of his head as he studied the unfortunate girl laying before him more closely.

"Was this young lady carrying any identification? Purse? Driving licence?"

"Nae, Sir." St John spoke up, screwing his face up slightly as he recalled from memory, still juggling the two polystyrene cups of steaming, hot 'something'. *"Nae ID in her handbag. Juss some personal effects."*

"Well, what are they Sebastian?"

The Guv'nor was now beginning to become agitated and somewhat impatient. *"Berk,"* Duncan whispered under his breath. Quickly stopping a passing WPC and making her hold the two hot beverages, St John opened his notebook, flicked a couple of pages, and began to recite.

"In her handbag wassa small amount of cash — £5.62 t' be exact" —

The Inspector interrupted, *"So robbery can be albeit discounted, then."*

St John continued, *"Some inexpensive cosmetics, a hair brush, an empty packet o' tights — American Tan in shade..."*

"So someone potentially used her own spare pair to restrain her? Or possibly took them as a trophy?"

Cavanagh interjected with this suggestion, but Nick reflected to himself such an idea would be good for her in the future, after damaging her own that evening. He then noticed something quite obvious no one else had mentioned as yet.

"But she's wearing American Tan colour tights. Right now."

Everyone stared at the dead girl. Duncan was correct.

"Possibly she's changed for some reason..." Cavanagh began to speculate, Edwards and Duncan replied in unison.

"Perhaps..."

St John began again, pulling a face at Duncan as though his interruption was not required.

"A started bag o' boiled sweeties, and a flyer from a Sikh temple on da Foleshill Road."

"Joan, make a note of the address — go there in the morning and see if there is a misper reported."

Cavanagh immediately reached into her handbag,

retrieved out her own notebook and began to scribble on one of the pages.

"I'd rather you perform initial enquiries, as to Duncan or St John. The community at the temple are much more likely to open up to a young woman."

"Yeah, Guv," the constable agreed.

"Right, let's leave SOCO to their business, while this young lady is taken away by Dr Tyler. Sebastian, you can give me a lift back to Highfield Road so I can collect my car."

"Aye, Guv." St John simmered as he spoke, in quite a slimy manner. He trotted over to the inspector with a spring in his step, disappearing into the darkness.

"Be careful at the temple in the morning, Joan."

"Why so, Sarge?"

"This could be a race crime. At the moment, all options need to be considered."

"Ahhh, of course. Nothing to be assumed as yet."

"Exactly. Where would you like dropping off?"

"Back at Little Park Street, please. My car is there."

"Sure."

Duncan began reaching into his pockets hunting for his cigarettes. It was only paces later, once through the cordon that Nick found his packet of Park Drive at the bottom of the first pocket he had searched a moment earlier. He began the same ritual trying to locate his lighter, but the constable spoke up watching the detective about to rummage through his clothing yet again.

"You couldn't find that earlier either."

Moments later heading back towards the city centre, Nick drove along once again with the driver's window down, exhaling the smoke from his cigarette straight out into the crisp night air. Cavanagh shuffled in the front passenger seat, making the plush beige leather squeak just as before. The constable pulled the collar on her coat up against her porcelain white chin, the near-freezing draught cutting through the interior of the car like a dagger.

"Just close the window, Nick. I'll put up with the stink — it's proper Baltic outside."

Duncan took one last, long draw on his tobacco, held it in for a few moments before blowing it out of the open window, before winding it back up. Promptly, he extinguished the stub in the ashtray.

"Well," Nick began, *"A pretty young woman of Indian ascent found strangled to death on a dark, secluded country lane."*

"I'll find out all I can from the temple in the morning."

"Either way, we should know her identity by tomorrow night — as long as a misper report is lodged. From my dealings with the Sikh community in the past, they're bordering on obsession with their families, and fiercely protective of them."

The Sergeant spoke from experience — gaining the confidence and trust of all victim's families in a case was absolutely essential, but even more so with the ethnic minority groups across the city who may feel their plight was not being taken as seriously as that of others.

Pulling away from the traffic lights outside the General Wolfe pub, a Mini Cooper rapidly followed by a Hillman Imp darted out of a side street, turning across the bows of Duncan's Alvis. Nick was forced to execute an abrupt emergency stop to prevent a certain collision, braking so intensely he locked the wheels up to such an extent, he stalled the engine. Cavanagh was thrown forwards, just preventing herself from slamming face-first into the walnut inlaid dashboard at the last second.

"*Fucking idiots!*" Duncan exclaimed, before his attention was drawn to Joan as a crumpled heap in the footwell.

"*Are you all right?*"

"*Yeah, I'm fine.*"

The constable rubbed her left shoulder, wincing slightly.

"*Used to be the bane of my life when I was on traffic back in Bootle. Scallys in fast little cars who believed they're auditioning for 'The Italian Job', racing through the Mersey Tunnel.*"

"*Yes, I've had my own fair share of seeing the aftermath of over-exuberance behind the wheel, and lack of driving ability.*" Nick stretched down towards his colleague, grabbing hold of her and lifted.

Duncan leapt out of the Mk II Jaguar pursuit interceptor as quickly as he could, and sprinted over to what was left of the MGB GT. He flicked his torch on to illuminate the scene in front of him, but it was of hardly any assistance, more of a hinderance. The beam bounced up and down as he ran, plus was being reflected back at him off the falling snow. The only light source around was from the spinning blue emergency light on top of the police car. Wreckage from the MG and road side signage it had hit was strewn here and there across the grassy verge it had come to rest upon, in the middle of the traffic roundabout. It resembled the aftermath of a war zone.

As Nick ran towards the car, trying not to slip on the now settling snow, he could clearly see the front of the MG had borne the brunt of the impact with the high kerb

51

around the island. Before completely coming to a stop, it had demolished the sign which informed motorists Solihull, Birmingham and Elmdon Airport were only a small number of miles away. Racing towards the crashed car as fast as his legs would carry him — nearly falling over on two occasions, his cap blew off his head, landing in a nearby drift. This was the least of his worries, he could already see smoke or more hopefully steam emanating from around the edges of the bonnet.

As he got closer to the crashed car, Nick's biggest fear was confirmed — he could smell the pungent unmistakeable aroma of petrol. Intensely. Duncan wondered as he arrived alongside the driver's door whether it was a severed fuel line, or had the tank been split during the collision ? He had to act fast. It was then, the Constable noticed something terrible. Something he'd didn't expect to see — several yards in front of where the MG had come to its abrupt halt was a young woman lying face down in the long, snow-covered turf. With the windscreen of the car totally smashed, it was clear she'd been thrown from inside, through the glass and over the bonnet.

"Sarge! Sarge! Radio for an ambulance — quick!"

Sergeant Noel Ribbons moved as quickly as he could towards the crash scene in his lumbering gait, his own torch swinging its beam left to right like a broken street light in a storm. He gave an over-elaborate thumbs up. Sliding to a stop in the slush, he ran back towards the police car.

As quickly as possible through the shin high sodden grass, Nick made his way towards the injured young woman. Upon reaching her, he dropped down to his knees and checked for her pulse. This was made all the more difficult due to the falling snow increasing in strength. She was so young — barely fourteen or fifteen years old — her injuries were terrible, primarily to her head and face. Duncan checked again for a pulse as he couldn't find it. He tried elsewhere on her body — her neck, her wrists, slowly coming to the realisation she no longer had one — she had passed away. Nick stood up, removed his overcoat and laid it over her as a mark of respect. What a total waste of life, he lamented.

"Mike One, this is Mike Indigo Three, over."

Ribbons could be heard in the distance on the radio to control. Scratchy static and white noise was all the sergeant received in reply.

"Mike One, Mike Indigo Three calling, please respond."

The gravity of the situation all too clear in the Sergeant's voice. After yet more static, the radio erupted into life.

"Mike One receiving — go ahead Sarge. Over."

"Urgent medical assistance required at RTC on Stonebridge Island — junction of Coventry Road A45 and Chester Road A452, vehicle we were in pursuit of has crashed. Over."

The cold of the falling snow against his face brought Nick out of his daydream as regards the dead girl, and turned his attention to the driver. Striding around to the driver's door of the car, the stench of petrol was more pronounced now. Duncan grabbed hold of the door handle, squeezed in the button, and pulled. Nothing. He tried again, this time with more force. Still nothing. Then, the one thing he feared the most happened — a tongue of flame licked out of the bonnet edge against the front bulkhead.

Nick tried the handle yet again, with even more vigour. The door still wouldn't budge. Taking his truncheon out of the pocket running along the outside of his right leg, Duncan swung it with some force at the window, smashing it instantly. He reached inside and tried the internal door handle. With severe persuasion, it worked. Pulling the door open as wide as possible, Nick reached inside to the driver — another teenager, a little older than the deceased girl. He was lying over the steering wheel, part way over the dashboard. If it wasn't for the fact the wheel of the sports car was low slung, he'd be lying on the snowy grass next to his girlfriend now. The Constable checked for a pulse on the young man's neck — it was there! Weak, but there. Duncan had no time to lose, the flames were now growing in size and intensity.

He took hold of the young man on either side, and hauled him out of the car. Nick was aware he could have serious injuries that meant he should have been left where he was until the ambulance crew arrived, but with the car now on fire, that wasn't going to be feasible. He heaved with all his worth, pulling the driver out. He was a dead weight being unconscious, but Nick wrenched him clear and continued to haul him away from the burning wreckage — just as the bonnet burst back on its hinges with a loud 'pop' and slammed onto where the windscreen was, exactly where the injured young lad had been. The small explosion caused Duncan to lose his footing on the quicksand-like soft ground. He fell backwards, pulling the

driver partially onto himself. Lying in the snow, Nick glanced down at the young man, but he was no longer there. He had Joan Cavanagh in his hands, hauling her upwards.

Nick reached over, and pulled the Scouse detective back into the passenger seat of the Alvis. Cavanagh straightened herself up, still rubbing her shoulder.

"Are you sure you're all right, Joan?"

"Yeah, I'm fine. No need to fuss."

The sergeant nodded, and re-started the engine.

"Fancy going for a swift half in the Hare and Squirrel? That's if you're in no rush to get home, like."

Duncan's face mirrored how awkward he suddenly felt, not his usual confident, assured self. Not sure how to reply to the young woman, he managed to stammer out a few words after what felt like an age.

"No thanks Joan. I need to get back. Plus, the Guv'nor will expect us back in early tomorrow morning."

Joan stared at her feet, disappointed. But a sense of realisation Nick's words made sense made her nod in agreement.

"Another time, eh?"

"Yeah, another time."

Duncan smiled nervously back at the Merseysider, as they arrived at the police station car park. Nick brought his car to a stop next to a scarlet Singer Chamois Coupe.

"I'm still surprised you haven't got a Mini or similar. Surely that's more 'you'."

"Stop knocking my motor! There's nothing wrong with her!" Joan glared at the sergeant as she defended her car.

55

"I found living in Anfield, despite how easy she is to break into, she'd be left alone by thieves. She may not be as plush as this mobile palace, but she suits me fine."

Duncan carried on giggling, which did nothing to quosh or deter her rant.

"She's only three years old too — cost me a small fortune, but I love her." Opening the passenger door of the Alvis, Joan bid goodnight to her colleague, and started to delve into her handbag for her keys. *"See you in the morning, Sarge."*

"Yeah, see you tomorrow, Joan."

The policeman bid his farewell and began to feel relieved. The prospect of the after-work drink with a work colleague appealed, but he didn't wish to give the young woman the wrong impression. During the eighteen months they'd worked together, he'd endeavoured to convey this stance. Nick liked her forthright manner and found her an exceptional detective, just didn't see the constable as anything more than that. He waited as Joan walked to her car, letting herself in. The graze on her leg she'd received earlier now quite pronounced and visible under the car park floodlights. He tooted the horn, waved, and drove off into the night mulling over the events of the evening in his mind.

Reaching across the dashboard, Nick flipped open the walnut veneered glove box, stretching further inside he found two 8 track cartridges. The labels on each revealing the contents — one contained Eddie Cochran songs, the other Billy Fury. He removed the Gene Vincent one from the player, replacing it with the Billy Fury cartridge. The interior of the Alvis was immediately filled with Fury's song *'A Thousand Stars,'* to which Nick began tapping the steering wheel in time to. *"He's only seven months older than me,"* the detective said to himself. He caught his reflection in the rear-view mirror, smiling slightly at the realisation his hair was in a similar style to that Fury had when he first became famous. Reaching into his inside pocket, Duncan found his packet of cigarettes, and with the tip of his thumb lifted one upwards, leaning forwards slightly as he grabbed the tobacco between his lips. He then pushed the inbuilt cigarette lighter into the dashboard again to heat up.

As he drove the relatively short distance towards his home in Earlsdon, the detective dwelled over a few of the details. The unfortunate Indian girl that had been strangled was wearing hosiery, same shade as the empty packet in her handbag — did she get changed? How come? Where was she going? Was she meeting someone? And where were the missing hosiery from earlier in the day, if she had gotten changed? Plus, that cigarette butt — as Edwards had stated, rather extravagant for a Coventry smoker. Nick drew on his own tobacco as he placed the lighter to its tip.

As he arrived onto the sloping drive outside his home, and walked the few short steps to his front door, considering the oil drip trail too. It might be a wild goose chase, as many vehicles leaked lubricant, but the substance on the tarmac might not be engine oil — his own mechanical experience told him that. The detective wondered how many cars might be prone to leaking oil — from wherever on the engine, gearbox or rear axle. Most likely too numerous to mention, he concluded.

Letting himself into his house, Nick fumbled around in the darkness for a few seconds, till he found the light switch. As the hall light killed the inky blackness, he was greeted by the same thing he always was when he came home, a huge poster of his hero — American Rock N' Roll legend, Buddy Holly. Unexpectedly, he felt something brush against his ankles, causing him to look down. It was his overfed tabby cat, Stirling. The cat purred at being let back into the house and continued to rub against his owner's legs requesting attention or feeding. Or most likely both.

"What do you think, my friend?" the policeman addressed the forever hungry feline as he took another long, slow draw on his cigarette.

CHAPTER TWO
WEDNESDAY APRIL 18th 1973

Hiding behind the current copy of *'Motorsport'* magazine, a fine picture of Swiss Formula One driver Clay Regazzoni on the front cover at the wheel of his race car, Duncan sipped at his cup of tea. Carefully Nick placed the tea cup back onto its saucer, moving his hand to a nearby ashtray to find his cigarette, and took the final draw on the tobacco before stubbing it out. All of this the detective did without taking his gaze from the magazine, concentrating solely upon the South African Grand Prix analysis from the previous month. So intense was Nick's focus upon the race report, he barely registered someone sliding into the seat on the other side of the table. Suddenly, the magazine the detective was holding was prodded from opposite, causing him to look up. A smartly dressed man sat in front of him, a few years older than himself, smiling the cheesiest of grins.

"Morning Alex. Fancy meeting you here."

The detective greeted the gentleman, giving him a deliberately over the top broad, fake smile.

"Still dreaming of becoming Stirling Moss, little brother?" Alex gestured at Nick's choice of reading material.

"Nah, Jim Clark will always be my favourite."

Nick slowly closed the magazine and placed it upon the table.

"I thought I'd find you here. Best cup of tea in the city."

Alex gestured around the café and at all the other clientele present. Three double decker buses emblazoned in maroon and cream livery passed the entrance to the café, shaking the building to its foundations. Crockery and glassware behind the counter jangled and tinkled against itself for a few seconds until the large vehicles had passed.

Nick reached into his coat draped over the chair next to him, pulling out his packet of Park Drive. Sliding the right side upwards, he offered his brother a cigarette to which he took one. The sergeant selected one himself, slid the packet closed, tapping the end of the tobacco several times on the front of the closed box.

"What brings you here, Alex? This place isn't exactly on your most direct route to work."

The detective began searching through his pockets one-by-one, trying to locate his lighter.

"Mum was saying on the phone last night she hadn't seen you for a few weeks."

Alex slightly chastised his younger brother, waiting for a light. Nick continued to rummage through his pockets, now searching through his overcoat on the chair beside him.

"I'll pop round at the weekend — work has been silly busy recently."

The elder Duncan peered over his shoulder, whispered something to an elderly man sitting behind him, to which he offered his disposable lighter. Alex took it, nodding thanks. Swinging back, he leaned across the table offering the lighter, igniting it at the same time. Nick ceased searching through his pockets for the third time, leaned forwards and lit the tobacco, inhaling deeply upon the first few draws.

"I'm taking Ellis away for the Bank Holiday next week, and Mum said she'd look after the girls—"

"And you wondered if you could borrow Alice?"

Lighting his own cigarette and taking a long slow draw upon it, Alex sheepishly grinned and nodded.

"Well, you know how it is. Pulling up outside some swanky hotel in the Worcestershire countryside, in a rather tired Standard Vanguard estate is a major social faux pas."

"But arriving in an Alvis crates the required gravitas?"

Alex smiled slightly awkwardly back at his brother. Nick sucked on his tobacco, staring at his brother with a poker face. He held the vapour in for a few seconds, still maintaining eye contact, before slowly exhaled.

"Oh, go on then."

"Thanks Bro—" Alex began, his smile growing rapidly, but Nick interrupted him mid-flow. Adding like a scolding parent while thrusting his cigarette at his older brother to emphasise his point.,

"But this time bring it back without it looking like it's been competing in the RAC Rally."

The elder sibling grinned.

"Twice!"

As Nick finished, glaring at his older sibling, Alex's smirk grew even larger. *"If his grin gets any broader,"* he debated to himself, *"I'm going to hit him!"*

A polite but loud female cough cut through the air. Alex and Nick both turned in the direction of the deliberate attention grabber to find Cavanagh standing there.

"Mr Duncan, Sarge." Joan greeted the two seated men.

"Hello Joan." Alex cheerfully returned the greeting,

shuffling across to the seat on his left, patting the chair he has just vacated.

"Ta Mr Duncan, but we need to be on our way."

The female detective graciously declined, while at the same time trying to gesture subtly to her colleague.

"Don't we, Sarge..."

To emphasise the point, she prodded Nick on the shoulder. The sergeant pulled a face at the constable, and began to rise from his seat collecting his personal effects.

Stepping out of the café onto the footpath, Cavanagh began, *"I managed to find a few details relating to last night, Sarge."*

Nick stared back at Joan, raising his finger to his lips, gestured with his eyes in the direction of his brother. Silently, Cavanagh acknowledged what her colleague meant.

"Would you like a lift, Alex?"

"Yeah, thanks. Saves on shoe leather."

They wandered through the bus station into a public car park, where Nick's Alvis awaited. On the dashboard of the car for all to see, was his warrant card.

"You really will do anything to avoid paying for something when you don't have to."

Alex chuckled, pointing at the warrant card.

"You're only jealous." Nick quipped back.

As the passenger door opened and Alex stood back to allow Cavanagh access to the backseat, Nick couldn't help himself.

"Don't ladder your tights again, Dear."

The female Detective glared back fiercely as she climbed into the car.

"Why did you think I'm wearing trousers and boots

today?"

Alex had immense trouble keeping his eyes off Joan's purt behind encased in fitted black slacks. Nick caught his brother giving his colleague the once over, and began to tut.

"What?" A cheeky smile flashed across Alex's face.

"Remember — you're married."

"But you're not interested, anyhow."

Alex flicked his eyes in Joan's direction a couple of times. Nick slowly shook his head in a silent 'whatever' motion.

Moments later, the Alvis came to a halt outside the Council House.

"Thanks for the lift, Nick. I'll give you a ring about Alice near the weekend."

"Yeah, yeah. Go on, piss off before I change my mind."

Alex smirked back at his brother, and climbed out of the car.

As Nick moved away towards the station, Joan spoke.

"Why did you tell me to shut up outside the café, Sarge?"

"My brother works for the council. He'll find out soon enough there's been a murder in the city, without hearing it from us."

"Soz — I just... I've found out who the dead girl is."

"Joan, we're nearly at the office now. Edwards will be holding a briefing shortly. Tell the entire department at once, not just me. But thank you — wanting to share the news with me first."

Nick manoeuvred the Alvis into Little Park Street and slowly drove the four hundred yards or so to the police station at the end of the street. Climbing out of the car, he paused, turning towards the constable.

"Coming from you as well, Edwards will think you're the

cat's pyjamas!"

As this began to sink in, Joan smiled uncontrollably.

Duncan and Cavanagh wandered into the CID office with its dower and drab decor, that did little to inspire or motivate the police officers that used it. Nick felt the resemblance the office had to the ones he used while in the Navy was uncanny. A blue tinged fog hung in the room, giving the appearance of an opium den as a result of the copious chain-smoking within.

"Good morning! Nice of you to join us!"

The inspector called across the room, having already begun his briefing before their arrival.

"Guv."

"I'm only trying to conduct a Major Incident briefing here, that's all!"

Nick acknowledged his superior, flicking a brief sheepish smile in his direction in an attempt to pacify his sarcasm. All the other detectives in the room stared in Duncan's direction.

"I see yous got yer muse in tow."

St John nodded towards Cavanagh trailing in Duncan's wake.

"Eh, why not? Sergeant Duncan's aftershave has a much better fragrance than yours, ya Meff! If I'm not mistaken what you're wearing is that famous natural brand, B.O."

St John scowled back at the constable, as the others in the office began to laugh at his expense. Giggling excessively was the detective constable seated directly opposite the Scotsman who partnered him predominately, the quite average in appearance but carried that permanent attitude that said he considered himself God's gift to women, Dermot Ward.

"People, people — please, the matter in hand."

Edwards abruptly interrupted the hilarity trying to focus

his officers' attention, clapping his hands together loudly. Duncan and Cavanagh squeezed past the other detectives and uniform constables in the room until they made their way to two empty desks, placed facing each other.

A typewriter was positioned to one side of Nick's desk, a large, blank notepad waited patiently nearby. To the rear of the desk were two picture frames, one containing a black and white photograph of a man in wartime police uniform, sergeant stripes on his sleeves, smiling broadly. The other being the insignia of the Royal Navy Regulators. Duncan gazed at the photograph of his father again, admiringly. It was at this very desk he had received that horrible phone call three years earlier, he'd never forget no matter how hard he tried.

Nick finished his paperwork, removing the document from his typewriter and signed the bottom of it with his silver cased pen his parents had given him — a 'well done' gift upon his promotion to Detective Sergeant a couple of years previous. Mum and Dad had even had three sergeant stripes engraved into the barrel, along with 'Det. Sgt. Nicholas Duncan'. Abruptly, the telephone on Duncan's desk began to ring. Nick sighed at the disturbance, leaned forward and picked up the receiver.

"Warwickshire Police Little Park Street CID, Detective Sergeant Duncan speaking."

The phone line was quiet, but the detective could hear someone breathing at the other end.

"Hello, can I help you?"

The person at the other end of the line was now sobbing softly. He could make out it was a man too.

"Hello..."

The sobbing continued. After a couple of sniffles, the man spoke.

"Nick... it's Alex."

"What's the matter, Mate?"

Nick rapidly enquired, quite concerned. The line fell silent — the detective assumed his brother was trying to regain his composure, but muffled shuffling, scuffling sounds suggested the receiver was being taken by someone else. Nick spoke again.

"Hello... Alex...?"

A variety of images raced through his head — had something happened to Ellis, or his nieces? Was Alex in trouble and his brother was the only person he could turn to?

Completely unexpectedly, a woman's voice replied. With her slight West Country twang, he knew straight away who it was.

"Nick, It's Ellis. Alex was phoning you about Bob...er...your dad. The Doctor has said he hasn't got long left — I'm so sorry, Nick. Can you get here as fast as you can? Please."

The colour drained from the detective's face at hearing these words. His father had been ill on and off for the last couple of years — he'd attended several hospital appointments with him — as had Alex — but knew what was coming, pushing the inevitable out of his mind. The sergeant began to choke on the lump now appearing in his throat. He could barely speak.

"I'll be right there — I'm... I'm on my way."

Nick put the phone back onto its cradle, rose from his seat as though in a trance, and reached for his coat.

Edwards breezed into the office, and straight away could see all was not what it should be with his young sergeant — Duncan was fighting to put his coat on, in a manner that suggested he'd completely forgotten how to get dressed, but had to as quickly as possible.

"Is everything in order, Nick?"

Having known him since he was in short trousers, Duncan knew the Guv'nor would quickly notice when he was behaving out of character — like right now.

"Guv, I've got to go — I'll... I'll be back later."

The Sergeant, flummoxed and distant, began to make his way to the door.

"Nick, what's the matter? Something is really troubling you — tell me — please."

Duncan paused briefly, now trying to hold back the tears he wanted to cry. This wasn't lost on his Inspector either.

"Albert, it's Dad..." were all the words Nick managed to stammer out. Edwards rapidly grabbed his own coat and hat from his office.

"Come on — I'll drive — you're in no fit state."

Moments later, the two men were in Edwards' Riley saloon, racing across the city. The inspector proved he'd lost none of his pursuit interceptor ability, as he drove the wheels off his car, driving like he never had before. Duncan, with tears welling up in his eyes, was too preoccupied to notice his superior's prowess behind the wheel.

Arriving outside his parent's home, Nick leapt out of the car and ran to the front door. The door opened as he approached, a woman a little older than himself standing there with short auburn hair. The moment Duncan saw his sister-in-law he crumbled. He threw his arms around her and held her tight, starting to sob silently. Ellis reciprocated the hug, stroking the back of Nick's head in comfort, while trying to with-hold her own grief and upset .

"Your dad's upstairs, Nick."

After what appeared like an age, he let go of Ellis and made his way upstairs

Nick reached the doorway to his parent's bedroom, finding Alex standing there, looking at their father lying in bed. Dressed in his favourite sky-blue pyjamas, Bob was partially under the covers. Next to him was his wife and the brother's mother, Georgy. Alex leaned against the doorframe, hand to his mouth, biting on the knuckle of his index finger trying his best to hold back his tears. The Detective put his arm around his brother's shoulders, and hugged him tight. Alex buried his face in his brother's neck and sobbed for a while, until Edwards appeared and placed his hands on the backs of both young men. Nick released his embrace, and moved into the room.

"Dad... Dad... it's me... Nicholas..."

Nick spoke out to his father, kneeling beside the bed and taking his hand. After a few moments, the policeman could feel his father slowly squeeze his hand. The gravely ill man gradually opened his eyes.

"Hello Son — how's work going?"

Between sniffles, and summoning an inner strength from he didn't know where, Nick replied.

"It's going well, Dad. Busy, but going well."

"Good — good. I knew you'd be an excellent copper, Nick — even before you joined the Navy."

The detective squeezed his father's hand at hearing this praise, rubbing his forearm with his other hand.

"Dad, Albert is here. Here's come to see you too."

"Albert?"

"Bob — Sarge — it's me!"

The older detective greeted his former superior, stepping into the bedroom and knelt next to Nick.

"Let's go watch City play this Saturday — United are coming to town!"

"Really?" Bob wearily asked. *"That would be nice."*

"We could have a couple of pints in the Binley Oak before kick-off, and go to the chippy on the way home."

Emotion began to overwhelm the older detective as well, as he stammered the words out, sounding more like a desperate child.

"Are you paying?" Bob softly put to his former Constable, with a silly smirk on his face.

"Of course, Sarge!"

The ill bed-ridden man smiled, and snuggled slightly more into his wife next to him.

"Georgy..."

"Yes, Love?"

"I feel so tired..."

Bob's voice was a faint whisper, which promptly fell silent.

Nick was the first to notice. His father's grip slowly diminished to nothing. He knelt there hanging onto the man who had raised him, taught him right from wrong and the initial way through life. Former Police Sergeant Robert Duncan — Bob to all those who knew and loved him — had passed on. Unable to hold back the tears, they flowed down his face.

"Dad... Dad... Dad!"

Nick began, as though calling his father would bring him back, squeezing his hand and shaking it at the same time. He watched as his mother cuddled up even closer to the man she loved, squeezed him even tighter, and began to cry uncontrollably.

"Bob, you silly sod! I love you so much."

The Detective became aware of someone kneeling on the opposite side of the bed from himself, the tears in his eyes clouding his vision. He reached up to his eyes and wiped them away — who was that the other side of the bed? As his sight cleared, he could see Joan Cavanagh looking back at him in a concerned manner.

"Nick — Are you all right, Lar?"

Duncan spun his silver cased pen between his fingers, stopping occasionally to stroke the engraved sergeant stripes, his rank and name upon it.

"Yes Joan. I'm fine."

The policeman snapped out of the memory he had painfully revisited, rapidly trying to regain his composure. He pulled his notebook towards him, and began to write bullet points into the first page.

At her own desk, Nick watched as Joan contemplated its untidy and messy state, completely strewn with paperwork. At the rear of her desk stood a solitary picture frame, which had the Liverpool F.C club crest displayed within. She too began to take notes as Edwards spoke, but not before Duncan noticed her manner turned furious.

The Scouse detective leaned towards the picture frame,

violently ripped a piece of paper adhered to it, the offending leaf displaying an image of the Celtic Football Club emblem. Cavanagh theatrically screwed it up into a ball and threw it angrily at St John. Sebastian ducked, the paper ball missing him by a fraction. He stared at the constable and winked. Joan glared back, mouthing the immortal words *"Fuck Off!"* Duncan put his hand to his mouth, spluttering as he stifled his laughter.

"Now that I have your full attention ladies and gentlemen," the inspector continued, *"You have no doubt heard a young adult female of Asian ascent was found on Bedlam Lane. She'd been strangled."*

Edwards turned around to a notice board behind him, which had a map of the city upon it. A large red marker was pinned to the location where the unfortunate young woman had been found, plus alongside the map was a series of photographs of the said girl in question. Duncan eyed the images with discernment, wondering how come victims always looked a hundred times worse in SOCO photography? The pictures appeared to be something you'd expect to see in a horror movie.

"At the moment we estimate the victim is in her early twenties, and still trying to gain her identity. We have very little else to go on at the moment."

The inspector gestured towards St John.

"Have any missing persons matching this girl's description been reported, as yet?"

"Nae-one matchin' da details o' dis woman, Guv. Juss a laddie in his twenties still unaccounted fa."

Cavanagh began to cough deliberately, gaining the attention of all present. All heads turn in her direction.

"Er, actually Guv, I went to the temple earlier that was named on the flyer in her handbag, and learnt a twenty-four-year-old — an Arosha Rana — did not turn up last night to assist in cleaning up after the Vaisakhi festival."

"Did you gain a home address?"

"Yes, Guv. I wanted to inform you first, as to approach the family like."

"Good thinking, Constable. Go with Duncan and speak to the family. Break it to them as gently as possible — I know it's going to be an enormous shock to them — "

"But Guv..." St John interrupted, getting to his feet. The seasoned detective glared at his Sergeant due to the unwanted intrusion.

"Sebastian, at times you have all the subtlety of a fart in a crowded lift. That's why Duncan is more suited for this duty."

"Juss cause hissa da Golden Boy! And Little Miss Canna Do Wrong."

"Sebastian!"

Edwards snapped, pointing at him. The aggrieved Sergeant sank back into his seat.

"Dermot and yourself can accompany me to the hospital — we're attending the post mortem examination."

The Inspector gestured to a uniformed female constable standing close by.

"This is WPC Rachel Ryce, she'll be your liaison with uniform downstairs and 'Our F.L.O'."

A highly fetching long-haired brunette, who was buxom enough to make her tunic appear tailor-made fitted stepped forward, and nodded once politely. Duncan noticed her make eye contact with Cavanagh and smile, plus saw the scouser wink back in return. Nick leaned forwards to the Merseysider.

"*Do you know her?*"

"*I should say so, — she's one of me housemates.*"

Duncan could see several of the other male detectives were already eyeing her up, with a soft wolf whistle being heard from an as yet undetermined source. He could've sworn it emanated from Dermot at the next desk.

"*And look into this car that's leaking oil — which models are more prevalent to do so, plus check with local garages — has anyone booked their motor in for such a repair. If you can't get hold of myself, inform Chief Inspector Spencer. Right, let's begin.*"

Right on cue as though it had been scripted, Detective Chief Inspector Thomas Spencer breezed into the office. Taking his pipe from his mouth, he addressed all.

"*Morning Each — a little bird has told me we have a slight situation.*" The Chief Inspector stepped back to absorb the information on the notice board.

"*That's one way to put it, Tom.*"

"*Hmmm... strangulation, eh? We haven't had something like this for quite a while.*"

Spencer popped his pipe back in his mouth and puffed upon it, absorbing the information. As the entire CID team began to scatter and go about their duties, the Guv'nor suddenly paused.

"*W.D.C Cavanagh...*"

Joan glanced over her shoulder to see her superior officer beckoning her towards him.

"*Yes, Guv.*"

"*Good work this morning. Keep it up.*"

Edwards praised the constable. Cavanagh smiled broadly, and was just about to say thanks for the compliment, but the inspector continued.

"Oh, and one other thing..."

"Yes, Guv..."

"Next time I see you, be wearing a skirt or a dress. Trousers on a female detective constable are not appropriate or standard practice."

"Yes Guv. Of course."

The scouser's expression darkened, sulking slightly like a told off child.

"Good. Glad that's clear."

"Guv..." Duncan called after the inspector, to which Edwards paused and turned back towards the sergeant as he is about to leave the office.

"I'm in court later today — remember the cannabis farm in the student house case?"

The realisation of Nick's words were acknowledged on the inspector's face.

"Well, I think you'll have time to see the family before you go to court. What time is the case being heard?"

"1.30 this afternoon."

"Plenty of time. Best of luck with the family both of you."

"Thanks, Guv," both Duncan and Cavanagh replied

Walking out of the police Station back towards the Sergeant's car, Joan quizzed Nick out of curiosity about the remarks thrown in his direction recently.

"Why does that blert St John keep saying what he does about you, Nick?"

Duncan paused before answering, beginning to rummage through his pockets, and for a refreshing change found his cigarettes quite quickly.

"Sebastian has got issues with me over how quickly I was

promoted, Joan." Nick placed a cigarette between his lips and continued to explain. *"I was made a sergeant in late '68, a couple of months after my twenty-ninth birthday. In all fairness, I hadn't been a Detective Constable that long, having joined Coventry Police in early '63 after leaving the Navy. I was only a uniform bobby for eighteen months before joining CID."*

"The Navy? Were you a sailor?"

Duncan tittered, as he now began the ritual of scouring his pockets for his lighter.

"No, not a sailor. But I have briefly served on a ship. I was called up for National Service in late 1957, and initially was ground crew, repairing jet fighters and helicopters. My father was a bobby here in Coventry — a Sergeant by the end of the War. So, I always had an interest in Police work. As my National Service came to an end in mid-1959, I joined the Royal Navy Regulating Branch".

Still searching his pockets, Duncan gave up as two uniformed constables walked towards him. Gesturing with his cigarette, one of the officers smiled and produced their lighter. Looking most appreciative, he lit his Park Drive and returned the lighter to its owner, thanking him.

"Royal Navy Regulating Branch?"

"Naval Military Police — Shore Patrol."

As the sergeant explained, he took a hasty draw upon his tobacco. *"I started out in the Regulators based at an air base in Somerset, then briefly onboard a ship for a few months, followed by Devonport in Plymouth. I eventually ended up based in Malta."*

Finding his keys with an ease that begged the question why he couldn't find his lighter a few moments ago, Duncan unlocked his car.

"How did you end up here with the Warwickshire Police? You've never said before."

"I left the Navy in early '63 and came home. Dad advised me to join the local Police, so I became a Bobby here at Little Park Street. A position appeared in CID in summer of '65, and with experience of this type of work when I was a regulator in the Navy, I was a shoe-in."

"Is that why St John is always indifferent towards you?" Edging the luxury car out of the city centre, Duncan continued.

"Sebastian has an issue not just with my rapid rise up the ranks — remember, he's been a Detective Sergeant longer than me as well — but my family connection with the Guv'nor."

"You're related to Edwards, as well?"

The sergeant laughed, choking on the cigarette smoke he'd just inhaled.

"No, no! He joined Coventry Police after the War, as he'd been military police in the Royal Marines. My Father was his uniform sergeant showing him 'the ropes' of civvie policing."

Heading north easterly out of the city, the detectives entered a suburban area now predominantly inhabited by the influx of Indian and Pakistani families that had emigrated to Britain over the last twenty years.

"I guess Sebastian feels I receive preferential treatment, due to the Guv'nor being a good friend of Dad's."

"Hmmm, possibly." Joan did not seem entirely convinced. *"From what I've seen, the Guv'nor seems to come down on you the hardest."*

The Liverpudlian studied Duncan with a pondering expression. He could see her doing such in the corner of his eye. Nick wasn't sure whether Joan was convinced this was the reason for all the animosity between St John and himself. He knew the constable was too good a detective not to 'feel' there was more to the situation than met the eye.

"This is the one part of this job I absolutely detest," Duncan announced, as he solemnly drove the car. *"You'd think it would be a little easier each time we have to inform a family of what's happened to a loved one — but it isn't."*

"Yes, it's horrible." The constable regrettably agreed.

"I wish I'd met many of the people I have through my career in much better circumstances. Giving nice, decent people terrible news is beyond awful."

"It is." Duncan recalled with deep sadness his first time he had to undertake this part of being a policeman.

The constable wandered across the car park towards the Ford Anglia 105E patrol car awaiting him. Walking double-time to catch up with him was his Sergeant, Nathan Slater. He placed his protective hand on the nape of Nick's neck once alongside him.

"I'd like to tell you this gets easier, but it's one part of our job that stinks."

Duncan nodded his head, looking solemnly at his feet, not really where he was walking. Arriving at the car, Nick dwelled on the irony of the car's colour scheme suited the occasion — the Anglia painted entirely in the darkest navy blue, in some lights it appeared 'black' — just like a hearse.

"Whereabouts are we heading to, Sarge?"

"An address in Wyken." Slater checked the document file under his arm to confirm in his own mind he was correct.

"I take it you've never had to do a 'Next Of Kin' visit

before, Nick?"

Taking his helmet off before getting into the police car, Duncan slid behind the wheel.

"No, I haven't. During my time with the Navy Regulators other members of staff did this job, I just enforced base rules and investigated."

Leaving Little Park Street, Nick drove past the Council House, and downhill towards Far Gosford Street.

"I'm sorry to say it never gets any easier, no matter how many times you have to do this."

Duncan heard the sergeant's words, but concentrated on driving. He could see in the corner of his eye Slater was looking at him, concerned.

"You're Bob Duncan's lad, aren't you?"

"Yes, Sarge."

"Bloody good copper, your Dad. If all policemen were like him, there wouldn't be any crime in Coventry."

Nick swelled with pride at hearing this high-level praise for his father.

"The biggest irony is I'm only based here at Little Park Street, as Dad retired the month before I started. If he'd stayed on, I'd have begun my career elsewhere."

As they passed the Devonshire Arms on Sewall Highway, Nathan instructed the constable.

"Pull up along here where you can, lad."

"But we haven't reached the address yet, Sarge."

Gradually, the Anglia came to a halt. Slater reached into his left breast pocket of his tunic, retrieving a packet of new Embassy Filter cigarettes. Flipping the hinged top of the packet, the sergeant offered the constable one. Duncan placing the tobacco between his lips as Slater offered him a light.

"Steady your nerves, lad."

The older, more experienced policeman lit his own smoke, taking a lengthy first draw. Nick drew on his burning cigarette. It tasted good, if a little different in flavour to his own Park Drive.

"The trick is," Slater began, *"Is to detach yourself from the situation anyway you can. As you already have experience of police work, you get the idea."*

Duncan nodded his head in agreement, exhaling his tobacco smoke out of the open window.

"If we get too close to all those we help, we'd be bogged down with so much emotion it would be impossible to do the job."

"I understand, Sarge."

"Be caring, be compassionate, but don't take it to heart or carry other's problems with you."

Slater blew his own vapours out of the window, and stubbed his tobacco out.

"Come on, lad. Let's get this done."

Moments later, they arrived at the home of the unfortunately recently deceased, Ken Balham. His home was a tidy looking house, well maintained in appearance. The two policemen glanced at each other pensively, and approached the dwelling. Placing their helmets back on and straightening their tunics, they knocked the well painted green door before them. Straight away, they could hear a dog barking inside — not a large breed by the sound of the animal's voice, Nick contemplated.

The door opened slowly, to reveal a pretty long-haired blonde. But it wasn't her good looks that grabbed the attention, it was something else. She was pregnant — heavily so. *"Oh, no!"* Duncan muttered under his breath, a lump emerging in his throat from nowhere. The sergeant found his voice first.

"Mrs Balham?"

"Er, yes. Can I help you?"

The young woman looked puzzled, at the same time rubbed her large pregnant belly.

"May we come inside, please? We have an important matter we need to talk with you about."

The pregnant woman's expression was even more perplexed and confused, now.

"Please," Slater added.

"Yeah — all right. Do come in."

Entering the living room, Duncan found the Balham residence modest, but tastefully decorated to what could be achieved on a minimal income. Following the policemen into the room, Susan Balham gestured at the sofa, to which the two men sat down.

"Pardon me for being a bit thick, but I'm surprised to be visited by two coppers. Why are you here?"

"Would you like to sit down, Mrs Balham?" Nick rose from his seat as he could see the pregnant woman's movements were quite an effort.

"No, it's fine." Susan gratefully declined, holding onto the edge of a gate legged table.

"Have you long left?"

Duncan pointed at her bulging tummy. He stood up, pulling out a chair regardless. Susan sat, her breathing quite shallow and laboured.

"Not much longer." She slightly winced, rubbing her

enlarged abdomen once again. *"So what can I help you with?"*

"Mrs Balham, we're here regarding your husband"

The sergeant began, but he barely finished the sentence as Susan interrupted.

"What's the matter? What's happened to my Ken?"

The pregnant woman erupted extremely agitated, which was increasing in ferocity by the second. She rose to her feet instinctively. Nick visibly showed his concern, it was upsetting to see her reaction. He felt it was as though she somehow knew what Slater and himself were about to tell her.

"Mrs Balham, please sit down!"

"No! What's happened to Ken? Tell me!"

Susan began to scream, tears welling up in her eyes.

Without warning, Susan grabbed her pronounced large pregnant stomach, bent forwards and cried out in pain. Gradually, growing in size at a speed barely negligible like the hands moving on a clock, a small dark mark appeared on the front of the skirt of her dress. The grey fabric darkened to near black.

"Fucking Hell!"

Slater leapt from his seat and straight to the pregnant woman, throwing his paperwork to floor.

"Nick! Phone for an ambulance! Quick!"

The Sergeant barked at his Constable, but Duncan could already see the severity of the situation.

Through gritted teeth due to the pain, Susan managed to utter, *"We haven't got one. I have to go down the road to Iris and use hers"*.

"I could radio control from the car."

"Good thinking, lad — go on!"

From out of nowhere, Susan let out an earth-shattering scream, doubling her up even further in agony.

"Nick!"

Slater called after the younger man. Just about to leave the house, Duncan retreated to the living room, finding Nathan holding Susan in his arms. *"Sod the radio — we'll take her to hospital!"*

Nick, opened the front door and dashed to the car. Glancing over his shoulder he was greeted by the sight of Slater carefully semi-carrying the highly distressed and in severe discomfort Susan.

"Don't worry, sweetheart — we'll get you to hospital. What's your name, love?"

Between grimaces, the pregnant young woman announced *"Susan."*

"I'm Nathan. And this wet behind the ears eager to please youngster is Nick."

The constable pulled a comedy face in the manner of *'Are you talking about me?',* to which Susan smiled slightly.

"I wish Ken was here."

The two policemen stared at each other, unsure as to what to say.

"Let's get you into the car, eh?"

With much effort and some assistance, the pregnant woman got into the front passenger seat of the police car. Quickly, the two policemen leapt in, Duncan taking the wheel.

"Get us there as fast as, eh lad?"

Nick nodded.

Firing up the engine, he pulled away as though he was

starting a Grand Prix. Immediately, the constable turned on the two-tone siren and blue flashing lights. Bombing along, traffic pulled to one side to allow them through. Slater tried to comfort Susan, rubbing her shoulders and stroking her hair.

"We'll soon be there, love. Nick doesn't hang around."

"Good! I can't stand much more of this!"

The experienced policeman reached for the radio receiver, placed it to his ear.

"Mike One, this is Mike Papa Four, over."

Nathan barked into the mouthpiece, in order to be heard over the racing engine and blaring siren. There was no reply.

"Mike One, this is Mike Papa Four, are you receiving? Over."

After a few crackles, a response.

"Mike Papa Four, this is Mike One receiving. Go ahead, Nathan."

A mature female voice with a thick Black Country accent replied.

"We've attended the Balham residence in Wyken, Mrs Balham heavily pregnant and in need of immediate medical assistance. We're taking her to hospital in patrol vehicle, over." Slater was hit by more static and feedback. He paused briefly till the signal cleared. *"Can you inform the Cov & Warwick were on the way? Over."*

"Understood Mike Papa Four. Wot yer are, Cocker. Control out."

Slater gave the hand set a disbelieving face, shaking his head slightly.

Approaching the traffic lights at the junction with Bell

Green Road at speed, Nick needed to execute a hard left back towards the city centre. With the lights on 'red' and against him, he threw the car into oncoming traffic, performed a near impossible ninety degree turn hanging the tail of the Anglia out and drifted around the corner. Slater was thrown across the backseat and onto the floor, not hanging onto anything.

"Get us there in one piece, Lad!"

Nathan snapped at his Constable, trying to removing himself from the crumpled heap he'd unwillingly become. By the time Slater had managed to right himself back into a seated position, the car was belting along negotiating several more sets of 'red' lights, crossing from the correct to wrong side of the road and back again.

Rapidly, they approached the hump-back bridge where the road passed over the Coventry Canal. Hitting the bridge at several times the legal speed limit, the car couldn't help but become airborne — basic physics dictated that. The sight that came into view for Duncan and the others on the other side of the bridge made them all think their number was up.

While still in the air, they could see the street in front of them was blocked. A coal delivery lorry was unloading its wares outside a row of terraced houses, meanwhile the number 21 bus, one of the Coventry Corporation's plodding, lethargic old Daimler double deckers was on the wrong side of the road moving around said stationary coal wagon. There was nowhere, nor any space for the speeding police car to land and come to a complete stop.

The Anglia landed heavily nose first, bursting both chrome hub caps from off the front wheels. The moment the car's tyres touched the tarmac, Nick hit the brakes, but this was clearly futile as the entire underside of the police car grounded out. Like an inept welder at work showering sparks into the air, the Ford's exhaust grated along the highway. Plus, Duncan had other issues — the cross-ply tyres fitted to the car were barely offering any semblance of grip on the damp, greasy road surface.

Instinctively, the Constable grabbed the handbrake and pulled it up for all his worth. At the same time, he spun the wheel hard to the right. Slater threw his arms around Susan and the front seat, holding the pregnant woman in place as the car began to skid.

"NICK!"

Nathan hung on with all his strength, as the rear of the car flicked around. Duncan rammed the gearstick into reverse, causing the police car to shoot backwards towards the bus and coal lorry exiting its slide.

"We're going to crash!"

Susan screamed at the top of her lungs. A collision seemed inevitable.

"We're not!" Nick reassured her calmly.

Miraculously, the police car squeezed through the narrowest of gaps between the two large vehicles. Nick looked over his left shoulder as he steered, and did not notice — or at least appeared not to — that the gap was so tight the nearside wing mirror was torn clean off as it caught the side of the parked coal wagon. He had no time to worry about this, as although the car was now facing the right way with flow of traffic on the correct side of the road, it was accelerating into said traffic. In reverse.

Once again, the young policeman pulled on the

handbrake and flicked the wheel. As the Ford slewed yet again into a slide, the constable forced the gearstick into 'second', let out the clutch, and straightening the steering. Somehow, the Anglia was now facing the correct direction of travel. He buried his right foot into the carpet, shooting the car down the road.

"Where the fuck did you learn to do that, lad?"

Duncan glanced back at his Sergeant with a sheepish grin. The truth was, he hadn't a clue — it was all just incredible good fortune. A pure fluke. Lady Luck had favoured them all with her smile on this particular afternoon.

Then, the Coventry & Warwickshire Hospital loomed large on the right. Nick threw the Ford along the 'Ambulances Only' access, coming to a full emergency stop directly outside the main entrance. He leapt out of the now battered police car, and ran around to the passenger side, opening the door just as medical staff emerged hurriedly. As they helped Susan carefully climb out of the car, Duncan happened to notice a pristine looking bronze Series II Alvis TD 21 passed the hospital, heading in the direction where he had just driven from.

Passing the hospital where he was born some thirty-three and a half years earlier, Nick did a double take. For a moment he was certain he had just seen an old police Ford Anglia parked outside the main entrance, with a uniform constable and two hospital staff assisting someone out of the car. He shook his head quickly and gazed again — there was an ambulance crew helping an old dear out of the vehicle's back doors.

"Are you OK, Sarge?"

Snapping back into reality, he returned his attention to driving the Alvis, and continued heading for Courthouse Green.

"Yes Joan — everything's fine."

Once close to the Coventry Morris engines works, he turned off into a Victorian-era housing estate. Negotiating several tight, blind junctions, he found the address Joan had sourced. The two detectives climbed out of the car, and approached the front door of a well-kept house. Duncan adjusted his tie in his refection of the gloss painted red door, pressing the door-bell. After a slight pause, the lock of the door was undone noisily from the inside. As it gradually opened, a short, comely Indian lady in her early fifties peered through the gap.

"Hello, can I help you?"

Both Joan and Nick performed a double-take — the woman in front of them bore more than a passing resemblance to the deceased woman found on the country lane the night before. Duncan quickly recovered his composure.

"Mrs Rana?"

"Yes."

"Sorry to bother you, Madam. I'm Detective Sergeant Nicholas Duncan — Warwickshire Police, and this is Detective Constable Joan Cavanagh."

The Indian lady opened the door further, looking most puzzled. A striking and dapper man with well-groomed greying beard — obviously a Sikh from the turban he was wearing, and around the same age as the lady — appeared in the hallway.

"Is there a problem, Sergeant?"

"I think it would be better if we could come inside, Sir."

Both Mr and Mrs Rana stepped back allowing the detectives entrance to their home, looking even more confused and baffled than before.

Baljinder Rana cried. He sobbed from a broken heart, so shattered nothing during the rest of his lifetime would ever remove the grief and pain he felt. Tears flowed down his face soaking his beard and dripped to the floor. Gradually, he regained his composure, taking a few deep breaths. Between gasps and sniffs, Bal managed to speak.

"Yes Sergeant — this is my daughter, Arosha."

Joan put her arm around the distraught father trying to comfort him. Nick watched, knowing while her intentions were admirable, nothing would take away his pain. Lying on the table in front of them, the lifeless body of Arosha Rana was covered with a white sheet. Her father, choking upon his tears, gently touched her face, leaned forward and tenderly kissed her forehead. Cavanagh continued to rub his back, pity filling her face. Taking the edge of the sheet, Bal carefully lifted it, and covered his daughter's face.

"Mr Duncan..."

"Yes, Mr Rana..."

"Please find who did this. Find who took Arosha from us."

"I will, sir — I promise — you have my word."

Nick beckoned to their uniform liaison, Rachel. She approached slowly. Duncan whispered to her.

"Can you please take Mr Rana home. Arrange for victim support to offer assistance and care to the Rana family, plus respectfully explain how we need to gather information — see Arosha's room — it might give us some valuable clues."

"Sure Skipper — understood."

The WPC stepped forward. Rachel smiled as sympathetic smile as she could, and offered a hand towards Mr Rana. Bal took the buxom brunette's invitation, allowing himself to be led out of the room.

"I absolutely hate that — formal identification. I always end up putting myself into the position of the grieving family."

"I know, Joan. I remember when Dad passed away — that was devastating. But he died of cancer — seeing a loved one murdered…"

Nick stared down at his feet solemnly and shook his head.

"Could you liaise with victim support, plus go back to the temple — ask all the relevant questions, please."

The Merseysider nodded in reply.

"And inform the Guv'nor of all of this. We'll visit Arosha's home in the next few days, hopefully we'll find a few clues."

Just as the two detectives were leaving the unfriendly, cold and clinical examination room, Dr Tyler entered from a different doorway, attired in surgical scrubs.

"Morning Sergeant — Constable. Have you seen the post mortem report on this poor young lady?"

"Not as yet, Doctor. Could you tell me the details briefly, please. We'll read your report in depth when we get back at the office."

The Doctor stepped towards the examination table, carefully folding back the sheet covering Arosha's shoulders.

"No doubt she was strangled. If you look at her neck, you'll definitely see the bruising that shows 'cause of death'," Tyler began. *"What's worrying is the strangulation appears to have been performed by the assailant's hands."*

"Someone throttled her with their bare hands, like?"

"Yes, Constable. The perpetrator has wrapped both hands around the neck, crushing the trachea with their thumbs." Duncan's face said it all — he was disgusted at this information. Cavanagh put her hands to her mouth in horror. *"Yes, the method of asphyxiation is extremely intimate. Quite chilling, in fact."*

"Sadly, that's correct, Sergeant. Plus, as I initially noticed at the crime scene, she fought for her life — look at how she's dug her own finger nails into her neck trying to prise off the hands choking her."

Nick stepped forward, taking a closer inspection of the deceased girl. The bruising on the skin formed the shape of two rather substantial hands. Nick reached out, placing his own hand over the bruise on the side of Arosha's neck. The size of the hand that had left behind the mark was obviously much larger than the detective's, even though Duncan's hand wasn't exactly small.

"Whoever did this must have considerable strength — being able to crush her windpipe while fighting off her desperate attempts to save herself. Plus, would have received substantial injury to their own hands."

Dr Tyler nodded solemnly in agreement.

"It's an extremely brutal death, Sergeant. We need to catch this one."

Walking back to the car Duncan thought out loud.

"The size of those hands that strangled Arosha were huge. I'd say most definitely we're looking for a man."

"Or a woman with the biggest pair of dabs ever."

"Possibly, but unlikely. How many women have you seen with hands as large as those on an Irish Navvy?"

The Sergeant found his packet of cigarettes in his pocket,

and selected one. Placing the tobacco between his lips, he at once became aware of the Scouse Constable glaring at him.

"What?"

Joan gestured to his cigarette, making an over-elaborate mimed smoking action, coughing to draw his attention to it.

"Sorry Mum!"

Like a stroppy toddler being stopped from what they wanted to do, the detective sarcastically took the cigarette from his mouth and returned it to its packet, sliding into the car.

"I'm due in court shortly — that huge cannabis find at those student digs in Canley?"

"Oh, yeah — I remember — the greenhouse with the small holding inside."

"That's the fella. Huge amount for personal consumption — must be dealing."

"Yeah, I'd say so. There was a case I recall back in Wavertree in Liverpool that was similar."

"How long have you been based down here in Coventry now, Joan?"

"Oh, about eighteen months now. That reminds me, have you heard from Judy Young at all? How is she?"

Duncan chuckled as he drove back towards the city centre.

"Got twin boys and a third on the way!"

"Really? She was only preggy with the twins when I arrived!"

"I know! You were initially meant to be her maternity cover, but she never came back!"

She nodded her head in agreement at his statement, chuckling.

Nick edged the car towards Little Park Street, through the

obligatory slow moving, heavy traffic. Grabbing the detective's attention was what was advertised on the front of the Odeon cinema — the movie *'That'll Be The Day'* starring David Essex. Duncan exploded in excitement. Not looking where he was driving, he nearly introduced an elderly couple using the zebra crossing in front of the picture house to St Peter years earlier than they anticipated.

"That'll Be the Day? I hope that's the Buddy Holly story — it's about time that was made into a film."

Cavanagh peered at the front of the cinema, taking in the promotional posters, noticing other members of the cast.

"I don't think so. David Essex as Buddy Holly? Really? Plus, since when could Ringo Starr act?"

"Humph! His ability to play the drums is highly questionable, let alone 'act'."

"It's got Billy Fury in it!"

"What? Really?" Nick shouted in excitement, a huge grin began to spread across his face. The Detective peered back over his shoulder eagerly in the direction of the cinema. Cavanagh leapt across the front seat of the Alvis grabbing the steering wheel and give it a huge shove to the right, preventing the car from mounting the pavement and heading straight for a pillar box.

"Fuck me, Nick!" The constable's swearly outburst brought the sergeant back to the present.

Duncan brought his opulent car to an abrupt halt, still with a daft smirk on his face, which dissolved in a flash into one of mild disbelief. The clock on the side of the Council House cheerfully and reliably stated the time was just after quarter past one.

"Joan, could you take Alice back to the station, please —

I'll walk to court from here."

Without giving the scouser chance to remonstrate, he opened the driver's door and leapt out, sprinting to the other side of the road to avoid getting ran over. The driver blasted their horn at him to highlight their disapproval. Cavanagh slid across into the driver's seat, and moved Alice back into traffic. Nick was impressed with how Joan handled his car. He watched as she drove with a dexterity that suggested she was behind the wheel of the Alvis on a daily basis. But he couldn't help but grin at the sight of her head barely able to peer over the substantial wooden rimmed steering wheel.

Delving into his pockets, Duncan retrieved his packet of cigarettes again, and selected one. Placing it between his lips, he returned the packet to his pocket, before momentarily freezing on the spot. The realisation dawned upon him, he had no lighter and Joan had just driven off in his car. Walking towards him along the pavement was a man wearing a sports jacket, smoking his own cigarette. Nick politely stopped the man and asked for a light, to which he obliged.

Now satisfied with his lit tobacco, he darted across the cobbles alongside the ruined cathedral. The leather soles on his shoes occasionally slid and skidded underfoot on the smooth road stones, making him slow down and stroll more gingerly.

At the crossroads marked by the Tudor age public house, the Golden Cross, the County Hall was directly opposite. To signify its purpose further, a couple of obligatory police 'black mariah' prisoner transport vans were parked at the side of the aging Georgian building. Besides this, Duncan could see the brief leading the case for the prosecution he needed to liaise with. Attired in a smart secretarial style business suit, with her near-black hair tied back in a highwayman-esque ponytail was

Patricia Bayliss. To remind everyone of her nationality, she wore a gold broach on her lapel, in the shape of the Welsh dragon. Wandering towards her, the detective greeted his friend with a cheeky smirk.

"Hello Stranger. Fancy meeting you here."

"Ever the charmer, Sergeant." Sounding most sarcastic in her South Wales accent, she added *"I trust you're ready for a grilling from the Defence?"*

Leaning forward towards Duncan, she took his cigarette, gave him a peck on the cheek and took a long draw upon the tobacco. Nick stared at the barrister, puzzled. Patricia gestured with the cigarette in her hand towards a group of three men. One of which was a tall, slim fellow, a little older than Duncan and dressed just as immaculately, holding a folder of loose paperwork.

"Who's that?"

His tone of voice clearly indicating his growing interest. Patricia smirked, taking another draw on the Park Drive.

"That's Harvey Wiseman. Very sharp brief. Someone has quite a few bob to afford his fees."

The detective continued to gaze in the direction of the defence barrister, unable to take his eyes off him. He managed to utter, *"I've heard his name mentioned around the office, but never had any dealings with him."*

"You'll have to be on top of your game today, Nick. He's extremely thorough."

Patricia's words though were falling on deaf ears, as Duncan appeared to be within a daydream, still gazing at Harvey as people would drink in an epic vista of a landscape, or a masterpiece in a gallery. The brief raised her hand up to the policeman's face and clicked her fingers repeatedly.

"Sorry, Pat — was miles away." Nick apologised as he snapped out of his self-induced trance.

"Yes. So it seems." The brief smiled a silly smirk. *"Shall we go inside, Sergeant?"*

"Good idea."

Around an hour later, Nick and Patricia re-emerged. The Welsh barrister's face said she was reluctantly accepting defeat, while the detective had the appearance of an incredibly intense and stressful exchange.

"Grilling? You weren't kidding!"

Duncan's face was flushed and red. He did not resemble his usual calm and unflappable demeanour.

"I did say Mr Wiseman would keep you on your toes." Patricia began to giggle.

"That's the understatement of the century! Last time I was on the receiving end of an inquisition like that was when I had my assessment to join the Navy Regulators!"

"I'm more surprised at the angle Mr Wiseman attacked the Prosecution from."

"Yes, the student was growing the plants as part of a research project still stinks of complete B.S to me. Even though that evidence the barrister produced from somewhere in the Ether which the University confirmed as legit!"

"Seemed genuine enough to me, Nick."

"Well, put it this way — if Daddy can afford the best briefs in Warwickshire, unexpected previously unseen paperwork tends to miraculously appear from nowhere in my experience."

Unexpectedly, someone placed their hand lightly on Duncan's shoulder, causing the detective to turn around and receive quite a surprise. Standing before him was Harvey Wiseman. Nick gawked at the barrister with a mixture of awe due to a certain *'je ne sais quoi'* about him, and the nasty taste in his mouth at being beaten. The sergeant's heart skipped a beat at being within such close proximity of the handsome brief, as the butterflies rose within his chest, he found Harvey even more attractive up close. What was that aftershave he was wearing? It piqued Nick's senses with excitement and wonder.

"Nothing personal, Sergeant. I always ensure my client has all the facts when faced with such strong allegations."

"How extremely thorough of you, Mr Wiseman."

For the first time in longer than the policeman could recall, he was struggling to keep his composure. Harvey was more softly spoken than himself, his manner and persona more genteel than his own. One thing they did have in common in spades and was immediately obvious, was a dedication to their respective professions that was single-minded and unshakeable.

"Thorough, Mr Duncan?"

"Yeah, exceptionally so. Finding evidence my team had not."

"Even the great Steve McGarrett of Hawaii Five-O doesn't gain all the information and evidence straight away. Sometimes, not at all."

"Quite."

"No hard feelings, Detective. Better luck next time."

Harvey patted Nick on the back, before breezing off towards a nearby dark wine-red Humber Imperial. Duncan's gaze followed the impeccably attired barrister as he sauntered with a slight, relaxed easy gait towards his immaculate motor. He could not take his eyes off him.

"You two have more in common than you both realise." Patricia snapped the policeman out of his daydream. He rapidly spun towards the Welsh brief, puzzlement emblazoned on his face.

"Really?"

"Indeed! Similar dress sense, similar taste in cars, same fierce determination bordering upon obsession to get their respective jobs done."

Duncan's poise changed, as he appeared to be a little awkward at the lady's words. He glanced at the Humber moving away, giving a partial wave-cum-salute with the two fore fingers of his right hand from over his right eye. Harvey smiled back at the detective, replicating his gesture.

"See. You both even acknowledge each other the same way." It rapidly dawned on Nick what the Welsh brief was pointing out. Uncontrollably, he began to blush.

"Come along, Sergeant," she cooed at the detective with a silly smirk on her face. *"Let's have a drink — we can have a bit of a natter."*

Linking arms with the detective, she dragged him in the direction of the nearby pub.

"Mine's a gin and tonic."

Before Duncan had chance to protest, he was already at the entrance of the Tudor age building and being dragged inside.

Sitting in a secluded snug, away from the bar itself and prying ears, Duncan returned from purchasing the drinks, setting them down on the archaic round table in front of them.

"Thank you, kind Sir."

Patricia took her drink, quickly swallowing a huge gulp of its contents.

"What have you had? I never knew you were a brandy drinker?"

The barrister pointed at Nick's beverage — a golden-brown coloured liquid contained inside a brandy snifter.

"Calvados, actually — French pear brandy. Not that readily available in Coventry. This place and a couple of others do stock it."

"Very exotic. How did you happen across that?"

"During my time in the Navy. Was a staple in the Officer's Mess."

They both took a sip of their drinks, Patricia finishing first.

"Tell me, how long have we known each other, Nick?"

The lady leaned into the policeman, taking his left hand.

"Oh, it must be getting on for seven years now, I'd say. You were representing the prosecution on the first case I had to attend in court as a Detective Constable."

"And in all that time I've never seen you behave this way, the way you have around someone — dare I say it — you like."

The detective remained silent. He reached out with his loose hand, picked up his drink and took a long, slow sip.

"Like Harvey," she continued. *"I understand the tell-tale signs of body language, and what we subconsciously reveal without realising."*

Duncan remained tight-lipped, staring at his drink as he swished in gently around in his hand.

"I'd even be as bold as to say you fancy the pants off Mr Wiseman. I had an inkling you might have been gay as I've never seen you flirt with any women. Not even a sly, crafty glance or double-take over your shoulder at a pretty lady."

After a short silence, Nick spoke.

"Is it that obvious?"

"No, not really." Patricia squeezed the detective's hand, stroking it soothingly with her other. *"Only to those few of us that fully understand body language and human behaviour."* The policeman continued to stare into his drink.

"It's not something I publicise. I had to keep that part of myself a secret when I was in the Navy, and even more so when I joined the police."

He placed the glass he was holding back on the table.

Nick put the glass he was holding back on the table, returning to typing up the report he had to finish before the end of his shift. He stabbed at the keys on the ancient machine, in time to a rather rude and somewhat amusing rhyme he had learnt during his basic training. Trying not to get his fingers caught in the old-style contraption, Duncan envisaged it had been brought to Malta some fifty years previous, maybe even been used to report the Gallipoli landings. His office was sparse to say the least, even by Royal Navy standards. The Master-At-Arms however, had brought with him his trusty table top transistor radio. This was no mean feat, as the radio in question was roughly the same size as a box of breakfast cereal — smuggling it onto a naval base took a tremendous amount of cunning and guile.

Completely unexpectedly, the office door burst open in a manner that almost tore it clean off its hinges. In leapt a man in his late twenties, attired in all white tropics officer's uniform, with the rank of 'Lieutenant' displayed his epaulettes.

"Ten — Shun!"

The man shouted at the top of his voice, stamping his left foot into the floor for effect.

"Tony, that wasn't funny the first time you did that."

Nick glanced up from his typewriter not flinching once. He smiled at the Officer, who broadly reciprocated the grin, and a slow wink.

"Haven't you finished those case files yet?"

Anthony Devereux rhetorically asked Duncan, still with a silly smirk on his face.

"Just about. One case of petty theft from a bar in Valetta by crew from HMS Aisne on shore leave, pretty straight forward. Rather boring for top brass to read in Admiralty House over brandy and cigars."

The warrant officer tried his utmost not to look up at the Lieutenant as he typed. In his trim figure, he was devastatingly handsome — and then some. Duncan speculated he must have the pick of the women. There was no way he'd be interested in a guy. And even if he was, definitely not him.

"The other an AWOL matter. A crew member absconded with a local girl from Mosta."

"Absconded?"

Tony repeated, curious. He slowly moved around Nick's desk, now standing alongside him.

"Yeah, the family say their daughter was seeing a British sailor, and she's vanished too."

Tony perched himself on the edge of the desk, right next to Duncan, severely hindering any immediate use of the typewriter. He peered up at his superior, trying his utmost not to blush or show how he felt.

"No fears of you absconding with a local dusky damsel,

eh?"

Now he did begin to blush. He knew he was, not just because his cheeks felt like they were on fire, but also due to the growing smirk on Tony's face and the glint in his eyes.

"I know this to be matter of fact. As when that 'Wren' Andrea Swan saunters about the place—"

Duncan, still flushed, gave the Lieutenant a puzzled look. Tony sighed.

"Short black hair, piercing blue eyes, infeasibly massive tits..."

Sudden realisation spread across Nick's face, as he grasped who Tony was referring to.

"You, my friend don't really give her a second glance. Most of the other blokes on the base flock around her as though we've received an unexpected visit from Princess Margaret!"

Devereux leaned right into the warrant officer, his mouth a fraction away from Duncan's right ear. Whispering, he concluded, *"I'd even go as far to say you don't like girls at all."*

Now so flushed in the face, Nick was close to the same hue as someone suffering from acute sunburn. Unintentionally, as Duncan turned to face the Lieutenant, he stared straight into his ice blue eyes.

"Is it that obvious?"

Tony made a shush sound, placing the index finger on his right hand on Duncan's lips. A moment later he removed it, before kissing Nick full on the mouth.

He had kissed a few guys in the past, but this was something on a completely different level, something Nick had never experienced before. It was beyond fantastic, as though energy was flowing between the two of them, ebbing and falling in intensity only to pique once again. Without realising it, the two young men were now on their feet — the warrant officer holding his superior's face in his hands, in return the Lieutenant pulled Duncan closer grabbing his waist.

They continued to kiss passionately, Nick pushing Tony against the wall. Instantly, Duncan felt Tony's substantial erection bulging in his trousers pushing into his own mid-rift. It lit his own desire, turning him on as his own package began to swell and push back into Tony. Devereux responded by sending them both scurrying across the room, the Master-At-Arm's back slamming into a filing cabinet, still clinging onto the Lieutenant.

The impact of their heated embrace caused Nick's trusty transistor radio to tumble from the top of the cabinet. The impact of striking the ground caused it to switch on, ironically blaring out the current single by American crooner Bobby Vee, 'The Night Has A Thousand Eyes' exactly as the up-tempo chorus began. Tony dropped into the chair behind the desk Duncan had vacated a few moments ago. Nick himself knelt down to attend to the radio, turning it off. The two men stared at one another sheepishly. Nick was first to speak.

"We could both be court-marshalled and dishonourably discharged for this sort of behaviour."

Tony smiled wickedly.

"Fun, isn't it?"

Duncan glared back at him, but couldn't prevent a grin from spreading across his own face. Standing up, he placed the radio back from where it had fell. Still smirking, he glanced in Tony's direction, but performed an immediate double take. He was no longer there. Patricia Bayliss was sitting at the desk, leaning forward to pick up her drink.

Patricia leaned forward and picked up her drink, taking another swig of the clear liquid.

"During my time in the Navy, if I'd announced my preference I'd have been dishonourably discharged."

"Well, thankfully attitudes are changing slowly."

"A homosexual in the CID. will still be frowned upon by many."

"Well, your secret is safe with me, Sergeant. Still, a shame you're not straight — I'd have been after a handsome guy like yourself years ago."

The Welsh lady gently patted Duncan's knee. The detective smiled at her, placing his hand on top of hers and squeezed it.

"Thank you."

Nick leaned towards the brief and gave her a peck on the cheek.

"Steady, Sergeant — people will talk about us next!"

The detective finished his drink in two large gulps, winked at his friend and stood up to leave.

Exiting the Golden Cross, Duncan headed towards the station. He pondered to himself who else may have figured out as regards his sexuality, as he stopped a passer-by for a light. While it was now no longer illegal in Britain to be homosexual, it was an immensely slow process for attitudes of society to change for the better. Many of the general public would not accept a gay policeman, regardless of how efficient and trustworthy he might be. Not just yet. It would still be regarded as too much of a taboo.

Approaching the station, the sergeant paused before crossing the road. He decided against it — continuing along the street he entered the tobacconists on the corner. Once inside the store, the bell attached to the back of the door jangled into life announcing his arrival. Still with his lit but near finished nub end between his fingers, he took one last draw on the cigarette before extinguishing it in an ashtray on the counter.

"Ahhhh, unless I'm very much mistaken, that's the fine aroma of a Park Drive," a voice from the back of the stop announced. Breezing into the shop through a beaded curtain appeared the owner. *"Sergeant Duncan! The usual?"*

"Hello Cyril — Yes please."

Cyril selected forty Park Drive, and brought them to the till where Nick was waiting. Duncan watched the shopkeeper going about his business, during which he suddenly performed a slight double take as the tobacconist passed a small selection of American tobacco. Amongst the Winston, Lucky Strike, Camel and More brands, the policeman spotted Marlboro, its distinctive red and white livery catching his eye. Next to these in their own rememberable gold and white packaging were Marlboro Longhorn 100s.

"Cyril, is there much call for the American brands?"

"The American ones? Well, there's a few regular customers hence why I stock them. Not everyone wants the British brands, like yourself. That'll be fifty pence please."

Nick retrieved a handful of change from a pocket, and paid the shopkeeper.

"Are you considering changing brands, Mr Duncan?"

"Oh, no — not at all. Just curious."

"Can I interest you in these new lighters, made by Calibri? Deliciously stylish, perfect for a gentleman of discerning taste such as yourself."

Duncan smiled.

"I've already got one, thanks Cyril. Somewhere......"

The CID office, with its dingy lighting and indoor haze which now more resembled an open coal fire had just been lit — and was just as stifling — now had a dedicated notice board outside Edward's office. Upon this was information about Arosha Rana, along with her photograph. Cavanagh was standing in front of this, studying the information intently. Her snug fitted jumper, combined with her fitted black trousers and knee-high brown boots were generating unwarranted attention, as the Sergeant noticed other members of the detective department effectively letching and leering at her. The occasional comment of a sexual nature was also being thrown in the detective constable's direction.

"Are you all right, Joan?"

"You know Sarge, you'd think some of those blerts have never seen a woman up close before."

Joan gestured over her shoulder. Duncan peered over towards a group of four detectives where the rowdiness was originating from. Detective Constable Dermot Ward was amongst them.

"Is everything in order, gentlemen?"

Sudden silence fell across the group of men. After a brief pause, Dermot responded.

"Yes, Sarge. Everything is fine."

"May I suggest you all busy yourselves with your duties, before either the DCI or the Guv'nor notice you're all just loafing about drinking tea and smoking during a murder enquiry. I'm sure some of you will be off this coming Easter weekend, so let's get all loose ends gathered, please."

"Yes, Sarge," one of the other constables acknowledged grumpily. The group began to disperse slowly, muttering under their breath.

"It's about sodding time they see you as a bloody good copper, not just a woman."

"Thanks for sticking up for me Nick, but I can deal with meffs like that myself. It always feels I have to be double the police officer of those sort of twats, to prove I'm equal to them."

"Trust me Joan, it is noticed."

Cavanagh smiled back at the sergeant. Abruptly, Edwards appeared from his own private office and addressed the pair of detectives.

"Ah, glad you two are here. I'd like you both to visit Arosha Rana's home tomorrow and see if you can find any leads or clues in her bedroom, amongst her personal effects. Did she have any secrets she was keeping from her parents? I know not all young ladies will tell their folks everything. If I'd found out half of what my daughter got up to when she was younger, I'd be doing a stretch at Her Majesty's Pleasure right now."

The scouser covered her mouth to hide her huge smirk. Duncan began to nod repeatedly, the hypothetical image of the inspector being incarcerated tickling his own sense of humour. The senior detective frowned at the pair, before beginning to realise the reason for their mirth and smiled broadly as well.

"Less of the giggling, children. Sebastian, Dermot and myself will visit her place of work tomorrow, one of the department stores in the city centre. We'll have a chat with her manager and some of her work colleagues."

"Yes, Guv."

Nick nodded. The inspector breezed across the office, and began to issue further orders and details to other detectives.

"I think the Guv'nor is right. Our best bet in finding a lead may well be in Arosha's personal belongings."

"Well, as a young woman myself I can understand where the Guv is coming from. I had several things I would blag my Arl Fella about."

"Really?" Nick's curiosity piqued. *"Oh, do tell!"*

"Oh, just daft little things. Who I had a crush on, where I was going, who I was seeing. The usual stuff teenagers keep from their parents."

"Who did you have a crush on?"

Blushing slightly, Joan opened up.

"George Harrison."

"John Lennon is more to my taste." The sergeant quickly realised what he'd said. *"Er, I mean I like his confidence, dry wit and what a songwriter!"*

Cavanagh looked at Nick with a sideways glance, a wry smile spreading across her face as she crossed her arms. Still trying to divert attention from his initial comment, he continued.

"I did see the Beatles when they played the Coventry Theatre about ten years ago."

The sergeant knew this had worked, as Joan stood open-mouthed in wonder as talk moved to the most famous rock group in the world who originated from her home city.

"You actually saw the Beatles? Live?"

"Oh Yes! The theatre was absolutely packed. And when I said 'saw them play', that's exactly what I mean. The four of them walked on stage to a huge welcome, so much screaming from the young women there, more than you could possibly imagine. They quietened enough for John Lennon to speak and introduce the band, welcome the audience. They played the introduction of the first song, I think it was 'I Saw Her Standing There', after which I heard nothing for the next hour or so, just constant screaming."

Nick pulled a bemused face. Joan couldn't help but allow her own disposition to change from awe and wonder to mirth.

"So you're saying you saw them live, but never actually heard them live?"

"Yeah, that's about the strength of it."

Even the sergeant was now starting to see the ridiculousness of his story.

"I was a uniform constable back then, so it was a miracle I had the evening off. Especially considering my colleagues were on crowd control duty that night to prevent over-excited fans mobbing the band."

Both detectives continue to giggle, smiling at each other. Nick swiftly became aware of other detectives in the office paying attention to them, wondering why he was laughing in front of a notice board with a murder case pinned to it. Duncan stopped chuckling abruptly, with Cavanagh following suit.

"How about that drink, Nick? You did say another time, like."

The Sergeant was about to reply to the Merseysider, on this occasion appearing more comfortable with the same question he'd faced the night before. However, Edwards

108

interrupted him as he passed the two detectives returning to his office.

"*Drink? How about you both go home and get an early night I need you on the ball when visiting the Rana's home in the morning.*"

"*Yes Guv,*" both Duncan and Cavanagh replied in unison. Edwards disappeared.

"*Another time, eh?*"

CHAPTER THREE
MAUNDY THURSDAY
THURSDAY APRIL 19th 1973

"Thank you, Mrs Rana. We'll do our best, and the information we've have found today will really help."

Cavanagh was almost apologetic as she spoke.

"It's all right, Constable. Just please find who did this."

Solemnly, Mrs Rana disappeared inside her home. Joan walked the few short steps to Duncan's car, stepped inside. Upon sitting down, she fidgeted and shuffled, straightened her skirt.

"How's your leg now, after the other night?"

The sergeant gestured at Cavanagh's knee-high boot clad legs.

"I'll survive. Although it's just as well the weather isn't great, so I can wear these to hide the wound."

Nick chuckled at the scouser's dramatic over-statement. He reached into the inside pocket of his jacket and pulled out a burgundy leather-bound diary.

"Hopefully this will assist."

"Arosha's diary? You brought it with you? Did you ask permission?"

"Indeed, it is."

He dropped the journal into the Constable's lap.

"What I do know of some young women, they'll keep some

sort of diary not just to record future appointments, but write their inner most thoughts and feelings, or in the case of this young unfortunate, most likely both. Remember what you said yesterday?"

Cavanagh began to look through the last few entries, as Nick started Alice's engine and moved away.

"Have you had chance to read any of this, like?" Joan asked flicking through to the last few handwritten pages.

"Indeed, I have. Arosha met someone a few weeks back. Also, she attended an audition. Possibly, they're both could be connected?"

Joan nodded in agreement, trying to read the diary at the same time as she listened.

"An audition?"

"Yes. At the end of last month. 25th or 26th I think."

The Merseysider flipped through the pages to these dates.

"Yes, she wrote — 'I can express myself and perform on stage at last!' But an audition where? And for what?"

"There are three theatres here. We'll need to get in touch with all of them as regards any castings. Plus, find out if any amateur dramatics societies had any auditions recently." Coming to a halt in traffic, Duncan gazed along one of the side streets. Amongst one of the derelict buildings which stood there, he thought he could see two little boys playing.

Scrambling across the rubble and semi-demolished houses, Nick chased after his brother as quickly as his little infant legs would carry him. He'd already fallen twice, his gas mask inside its case proving to be more of a trip hazard and hindrance, than the safety precaution it actually was. The large deep, red wound on his right knee was taking an

age to clot and scab over entirely.

"This is my castle, Nick — you can't come here — you're not allowed."

Alex taunted his brother, knowing he'd bite back.

"I am! I'll tell Mum on you!"

A few weeks shy of his third birthday, the younger Duncan was expanding his boundaries. The world had become a fascinating place to him. It was sometimes bewildering if a tad scary — the gas mask in its case thumping against his side reminded him something quite horrible was never too far away. Plus, with the air raid siren sounding at any moment, even in his young, innocent mind he knew something incredibly bad was approaching. Although, it was strangely fun when Dad would burst into his bedroom, snatch him out of bed placing him over his shoulder, and sprinted down stairs through the house, only slowing down as he reached the top of their garden and the Anderson shelter located there. Nick knew he'd be cuddled up safe with his father those nights.

Twilight was edging its way ever closer, but the street lights did not begin to illuminate the gloom — this was partially due to the Blackout regulations putting paid to that, but more so because this street in the Stoke Heath area of the city still bore the scars of the Luftwaffe's most recent fly past. Having gotten quickly bored visiting Auntie Eileen's home — who was not really an 'auntie' at all, but insisted on being referred to as such even though she was just a friend of Georgina Duncan. The two little lads ran amok in the bomb site. There was nothing like this at the end of their street, despite their home being just round the corner from the Daimler works.

"You can't catch me!"

Alex goaded his younger sibling, skipping through what was left of some poor unfortunate's kitchen, swinging his gas mask case on its strap round and round like an over-zealous windmill.

"Alex! Wait!"

Nick cried out at his brother's shadow, as the older Duncan darted this way and that through the debris. Nick's little legs unable to traverse the rubble with much finesse or speed.

"Come on Slow Coach! A snail can move faster than you!"

The younger Duncan heard his older sibling taunting him further. The little boy began to take risks, now leaping greater distances between ruined furniture and collapsed walls, in an attempt to catch up with his irritating older brother. That was until he over-estimated the gap he was trying to jump across. Slipping on landing, he tumbled to the ground and skinned his other knee in the process. Nick howled in pain, tears flowing down his cherub-like face. He took the strap of the gas mask case from around his neck, and threw the box as far away from himself as he could. It was that dreaded gas mask's fault he'd ended up as a heap in the rubble — again. Moments later, Alex appeared. As soon as he saw his brother sitting on the ground crying with a blooded knee, he burst out laughing.

"What have you done now?"

Showing no sympathy whatsoever, he continued to giggle. In obvious pain, the fallen infant yelled out between sobs.

"I want me Mum!"

This did little but fuel Alex's mirth further, who continued to titter and snigger. That was until in the distance the now familiar yet sinister and menacing sound began — the air raid siren.

Even in his infant mind, Nick knew this wasn't good. He got to his feet just as Alex climbed up to the highest pile of rubble he could find — a semi-collapsed chimney breast — and gazed into the sky in the direction of the siren. Slowly, other sirens closer to their location began, getting louder in intensity.

"Nick, they're coming!"

Alex bounced up and down in his child naivety, as he announced what was occurring. Both boys knew the sirens foretold the visit of many aircraft. Scary, nasty planes dropping their deadly cargo onto their city. It was frightening, yet exciting. Nick peered up at his brother, still snivelling as another siren — this one really close by — began to wail. The little boy attempted to climb up the derelict chimney to get alongside Alex and see what he could, but stopped dead in his tracks as he heard someone shouting, aimed in his direction. In fact, personally right at him. It was Mum!

"Nicholas! Alexander! Quickly, get here!"

Georgy shouted in terror as she ran down the street towards her two sons.

"Now, quickly! We need to get to Auntie Eileen's shelter!"

Both of the boys heard something in the sound of their mother's voice. Mum was speaking with much urgency and fear. This was serious. Scrambling across the rough ground and wreckage, they hurriedly made their way to her.

Meeting them on the kerbside, Georgy took their little hands and ran back up the road from where she had came.

"Mum! Mum! They're coming!"

Alex pointed at the purple sky with all the innocence only a child can possess.

"Come on!"

Now becoming incredibly distraught, Georgy lifted Nick up onto her shoulder and began to run for their lives. Alex, his mother holding his hand as tight as possible, was dragged along in her wake. His feet barely touched the ground as his mother ran for all her worth up the road, heading straight for the house with the front door still wide open from where she had burst out of moments earlier. The sirens gradually fell silent as they fled, which made the air heavy with an eerie, unnatural silence.

As the three reached the passageway between the houses that led to the rear back gardens, a low throb and drone grew in the distance, increasing in volume and presence — the BMW engines belonging to a squadron of Luftwaffe Heinkel He111's — on this occasion aiming for a nearby engine factory. To emphasise this, the anti-aircraft defence battery cannons based nearby opened fire into the heavens. Hurtling along the passageway, Nick peered down at his brother. Alex was now unable to keep up with his mother's speed or purpose. He hung onto her with all his might and drifted through the air. Nick himself found he has squeezed tighter than ever before in his short life, struggling to breathe at times as he bounced along.

They flew into garden, across the dug up and turned over lawn which was now a vegetable patch, to the entrance of the Anderson shelter.

"Thank the Lord you found them!"

Eileen was immensely relieved as the three of them appeared from out of the twilight, taking Nick from his mother's grasp and placed him on the top bed of an empty bunk.

"Nicholas! Where's your gas mask?"

Georgy was panic-stricken, beside herself what her youngest son was going to do during the raid should it be required. Trying to be helpful, but not all, Alex began.

"He dropped it when he fell, Mum."

"We'll go back for it later. He can use mine if need be."

Eileen tried to be positive, to ease Georgy's disquiet. This wasn't helped by the increasing crescendo of the aircraft engines, along with the anti-aircraft battery increasing in intensity. From out of nowhere, two RAF Hawker Hurricane fighters buzzed across the roof tops, climbing straight towards the incoming bombers. As they homed in on their target, they opened fire.

Nick watched this from his vantage point, the British fighters racing at speed to halt the attack from the enemy. As he watched the ascending aircraft, he performed a double take — they had become two civilian planes, two private Cessenas. The approaching throng of the Heinkel bombers had changed too, dissolving into nothing more terrible and imposing than a substantial, dark rain cloud. Nick looked at them again, rubbing his eyes, gesturing towards Auntie Eileen to ask her did she see what he could — only to find Joan Cavanagh sitting next to him.

"Are you OK, Sarge?"

Joan's question snapped Duncan out of his daydream, as

he watched the two small light aircraft fly off into the distance. Having not moved as the traffic had now begun to do so, the driver behind them sounded his horn in frustration.

Moments later they arrived back in the city centre. Duncan pointed out the Coventry Theatre just visible over the elevated ring road.

"Let's strike while the iron is hot." Nick smiled at his colleague.

He parked outside the theatre, looking up at the posters adorned to the walls of the art deco building. They notified the passing public of the up-and-coming concert to be held there by David Bowie, and a new musical *'Passport To Paris'* later in the year. Approaching an open service entrance at the side, the two detectives walked past a tatty Triumph Courier van with its back door flipped wide open like a gaping mouth, parked in front of this was a spotless Hillman Minx convertible. A tall, rugged, burly man unexpectedly appeared from inside the theatre, colliding with Joan and almost knocking her off her feet. Cavanagh was hardly a small woman, but this fellow towered over her.

"Sorry Sweetheart."

The big, curly haired man just managed to grab hold of the constable before she toppled over. The pair pirouetted around on the spot, in an impromptu ballroom dance move. Staring into the large man's eyes, the Scouse Detective began to smile. Duncan could see after the initial shock, Joan was transfixed straight away with the man she had just encountered, her eyes wide in wonder and quite possibly immediate, instant attraction.

"It's quite all right — really. My fault for not looking where I'm going."

The guy smiled broadly back at the Liverpudlian.

"No, all my fault. Absolutely. I'm Oliver."

"I'm Joan."

Bringing the young female Detective out of her lightning bolt moment, Duncan spoke up.

"Cavanagh — we're here on official business, not a social jolly!"

"Yes, Sarge."

Begrudgingly, Joan let go of the man she'd inadvertently met, and took a step back.

"Could you tell us where the manager's office is, please?" Nick addressed Oliver, but before the strapping fellow had chance to reply, a tall well-built woman appeared from the same side door. With long strawberry blonde hair drawn back off her face with a broad headband, and wearing a shawl over a dress she could easily be mistaken for a lecturer at an Art College.

"Mr Sparkes' office is along the passageway, bare to the right. His office is on the left. Who are your new friends, Oliver?"

The lady spoke in a slightly stuffy, if sarcastic tone. Oliver also took his own step away from Cavanagh quite hastily. His demeanour quickly changing at the sight of the woman, becoming uncomfortable and uneasy. Looking apprehensive, he turned towards the mysterious lady, possibly about to answer her query but Cavanagh spoke first and produced her warrant card.

"Warwickshire Police. This is Detective Sergeant Nicholas Duncan, I'm Detective Constable Joan Cavanagh. Just some initial enquiries."

"Well, I'm about if you need anything."

The woman frowned at Oliver as he spoke, snidely peering down her nose at the constable with distaste. *"I'm Alison McLeod. I'm the casting director here and stage manager."* The theatre director offered her right-hand, to which Duncan reciprocated the gesture and shook hands. The detective couldn't help but notice Alison had a minor injury to her hand — skin-coloured first aid sticking plaster was adhered along the side of her index finger and partially on her thumb.

"Had a little accident?"

"Oh, it's nothing really. My cat got a bit lively when I was trimming its claws."

As Nick let go of Alison's hand, he smiled.

"I have the same problem with my cat. I take him to the groomers — got fed up of losing chunks of flesh out of my hands."

Alison tittered.

Duncan missed nothing, as he watched Joan and Oliver make eye contact again, lingering for a few moments as they smiled at each other.

"Constable!" The sergeant snapped.

Cavanagh stroppily strode towards her senior officer, whispered an apology to Oliver before flicking a wry smile in Alison's direction as she passed. Once again, the theatre director looked at the policewoman in mild distaste. Nick was already several dozen yards along the corridor inside by the time Joan caught up.

"Sorry, Sarge."

Duncan stopped dead, turning on his heels to face the constable.

"Joan, I have no issue with you meeting people, chatting to men, maybe even arranging something discreetly for your personal life if you feel the urge, but please remember were on a murder investigation."

The Merseysider sheepishly stared down at her well-polished boots for a few moments, shuffling slightly from one foot to the other awkwardly.

"I know that, Nick. I'm not doing any harm — surely. You must've met people you like through the job."

"Of course! But there's a time and a place."

"Come on, Nick. We barely get time outside of work to do anything, let alone meet people. Take any opportunity that might arise, like?"

Duncan understood Cavanagh's point of view. If it wasn't due to the court case the other day, he would not have met the incredibly intriguing and exciting Harvey. However, his own dedication to the matter in hand over-rode his own personal feelings. Nick frowned at the constable, gently shaking his head. A slight smirk spread across his lips.

"Come on, Casanova — let's find this theatre manager."

The sergeant winked at the scouser, and gestured to the inside of the theatre. Joan smiled back meekly.

Walking along the corridor in the subdued light, the two detectives happened across a bashed about and scruffy brown painted door. Duncan knocked the door firmly twice, to which a muffled older male voice replied.

"Come in!"

Opening the door, the two police officers were met with the scene of an organised but drab office. The room was fastidiously clean, but filled with the blue haze and heavy odour of cigar smoke. *"American tobacco,"* Nick recognised instantly. Behind a desk which would have been more at home in the office of a bank manager, sat a middle-aged man who had a clear military air about him — immaculately trimmed and groomed greying 'salt and pepper' hair in a side parting, paired with an extremely well-kept moustache which was also greying away from its younger dark brown hue.

"Sorry, I only see agents and their clients by appointment only. You'll need to contact my secretary."

"Apologies for the intrusion, Sir."

The sergeant produced his warrant card and offered it towards the seated gentleman.

"I'm Detective Sergeant Nicholas Duncan, this is Detective Constable Joan Cavanagh."

The man straightened himself in his seat. Leaning forward, he extinguished the last couple of inches of his cigar in a nearby ashtray, and exhaled more blue-tinged vapour into the already heavy atmosphere. Cavanagh recoiled slightly, as more of this tobacco-induced fog appearing.

"Please take a seat. I'm John Sparkes, theatre manager here." The two detectives encroached further into the smoky room, sitting in the chairs in front of the desk.

"So what brings the Warwickshire CID to the theatre?"

"Just some initial enquires, Sir. Have you been holding any open auditions recently?"

Mr Sparkes began to relax in his chair, twiddling his thumbs as he spoke.

"Open auditions, eh? Why, yes, we have. Our new musical production which is due to open this August, 'Passport To Paris'. Is there a problem, Sergeant?"

"We'd like to establish who may have attended the auditions. We're interested in a young Indian female who may

have taken part."

The manager stroked his moustache thoughtfully.

"Hmmm, well I think our casting director, Alison McLeod should have kept details of such."

Abruptly, a series of knocks at the door echoed through the office. Without waiting for permission to do so, the door burst open. Alison partially leaned through the open doorway.

"We're off now, John. See you next week after the holidays." As quickly as the door had flew ajar, it slammed shut. Sparkes exchanged glances with his visitors, unsure of what to say next. An awkward silence briefly ensued.

"Er, that was my casting director, the lady I was referring to."

Both Duncan and Cavanagh spun around in their seats, completely surprised at the manager's statement. Joan found her voice first, leaping out of her chair as well.

"Eh, we need to speak with her!"

"Please sit down, Constable. I can access any paperwork you may need to see."

The detectives stared at each another, Joan retook her seat. Duncan found some diplomacy.

"That's very helpful of you Mr Sparkes, but we may need to speak with Miss McLeod also."

"Well, she'll be back on Tuesday should you require her assistance. I'll just find that audition list for you, if you'd care to follow me."

The two detectives followed the theatre manager through the labyrinth of corridors and passageways in the bowels of the building. After several twists and turns, they came to what initially appeared to be a broom cupboard. Opening the narrow door, Mr Sparkes stepped inside and rummaged through some of the files present.

"It's here somewhere..." The manager muttered as he eventually found a beige folder with *'Passport To Paris'* crudely scrawled on the front. *"Ah! Here we are! Sergeant — the full list of who auditioned."*

Sparkes leafed through the enclosed paperwork, and pulled out a series of pages paper-clipped together. The detectives immediately began scouring the long list of names.

"There!" Joan pointed at what quickly had caught her attention — the name of *'Arosha Rana'*. *"May we take this with us, Mr Sparkes? We'll return it like on Tuesday and we need to speak with Miss McLeod as well."*

"Why, without question, Constable!" Sparkes leaned towards Duncan and smiled.

"Anything to help a former serviceman."

"Former serviceman?"

Nick gave the older man a puzzled look.

"Of course! You're ex-military. It's as clear as day. Ex-Navy, at a guess." The policeman smiled broadly.

"Yes, I am! But only by virtue of National Service. Although I was military police for a few years. And I'd say you're ex-Army. Did you see any action during the War?"

"I certainly did. I was a 2nd Lieutenant in the 3rd Royal Tank Regiment. My men fought in the Normandy landings."

A somewhat sober and sad expression spread across the face of the Theatre Manager. Memories he carried were obviously still painful after all these years.

"What a coincidence! I was an officer too — well, non-commissioned — a Warrant Officer in the Naval Regulators."

"You must've been one of the youngest officers in the Navy during peacetime, Sergeant. How old are you, if you

don't mind me asking?"

"I'm thirty-three years old."

"I'd even be as bold as to say you're probably the youngest Detective Sergeant in the history of the Warwickshire Constabulary."

Duncan tried not to visibly gush, plus was attempting to stifle the growing smirk that was growing on his face. Sparkes continued.

"You must be very good. You know you're getting old when police officers are appearing younger and younger, as they say"

The Sergeant now began to blush.

"Well, if that's all you need for now, I'd best get back to my own paperwork. Correspondence with Mr Bowie's people requires my attention."

"Yeah, Mr Sparkes. Thank you for yer help. We'll be in touch next week."

Cavanagh spoke, as Duncan was still tongue-tied after all the compliments he'd just received.

"Anytime Detectives. Allow me to show you out — it really is like a rabbit warren in here. I think there still might be some Vauderville act from before the War still stuck in here."

Once eventually outside, Nick and Joan found the parked cars present from when they had arrived had departed, Duncan assumed Oliver and Alison had been travelling in them.

"Bloody Hell! He didn't just stroke your ego Sarge, he put his hand down yer pants and gave yer balls a huge squeeze!"

"Really?"

As the sergeant spoke, he struggled to contain his huge smirk.

"Oh, yeah! All the mutual respect society fluff about the

Armed Forces, made me think you two should just get a room, like. Plus, with achieving so, so much at such tender young years..."

Duncan's smirk grew larger, partially fuelled by what the constable was pointing out, and additionally by her Scouse sarcasm.

"Jealously isn't that flattering, Miss"

Cavanagh pulled a face at the sergeant, glaring at him.

"You're a bloody good copper, Joan. In my own humble opinion, you should gain your own promotion to sergeant inside the next four to five years."

"Humph! There's more chance of the country electing a female Prime Minister before the decade is out."

This fell on deaf ears, as Duncan's attention was grabbed and dragged elsewhere. On the road where the Triumph and Hillman had been parked — a small patch of oil, with a trail of drips.

"Look!"

Nick pointed at the splatter, drawing Cavanagh's attention to the small spill. The Liverpudlian crouched down, and touched one of the spots.

"They look similar to those we saw the other night."

"Yes. The only issue is we don't know if either of the two cars parked there left this — it could be any car that stopped here previously, or could even be a common problem with many motors."

Joan stood up, looking disappointed.

"It's hardly ever we get a red-hot lead at the start of a case, Joan. For the most part, being a detective is like trawling trough muddy water with a tea strainer. What we need to know is there, in plain sight — it takes time to clearly see it."

125

Duncan crouched down too, inspecting the oil drips. They appeared to be identical to those he'd seen the other night, but without knowing the source or was this liquid the exact same as the one found at the crime scene, this could merely be a coincidence. He stood up and shook his head. This potentially was nothing, sadly.

"That Alison seems full of herself. Typical showbiz type."

"Just because her dress sense isn't the same as yours!"

"Eh, if I was that large, I would never wear what she does!" Cavanagh turned her nose up at the thought.

Climbing back into his Alvis, Nick glanced at the clock.

"Bollocks! I'm late!"

"Late? What for?"

"I'm due to meet my brother at my house. I stupidly agreed to lend him Alice over the Easter weekend."

As swiftly as he could, Duncan drove to his home in Earlsdon.

"Wouldn't it help to use the Blues and Twos, like?"

The constable cheekily put forward this idea. Nick gave the Liverpudlian a look that said, *"Really!"*. Glimpsing at the clock again, Duncan realised his colleague had a point. He leaned forward, flicked two switches on the facia, turning Alice into the unmarked Police car she was under the detective's ownership. With blue lights flashing and tow-tone siren blaring, Nick buried his right foot into the lush carpet, and sped across the city. Cavanagh didn't stop laughing until they arrived outside Duncan's house.

Ellis, Alex and their identical twin daughters — Katherine and Charlotte waited outside Nick's house. Alex knocked the door again, but as his wife pointed out, this was rather futile — the

Alvis was not parked on the driveway.

"Daddy, how much longer is Uncle Nick going to be?" Katherine Duncan hopped from leg to the other, playing an impromptu solo game of hopscotch on the paving slabs leading to the front door of her uncle's home.

"Not long, sweetheart. He'll be here soon."

In the distance, a police car siren could be heard, rapidly getting closer, louder. Ellis and the two girls peered down the street, they could now see a police car racing towards them. The car had its headlights on full-beam, blue lights flashing in motion. Within seconds, said police car came to a screeching halt in front of them. It was Nick behind the wheel of Alice.

"Uncle Nick! Uncle Nick!"

Both of the little girls jumped up and down in excitement at the sight of Alice coming to flying halt in front of them.

"Apologies for my tardiness."

"I was beginning to think you might've become the world's first policeman who couldn't tell the time."

Nick gave his brother a smarmy smile, partially rolled up his left sleeve and pointed at his beloved Universal Polerouter wristwatch. Alex read his brother's watch for a moment.

"Perhaps winding it up might be a good idea, eh?"

The policeman performed a double take checking the timepiece, only to discover it was running and showing the correct time. He glared at his brother.

"Uncle Nick! Who's this with you? Is this your girlfriend?"

Charlotte asked her uncle inquisitively pointing at Cavanagh, as she closed climbed out of the Alvis. Alex and Ellis visibly bit their lips trying not to laugh.

"No, Charlotte. This is my work friend — Joan. She's a

policewoman."

He bent down and picked up his niece, giving her a big cuddle.

"Uncle Nick! Can we play with Stirling?"

Katherine dashed up to Cavanagh, beginning to tug at her skirt.

"Hello Joan. I'd like to be a policewoman too when I grow up."

"You're very forward for someone so young."

Cavanagh crouched down to speak to her. Nick put Charlotte down, who decided to join in with the conversation.

"We're twins."

"I hadn't even noticed!"

The Scouse Detective told them this with the same conviction as telling the girls Santa Claus was going to visit them personally this Christmas. Basically, she lied through her teeth.

"You talk funny."

"Not like Mummy." Katherine, followed by Charlotte, began to quiz the female Detective much to amusement of everyone else.

"That's because I grew up in a city called Liverpool, in the North. I think your Mummy grew up in a place called Hereford."

The twin girls glanced at one another, slightly puzzled.

"I think they speak a little differently there," Cavanagh continued.

"They're intrigued by your accent. You sound different to me."

Ellis interjected, over-hearing both of her daughters chatting. Joan smiled, realising the girl's curiosity.

128

Nick found it quite endearing the twins' attention to detail at a young age had already been piqued. *"Maybe one of them will actually be a copper in the future,"* the sergeant thought to himself.

As the constable kept the two young girls entertained, Nick gestured to his brother to come over to Alice.

"Just a couple of things. Firstly, please don't let the girls play with the switches on the dashboard — a police siren is all well and funny set off by mistake, but not when continually repeated bordering on a habit."

Straight away Nick regretted saying this, as his brother's eyes lit up at the prospect of such a prank.

"Secondly, any remote chance you can bring her back a semblance of 'clean'?"

Alex grinned a sly, naughty grin.

"Please."

"I know how James Bond felt now receiving his briefing from Q about his Aston Martin!"

"Well, one of those switches just might be the ejector seat — you don't want to lose your beautiful wife now, do you?"

Ellis appeared more aghast than at any moment in the years Nick had known her as she heard her brother-in-law's words. The detective quickly tried to save face.

"I'm joking!"

The older Duncan rummaged in his coat pocket, and produced his car keys.

"Swop!"

He attempted to throw the keys to his younger brother, but Nick's body language was all too clear. Reluctantly in a manner which seemed agonisingly painful, the sergeant swopped keys with his brother.

"Come on girls! We've got Uncle Nick's police car!"

Alex boasted at the top of his voice, to which the twin girls ran towards Alice with huge excitement and cheering. The three of them rapidly leapt inside the Alvis.

"Sorry, Nick."

Ellis began to apologise for her husband's outburst. Nick shrugged his shoulders and gave an indifferent look in his brother's direction.

"Don't worry. I wouldn't expect anything less from him, really."

The policeman flashed an indifferent glance towards his sibling.

Alex gave a cod salute now behind the wheel of his brother's car. The detective pushed his face against the side window, peering into the rear, watching his two nieces bouncing and jumping about on the plush leather of his Alvis.

"And keep your feet off the seats!"

His statement did little but fuel the two little girl's enthusiasm and vigour further. They quickly found out the same as Cavanagh had established, shuffling on the back seat caused hilarious flatulence sounds.

"See you on Monday. And thank you."

Ellis smiled as she leaned partially out of the open window, placing her hand on top of Nick's on the edge of the door, rubbing it slightly.

"Bye Uncle Nick!"

The twins bode farewell in unison and at the top of their voices, as another fake fart was heard from the rear of the car, followed by much hilarity.

"Nick, what does this do?"

Alex asked rhetorically, while at the same time flicking

one of the switches. Right away, the two-tone siren began. With a huge cheesy, childish grin, he drove off. Alice flew down the street at speed before the younger Duncan brother had chance to complain.

"Alex! You complete bastard!"

The detective shouted after his car as it vanished into the distance, the siren drowning out his words. Joan had given up trying to hold her mirth in, and began laughing out loud.

"Oh, shut up you! Or I'll make sure you're transferred to uniform traffic duties."

This did little to cease her hilarity.

"Demoted for laughing? I can imagine the grid on the Union rep at hearing that!"

Duncan began to chuckle as well, now seeing the ridiculousness of the situation. His humour was clipped as he remembered the keys in his hand. He turned his attention to the vehicle they belonged to — a shabby and unloved Standard Vanguard Six estate. Nick sighed heavily, which only caused Cavanagh to begin giggling again.

"Bit of a difference to your beloved Alice, eh?"

"I daren't wash it! I think it's all the muck that holds it together!"

The detective realised his comments were just making Joan laugh more. He decided it would be for the best to talk about something else.

"Get in the car."

Climbing into the Vanguard, Nick realised something straight away as he looked at the dashboard.

"Remind me to pick up a portable radio back at the station."

Arriving back at Little Park Street, Duncan felt awkward parking his brother's car. It clearly showed.

"Are you all right, Sarge?"

"Humph! Just about. This heap has no brakes, the heaviest clutch I've ever had the misfortune to have used, and handles like a yacht!"

"You're such a snob."

"Piss Off!"

Nick grumpily clambered out of the car, but his mood continued to darken. On the tarmac in front of him was a trail of oil his brother's motor had deposited. It appeared his initial hunch about this might be more common than he realised was true. The policeman sighed in disappointment.

In front of both detectives glided effortlessly into the car park one of the Warwickshire Constabulary's latest sleek interceptors, a barely year-old Jaguar XJ6. With its high visibility orange stripe the full length of the car along its flanks, and roof detail of signage and blue-flashing lights, the car in modern livery appeared a whole world away from the Mk.II Jags Nick used to drive as a humble PC. Duncan purred with approval and an uncontrollable silly smirk spread across his face.

"Boys and their toys…" Joan muttered, shaking her head.

Nick knew she didn't understand, seeing a guy going all weak-kneed over a piece of metal. But everyone has that one interest they are fascinated in. Duncan's was cars. As the patrol car came to a stop, he wandered over and took a good look inside. Much to his surprise, his former colleague Jack Hicks who was now a sergeant himself, grinned like the proverbial joyous imbecile back at Duncan. Nick opened the driver's door of the Jaguar.

Nick opened the driver's door of the Mk.II Jaguar with his left foot, juggling two teas in polystyrene cups. Trying to execute this as quickly as possible, he wanted to prevent the falling snow dropping into the beverages diluting them too much. As the snow steadily fell, Duncan felt the all-white bodywork of the patrol car would be like camouflage, hiding it to a degree to the casual observer.

"Here you is, Sarge."

The Constable leaned into the car, handing Sergeant Noel Ribbons a cup. *"Thank fuck for that,"* Nick muttered under his breath. They were beginning to burn his hands.

"Ooo, thanks, son."

As he slid behind the wheel, Duncan sipped at his piping hot, steaming tea. He glanced back at the chip shop he'd managed to blag the drinks from with a smidge of good-natured banter and flattery. In hindsight, maybe he should have bought a bag of chips and a piece of fish as well. They smelt delicious. Taking another swig of his drink, Nick partially burnt his top lip on the hot liquid. Perhaps allowing more snow to have fallen into it would have been a good idea after all.

From out of nowhere, a royal blue MGB GT raced past them in the opposite direction, travelling at several times the speed limit. Noel choked on his hot tea.

"Bloody Hell! He's not hanging about — where's the fire?"

Duncan didn't gain chance to reply or comment, as the sergeant opened the door, grabbed Nick's drink and threw it along with his own out into the night.

"Get after that prat, Lad. I'd like to know what his

problem is." The Constable started the Big Cat, which erupted into life with a roar. He quickly flicked the car around on the wet road and set off at speed after the sports car. With the siren howling and flashing blue lights being reflected off every surface they passed, Ribbons reached for the radio handset.

"Mike One, this is Mike Indigo Two, Over."

The Sergeant was greeted with static.

"This is Mike Indigo Two — Mike One are you receiving? Over."

Once again, Ribbons was met with heavy static. Noel's face was a study. He glanced at Nick, his face full of frustration.

"This sodding weather always plays havoc with the radio!"

He started to hit the handset against the dashboard repeated for good measure. Peering through the windscreen, Duncan turned the wipers onto a regular constant sweep, as the snow fell steadily against the glass.

The older man tried the radio yet again, as the Jaguar flew along the road, accelerating harder and harder.

"Mike One, this is Mike Indigo—"

Then, there was a reply.

"Mike Indigo Two, this is Mike One receiving. Over."

"Mike One, we are in pursuit of a blue MGB GT, heading south west on Holyhead Road towards Allesley. Currently travelling at fifty — five oh — miles per hour and gaining speed. Over."

"Received Mike Indigo Two. Out."

In the distance, Nick could barely make out the tail lights of the sports car through the wintery weather. He buried his right foot into the carpet, resulting in the Jaguar starting to prove why it was the fastest production saloon car money could buy. Approaching the traffic island at the end of the Holyhead Road, Duncan caught clearer sight of the MG. Steering into the curve he flicked the rear of the car out and held it there as they drifted around the bend, before straightening up.

"Steady, son."

A little perturbed, Noel reached over his left shoulder for his seat belt hasp, fastening himself into his seat with much haste. Motoring at a fair lick along the dual carriageway, the two policemen could now see the rear of the escaping blue car. The increasing speed of the MG clearly suggested the driver either didn't have a moment to lose or was out on the ultimate 'jolly'.

The MG sped around the next island, and up the slip road onto the A45 towards Birmingham. Nick followed suit, really opening the Jag up. The engine sung the sweetest symphony of speed, as the car darted forwards not phased or hindered by the soaked tarmac or inclement weather. Within seconds, the police car was right behind the escaping sports car. *"They must be aware we want them to stop by now,"* Duncan muttered to himself under his breath, but realised he'd actually spoken quite clearly out loud. The sergeant replied.

"I reckon our new friend here believes out running us is the best way to impress his girlfriend."

Ribbons picked up the radio handset once again.

"Mike One, this is Mike Indigo Two. Over."

Almost instantly, a female voice with a thick Black Country accent replied.

"Mike One receiving. Over."

"Mike Indigo Two still in pursuit of blue MGB GT. Vehicle refusing to stop. Now on A45 Coventry Road, heading westbound towards Birmingham. Now doing ninety — nine-oh — miles per hour. Over."

"Message received, Mike Indigo Two. Out"

Nick glanced down at the speedo himself, and saw first-hand the Jaguar's acceleration. A few short seconds after Ribbons had spoken to control, the car was now moving at close on 100 mph and still accelerating.

The Jaguar having caught up with the MG, was now staying on its tail as it attempted to pull away. The sports car initially appeared to be starting to slow down, as the turn for Meridian approached, but at the last moment it burst forward with sudden, unexpected purpose.

The snow continued to pelt against the front of the police car, causing Nick to switch the windscreen wipers onto their fastest speed to aid his vision.

"It might be for the best we call this chase off, Sarge." Ribbons glanced back at him with an old-fashioned expression.

"What the bloody hell for?"

"Er, safety..." Duncan replied in a tone that meant 'Isn't it obvious?'

"There's a reason why he doesn't want to stop and talk to us."

As the two cars raced into the darkness, Nick had a realisation.

"He's going to have to slow down shortly. We're approaching another island."

In the corner of his eye, Duncan saw Noel's face

quickly convey his smug, satisfied but thorough state of mind.

"Get alongside him, Lad. When he starts to slow down, get in front and box him up against the kerb."

Duncan obliged his Sergeant's request, pulling the more rapid Jaguar to one side of the MG, and began to overtake.

As the road began to run downhill to another traffic island, Nick covered the brake pedal with his right foot ready to slow down and stop. Unbelievably, the MG continued to accelerate on this downwards slip road. As the junction grew ever closer, the constable refrained from entering into a game of 'chicken' and began quickly to slow down. However, he found applying the brakes had little effect — the seasonal weather had had that magical effect of making tarmac into something rather lethal, more suited for winter Olympic sports.

Before Nick had opportunity to carry out the stop procedure his Sergeant had requested, the sports car began fishtailing this way and that, almost colliding with the patrol car.

"Bloody Hell!"

It was clear to the two policemen the driver of the MG was losing control. As the Jaguar's speed decreased, the sports car entered into a side-on skid. They could see the young male at the wheel sawing with the wheel, battling to straighten the car up within the amount of road left to manoeuvre. The same was true for Duncan. But not only did he have the same limited stopping distance, he also had to contend with the escaping car performing a pirouette in front of him.

"He's going to stuff that! I just know it!"

Nick was too preoccupied to reply to his Sergeant's solemn prediction. He already knew it was going to take a near-miracle to bring their car not only to a stop, but remaining in one piece as well.

As the MG managed to exit its skid, the constable had reduced the Jag's speed enough to such it was now a clear three to four car lengths behind. Duncan began to initially apply the brakes gently, as engine-braking alone was not going to be sufficient. Observing the sports car in the corner of his eye, Nick could see Noel's prophecy was going to come true. Having now locked all four wheels up in an attempt to come to a halt on the quickly reducing amount of road, the MG still continued forwards.

Both policemen looked on in horror as the royal blue car crashed into, then mounted the high kerb surrounding the island, and smashed through the direction signage present. The car itself continued to plough through the soft turf for a good ten to fifteen yards before coming to a sudden, abrupt stop as the tyres and crumpled front end dug into the sodden ground.

Duncan was snapped back to the problem in hand, as the tail of the police car slewed out. Noel grabbed the handle above his left ear and held on for all his worth with both hands.

"FOR FUCK'S SAKE, NICK!"

The constable knew if he steered into the skid, the Jag would straighten but would be heading in the exact, same direction as the now wrecked MG. Instead, he drove out of the slide, blipped the throttle, and sent the tail around in the opposite direction. This resulted in the car sliding side on towards the island and the crash scene. Duncan threw the wheel back into the skid and stamped on the brakes as hard as he could. Additionally, he grabbed the handbrake lever and pulled it as high as it would travel, thus locking the rear wheels. The Jaguar became stationary, almost facing the direction from which it had come.

Nick opened the driver's door and leaped out, snatching the torch in the door pocket and turning it on. He dashed into the feather-like snow tumbling from the heavens towards the stricken MG.

Duncan clambered out of the XJ6, and gently closed the door. He smiled a wry smirk as he gazed back inside the car, admiring its new equipment and contemplated how useful it would've been ten years ago when he drove the interceptors.

"Fancy a go, Nick?"

The detective snapped out of his recollection as the uniform sergeant spoke. Duncan smiled back at him.

"That'd be nice, Jack. Maybe when I'm not so busy."

A discrete female cough interrupted the conversation between the two male officers. Nick swivelled around to see Cavanagh standing with hands in pockets, gesturing with her head towards the station building.

"I've got to go Jack — see you soon."

Sergeant Hicks nodded, as the detective wandered inside with his Scouse colleague.

A few short hours later in the Hare & Squirrel public house, members of the CID Team amassed.

"I had a feeling the promise of a couple of drinks might

get everyone here."

Edwards briefly choked on the first swig of his pint at Spencer's words, almost spraying beery froth across all assembled as he did his utmost not to laugh at the same time as he swallowed.

"Surely not, Sir. The appeal of the exquisite company was the main draw."

Duncan winked as he finished his comment.

"Pish! Bytheway, ever since I came south of the border, I'm still trying to find somewhere that sells proper ale!"

St John wasn't entirely enamoured with his beverage, taking pathetically small sips of the brew.

"You could always go back. I'll help you pack."

"Awa' an bile yer heid!"

Nick caught sight of Joan sipping her vodka and tonic, trying not to laugh as he bickered with his Scottish counterpart.

"You're in a good mood, Sebastian. Anything the matter?" Despite his differences with St John, Duncan was willing to help a fellow copper. *"Sebastian may have a gruff, at times unlikeable exterior,"* the detective thought to himself, *"But he's a good policeman."*

"Humph! Yous didnae have to tell the rest o' the office tomorra wasnae Poet's Day! Yer can imagine their reaction!"

St John saracastically snorted, as he spoke.

"Poet's Day?"

Cavanagh queried what the sergeant said, confusion spreading across her face.

"Piss Off Early Tomorrow's Saturday," Nick explained the slang acronym, to which St John smiled and nodded.

"Ahhh!"

Both Joan and Rachel spoke in unison, giggling at the

same time.

"How did you get into CID., if you don't mind me asking?"

The Liaison Officer asked Joan, her long coat covering her uniform. She reached up to her neck and undid her cravat, which clearly gave away her occupation as it was finished in the all too familiar black and white sillitoe tartan.

"Well, it was like this..."

Rachel leaned towards the Merseysider as she spoke. Hearing anyone speak in the noisy pub was becoming somewhat problematic.

"I was the same as you — I joined the Bizzies—"

"Bizzies?"

"Oh, sorry, Police. I was first as a WPC. Then became liaison between uniform and CID. I found I had a talent for detective work and was noticed by a D.I. there."

"I really hope the Guv'nor notices me. I'd love to be a W.D.C. like you."

Duncan had his back to the two constables, but heard all of this.

"Rach, if you do what's asked of you, and if an opportunity or lucky break appears — take it! Best way to get noticed."

Joan paused for a moment, taking a large slurp of her drink.

"But please do one thing above all else."

"What's that, Joan?"

"Don't let your personal feelings — fancying a workmate — cloud your Judgement."

Rachel instantly became flushed, a little embarrassed and stared at her shoes.

"Can you tell that easily?"

"Afraid so. Sergeant Duncan noticed straight away you're sweet on Mr Ward."

"I certainly did."

The two young women glanced up, rapidly becoming aware the afore mentioned Sergeant Duncan had now joined the conversation. The Liaison Officer blushed even more.

"Sorry, Skipper."

"Just bare this in mind, Rachel. Becoming emotionally involved and attached to a fellow colleague is all well and good, but once the Guv'nor and Spencer get wind of any liaisons between Constable Ward and yourself, you'll be back directing traffic at Coundon Halt level crossing before you can say candle lit dinner for two!"

Nick rested his hand gently on Rachel's shoulder. The WPC glumly stared at the carpet more intently than before.

"No one wants to stop you having a life. It could compromise the integrity of an investigation having two people who are lovers working upon it."

"Yes, Skipper. That was made crystal clear during basic training."

"Exactly!"

The detective began to walk back to the senior officers.

"It's upto you. We have no control over who we fall for or fancy. Shame you have fallen for a guy who already has a girlfriend."

Rachel's face changed dramatically in the blink of an eye from self-conscious into shocked. As she stared at her housemate for confirmation of the sergeant's comment, the detective constable nodded slowly. Nick meanwhile walked directly into a debate over the case.

"Personally, I think we should not rule out the racist

attack angle."

Spencer popped his pipe into his mouth and drew on the tobacco vapours it emanated after his statement. Edwards and St John both nodded in agreement. Standing next to Sebastian, Nick was suddenly struck by the odour. Although it wasn't completely offensive, it wasn't a joy to behold either — cheap, mass produced after shave applied to a man's body that was still two or three nights away from his weekly bath. The cologne itself was one that came out of a blue bottle with a white gull adorned to it, Nick concluded. He considered maybe Cavanagh's comment earlier in the office had caused him to have a guilt trip.

"It cuss be, sir." St John agreed with the chief Inspector.

"Maybe a lover's tiff gone nasty?"

The other three men nodded once again.

"Was anything untoward gleaned from the visit to her place of employment?"

The DCI continued to puff upon his pipe as he spoke. Yet again, the Scottish Sergeant was first to respond.

"Arosha wa'popular with her work colleagues, socialised with some. Nae problems, issues or enemies as fa as we can tell."

Edwards swished his pint in his hand, staring into it, nodding.

"But there's a'odd job laddie — maintenance man around da store — been known to flirt with anethin' in a skirt — even twist a few arms to gew on dates."

Duncan couldn't help himself.

"Best you don't meet him in national dress, eh?"

Nick winked at Sebastian after finishing his quip. St John glared back, furious.

After stifling a snigger, Edwards announced, *"Sounds like a right Casanova! He's interesting already."*

Duncan took a large gulp of his calvados, just as the chief Inspector spoke to all gathered.

"Anything else to contribute, gentlemen?"

Swallowing the liquor as speedily as possible, while simultaneously trying not to wince at the burning sensation it brought to the back of his throat, Nick managed to find his voice.

"Sir, I've looked through her diary and noticed a few dates she'd marked, including the day she was killed." The three other officers stared at Duncan — their attention now entirely focused upon him. *"I've also asked her parents about any potential boyfriend. They're not aware of anyone on the scene."*

Spencer rubbed his chin a little and moved onto stroke his well-groomed moustache as he speculated.

"Maybe something clandestine occurring..."

"My feelings exactly."

Nick agreed with the chief Inspector. He felt this situation was already far from straight forward.

CHAPTER FOUR
GOOD FRIDAY
FRIDAY APRIL 20th 1973

Daylight began to seep into Nick's bedroom around the edges of the curtains, slowly bringing the detective out of his slumber. Groggily, he yawned and stretched, rolling over to face his traditional style alarm clock with twin bells attached to the top. It cheerfully informed him with its luminous hands visible in the sub-dued light the time was approaching five past nine, in the morning. Sleepily, he reached out towards the bedside cabinet. After gently slapping his hand around on the flat surface several times, he found his Polerouter wristwatch and peered at it with one eye. It told him the time was exactly the same as the alarm clock had already informed him. Satisfied, he snuggled down under the covers, not wishing to get up as yet. A well-deserved lay in was required. Duncan had been looking forward to this for some time now — a whole weekend off to do with as he pleased. He closed his eyes with a contented sigh, and drifted back off.

Something appeared on the bed next to Nick, causing him to awake with a start. The four blunt paws walking over him could clearly be felt through the blanket and eiderdown. They left the detective with no doubt who it was.

"Morning Stirling."

The sergeant greeted the plump tabby, which now lay

across his chest. The feline began rubbing its face and whiskers into Duncan's features, purring the same way a low horsepower combustion engine can, but required its timing readjusting. Stirling bumped his head against his owner's, to emphasise his desire the human should get out of bed and attend to breakfast.

"Ok, Ok! I get the message!"

The detective protested to his pet, but the hungry feline was persistent in its need to be fed right here, right now. Throwing back the covers, Duncan reluctantly got up and headed downstairs.

After opening a tin of the most revolting and repulsive smelling fish pate that was masquerading as the latest in haute cuisine in feline feast, Duncan scooped a few large spoonsful into Stirling's stainless-steel bowl. Nick headed to the phone in the hallway as the ravenous tabby slurped and snorted away at his breakfast. Lifting the receiver, he dialled a number from memory. After a couple of rings, a woman's voice answered cheerfully.

"Hello…"

"Hi Val — it's Nick."

"Hello, you!"

Val cooed, extremely pleased to hear from the sergeant.

"Are we still on for tomorrow night, Constable?" Nick laughed politely, humouring his old friend. She always greeted him like this.

"Of course, Miss Myers! Spare room ready and waiting as per usual. And I'm a sergeant now — I keep telling you."

She giggled in return, teasing her friend.

"I've got a couple of new LPs you may like."

Duncan was distracted for a moment, as he heard

something at the front door.

The brass door knocker thudded against its strike plate twice in quick succession, echoing along the hallway of the house. Nick darted out of his bedroom to peer through the spindles of the banister to see who was the caller was. His father strode to the front door from the back room, hastily putting his dark blue tunic on, still doing up the silver buttons as he opened the heavy wooden door.

"Hello Valerie. My, you look sharp. Is that for the street party?"

"Hello Mr Duncan. Thank you! It was a gift from my Auntie Linda and Uncle Wilbur."

Nick craned his neck around the banister to see what exactly Val was wearing, but all he caught sight of was the back of his dad.

"Are you going to the party, Mr Duncan?"

"No, Valerie. I'm on duty I'm afraid. I should see some of the ceremony on the TV at the station. He's upstairs I'll see if he's awake."

"Thank you — if you don't mind."

Nick watched his father back away from the door and turn in his direction. He quickly retreated from his vantage point into the opening of his bedroom door.

"Nicholas!" The police Sergeant's voice boomed through the house. *"Your girlfriend is here!"*

The young Duncan leapt across the landing, and proceeded to remonstrate.

"She isn't my girlfriend! She's just a mate!"

Bob strolled back into the house, chuckling. Nick hurtled down the stairs as fast as his teenage legs would

147

allow, jumping over the last three steps in one exaggerated large stride. His appearance was so sudden, Val took an evasive skip to the side in surprise.

"Hello, you!"

The young woman Nick greeted was his closest friend, attired in a sleeveless pale honeysuckle yellow dress. As was the fashion, the garment had a stiffened petticoat under the skirt, to emphasise the 'A line' design. It reminded Duncan of a meringue dessert, especially as she spun around allowing the skirt to bellow out and fully reveal the huge petticoat.

"Do you like it? Matching headband and shoes too."

"You look great."

"Latest thing from America. My Auntie and Uncle brought it back for me. And these..."

Val opened her substantial handbag, revealing a dozen or so seven-inch singles. Nick reached in and pulled several out.

"Bill Haley and The Comets, Little Richard, Jackie Brenston and his Delta Cats, Fats Domino..."

"They're brilliant, Nick. Like nothing you've ever heard before. Let's go upstairs and listen to a few." The young Duncan couldn't help but allow the huge grin spread across his face. He really wanted to hear this new style of music. They both began to climb the stairs, when the teenage boy let out a cry of disgust.

"ERRRR! Mum! Dad!"

At the end of the hallway, Nick's parents were enjoying an intimate moment. Arms wrapped around one another, they were savouring a somewhat steamy kiss.

"You know I always kiss your Mum 'Ta-Ra' when I leave

for work."

"You'll be doing the same in years to come, young man." Georgy defended her own behaviour in as motherly way as possible. Nick gave his parents a *'Really?'* expression.

"Come here give your old man a kiss." Bob tormented his son, starting to move towards the foot of the stairs in what seemed like the beginning of a chase.

"Sod Off!" Nick protested, dashing upstairs.

"Remember, you promised Alex you'd help move those tables and chairs into the street!" Georgy shouted after her son.

"I think it's lovely." Val smiled as she watched Georgy put her arms around Bob's waist, pulling herself into her husband, resting her head on his shoulder.

"You look fantastic, Val. Your sister was just as swish in her blue outfit. I saw her down the shops earlier."

"Awww, thank you Mrs Duncan."

"You best get yourself upstairs, before his Lordship sulks!" Bob tried not to laugh as he spoke.

Sniggering, Val followed her friend into his bedroom at a more sedate pace, finding him sitting on the edge of the bed, readying his record player.

"Bloody soppy pair. They're always doing that."

"I think it's beautiful."

"Humph!"

"Are you jealous?" Val asked Nick between giggles.

"No!"

"You are! I think you'd love to have a girlfriend who'd cuddle and kiss you."

Before the young teenage boy had chance to remonstrate with his friend to the contrary, Val plonked herself next to him, threw her arms around his neck and kissed him full on the mouth.

Taken completely off guard, Nick didn't have a clue how to react. It felt nice, pleasant even, but no tingle of excitement or a zoom of good feeling. It felt the same as when he gave his mother or Auntie Alice a kiss, but with a huge awkward edge. He wanted it to end immediately, but didn't want to push Val away. Within his mind, it confirmed something.

In Alex's bedroom, he had pictures of his favourite Coventry City footballers, and world champion boxer Rocky Marciano. He also had pictures of several Hollywood starlets — Nick knew his brother carried a torch for one actress in particular, Rita Hayworth. In his own room, the wall decoration included his own sporting heroes from the world of Formula One, and his treasured Coventry Bees speedway pennant which were fighting for attention with his choice of Hollywood 'starlet' in Tony Curtis, Clark Gable and Rock Hudson (the latter being his own personal favourite). He now knew something for certain he had for several years. He was not attracted to the opposite sex. He was attracted to his own gender.

"Are you all right?"

Val peered at her friend slightly concerned, still with her arms around his neck. The young Duncan tried to appear as though everything was all right.

"Yes. Yeah, I'm fine. Thanks."

"You don't seem so."

Nick not only appeared awkward, but felt so in droves. He really did not know what to do with himself. He glanced at the picture of Rock Hudson on the wall behind Val, mentally asking for advice. Gradually, she relinquished her embrace.

"Really. I'm OK."

He nervously giggled too, hoping that might assist in defusing the situation.

"I'm sorry if I've upset you, Nick. I just wanted to kiss you, because I...I really like you."

The teenage girl blurted out her confession, opening up in a manner that not only completely surprised Nick but he instantly admired her bravery and candour.

"I like you too".

Duncan tried not to upset Val, either. The thing was, he meant he liked her as a close friend — like a sister — nothing more. Nick knew the young woman was suggesting something more romantic and intimate. Thinking fast, he tried to find something to divert attention away from where they were at.

"Are you wearing stockings, Val?"

He hadn't registered everything she was wearing after all the banter with his father. While appearing a sun-kissed, golden-brown hue, Val's legs had a matt finish to them.

"Yeah, Auntie Linda gave them to me. She said they go with the dress and shoes. My first pair. Do you like them?"

"They're very nice."

Nick tried to remain as neutral as possible under the circumstances. He had barely finished speaking, when Val lifted the hem of her skirt to reveal the dark brown stocking top around her right thigh, complete with white clasp attached to suspenders that vanished under her dress. This was far from the distraction the young Duncan had in mind.

Moving faster than at any other point in his short life, Nick leapt to his feet.

"Let's have a listen to some of those records."

He felt this might quosh Val's amorous advances. Rummaging through her bag, Nick pulled out the disc with Jackie Brenston upon the label, and placed it on the turntable. Moving the stylus towards the spinning vinyl, he placed it on the edge. The song *'Rocket 88'* began. Nick beamed a huge grin in approval.

"This is brilliant!"

"Told you so."

Abruptly, the door flew open in a manner that nearly removed it clean off its hinges. In stepped Alex.

"Come on Lover Boy — let's get those tables and chairs onto the street."

Normally, the younger Duncan would have exploded in fury at his brother for not only ordering him about, but bursting into his own private domain uninvited. However, today he did not mind one iota. This was exactly the diversion he needed.

"Sorry Alex. Did you want help right now?"

"If you don't mind, Bro."

Nick didn't need asking twice, and dashed out of the room in his brother's wake.

Leaning into the hall, the policeman saw the morning

newspaper protruding through the letterbox.

"So what's these new LPs you're eager to plague my ears with?"

"Cheeky! I'm not the one who owns all of Elton John's albums!" Val giggled down the phone at her friend.

"I do not! I borrowed them off Alex!"

"Someone doth protest too much."

The two friends laughed at each other down the phone. After a few moments, Val answered Nick's question.

"I've got the new albums by Pink Floyd — that's superb — and David Bowie's latest."

"That's a point, actually. Are you still up for seeing Ziggy when he comes to the Cov Theatre?"

"Oh, yeah! As long as I can bring someone along with me."

"Please not your sister, Esther." Duncan retorted quite seriously, it was obvious he didn't want Val's sibling tagging along. She began to giggle again.

"No, no! It's someone else, someone I've met."

"Ooooo! Oh, do tell!"

"Well, he's a couple of years older than us, he lives not too far away from me in Cheltenham, works as a fireman."

"Sounds good so far. Has he ever been married? Any kids?" Val laughed as he questioned her.

"I knew I'd be on the receiving end of one of your interrogations, Detective."

Duncan began laughing too. It did sound like a softly — softly approach line of enquiry he was giving his friend.

"He's lovely, Nick. We've been seeing each other now for close on three months."

"Three months? You've never said anything before! How

come the big secret?"

Val burst out laughing, and continued to titter at the policeman's reaction.

"Because of all your questioning! You're worse than my mother!"

"I am not!"

"You so are, Nicholas Duncan!" Val continued to giggle at her friend. *"Well, before you start his name is Richard, he's a bit taller than you, a bit thicker set, and Yes — you'll no doubt fancy him, but he's not interested in 'boys'."*

Nick was impressed Val said all of this without coming up for air, which only fuelled his own mirth further.

"So, if it's all right with you, I'd like you to meet him. In fact, this weekend if that's OK."

Feeling quite flattered his friend wanted him to meet her new beau, someone so important to her, Duncan agreed.

"I'd love to, Val. He sounds fantastic."

"May I be cheeky? Can Rich stay over at yours with me tomorrow night?"

"Of course. You can share with Stirling. Richard can have the spare room."

"Very funny! Since when have you been a comedian?"

Once again, the two friends laughed warmly at one another.

"Well, I've got to go — a few chores to do. See you tomorrow, Constable."

"Oi! Sergeant, if you please! Yeah, I've got a few things to sort out too. Firstly, persuading Stirling to share his bed with you."

Val laughed again. Their sense of humour was virtually identical.

"See you tomorrow, Dave Allen."

"May your God go with you." He heard his friend laughing once again, as she gently hung up the phone.

Straight away, Nick had the feeling he was being watched, being observed by something on the hallway carpet. It was Stirling, staring straight at him with a disapproving, frosty stare.

"I suppose you want feeding again, Sire."

The near-permanently ravenous feline followed his owner into the kitchen, rubbing around Duncan's legs purring loudly, tripping up his owner twice in the process. Half-filling the cat's bowl from a nearby tin, the detective screwed up his nose in disgust at the sight of the cat food. He read the label out loud.

"Salmon and trout."

Peering at the slop, Nick prodded it with a fork.

"Could've fooled me, Stirling."

The tabby simply could not wait any longer, and leapt up onto the table. Finding his bowl awaiting, the cat began eating the contents greedily. Nick tried not to heave. It smelt even more revolting than earlier that morning.

While washing up, Duncan switched on the portable handheld radio he had borrowed from the station. Partially so he could be gotten hold of easily should the need arise, but mainly so he could be nosey and listen in on any developments. All he had heard so far was news of a burglary last night in Holbrooks, a domestic in Alderman's Green, and a car theft in Tile Hill. Nothing related to the murder case. He began to busy himself around the kitchen and turned his own transistor radio on, fortuitously at the moment the local news headlines were announced. An older male newsreader with the plumiest, cut-glass British accent spoke.

"On the hour, here is the news from BBC Radio Birmingham. Consumer lobby groups are urging the Government to re-think the criteria of the Value Added Tax system it introduced at the start of the year. The tax adds 10% of the purchase value to non-essential and luxury goods, however as this includes all adult clothing and ladies' sanitary products, it is seen as unjust and unfair.

The funeral of Spanish artist, Pablo Picasso has taken place near his home in Southern France. The Impressionist passed away last week aged 91, and is survived by his third wife and four children.

The American space agency, NASA, has announced its interplanetary probe, Pioneer 11 which was launched from Cape Canaveral in Florida two weeks ago, is functioning well above expectations. The spacecraft will pass through the Asteroid Belt in twelve-months' time, enroute to a liaison with the planet Jupiter in the Autumn of next year, before travelling on to meet Saturn in early 1979.

Rumours are abounding, an announcement is imminent from Buckingham Palace over the possible engagement of Her Royal Highness Princess Anne and Lieutenant Mark Phillips. The couple have been attending Royal functions and social gatherings together since they met five years ago.

In local news, Warwickshire Police are appealing for any information into the mysterious death of a young woman. A body was found this week on a secluded country lane in North Coventry, with Police eager for any member of the public with any relevant information to please come forward.

On a lighter note, open auditions are currently taking place at the Coventry Theatre for a new musical, 'Passport To Paris'. We'll be speaking later with director and *choreographer Alison McLeod. In our sports report in twenty minutes, we'll preview this weekend's football and speedway fixtures."*

Football bored the pants off Duncan, so he attempted to retune the radio onto a music channel. Sadly, the feature on motorcycle speedway would be relatively brief, with more bias given to football. As the static hissed and popped, he dwelled over the request to the public for information he'd just heard, wondering if it would prove fruitful. Amongst all the somewhat useless, daft, weird and gormless phone calls CID will receive from some sad and lonely members of the public attention seeking, there might be something that would assist in solving the case.

The detective was particularly impressed with the choice of words in the news article — *'mysterious death'*. This sounded much more palatable than the truth — *'murdered'*. After an age, he found something being broadcast he liked — Ricky Nelson singing his hit song *'Mary Lou'* burst through the air. *"That's better!"* He whistled in time to the tune, as he scrubbed at Stirling's bowl. The sergeant speculated in his mind over who might have killed Arosha, and why.

Could it have been someone from her own family? Duncan had heard of sometimes people couldn't accept a child had become grown up, living an adult's life, undertaking all responsibilities and privileges that entails. Or possibly a family friend, maybe a member of the community, a neighbour, even a work colleague who had designs on her and could not contain themselves no longer. There was also the infamous 'crime of passion' angle that could not be disregarded. Could an over-possessive lover or highly jealous ex-partner have done this? Or possibly a potential suitor who

Arosha had rebuffed? There was also the cultural / race issue. Was the incident racially motivated? Was Arosha secretly dating a white guy, and someone disapproved from her family or temple, or even from his community? Robbery wasn't the motive, due to her belongings still being intact.

All that Nick knew, some individual wanted to either silence Arosha, or remove her from a situation. After contemplating for a few minutes, his police radio crackled into life. Nick heard uniform trying to locate teenage shoplifters in the city centre — nothing to concern himself with, kids pinching sweets from the pick and mix section in Woolworths. Recalling what he promised his brother earlier in the week about visiting their Mum, he began tidying away, then ventured upstairs to get dressed.

As he drove across the city to his parent's home, he dwelled upon a personal matter of massive importance — should he tell his Mum he was gay? Duncan had tried to on numerous occasions, but never succeeded for differing reasons. On some, he'd lost his confidence. Maybe his Mum would react horribly to the news, and want nothing to do with him. At other times, something else was happening around his mother, causing Nick to feel it wasn't the right time. He geed himself up, thinking now would be a perfect moment to tell her. Surely, she must realise, after all he'd never had a girlfriend as such, and since his teenage years he'd never spoken of or referred to any lady on a personal level. Yes, this afternoon would be good — Alex, Ellis and the girls were away, he was off work, and baring the Queen passing on within the hour, nothing would divert anybody's attention.

Nick eventually arrived at his parent's house, still taking a good couple of miles to become accustomed to his brother's car. The steering was so vague at times, he needed to use all of his detective skills to establish in which direction the front wheels were actually pointing. It probably appeared to the innocent bystander he couldn't drive at all, he contemplated. He began to wish he'd never agreed to Alex's request of taking Alice. She was much easier and more refined to drive.

Stepping out of the car, he took in the view of the old semi-detached house. Not much had changed since he had lived there, save for different colour paint on the front door and window frames. Using his key to open the front door, he knocked the door as well to notify his arrival.

"Mum! It's me!"

As he closed the door and entered the hallway with its highly polished parquet floor, an elderly lady with long, dark hair emerged from the back room. The woman, despite being in the twilight of her life, had a natural air of sophistication and elegance women decades younger strived to obtain, but never would.

"Hello Sweetheart. I was just about to put the kettle on."

"I'll do that, Mum. You go sit down and take it easy."

He embraced her dearly, giving her a kiss. Nick felt her small arms wrap around him and squeeze. It felt like heaven. The sergeant reflected on his mother's appearance. He knew Dad would approve in spades — fitted grey jumper, black pencil skirt, tan hosiery and black heels. Her hair was just so too.

"Are you off out somewhere nice?"

He had to comment on how his mother presented herself. He always did. Nick knew she wasn't going anywhere — she always dressed in this manner. Georgy Duncan giggled.

"I'm not going any place, silly."

The detective smiled in reply, removing his jacket. He gently placed his hand on the small of her back and escorted her into the back room-cum-lounge.

On the ornate mantelpiece still sat the art-deco clock, which resembled the exact same shape as the hat worn by Napoleon Bonaparte. Nick smiled further as he recalled the too numerous to mention occasions Dad had lovingly explained the clock had been a wedding present from Auntie Alice and Uncle Eddie. Besides the clock over the fireplace, resided five framed photographs in decorative frames that matched the style of the mantelpiece upon which they sat.

Duncan loved to lose track of time staring at these pictures, adoring the memories these images evoked. The photos showed Ellis and Alex on their wedding day, the twin girls Charlotte and Katherine in the obligatory school pic, himself in his Royal Navy Regulator uniform, his parents on their wedding day, plus a single, solitary image of his father attired in his police sergeant uniform — the very same picture he had on his desk in the office. Nick was convinced this photo of his dad in his parent's home had a permanently greasy smudge across his father's face, interestingly the exact shade and hue of his mother's lipstick. He missed his father terribly, but knew this was nothing compared to the huge chasm his mother felt since his passing. She had never been the same since that awful day.

As he watched his mother seat herself in her favourite armchair, Nick pondered over his announcement. Would now be the right moment to tell her of his sexuality? He wanted to, knowing the heavy burden of secrecy that he felt would ease the moment he opened up.

"Er, Mum…"

"Did Alex tell you he's gone away for Easter? Took Ellis somewhere really fancy, by all accounts."

"Yes, Mum, he said. He's borrowed Alice. Mum, there's something I want to say."

Her son's words not fully registering, Georgy continued.

"Oh Yes, Alex mentioned he'd taken your car. Where did he say he was going?"

"Somewhere near Worcester. Mum, can I say something?"

"Really? Worcester? Oh my! Silly me. Of course! Katherine and Charlotte are staying with me tomorrow night. They're with Ellis' parents today." Georgy sighed light-heartedly, smiling. *"Lovely little girls. Maybe you'll be a father one day, Love."*

The detective tried his utmost to supress the horrified expression which was rapidly spreading across his face

"Er, who knows Mum. I'll just go pop the kettle on."

Making a hasty exit to the sanctuary of the kitchen, Nick began to curse his luck. At the last count, it was now fourteen separate occasions this year alone he'd attempted to explain to his mother about his life. And each and every time there had been a distraction so he couldn't hold his mother's full attention.

"Are you all right in there, sweetheart?"

"Everything's fine. Turn the telly on — there might be a decent film on or something."

Moments later, the policeman re-entered the lounge carrying a tray containing a tea service, and carefully placed it upon the coffee table.

"I see you've found your favourites."

Georgy tittered, and pointed at a side plate on the tray

which was loaded with copious chocolate bourbon cream biscuits. Nick childishly smirked back at her, as he pinched one and placed it wholesale into his mouth.

"Shall I be 'mother'?"

Mrs Duncan giggled at her son, as he lifted the teapot with its slightly steaming spout and slowly swished it in mid-air to stir the contents. The detective began to pour the golden-brown stream of hot liquid, gradually filling two china cups.

"Why do you always do that?"

"Do what?"

"Pour the tea first, before the milk."

Nick paused, stared at the teapot for a moment, before continued to pour.

"Your father always put the milk in first. Heaven knows where you get it from."

"Maybe I was an Aristocrat in a previous life."

Georgy burst out laughing, to which Nick joined in. It felt wonderful to share something daft and silly with her. She reached forward for her drink, only to be met by an expected voice emanating from the hallway.

"Mike Zulu Two, this is Mike One. Are you receiving? Over."

Duncan leapt to his feet, and headed into the hall towards where his coat was.

"Sorry Mum. It's my portable radio."

Nick returned to the lounge with the device, picking up the handset towards his face to respond.

"Oh, your father never had one of those. Just a whistle attached to his tunic."

Once again, the radio spat out its message.

"This is Mike One, Mike Zulu Two are you receiving?"

Over."

"Mike Zulu Two receiving. Go ahead. Over."

Georgy watched her son concerned, as he awaited a response.

"Can you phone the Office asap please, Sarge. Over."

"Understood. Mike Zulu Two Out."

Nick could see the worry and concern on his mother's face.

"May I use the phone, Mum?"

She nodded quickly.

"No need to worry."

The detective patted his mother's shoulder in reassurance as he passed, and spoke as calmly as possible.

"Most likely further details about the case I'm working on."

Picking up the receiver, Duncan dialled the CID office. It rang a couple of times before being answered by a female voice.

"Warwickshire Police, Little Park Street CID."

Nick recognised the voice straight away.

"Hello Rachel. It's D.S Duncan. I've been radioed by Control and told to speak with the Office."

"Yes, Skipper."

She paused briefly, Duncan thought perhaps she wasn't used to this so had to compose herself.

"Another body has been found."

"Another one?"

"I'm afraid so, Skip."

"Whereabouts?"

"Coombe Abbey. In the children's play area."

"Fucking Hell! Oh, sorry Rachel."

163

Nick apologised for his sweary outburst. Rachel tittered briefly in reply. He felt his mother's stare burning into the side of his head, akin to the sensation of falling asleep while sunbathing.

"Sorry Mum," he silently mouthed to her.

"Can you tell the Guv'nor I'm on my way. Should be there in ten to fifteen minutes."

"OK Skipper. Bye."

Hanging up the phone, Duncan picked his jacket up, putting it on swiftly.

"I've got to go — something's happened."

"I guessed as much."

Georgy emitted a long, disappointed sigh as her son stepped forwards and wrapped his arms around her, embracing her tight.

"Take care, Love."

"Hey! It's me!"

The mother stared up at her son, making eye contact with him.

"That's what I'm afraid of."

She reached up and tapped the end of Nick's nose with her index finger.

"You've got the same fearless attitude as your father, for justice, solving crime, saving and protecting the victim."

Nick smiled back at his mother broadly.

"Bye Mum. See you Monday."

He kissed her, squeezing her close once again.

Walking out of his parent's home, he knew he could get across to eastern side of the city where Coombe Abbey was in less than ten minutes. Turn on the *'blues and twos'*, no problem.

The detective abruptly stopped dead as he made his way to the car — he remembered he had Alex's motor, not his own.

"Bollocks!"

Once again, he felt that all too familiar burning stare from his mother, scorching its way into the back of his head. As he spun around on the spot, the policeman was greeted with the vista of his Mum, arms folded, with a far from pleased expression on her face. *"Last time I saw her look like that, was when I returned home blind drunk after Alex's stag night,"* flashed through his head.

"Sorry Mum."

The sheepish looking sergeant waved, climbed into the Standard and drove off at speed.

The journey across the city was easier than Duncan had initially contemplated, considering it was the first day of the Easter break. He drove as briskly as he could, cursing further as he inadvertently crashed the gears. He snarled as he sucked on his cigarette. The smoke calmed him down — not from his fight with his brother's car, but after getting mentally set to explain to his mother about his life. Nick felt mixed emotions. Frustration, as he hadn't said what he wanted, but relief at not having caused a scene and upset Mum — or worse. His biggest fear was Mum wouldn't accept he was gay, and turn her back on him. All he wanted, the one thing he craved more than anything else was to be accepted for who he was — warts and all, just as Alex was. Basically, they were the exactly the same — male, from the same family, grew up in the same city, even attended the same schools. The only difference was their sexual orientation. Duncan had pondered on this over and over. Why on Earth did this one thing — the gender of who he chose to sleep with — matter?

Passing through the eastern suburb of Binley, the detective barrelled along a twisty country lane before he reached the ornate gateway to the Abbey — once a monastery, then a private country house for the gentry, now a country park for the residents of the nearby city.

Approaching along the long gravel driveway, he found the amassed group of Police vehicles next to the main buildings and the cordon. All the activity was, as the sergeant had already been informed, on the children's play area. This was effectively two courtyards of the former monastery, separated by a large, thick wall. As Duncan stepped out of his brother's car — only after stalling the wretched thing to bring it to a stop, — he caught sight of Dr Tyler. The physician was removing her large leather bag from the boot of her Sunbeam Alpine. Nick smiled slightly, as her car displayed a *'Doctor On Call'* sign on the dashboard.

"We need to stop meeting like this, Doctor."

"My sentiments exactly, Sergeant."

The Doctor firmly closed the boot lid of her car, picked up her bag and walked alongside the detective.

"Can I carry that for you? Your bag?"

"My, chivalry isn't dead after all! I'm impressed! After being married for close on sixteen years, I was beginning to think it was."

Entering the children's play area, Nick straight away caught sight of the officer in charge, tonight's CIM. Attired in his trademark tweed jacket, cravat around his neck, pipe in hand, DCI Thomas Spencer. Duncan pondered where Joan was, as he couldn't see her, yet had noticed her car parked close to where he 'abandoned' his brother's Vanguard. Dermot was with members of the SOCO team, crowded around one of the small tunnels which children used to get from one side of the play area to the other. Essentially, a large drainage pipe pushed through a thick wall, to add some interest to an otherwise boring and unimaginative recreational yard.

As he approached the crime scene, he over-heard Spencer and Dermot speculating.

"I'd say we're looking for two people involved in this."

The constable scribbled into his notebook, as the chief Inspector voiced his viewpoint.

"What makes you say that, Sir?"

Spencer opened his mouth to speak, but a Scouse female voice echoed out of the pipe where a young female adult was laying on their back, their legs dangling out.

"Well, you're gonna struggle on your own to stuff a body in here!"

"I knew it!"

The senior Detective clicked his fingers and nodded in confirmation.

"What have we got, Sir?"

Duncan asked his superior as he arrived. Dr Tyler knelt down next to the woman in the pipe, and opened her leather bag.

"Another young lady murdered."

"Same M.O as Arosha Rana the other night?"

"Strangled, yes. Exactly the same as Miss Rana's cause of death, unknown — yet to be established. Could just be a horrible coincidence."

"Or perhaps not..."

"We'll know for certain once Dr Tyler has concluded."

"Do we know who she is yet, Sir?"

"Dermot..." Spencer beckoned the constable over. *"Could you briefly tell Sergeant Duncan what we know, please."*

"Yes, Sir." Dermot began to dictate the entry in his notebook.

"Well Sarge, from the ID we've found in her handbag..."

"ID?"

"Her driving licence. This is Wendy Kroy, twenty-three years old, home address in Baginton."

"That's got to be her parent's place — a twenty-something living in an expensive and exclusive part of the city?"

"Yes, Nicholas. I have to concur on that point."

"Anything else of note?"

The sergeant craned his neck in order to read Dermot's handwriting himself, rather than wait a few seconds for it to be read aloud.

"Er, a small amount of cash, a bunch of keys, some till receipts, an open and started packet of fags..."

Nick interrupted, his curiosity getting the better of him.

"Which brand?"

"Embassy."

"OK — sorry for the interruption. Do continue."

Ward sighed. *"Interestingly she did not have a lighter, only a box of matches in her bag from the Swanswell Tavern."*

"OK, anything else?"

"Er, not really. Oh, just one more thing — packaging from a pair of tights, American Tan in colour."

"Really?"

Duncan glanced at Spencer, who returned his intrigued stance. Both of the detectives raised their eyebrows simultaneously.

"Now, there's a coincidence!"

The revelation was not lost on anyone, but the chief Inspector spoke first, placing his hand on the constable's shoulder.

"Did the Office inform Inspector Edwards of this situation?"

"Yes, Sir. He's with his wife, seeing her family in Hinckley. Said he'd get here as fast as he could."

"And Sergeant St John?"

"He's over there."

Dermot spun around and pointed at the SOCO incident unit. Spencer and Duncan turned as well, to see St John once again carrying two polystyrene cups of steaming hot something, but had paused to chat up one of the WPC's present.

Nick returned his attention to the deceased woman in the pipe. He leaned into the child-size tunnel to see for himself the deceased girl, only to be blinded in the darkness by the rapid fire of a camera flash in close proximity. The sergeant staggered backwards, blinking profusely.

"Sorry Sarge. Didn't see you there."

"No problem, Joan. I'll come around the other side."

Duncan strolled around to the opposite side of the thick wall, just as Cavanagh eased herself gingerly out of the pipe.

"Take hold of this, Nick."

The Merseysider offered the detective the Leica she had been using. Clambering out, she stood up straight with some effort, after the contortionist act she'd just had to endure. With her hair tied back in a ponytail, and dressed in an all-in-one overall, Nick couldn't prevent the huge smirk that was spreading across his face at a fair rate of knots.

169

"I'll wipe that grin off yer chops, if yer don't stop it."

This did little to deter Nick's hilarity. And even more so as Cavanagh bent down, rolled up the right leg of the overalls to reveal her shapely leg encased in hosiery and knee-high boot — but the knee of her tights had been put through. A large hole was now present.

"Bollocks! I'm putting a claim in for expenses!"

"Why did you have to climb in there? Couldn't one of the SOCO lads have done it?"

The scouser rubbed her knee, feeling the hole in the nylon, and made the rather futile step of trying to pull the material 'closed'. Additionally, the latex gloves Joan was wearing made this all the more difficult, as they tended to briefly adhere to the soft fabric.

"Why was I in the pipe? Well, now let me see...Oh, yeah! All the SOCO investigators are such fat bastards they couldn't fit!"

Just as Duncan burst out loud laughing, a voice echoed towards them through the pipe.

"Detective Constable! Some dignity, please. A deceased young lady lies here, just in case you'd forgotten."

"Sorry Sir."

The two detectives wandered back to the other side of the wall, rejoining the rest of the incident team.

"What do we know about this young woman?"

"Early twenties Caucasian, took great care of her appearance. Dermot has noted what personal effects she was carrying."

"Spencer said she's been strangled."

"Yeah. From what I've seen up close, that's right."

"Well, it didn't happen here, this is a deposition site, not

crime scene. She wasn't killed here, unless she laid on her back inside a pipe and allowed herself to be murdered."

Cavanagh slapped herself on the forehead.

"Of course!"

"And if this woman's demise is connected to the Indian girl the other night, that means she was dumped in a quiet, country lane, as to being attacked as she walked alone in the dark."

Making their way towards the incident unit, they both heard a voice behind them.

"Sergeant, Constable..."

Recognising who it was, they stopped and greeted the chief Inspector approaching them, who was trying to drink scorching hot liquid from a polystyrene cup.

"Sir?" Nick thought his superior wanted to discuss an aspect of this new case, or a development with Arosha Rana.

"Just a brief word with both of you..."

Duncan and Cavanagh glanced at one another puzzled, .

"I know through our work, we all too often see the unpleasant, distasteful and uncivilised side of society. I understand we all need a 'release' when matters become most unsavoury, but I expect my officers to conduct themselves in a professional manner while on duty."

Both of the young detectives appeared sheepish, and could do no more than stare at their feet. The DCI flicked disapproving glances at them in turn, like a headmaster scolding disruptive pupils in class.

"The old saying is true as regards if you can't take a joke, you shouldn't have joined the police, but how would you feel if that was someone you love there lying dead and knew the investigating officers were larking about?"

Spencer removed his pipe from his mouth, and took a large gulp of his drink while alternating his gaze between the two detectives. This was the first telling off Nick had received in years, the first since he was in the Navy. An uneasy silence fell over the three officers, only disturbed by distant, feint radio chatter from the portable sets carried by uniform constables present.

"I understand, Sir. Apologies."

"Glad to hear it, Sergeant." Spencer's tone began to soften. *"Right, I'll oversee matters here and speak with Dr Tyler."*

Duncan could see over the DCI's shoulder several SOCO investigators, a few uniform constables, along with St John were carefully removing the body of Wendy Kroy from the small tunnel, and gently laying her onto a light-weight gurney.

"You two can get off home. I'll see you in the office in the morning."

"Yes, Sir. We'll just hand this camera into the incident unit and we'll leave."

Joan pointed at the Leica Nick was carrying. Spencer nodded, and headed back to where Dr Tyler was now performing an initial inspection of the deceased. Once the senior detective was out of earshot, Nick performed a quick fascist salute and clicked his heels together. Cavanagh appeared as though she was going to burst holding her laughter in, and headed rapidly towards the incident unit.

As Cavanagh disappeared inside, Duncan heard someone behind him.

"Nick..."

The Detective glanced over his shoulder to find Dermot approaching him.

"Yes, Dermot..."

"I was wondering if you could help me, Mate."

The sergeant pondered at the constable, somewhat intrigued yet puzzled.

"Help me with my Sergeant application, if you don't mind." Nick's demeanour changed to that of understanding.

"I've applied three times over the last five years, but keep getting nowhere."

"Didn't you apply the same time as me? Back in '69?"

"Yeah, but you just edged it."

Duncan became aware Ward's attention wasn't solely on their conversation — the detective constable was distracted by something happening behind the sergeant. Dermot craned his neck, leaning this way and that to peer around his superior. Nick spun around, curious to see for himself what was so interesting. All he was greeted with was the Ford Transit incident unit, with its side door open. Duncan then saw what Dermot was so eager to observe — Joan fighting her way out of the overall, revealing she was wearing only white lingerie, damaged tan-coloured tights and knee-high boots. The Scouse detective was all fingers-and-thumbs as she got dressed in the cold air. Nick sighed, finding Mr Ward's ability to ogle the fairer sex somewhat irksome and tedious.

"Manners maketh the man, Mr Ward. A true gentleman would avert his gaze."

Dermot smiled a big gormless grin.

"And where would the fun be in that? Besides, you're hardly disliking the view yourself."

"Nah!" The Sergeant screwed his face up in distaste. "She's not my type."

Dermot raised his eyebrows as he stared his colleague

disbelievingly, gesturing with his eyes in Cavanagh's direction. When Nick saw what the constable was trying to draw his attention to, he now saw Joan wearing a brown fitted turtle-neck jumper and climbing into her skirt as speedily as possible.

"When we've got a moment, we'll go through your application paperwork. See you in the morning."

"Yeah, see you tomorrow, Sarge."

Duncan wandered towards the incident unit, handing the camera in. As they walked back to their cars, he decided he'd tease Joan a little.

"I've found you have a secret admirer!"

"Who?"

CHAPTER FIVE
EASTER SATURDAY
SATURDAY APRIL 21st 1973

"Are you thinking of staying for a fortnight?"

Nick struggled with Val's suitcase, as he climbed the stairs.

"Stop moaning! I've only packed the bare essentials."

"Have you ever heard about 'travelling light'?"

The issue Duncan was having with his friend's luggage wasn't its size or shape, but its weight. With much effort, the detective eventually made it to the top, and took a moment to catch his breath.

"You know, it would be easier to push those stroppy elephants from the Dumbo cartoon up a flight of stairs!"

Val couldn't help but burst out laughing at this, as she followed her friend carrying much lighter 'hand luggage'. At the bottom of the stairs stood Richard Abbott, Val's partner. From his vantage point, Duncan could clearly see Rich struggling to keep a straight face. Having only just met, Nick deduced he was trying his utmost to show good manners and be a gentleman, when it was clear he just wanted to laugh out loud.

"Be careful with that case, Nick. David Bowie is in there!"

Val fussed, as Nick walked into a banister.

"He's shrunk in the wash, if he is!"

Val and Nick chuckled at Richard's quip. He looked upwards at them, smiled and winked.

The policeman liked Rich. He spoke with a gorgeous, lush West Country accent not too dissimilar to Ellis. Val's fella was quick witted and saw the silly side of life in most situations, which was mainly due to his occupation. Like Nick, Rich was employed within the emergency services , and possibly due to people working in such extreme and intense circumstances, they develop a somewhat 'warped' and daft sense of humour as a coping mechanism. The two men adored the same jokes and japes. Duncan thought to himself it was such shame Rich was attracted to the fairer sex.

"Are we in the front room, Nick?"

Val walked towards the mentioned spare room, not waiting for an answer.

"Well, it might be a bit of a squeeze all three of us in the same bed!"

Rich couldn't help himself with another quip. Nick's eyes lit up at the idea. He laughed out loud, as his imagination raced away.

"I don't know — might be kind of fun."

Duncan couldn't help but wink as he finished speaking. All three burst out laughing. *"If you only knew,"* Nick uttered under his breath, eyeing up the off-duty fire fighter once again.

"Are you two up to anything tonight? Fancy going out for a few drinks and something to eat? Could even go to the cinema — there's a David Essex film out, plus that documentary flick about T Rex. Promise I won't squeeze your knee."

Both Val and Rich giggle at their host.

"We'd love to, Nick but I promised Mum we'd go see her while we're in Coventry. Rich hasn't met my Mum yet."

The sergeant was deflated at hearing Val's words, but understood.

"Are we all still going to the Locarno tomorrow night?"

"Of course! Rich has been boasting about his smooth moves on the dancefloor for ages, so it's about time we let him strut his funky stuff."

Right on cue, Rich began to sway and shuffle with his eyes closed, dancing to a tune in his head only he could hear. Val giggled at her boyfriend's impromptu star turn. *"Oh, you little tease,"* Duncan said to himself watching him shimmy around.

A car horn tooted outside, causing Nick to peer out of a nearby window. On the street was a scarlet Singer Chamois he instantly recognised. A few moments later, three short sharp knocks were heard from the front door. Cavanagh had arrived to take Duncan to work.

"Please excuse me, I have to go into the office this morning. We have a few things to deal with at the moment."

Nick ran downstairs, opening the front door.

"You took yer time. Were you on the bog or something?"

"Morning Joan." Duncan decided to embarrass his colleague slightly, after her blunt greeting. *"This is my close friend — Val, and this is her partner — Rich."*

The couple appeared behind the policeman, and smiled at Cavanagh. The detective constable smiled an awkward smile in return.

"Hullo — I'm Joan." The scouser stepped forward into the hallway, and shook Val's hand who giggled as she reciprocated the policewoman's greeting.

"Don't worry, Joan. I frequently put my foot in it when I first meet someone. Normally through a door to rescue them, but just as awkward nonetheless."

Duncan saw Joan instantly become more at ease at Rich's introduction, and felt more comfortable too, knowing all his closest friends — those he trusted implicitly — would get on.

"Are you ready, Sarge? You know what a stickler for time keeping the Guv'nor is."

"Oh, Crikey!"

Nick quickly glanced at his wristwatch, and saw time was getting on.

"Sorry folks, must dash. Help yourself to what you like. You know where the spare keys are, don't you Val?"

The lady nodded in reply, as the detective slid his coat on.

"Don't you worry! We won't run off with the family silver!" Rich winked at the policeman as he left the house. Duncan winked back and smiled in return.

Climbing into Cavanagh's small car, they set off towards Little Park Street. Almost immediately, Nick nearly caused a fist-fight. Absent-mindedly, he reached into his inside pocket and retrieved his packet of cigarettes, slid open the left side and placed one between his lips.

"For Fuck's sake, Nick! No, not in here!"

"What?"

"Your fag! Put it away! Can't you wait five minutes till we get to the station, like?"

Like a scalded child, the sergeant removed his tobacco from his mouth and returned it to its packet. Seeing this, Joan calmed down slightly.

"What you get up to in your own car is your own business. But this is mine."

178

"Sorry, Ma'am."

Joan gave her superior a black look, not finding his sarcasm remotely amusing. Nick leant forwards and switched the radio on to ease the situation. Already pre-tuned to BBC Radio 1, the interior of the car was at once filled with the irritating cheerful song *'Power To All Our Friends'* sung by Cliff Richard. Duncan began to over-elaborately mime to the track, in full gospel church choir style including over the top arm movements. Cavanagh's harsh mood almost instantly evaporated, as she smiled broadly and shook her head at her colleague's silliness. In the blink of an eye, Duncan ceased his mime act and sat bolt upright, looking forwards in the direction of travel, completely silent. Joan glanced at the sergeant, wondering what the matter was. Why had he stopped? The song hadn't even finished.

"Remember what the DCI said — professional at all times!"

Nick continued to sit still, holding the most serious poker face. After a few minutes, Cavanagh crumbled, her grumpy persona thawed. The constable began to giggle as she snatched the occasional glimpse of her friend as she drove.

"Now, now. That's not professional at all, is it Detective?"

This simply made the scouser laugh further.

Parking at the station, Joan managed to regain her composure.

"Seriously like Sarge, do you think these murders are linked?"

"Linked? I'm not sure. Obviously, evidence will confirm or disprove this either way. But my gut feeling is yes, they are."

Passing the landing on the first floor, Duncan caught sight of someone using the wall-mounted telephones, contained in the small booths that barely covered the user's head and shoulders. The person turned, wrapped up in a conversation with someone. Nick recognised who it was instantly. *"Why is Dermot using a phone down here, as to the one on his desk upstairs?"* the sergeant pondered to himself.

Entering the office, Nick knew the gravity of the situation with the unprecedented circumstance of two consecutive murders in the city so quickly. The last time people had been killed this rapidly in Coventry — aside for traffic accidents — was during the War. This was compounded when the notice board in front of Edwards' office was now displaying the details of the two women who had had their lives cut short. Plus, DCI Spencer was thoroughly perusing all information collected there. Duncan knew this was serious, as the senior detective had removed his tweed jacket and stood commandingly with his shirt sleeves rolled up, hands on hips, puffing away on his pipe. As the Chief Inspector began to open the briefing, Dermot darted into the office, taking his seat at his desk. Spencer glared at the constable.

"Right then, Ladies and Gentlemen. This was meant to be an update on the young lady found strangled on Tuesday night, but as you've most likely heard, another young adult female was found yesterday. Due to us having two murder cases on our hands in uncomfortably quick succession, I'll be working alongside D.I Edwards as joint C.I.M."

Duncan sensed the gravity of the situation, *"This is serious. Never known the DCI step up to the plate before."*

"At the moment we can't be certain if the two cases are linked, so that's one obvious line of enquiry."

Spencer pointed to several new photos, all as equally horrific as the ones already present of Arosha Rana. Cavanagh had caught every unpleasant detail with her session as photographer.

"This is one Wendy Kroy, aged twenty-three. She was found stuffed rather unceremoniously into a small tunnel in the children's play area in Coombe Abbey. All we know at the moment is she was strangled, plus a nightwatchman at the Abbey — building work was on-going — did see an estate car leave the scene around 1am yesterday morning."

"Did he sees wha' make? Model? Colour?"

All eyes in the room instantly fell on St John. Nick considered his questions were spot on — he was thinking the very same. Perched on the edge of a nearby desk, Edwards picked up a file and opened it, reading what was typed inside.

"The bloke said the vehicle had — I quote — 'was dark in colour and had pointy tail lights, with number plate across the middle of the rear.' So we can confidently say it wasn't a Ford Cortina or Morris Minor Traveller."

"Is it too much to ask he made out the registration?"

Nick spoke up, hoping above all hopes this vital piece of information had been gained.

"Sorry Nick — nothing."

Spencer removed his pipe from his mouth and frowned, not best pleased at the interruption.

"Well, as that's another matter to be investigated, the post mortem will tell us more for the time being once we receive the report. But as I've already said, we'll definitely be keeping an open mind as to whether these unexplained deaths are connected".

The chief Inspector continued, re-lighting his pipe. *"Open mind, Each. This car could merely be a courting couple trying to find somewhere secluded."*

"OK folks, while the chief Inspector and myself dwell and ponder on the information we have so far, plus have an unpleasant meeting with the Super to update him on matters, you lot can be doing the following."

Edwards stood up, and began to issue tasks.

"Sebastian, go to Wendy Kroy's home address. Take Dermot and Rachel with you. Wendy hasn't been registered as 'missing' as yet, so being away from home this long might be nothing out of the ordinary."

The inspector leaned forwards, over St John's desk.

"Break it to them gently, please."

The Scotsman smiled his trademark smarmy smirk, and nodded twice.

"Nick, go to the hospital, take Joan with you. See what Dr Tyler has found out at the post mortem."

"Yes, Guv."

"The SOCO report should be with us today, tomorrow morning at the latest. Which brings me onto that. Everybody in tomorrow, please."

A huge groan went up through the office, along with mutterings of disbelief.

"Oi! Oi! Calm down, calm down!"

Spencer interjected, *"I appreciate it's a public holiday, and you've all made arrangements with your friends and families, but if we go and tell the Superintendent two-thirds of the CID department are off on their jollies when two young women have been murdered in the city, he's not going to be a happy camper!"*

The grumbling gradually eased, as a sense of resignation to the circumstances spread through the office. *"Well, that really cuts into the small amount of time I already had with*

Val," Nick cursed to himself. He absolutely adored his job, but it was Sod's Law something always cropped up that meant he had to curtail events in his private life. No wonder he'd been single for an age. He recalled how his father had fore-warned him of such. A cup of tea was in order to soften this disappointment. Duncan wandered over to the corner of the office where the kettle was kept. *"Charming! Some kind member of Society has used my mug and not washed it out afterwards!"*

Duncan took the briefing handout from Cavanagh as she wandered towards him, and picked up another mug beginning to make himself a tea. As he read the information enclosed, Spencer continued to address the assembled team.

"On the handout in front of you, I have arranged for WPC Ryce to correlate the details of the two young ladies who have perished. You'll find all the details of location, their condition, personal belongings and the first post mortem report."

Nick began to skim read the information, with Joan absorbing the details herself alongside. Straight away, something caught Duncan's eye. He nudged his Scouse sidekick, and pointed at what he had seen.

"BHS receipts?"

Joan was somewhat puzzled. Her face said it all — *"So what?"*

"Yes, British Home Stores receipts. With a discount taken off the price. The question is, why would not just one woman but two receive a discount at one of the countries' most famous department stores."

"In store promotion?"

"Possibly. I was more thinking who always but always receives a discount?"

Joan appeared even more mystified by the sergeant's question.

"Company staff! Arosha Rana was. I wonder if Wendy Kroy was also."

Realisation washed across the Liverpudlian's face like a tidal wave, just as Edwards approached.

"Right then, Peters and Lee…"

The two younger detectives glanced at one another, puzzled by the inspector's latest nickname for the pair of them.

"Like I said, could you pair go to the Hospital. The post mortem should have been carried out by now. Have a chat with Dr Tyler if she's free and see what she has to say."

"Yes, Guv."

Edwards nodded, and moved onto St John and Dermot.

"Right, Morecambe and Wise…"

Once the inspector was out of earshot, Duncan whispered to Cavanagh.

"On the way back, I think we need to take a shopping excursion to British Home Stores."

The constable's face lit up with a huge beaming, ear-to-ear grin.

"Are ya gonna treat me to a new frock?"

Cavanagh brought her car to a stand-still on Queen Victoria Road, outside the Green Shield Stamps exchange store.

"Stop here, Joan."

"Aren't we parking on double yellows?"

"Well deduced, Nancy Drew."

"Well, we can't park here — can we?"

"Have you got your warrant card on you?"

"Er, duh! Of course!"

"May I?"

The Scouse Detective reached into her coat pocket and retrieved the folding slim wallet. Duncan immediately opened it, and laid the ID photo side up on the dashboard.

"See! Perfectly legal now!"

Nick beamed a huge gormless grin at his colleague. Joan climbed out of her car rolling her eyes.

Walking through the Lower Precinct, the two detectives happened upon the flying saucer shaped burger bar, polluting the immediate vicinity with essence of fried onions and overdone grilled beef. This, combined with the fragrance of stale urine in the more secluded parts of the concrete brutalism the precinct was styled within, made the stroll an assault on the senses.

"So, Dr Tyler can confirm Wendy Kroy was strangled the same way as Arosha Rana."

"Yeah, it appears so. I could hear the dread in the Guvnor's voice when I phoned him from the hospital. Last thing anyone anywhere needs is a serial killer on the loose."

The detective constable stared solemnly ahead. Nick knew she had grasped the severity of the situation. Entering the British Home Stores branch, Duncan found the shop's manager.

"I understand some of my colleagues have already been to visit you?"

Nick produced his warrant card and unfolded it for the lady to read.

"Yes, Sergeant. Is there anything else we can help you with?"

Store manager Mary Randle gave the two police officers a curious, but confused stare.

"Yeah, there could be," Cavanagh began. *"Do you have a young woman employed here by the name of Wendy Kroy?"*

"Er, yes. We do! I think she works within haberdashery. I'll just check."

They followed the manager through to the relevant department, to where Mrs Randle went to speak with a male colleague. The man pondered for a few moments, recalled something, shook his head several times, and shrugged his shoulders.

"What's taking her so long?"

Curiosity was getting the better of the Merseysider. Duncan shrugged his shoulders too. In return, he received a frosty glare from his young female companion.

"I'm sorry for keeping you waiting, Detective. Wendy is no longer employed here. She left a couple of months ago."

"Oh, I see. Thank you."

"Apparently, she left under a bit of a cloud. There were suspicions of her being involved in stock going missing, but she moved on before we could investigate fully."

Duncan and Cavanagh exchanged surprised glances.

"Do you know where Miss Kroy is employed now, at all?"

Joan retrieved her notebook from her handbag, and began to scribble.

"My colleague said he thinks he heard she'd found work either at Owen Owens or C&A."

"Thank you, Mrs Randle. Did Wendy have any friends when she worked here?"

The manager dwelled on the query for a moment before answering.

"Well, she got along with everyone. Friendly girl, approachable. And I don't mean to pry into people's private

lives, but I think I did hear she had a couple of dates with one of the maintenance lads here. Don't know how truthful that is, or if it's just staff room gossip."

The detective constable continued to write, as Duncan watched. The manager fidgeted slightly, becoming a tad awkward in her manner.

"Er, is Wendy in trouble?"

"Everything's fine, Mrs Randle. We're just following a line of enquiry."

The store manager began to appear less worried, but not entirely comfortable as Duncan did his utmost to conceal the true nature of why they had actually visited the shop.

"Thank you for your time."

Returning to the constable's car, Duncan began to chuckle as he climbed into the passenger side.

"You said I wouldn't get a ticket parked here!"

Between guffaws, the sergeant pulled a wistful face and placed his hand on his chin.

"Hmmm, that never happens to me when I park here..."

For not the first time, Joan gave her colleague a dark look. She removed the ticket from under the windscreen wiper and placed it in her handbag.

Back at the office, Duncan amended the notice board with the information he had learnt from the post mortem and the visit to the department store.

"Anything of interest I should be aware of?"

Edwards peered over Nick's shoulder at the new items the sergeant was adding.

"Looks like your interest in the odd job guy may well be warranted."

Duncan pointed at the link he'd just placed next to the two

deceased woman. The inspector adjusted his spectacles, read the displayed details, before taking a step back to contemplate. *"Go and pay this fellow a visit, Nick. Find out what he has to say for himself."*

"I'll try and contact the store to get his address, but might not have any joy till Tuesday."

Edwards gazed at his Sergeant in slight confusion.

"It's the Easter Bank Holiday weekend."

The inspector nodded and smiled, slightly waving an index finger in understanding.

"Most likely Tuesday."

"But it could be one of those coincidences, you know. Just one of those things."

"Well, you'll know for certain once you've had a word."

Edwards patted Duncan on his back, wandering off to his private office. Many times, Nick compared working with the Guv'nor, was just like performing chores for his own father. He smiled a wry smirk. It felt good. It felt as though Dad was still around. Looking down at his open diary on his desk, he remembered the Coventry Bees were racing at home tonight.

"Let's go watch the Speedway tonight, eh Dad."

The car park at the Brandon Stadium was busier than normal, Duncan put this down to this weekend being the Easter break. Plus, the motorcycle speedway fixture tonight was against local Midlands rivals, Cradley Heathens from Dudley. He made his way to his favourite vantage point to view the racing — towards the back of the main stand, with the restaurant behind. From where he sat, Nick had full view of the entire track and the pit area. He loved seeing the riders prepare their machines, roll out to the start line, and roar off in a shower of shale as the tape lifted. The policeman adored motor racing in all its forms, so to watch some live action in his home city was a huge boon.

The detective sat back in his seat, drawing on one of his beloved Park Drive, exhaling the vapour into the night air. Even through his cigarette smoke, the heady elixir of pure methanol the bikes ran on, blended with the aroma of fried onions and hot dog sausages was still noticeable. As a couple of engines fired up, Nick realised how intimate speedway was. The riders performed a pre-race parade at slow speed, travelling with their helmets off waving to the crowd, 'high-fiving' teenagers hanging over the track-side fence. This would never happen before a Formula One event. He smiled and applauded along with all those around him, even waving a little too, as his current favourite Coventry Bees riders were in the welcome — John Harrhy and Les Owen. Duncan peered down at the fixture programme in his hand, flipping through to find the schedule and the yet be filled in scorecard.

"If those two, ride to what they're capable of, we'll win tonight."

Nick initially didn't realise he'd shared his viewpoint with all around him again, until a male voice behind him replied.

"We didn't fare too well in Scotland last night. Coatbridge were all over us."

The policeman paused for a moment — he scoured his memory. He recognised that voice. It was someone he knew. Curiosity got the better of him. Spinning around, Nick was met with the deep brown eyes of Harvey Wiseman. Duncan looked straight into them, and fell into them.

"Good evening, Sergeant."

Like a lightning bolt screaming down from the heavens to strike the tip of a church steeple, the sergeant experienced a rampaging rush internally. His heart rate quickened, his blood pressure rose, his pupils dilated. To coin an old romantic ideal, butterflies were performing an aerobic display inside Nicholas Duncan the Red Arrows would have been envious of.

"Hello Mr Wiseman. Fancy meeting you here!"

The detective struggled to keep his composure at finding Harvey right next to him, hoping he appeared calm and relaxed, instead of excited, pent up and nervous as he really was. The brief moved from his seat, to one beside Nick.

"Small world, as they say."

"I never realised you were a speedway fan?"

Harvey chuckled. *"Why Sergeant, you never asked!"*

Duncan found he was a little lost for words, which was quite unlike him.

"Don't worry, Detective. I won't give you a hard time like last time we met."

Nick partially glared at the barrister, which melted immediately as he made eye contact once again. He still tried to appear casual and friendly, but this was a severe uphill struggle. Duncan knew Harvey had already realised this. He must have. The policeman eventually found his voice, after what seemed like an age.

"I'm glad to hear it. I wouldn't want to face that every time I have to take the stand."

Nick could see in the corner of his eye his legal nemesis was having difficulty suppressing his own smirk.

"Last night's fixture was a tad too far to travel to for a night race, especially with my duties at the station."

"Indeed, southern Scotland is somewhat excessive for an overnight jolly."

"I don't know — depends who you're with!"

Duncan had voiced the slightly cheeky quip without a second's thought. He gave Harvey a sheepish grin, but straight away saw the man he had designs upon found it amusing in the right way.

"Very true. Beats an evening on your own in the Black Country."

The solicitor tapped the front of the programme Nick was holding, pointing at the Cradley Heathens' name. They both chuckled at the silliness of the suggestion.

"How long have you been following the Bees, Mr Wiseman?"

Harvey began to laugh.

"No need to be so formal, Sergeant. We're not in court! Call me Harvey."

"Nick."

The policeman put out his hand, to which the brief took and shook. The surge of feeling Duncan felt starting in his hand, gathered pace and rocketed up his arm. He tried to keep his face and manner as neutral as he could, but it was proving near impossible — the sensation was exquisite. The two men smiled at each other, sharing a long lingering stare. Nick fought a near over-whelming desire to kiss Harvey's purt lips in their slightly upturned pout. Wearing what was still a fine piece of tailoring, but more casual than the other day, the solicitor's demeanour was divine.

"So how did you get into speedway?"

"Oh Yes, you were asking."

Harvey pointed across the shale track at something. Peering in the direction he gestured, Nick was slightly unsure as to what the barrister wanted him to notice.

"The advertising hoarding — for my father's practice."

The detective became aware of what Harvey was referring to, cursing himself for not noticing straight away. *'Bartholomew & Wiseman — Legal experts, Solicitors, Advice'* the sign told all, above the practice's contact details.

"I've been visiting Brandon since I was eleven."

Duncan couldn't help himself, becoming overcome with excitement. The man he fancied was also a speedway fan!

"Really? You must've started coming here when we first joined the National League!"

"That's about right. My grandfather used to bring my brother and myself after the War."

"Do you remember Johnnie Reason?"

Harvey's smile grew larger as Duncan recalled the speedway rider from yesteryear, his excitement now equalled and bounced off that of the detective.

"Do I? Oh, yes! He used to come to our table after meetings on many occasions."

"Your table?"

"Er, yes."

As Nick asked questions in disbelief, the solicitor came across as self-conscious and uncomfortable.

"My grandfather used to have the same table in the restaurant, overlooking the track for every race upto when he passed on twelve years ago."

"Blimey! It's surprising our paths haven't crossed before now."

"It is! But I bet you had the better deal, not cooped up in some stuffy cod-silver service wannabe."

Duncan didn't see Harvey's point that way. He had met riders, officials, speedway royalty effectively. Nick had not, and his face showed this.

"Nick, I bet you stood right on the perimeter fence, your father holding you steady, tasting the exhaust fumes and shale on your tongue."

"Now, hang on tight, Son — they'll be starting any moment!" Nick held the top rail of the fence tightly in both hands. Well, with one but only vaguely with the other as he held the fixture programme as well. He felt his father place a protective arm around him and hold him firmly in place. He could barely hear Dad speak, as the engines of the four bikes grew louder and louder as they passed. Staring down the home straight, the young Duncan could see the blue-tinged fog appearing around the four racing machines as they appeared out of the nearby pits and flew around the track, only slowing down as they reappeared out of the final bend approaching the start / finish line. The bikes angrily growled and snarled like restrained beasts who wished to be free and roam where they pleased. Even to Nick's innocent and immature mind, it seemed they were all straining at the leash, desperate to be let go.

"Which ones are our riders, Dad?"

He bellowed at his father partially out of excitement, and also because the noise was deafening at their vantage point next to the pits.

"The Bees lads wear black with yellow stripes, and have red or blue helmets. We're racing Norwich tonight — they're wearing all green with a yellow star on their back. Their riders have white or yellow helmets."

The young Duncan beamed with joy, listening to his father's words as he near shouted straight into his ear. This was a birthday treat beyond anything he'd received before in his short life, but as Mum and Uncle Eddie had put it, he was into double figures now — ten years old no less. He could still recall Dad taking Alex out for his tenth birthday treat about three years earlier, they went and watched Coventry City play a match. Nick's brother had returned bursting with pride and enthusiasm after the Bantams had beaten West Ham that late November. He'd felt so envious, wishing he was older, then Dad could take him too. But his father had promised his day would come. And true to Bob Duncan's word, today was his turn.

"Dad, what make are the bikes?"

Nick had sat straddled over the tank of his father's Francis-Barnett Cruiser, being held in place between his arms for the short journey from Radford to Brandon. His favourite part was once through Binley, Dad had opened up the bike and belted along the country lanes. With the mobile 'anchor' of the sidecar removed at the moment, it felt to Nick they were moving faster than the fighter planes he had seen in the Pathe news reports at the cinema during the War.

"The Bees ride Excelsiors. Superb sports bikes."

The little boy watched with anticipation the four riders on the start line, a couple of them fidgeting around on their machines, making sure everything was perfect before the heat began. Suddenly, one of the Bees riders flew forwards a few yards in a crescendo of noise and huge shower of powdery dust, before pushing himself backwards into position alongside the others.

"Ladies and Gentleman, welcome to our first heat tonight. As you can see, the riders are seating themselves in their gates and we'll be underway shortly."

Nick could hardly wait. The announcer made his excitement pique even higher with his greeting.

"Lining up for the Bees tonight in this heat with the red helmet is our adopted Australian, Les Hewitt, and a big cheer for our local lad, wearing the blue helmet, Johnnie Reason!"

The crowd in the stadium rose to their feet, cheering and applauding. Still with his eyes glued to the four bikes on the start line, Nick saw the rider with the blue helmet raise his hand, and give the crowd a thumb's up signal. As the four racing machines idled, popping, coughing and spluttering, being revved slightly by their riders, the tape was lowered in front of them. The riders edged their bikes as close as possible to it, as not to give any advantage to the others.

Nick didn't realise the tape had been lifted and the heat had begun, until both of the Bees riders had accelerated away from the line and within the blink of an eye had begun to power slide into Turn One. The noise was intense, the racing closer than close. Boggle eyed, the young Duncan could not believe how close the bikes got to one another, riders regularly clashing elbows and handlebars, barging one another out of the way, at times appearing as though they wanted to swop bikes while moving as they hit fantastically fast speeds on the straights. And every time they drifted past hanging the rear wheel out, he received a face full of shale dust. He loved it. Nicholas Duncan had been bitten by the bug called 'Motorsport'.

As the chequered flag was waved, the crowd applauded and cheered as one, as their favourite Johnnie

Reason crossed the line in first place. Raising a pointed finger to the heavens, the racer acknowledged the adulation as he slowed down.

"Yes! Great start! Johnnie wins for the Bees! Open the programme Nick, and I'll show you how to fill the scorecard in."

The ten-year-old attempted to pass his father the magazine, but clumsily dropped it. Climbing down from the fence, he attempted to retrieve it. However, once on the ground Nick couldn't find it anywhere. Had someone taken it in the few seconds before he had gotten down from the fence? Had Dad picked it up, seeing it fall from his grasp? Completely unexpectedly, the programme was offered to him by an adult man. Nick took the magazine back slowly, looking up straight into the smiling face of Harvey Wiseman.

Harvey dusted off the fixture programme after its tumble onto the ground, and handed it back to the detective.

"Thanks. Yes, my childhood was something like that."

The rising crescendo of four bike engines drew their attention back to the track. Just in the nick of time too, as the tape flew upwards and the heat began.

Barely a minute had passed, and the heat was over. The two men were speechless watching the break-neck speed of the racers, how at times the riders were shoulder-to-shoulder leaning on each other as they drifting through the turns.

"Winner of the first heat, for Coventry Bees, Les Owen! Ladies and Gentleman, show your appreciation, please!"

As the stadium announcer informed the masses of the result, Nick and Harvey joined in with the rapturous applause.

A rider in Bees colours with a blue helmet stood up on the foot pegs of his machine during his victory lap, punching the air with his right fist. Gradually, the sound of the bike engines dissipated as the riders completed their cool down circuit, to which the two men moved towards one of the hot dog stands.

"It never ceases to amaze me how much faster these modern bikes are, compared to the ones I first saw in the late forties."

Harvey nodded in agreement. *"It's these new bikes from Czechoslovakia, that's why the lap record has tumbled over the last few years. Coffee?"*

The barrister offered Nick a plastic cup of some sort of hot beverage. Duncan grimaced after taking a swig of its contents.

"That's not what I'd call it!"

Taking a pre-cautionary sip of his own drink, Harvey rapidly came to the same conclusion.

"Ahem! Shall we head over to the bar?"

Nick chuckled and nodded.

"Tell you something, it's really nice to find someone with like interests. Do you follow Formula One as well?"

"Oh, indeed!" Harvey's face lit up at the mention of the sport. *"I remember Mike Hawthorn becoming the first British driver to win the World Championship. That felt incredible."*

The policeman nodded in appreciation at the solicitor's memory, a massive smirk spreading across his face.

"I was undertaking my first year of National Service. We used to get the news reels before they were shown on TV or at the cinema. I remember seeing the reports, and the celebrations when Hawthorn took the title, but felt so sorry for Stirling Moss who missed out by one point."

"Yes! I remember that too! And weren't all of the drivers that finished in top five of the Championship that year British?" Duncan was seriously impressed with Harvey's knowledge of motor racing. He didn't know that snippet of trivia himself.

Reaching the bar entrance, the two men stood to one side as a group of older, gobby teenagers barged their way through. The policeman reached out to push the entrance door open, still struggling to keep his eyes off the solicitor.

"Do you reckon Jackie Stewart will regain the title this season?"

Harvey did not get chance to continue the conversation, as the instant his hand touched the door handle, they became aware of an announcement over the stadium tannoy.

"Sorry to interrupt tonight's racing, but we have an urgent message for one of our spectators. Could Nicholas Duncan please contact the Office immediately. That's could a Nicholas Duncan please contact the Office immediately. Thank you."

Nick and Harvey exchanged concerned glances. The barrister spoke first.

"That sounds serious."

"Yes, I best find a phone. Excuse me."

The detective dashed off towards a pair of red telephone boxes, entered one, and dialled the office at the station. As a male voice answered, Duncan pushed his five pence piece into the coin slot.

"Warwickshire Police, Little Park Street CID."

"Dermot?"

"Yeah, who's that?"

"It's D.S Duncan. I've just had a message to contact the Office."

"Yes, Sarge. I hate to say it but it's happened again."

The sergeant's heart sank. He knew exactly what the constable was about to inform him, but had to hear it regardless.

"What's happened again?"

"Another body."

"Oh, for Fuck's sake! Whereabouts this time?"

"The Zoo. A young woman has been found in the maintenance area."

Duncan sighed heavily, closing his eyes and putting his hand to his forehead in disbelief.

"OK, Dermot. I'm on my way."

"OK, Nick. I'll let the Guv'nor know."

Re-emerging from the phone box, the detective found Harvey loitering in close proximity.

"Sorry Harvey, I've got to go."

Duncan patted the solicitor on the shoulder, wishing he could spend the whole race meeting with him, and exchange some of their favourite memories in motorsport. Harvey gestured he understood. He reached forward with both hands taking Nick's other hand, embracing it with both of his.

"Take care, Sergeant. I hope it's nothing too serious."

The policeman glanced down at the barrister's hands wrapped around his, gradually feeling their fingers beginning to entwine. It felt divine. He didn't want it to stop. The sudden roar of four bikes re-entering the circuit in preparation for the second heat snapped Duncan out of his daydream.

"Thanks. I'm afraid to say I've gradually become used to it. It's my job."

The two men released one another — Nick being pleasantly surprised Harvey was equally reluctant to do so as himself.

"Give me a call, Nick. I'm sure your office has my number." Duncan peered over his shoulder and smiled, saluting the solicitor as he made his way briskly back to the car park.

It took the detective around fifteen minutes to traverse to the other side of the city. As he closed in on the animal sanctuary in the darkness, Nick headed towards the glow and repeated flashing of blue lights emanating over the tree tops. Parking the Standard behind the queue of Police vehicles along the narrow lane, he walked towards the cordon and continued towards the scene. Temporary arc lights already in place, Duncan could see attention was focused on a group of industrial size dustbins, a large heap of black refuse sacks and some discarded equipment.

"What have we got, Guv?"

"Ah, Nick! Well, another deceased female. Found by zoo security. Well, they spotted a group of foxes having a party in the rubbish. They had a closer look and found this poor unfortunate. St John can fill you in with the rest."

Edwards gestured in the direction of the other sergeant, who was talking to Cavanagh as the two of them jotted into their notebooks. Nick moved over to his colleagues to gain more information.

"Do we know who this lady is, folks?"

"Yes, Sarge." Joan flipped a few pages back in her notebook. *"ID found in her handbag says she is a Chinese national, name of Zhen Wheng."*

"Chinese?"

Nick raised his eyebrows in surprise. Sebastian chipped

in, reading from his own scrawl.

"*Aye, Chinese. From bits an' pieces in her bag, a student at University o' Warwick down the road. We're gonna need a' interpreter too. There's hand-written notes an' a wee diary, all in Chinese.*"

"*You mean 'Mandarin' or 'Cantonese', Sebastian. There's no such language as 'Chinese'.*"

"*It all looks like scribble on a takeaway menu t' me.*" Sebastian dug himself further into his hole with his blinkered, tired and old-fashioned opinion. The other two detectives glared at the Scotsman.

"*An' another thing — she's bina here fa a while.*"

"*Seriously?*"

Nick spun around on the spot, staring at the floodlit area. Fellow officers from SOCO were now on scene, taking photos, gradually moving bagged rubbish and disused maintenance equipment out of the way. Edwards was conversing with different people, showing an extreme concern on his face and through his body language, asking numerous questions.

"*Aye, Golden Bollocks. She's been lying there a few days now.*"

Duncan continued to look aghast.

"*That's why the foxes were digging amongst there, Sarge.*"

"*Yes, I'd say so Joan. I bet most of the animals close by could smell the decomposing body too. Like the girl found at Coombe Abbey, this young lady has been dumped here. This isn't where she was killed. There might be a pattern forming...*"

All of a sudden, Nick became aware of someone joining them.

"People, we're going to have to raise our game after finding this young lady."

The inspector addressed his detectives. Duncan had never heard his boss speak so seriously and gravely.

"Do we know the cause and the time of death yet?"

Duncan reached over to Cavanagh, taking her notebook and pen, beginning writing his own observations and considerations. The scouser glared at the sergeant with an expression that at its most polite said *"Charming!"*

"We don't know exactly as yet, Nick. Dr Tyler will be able to say for certain once she's conducted the post mortem. Her colleague Dr Basra is enroute as we speak."

The three junior detectives glanced at one another, then the inspector, all looking surprised yet puzzled.

"Apparently, Dr Tyler is attending a health care fundraising evening in Birmingham tonight."

"Eyeza be surprised da Doc canna establish anything wiv wassa left o' da woman."

Everyone stared at the Scotsman after his somewhat gory comment.

"Issa true! Duze foxes have already eaten her fingers anna one of her hands."

Nick could see the disgusted and uneasy face Cavanagh pulled, as St John pointed this out.

"She's been here a few days for sure, I'd say."

Edwards said what Duncan was thinking. In fact, the sergeant knew for certain to have decomposed to such a level wild animals would be attracted to it, the likelihood was the poor young woman had been deposited unceremoniously where she was found for the best part of a week and half.

"I would say good evening, ladies and gents, but it's far

from one."

The group of detectives turned at the sound of the voice addressing them, finding Detective Chief Inspector Spencer approaching.

"My thoughts exactly, Tom. This is now getting ridiculous."

In the eerie semi-darkness, Nick could clearly see the DCI give Edwards a glance that agreed with the inspector's comment. In the corner of his eye, the sergeant caught his young Scouse colleague gazing upwards at the giant zulu warrior towering over the zoo entrance. Screwing up her face, Cavanagh appeared somewhat perplexed. Duncan could understand her mystified state of mind — he never understood why the animal sanctuary's owners had the thirty-foot tall effigy there. Holding a spear in its right hand in attack pose, it was quite a disturbing sight in the partial dark, as the flashing blue lights of the emergency vehicles illuminated it.

"I'm cancelling all leave now. One murder on my patch is completely unacceptable, but now three in rapid succession — inside one week..."

Needless to say, Spencer grabbed all of the other detective's attention quicker than quick.

"Cancelling all leave?"

St John spoke first, only to be shut down instantaneously by the DCI.

"Yes, Sergeant. The severity of the situation dictates such. The Super wouldn't expect otherwise."

The Scottish Detective sighed heavily.

"Apologies for impinging on your personal life Sergeant, but I'd say these investigations far out way any drunken social gathering you were planning."

"Aye, Sir."

"Right then, folks. Less of the belly-aching. The DCI and myself will see you all in the morning, bright-eyed and bushy-tailed."

"Guv."

Nick acknowledged the inspector. He tugged at Cavanagh's arm, gesturing towards their parked cars with a slight flick of his head. The scouser looked puzzled, but followed the sergeant.

"A Chinese student?"

"Yeah. The Guv'nor has already asked Dermot to inform the Home Office and the Chinese Embassy."

"Well, I think the Home Office will deal with that themselves, as to us. We'll have to expect a visit from them both now."

"Bloody Hell! I didn't think of that!"

Duncan froze to the spot, staring at the constable. A curious and slightly confused look on his face.

"Joan, what on Earth are you wearing?"

"What?"

The young female detective peered down at herself, studying what the sergeant was referring to. From under her coat, it seemed she was wearing deep purple, loose fitting satin trousers. Her knee-high boots covered them around her shins.

"Oh, my pyjamas!"

Undoing her coat and opening it wide like a flasher exposing themself, she revealed the satin jacket of the nightwear, that perfectly matched the bottoms.

"Off to some sort of kinky party?"

"Humph!"

Cavanagh closed her coat, buttoning it back up tight

against her chin.

"Chance would be a fine thing! I was getting ready for a cosy evening in front of the telly when Dermot phoned."

Nick chuckled, reaching into his jacket pocket for his cigarettes.

"Well, apologies for disturbing you from tonight's episode of Crossroads.*"*

"Crossroads *my arse! I was watching that Petula Clark thing, before* Match Of The Day *came on."*

"How did Liverpool get on today?"

"Shite! Lost 2–1 to the bloody Geordies. But should win the League on Monday if they beat Leeds."

Duncan's eyes began to glaze over as the constable talked football, which he tried to disguise as he placed one of his cigarettes between his lips. He began his ritual of trying to find his lighter, as the Merseysider shook her head and wandered off back towards her car.

CHAPTER SIX
EASTER SUNDAY
SUNDAY APRIL 22nd 1973

Of all the paperwork Nick had to read and digest, post mortem reports were his least favourite by a country mile. He could never become accustomed to medical jargon, wishing doctors spoke in clear, concise normal English. Although 'medical speak' was essential in court, especially when bamboozling a wet behind the ears brief.

"Yes, Sergeant. The deceased has experienced the same method of death as Miss Rana and Miss Kroy — asphyxiation by strangulation. If you look here…"

Cavanagh and Duncan looked up from the report the constable was holding, and in the direction of where the Doctor wished them to.

"…You can clearly see the contusions in the neck tissue which caused the excessive constriction and compression of the trachea." Dr Tyler pointed at the hand-shaped bruising around Zhen's throat. *"As I've already mentioned, identical to the other young ladies."*

Duncan again reached out with his right hand, comparing it against the marks on the Chinese girl's neck.

"Very similar in size to those on Arosha."

"Really, Sarge?"

"Sadly, yes. I'd even be as bold as to say we're looking

for the same guy now. We have a serial killer to catch."

Solemnly, the Scouse Detective nodded in agreement.

"I hear you found her last night at the zoo."

"Unfortunately, yes."

"You and your crowd don't like making things easy for me."

"Trust me Doctor, despite how delightful your company is, I'd much rather not visit here at all. Let alone for the third time in a week, or on a public holiday."

Tyler smiled pensively and nodded.

"I haven't been called in here during a major holiday for a long time. I should be taking my daughters to church later for the service."

Duncan and Cavanagh exchanged glum looks with the Doctor.

"We need to get back to the station. Thanks for all of this."

Joan gestured with a copy of the report. Nick smiled at the Doctor thoughtfully.

Heading back towards the city centre, Joan was trying to suppress her attack of the giggles. This did little to aid Nick's state of mind, as he crashed the gears once again of his brother's car, and stalled as he approached a set of traffic lights.

"Oh, shut up!"

Duncan glared at the constable, not finding the situation remotely amusing. He knew straight away this would only fuel her mirth further.

"Don't you adore cars and used to be a mechanic, like?"

Joan managed to utter a coherent sentence between guffaws.

"I do! It's this shitty thing! Christ knows what Alex has

done to it!"

After more tittering, Cavanagh became more brazen.

"Are you sure you learnt to drive?"

"Fuck Right Off!"

"Maybe it would be better if I drove."

"Be my guest! I'll be glad when I get Alice back!"

Joan didn't need asking twice, leaping across the bench seat, landing on Duncan's lap.

"Move over, then!"

The constable squirmed to her right, as Nick shimmed to the left. The sergeant found the brief physical contact quite pleasing and enjoyable, the Liverpudlian inadvertently rubbed her peachy derriere into his genitals. Nick found his colleague had a fairly purt and shapely behind as she slid across. It reminded him of his illicit Navy 'squeeze', Tony Devereux. The two things that threw his naughty memory into touch were Cavanagh's soft, long brown hair brushing against his face, and the fragrance she was wearing — the new *'Charlie'* perfume, if he wasn't mistaken.

Once behind the wheel the Merseysider re-started the engine, and moved away into traffic. Straight away, Duncan could see his colleague was driving the wretched thing with aplomb. She accelerated with ease, changing gear in such a slick and smooth manner, even slowing comfortably at junctions.

"How the hell did you manage that?"

Cavanagh turned to look at the sergeant with a huge beaming grin.

"I learnt to drive in one of these. My Arl Fella has a Vanguard, owned it for yonks."

"For a moment, I was beginning to believe you were one

of those rare people who can drive anything!"

Joan laughed out loud.

"Believe me, learning to drive in one of these makes it feel that way. Your Alvis is much more refined than this antwacky heap. Alice is much easier to drive."

The sergeant smirked and nodded in agreement.

"I'd say, it appears both Arosha Rana and Wendy Kroy were killed by the same person."

"Well deduced, Jane Marple."

"Oi! Less of the sarcasm! Do you reckon this Chinese girl is connected to the others?"

"Not directly, but my gut feeling is it's the same killer."

"The same killer? What makes you so sure, like?"

"Zhen Wheng's personal effects were still intact. Plus, have you noticed something about their appearance? What have all of these unfortunates have in common?"

Cavanagh screwed her pretty face up in a manner you wouldn't expect from a beautiful young woman, her eyes bulged in confusion.

"Er, Sarge just in case it's slipped your attention, these three women are all from different ethnic backgrounds…"

"I know that! But they're all around the same age, same height, same hair colour in near as damn it the same style…"

"Fuck me! You're only bloody right!"

"And as I've said before, the guy who's done this has dabs bigger than mine."

Duncan lifted both of his hands up, wiggling his fingers jazz-hands style.

"I hope Wendy's family has been notified by now, Nick."

"I'm sure it'll be sorted today, along with the situation with Zhen Wheng. I bet due to the Bank Holiday, we won't be

able to get in touch with the Home Office proper till Tuesday."

As they passed the Council House and entered Little Park Street, something grabbed the sergeant's attention outside the station. Parked a few hundred yards away from the main building, was a dark blue Daimler saloon. Duncan knew full well who the owner of the immaculate luxurious motor was, the private registration plate confirming this.

"What on Earth is he doing here?"

"Who, Sarge?"

It was only Cavanagh's reply that made the sergeant realise he was thinking out loud.

"Oh, no one important. I thought I saw someone I know."

Nick continued to stare at the stationary car as Joan drove into the station car park. The twin exhaust pipes of the Daimler gently emitted visible warm vapours, the engine on tick over. This time, he made sure he didn't 'think' out loud. *"Why would he be here?"* After clambering out of the car, the detective strode back to the street to ponder once again over the Daimler and its owner, only to find the car had moved on. Nick scratched his head, baffled. *"When was the last time I had to speak with him?"*

"Are you all right? You look like you've seen a ghost."

Joan caught up with the sergeant, concerned.

"Yeah, I'm fine. Let's go inside."

Assembled in the CID office were the whole team. It was crystal clear many would prefer not to be there, stuck at work on Easter Sunday. Some appeared to believe having to report to the station on a public holiday was carte blanche to wear their own 'casual' clothing, which had descended further into sportswear for some. Duncan himself felt this was not befitting the grave, seriousness of a murder enquiry. Edwards had taught him well as regards discipline and professionalism. It had to be upheld at all times, no matter what. He glanced at the noticeboard, already amended with additional items and a whole new section had now been included for the unfortunate Zhen. Besides the distasteful and unpleasant pics of the women in the state they'd been found, mercifully images of Arosha and Wendy when they were alive had been sourced. Nick couldn't wait for a lovely photo of Zhen to be found — he really did not wish to be reminded of the state she was when they found her.

"Right folks, once the DCI gets here, we'll begin. But in the meantime, make yourselves familiar with all of the latest information on the noticeboard." Edwards addressed the room, removing his coat and hat as he spoke. *"Apologies for dragging you all into work on a public holiday, but as you're all aware we have a massive situation."*

Through the nicotine laced fog which was growing in intensity, the sergeant could see all eyes were on the inspector.

"People, we're after a serial killer or killer with accomplice. As confirmed by Dr Tyler in the post mortem reports, we have several similarities too much alike to be a fluke."

"Cus b' a copycat killer."

All eyes in the room turned towards St John as he uttered his hypothesis.

"Copycat!?!?! What are you yappin' about, you blert!?!"

Cavanagh was far from impressed with her Scottish colleague's idea.

"Aye, copycat. Remember that Boston Strangler in the States about ten years ago. Tony Curtis was in da film."

Nick chuckled and interrupted.

"Alfred De Salvo was strangling women with their hosiery, not his barehands, Van Der Valk !!"

Sebastian huffed.

"Jus fort it cus b' sumat."

Duncan quickly noticed Dermot sitting towards the front of the assembled mass next to Rachel, pointing items of interest out on the reports spread out in front of them. *"They're becoming rather cosy..."* he began to mentally note.

"If I'm allowed to continue !!"

The Inspector paused for a moment, glaring at his team.

"We now have the report for the young lady found last night, full name ZhenZhen Wheng, aged twenty years old. It would appear our killer or killers have good local knowledge, due to the secluded places the deceased have been left. We're fairly certain were looking for a man or two working as a partnership due to the bruising on the women's necks in a hand shape..." Edwards pointed at several photos on the noticeboard of the strangled girl's necks. *"...which is quite large. Bigger than my dabs, I'd say."*

Just as the inspector held his outspread hands towards his detective team to emphasise his point, DCI Spencer entered the office, puffing away on his pipe with vengeance.

"Morning Each — Happy Easter, under the circumstances."

Several replied a near simultaneous response, but it was more staggered and sounded like a rabble with a severe hangover.

"Morning Tom. Just informing the team of everything."

"Oh, do carry on. Don't mind me."

"Where was I? Oh, yes. Two people. We know this, as one

person would have found it near impossible to carry and stuff Wendy Kroy into that small tunnel on their own. " Edwards pointed at a new section on the board, under Zhen's name.

"We're trying to rapidly gain a translator to read some notes and a pocket diary amongst her personal effects. There could be something critical amongst her scribble. Rachel, have we sorted out a translator?"

The inspector turned to the liaison officer, but she was distracted — miles away, sharing sweet nothings with Dermot.

"Rachel..." Edwards tried again. She was still elsewhere mentally, batting her eyelashes at the detective constable.

"WPC RYCE!"

"Oh! Sorry, Sir!"

"Miss Ryce, if I wanted to see a young couple flirting, I'd have stayed at home and watched my daughter and her boyfriend fawn over each other. Our translator? Any news?"

The older man spoke in a rather condescending and patronising tone, not lost on others in the office. A few sniggers flitted around the background.

"Oh, yes! I've been in contact with the University of Warwick, they said they'd send over a lecturer from the School of Languages who teaches Chinese."

Duncan shook his head at Rachel's words, recalling what he said to St John the night before about Mandarin and Cantonese. Spencer spoke up.

"When will they be here, Rachel?"

"Hopefully tomorrow afternoon. The University said they'd get in touch with him today, and stress its urgent."

"Tomorrow?"

"It is a Bank Holiday weekend, Sir."

"Humph! Haven't we got any officers who are fluent in

this dialect?"

"Not here, Sir. There might be over at one of the central Birmingham stations."

"Well, could you find out please! Speed is of the essence."
"Yes, Sir."

Edwards conveyed his own query.

"And has the Home Office been informed?"

"Yes, Sir. The Telex was sent last night."

Both of the inspectors nodded in approval.

"Right folks, we do have a couple of leads. A chap who works at a department store where Arosha and Wendy worked, plus similarities in the women's personal effects."

The inspector picked up a nearby mug and took a huge swig of the contents, to wet his whistle.

"OK then, before you all return to your homes to stuff yourselves stupid with chocolate a few matters to deal with. The 'large hands' angle — which professions traditionally do the workers have huge dabs? I want you to contact builders, carpenters, plumbers, garages with mechanics, butchers, farmers — I know it's a long list, but we could find something. Others of you contact gymnasiums, local community centres, youth clubs — any amateur boxers or martial arts participants with big hands? Duncan and Cavanagh — go visit the University, find where Zhen was living, take Rachel with you for 'house-to-house' enquires. St John and Ward — go through the personal effects Zhen was carrying, is there anything of note, any connection or similarity to what the other girls were carrying. And the rest of you, go over everything again — look for similarities or anything that sticks out like the proverbial. Go through the information uniform has found for us on their 'house-to-house' calls again, cross reference it with the details

we already have and know. Right, any questions before we go about our duties?"

After a brief moment's quiet, Rachel spoke up.

"Er, Sir...visiting Zhen's place of residence?"

"That's correct, Miss Ryce. If you don't mind."

"Will the university be open? It's the Easter holidays, after all."

"Hmmm, that's a point. Didn't think of that."

Edwards scratched his head and raised his eyebrows, glancing at the chief Inspector.

"Guv?"

"Yes, Nick."

"I think students from overseas remain on campus during the holidays. There isn't enough time for them to visit home and return. And then there's the cost."

"Of course! That would explain a lot. See what you three can find out when you're over there."

"Guv."

Sebastian screwed his nose up and glared at Duncan as he finished speaking with the inspector. The Scotsman mouthed the words *"Smart Arse!"* Nick smiled smarmily back, and winked.

A while later, the Standard Vanguard owned by Alex Duncan arrived outside one of the halls of residence blocks on the University of Warwick campus. Cavanagh stepped out of the car from behind the wheel. She looked at Duncan, smirked and winked. The sergeant returned her gaze with an appreciative smile and nodded.

"Miss Wheng is living in this block, Detectives."

The warden escorted the police officers into the building,

up a series of flights of stairs and onto the first floor.

"Do many overseas students remain here during the holiday periods, like?"

"Most do, Constable. Except at Christmas. Then there's barely anyone here."

The group passed by other students on the landing, all of Far Eastern ascent. Duncan noticed they eyed them, specifically Rachel in full uniform, quite worryingly as the warden jingled through his keys trying to find the correct one. The sergeant peered at the warden's name tag, pinned to his tie. It appeared as though it had been placed there in a hurry, its slightly jaunty angle making the observer 'cock' their head to read the university logo and his name, Charlie Saunders.

"Ah! Here we are."

Mr Saunders unlocked the door to the student bedsit, allowing the detectives access.

Straight away, Duncan was hit by the fragrance of stale air, a bed that required changing and most likely over-ripe fruit.

"Oooo! Someone hasn't eaten the bananas they bought!"

Rachel was first to comment. Both of the detectives glanced at her. They were too well experienced to comment on something as trivial as the pungent aroma of over-ripe tropical fruit. Nick had a brain-wave — this was an opportunity for the sergeant to point out a few detective techniques to the wet behind the ears WPC.

"Rachel, here's a tip. When first entering a room, take in as much as you can mentally. Take notes if you wish. These initial moments can give major pointers as to what's happened here or relates to matters elsewhere."

The uniformed constable's face swiftly changed as she

absorbed the sergeant's words, and rapidly found a notebook in her handbag.

"Is there anything specific you're looking for, Sergeant?" Mr Saunders voiced his own curiosity, in a semi-helpful way.

"Just anything that may help us with our enquiries." Entering the bedsit, Duncan noticed it was a typical student digs. More tidy and clean than what he was expecting, only had the lingering odour of being shut up for a couple of weeks. And those bananas. Across a desk, several text books were strune.

"Modern Languages." The sergeant picked one up, and leafed through. This particular book was printed in English, most of the others were Mandarin/Cantonese, with a couple in French and German.

"I take it she was multi-lingual." Rachel began scribbling in her notebook. Nick saw Cavanagh gave her friend a slightly sarcastic glance, but the liaison officer was too busy to notice. On a noticeboard over the desk, was displayed Zhen's timetable many little pieces of paper. Most were in her native tongue, a few in English. Alongside these, was something that really caught Duncan's attention — a newspaper clipping. An article announcing the auditions at the Coventry Theatre for the musical due to be opening there in a few months' time, *'Passport To Paris'*.

"We'll need that translator in here too." Joan peered at the noticeboard as well, while Nick leaned forward and removed the press clipping.

"Yeah, good idea. I expect all of these are just bullet-point prompts, relating to her studies."

"What have you found, Skipper?"

217

Rachel watched as Nick held the piece of newspaper, the detective contemplating its content material.

"I think we need to visit the theatre again."

Cavanagh nodded in agreement.

"Rachel, could you go knock a few doors along this floor, ask the relevant questions please."

"OK Skipper."

Duncan surveyed the room once again. First thing that caught his keen eye, were a group of photographs adhered to the wall next to the bed. Not actually having seen an image of Zhen, Nick could see the same face in different pics.

"That's her! That's Zhen Wheng."

The sergeant pointed at a pretty young woman in the pictures, adorned in well-appointed cosmetics with her black hair styled in the popular 'bob' cut. The detective constable leaned forwards and carefully removed a photo from the wall, inspecting it closer.

"I wonder who the other girl in the pic with her is?"

Cavanagh tapped the photograph with her index finger, looking at the white young woman who also had make up just so, her shoulder length black curly permed hair perfect.

"More to the point, whereabouts was that taken? I swear I recognise that pub they're standing in."

The two detectives scrutinised the image. The background sure did look familiar. Where the hell was it? Nick was certain he'd been there.

"I think I've been there too, Sarge. It looks like somewhere I should know."

"Bring that picture with us. We need that for an accurate likeness of Zhen, and to work out which bar that is."

The detectives examined the other photos. One showed

Zhen with what was clearly her family, another with a group of other people her own age on what they assumed was the Great Wall of China, but one in particular grabbed Nick's attention. Zhen was once again amongst a group of people her own age, but this time standing amongst the cathedral ruins in the city centre.

"Excuse me, Mr Saunders. Maybe you can help us. Do you recognise the people in this photo?"

The warden retrieved a pair of spectacles from his shirt pocket, sliding them onto his face. He studied the picture.

"Er, not as such. I've seen some of them around campus, I think. Some I don't know at all."

"What about the young woman with Zhen in this one?"

Nick gestured to Joan to remove the pic in question, and offer it towards Mr Saunders. The warden fiddled with his glasses again, squinted and rubbed his chin as he considered what he could see.

"Not really. I might have seen her around. Young girls all look alike and dress the same."

"Thanks all the same. We'd best be getting back to the station."

Joan politely spoke, before both detectives made their way towards the door.

In the car on the journey back to Little Park Street, Nick began leafing through Rachel's notebook.

"Crikey! I was always told when I passed through training to take copious notes, but this is something else!"

Duncan spun over page after page of the liaison officer's hand-writing. He could see she'd scribbled down everything there was to see, smell and touch about Zhen's room.

"You should consider transferring over to SOCO. They'd

love this much attention to detail."

"Really, Skipper?" Rachel smiled broadly.

The sergeant cleared his throat in an over-elaborate, theatrical style, about to read aloud but was cut-short.

"Leave Rach alone. At least she's thorough."

Duncan caught Joan in the corner of his eye look into the rear-view mirror, and wink at Rachel in the backseat. Nick smiled. Yes, the liaison officer was very thorough, but prone to the odd gaff due to trying too hard to impress. And there was the distraction of fellow male colleagues. He knew she was sweet on Mr Ward. If Rachel could deal with this better, Duncan felt she'd make a damn fine Detective Constable.

"Joking aside, keep this attention to detail up. You'll make a bloody good detective if you do."

Nick shuffled around in the front passenger seat to look over his shoulder at the WPC, smiling the same way a teacher does to a pupil who has potential and was starting to achieve it. Rachel grinned back at the sergeant appreciatively.

"Thanks, Skipper. That's kind of you to say."

Duncan turned back to face their direction of travel, and began thoroughly inspecting the photos they had borrowed. Something struck him as clear as day, something he felt he should have noticed earlier — the young brown-haired woman in the pic with Zhen, was also in the group pic at the old cathedral. The two women were standing amongst the group, their arms around each other. He pointed his 'find' out to his colleagues.

"Look at this!"

Cavanagh tried to glance at the images being shown to her, while not taking her eyes off the road for too long.

"Oh, yeah! We need to find her then. See if she knows

anything. "

"*Exactly! And find out where the photo of the two of them was taken.*"

"*We'll get on it, Skip. I'm sure I've visited that bar, but where is it...?*"

"*There's something else I noticed in her bedsit...*"

Both women gazed at Duncan, intrigued with what he was about to reveal.

"*I noticed something that isn't there. There's no pic of Zhen with a potential partner or boyfriend.*"

Realisation spread across the two Constables, as they glanced at each other. Rachel pondered a possibility.

"*Maybe she hasn't currently got one.*"

"*Hmmm, perhaps...*"

Nick continued to study the images. "*Unless the young brunette is Zhen's partner,*" he muttered under his breath. The detective had visited that bar as well. He knew it. It was located in the city somewhere. Only, he couldn't recall which one.

Duncan sung to himself the Buddy Holly song, *I'm Lookin' For Someone to Love* as he got dressed, looking at the framed pic of the Rock N' Roll singer he kept on his chest of drawers. Reattaching his Polerouter to his wrist, Nick followed this by carefully folding his cuff into the perfect position, and passed a gold cufflink through the holes in the high-quality fabric. Admiring his reflection, he did up his black, silk tie. It complimented perfectly with the three-piece suit he was in the process of climbing into. The suit itself was sharper than sharp, and was the reason why he never took a decent holiday in 1968 or the year after — partially due to the series of appointments in London he had to keep at an exclusive Saville Row tailor and partially due to the cost. Ever since Sean Connery had worn one in the James Bond movie *'Goldfinger'*, he had to have one.

The policeman slid into the waistcoat fastening the buttons and adjusted the rear cinch. Finally, the jacket. After slipping it on, he adjusted his shirt cuffs so they protruded just the desired amount — no more, no less. The sergeant was now ready. Well, almost. He pondered over which aftershave to wear tonight. He usually wore Acqua Di Selva for work as it had longevity and it was powerful enough to be smelt over his self-generated tobacco smoke. This evening was no different, especially being in the confined space of a nightclub and all the dubious fragrances and aromas that entailed. Selecting the Chanel bottle, he sprinkled a few drops of the gold liquid onto his left palm, and rubbed it against his right. He patted his face, throat and nape of his neck with both of his damp, fragrant hands.

"Are you ready yet, Constable?"

Val knocked the door of Nick's bedroom, eager to get going for their evening out.

"Just coming."

Duncan emerged from his personal sanctuary to receive long wolf-whistles from his friends.

"Hark at you! Someone is out on the pull!"

Nick put his hands at a rakish angle from his body, while keeping his arms perfectly straight along his sides, slowly shuffled around on the spot performing a daft 'twirl' showing off his three-piece suit. As the detective finished his full turn and returned to facing Val and Rich, he could see they were attired in their best bib and tucker as well.

"Are we driving there?"

"Eh? In my brother's bag of bolts? No fear! I've booked

us a taxi!"

Nick darted downstairs and into the lounge, rubbing his hands together.

"Let's have a drink."

Opening a cabinet in the sideboard, Duncan found three 'highball' glasses, filling each glass about an inch with vodka. Adding a golden Italian liqueur to the glass, Rich's curiosity piqued.

"What are you making us, Mate?"

Nick replied only with a wink. Carrying all three glasses wedged between both hands, he headed for the kitchen. Reaching the fridge, he found some orange juice, topping up the glasses and stirred them thoroughly. Picking up two of the drinks, he offered them to his guests.

"Oooo! What's this, Nick?"

Their host returned to the kitchen, reappearing with his own liquid refreshment.

"You're holding — and hopefully will enjoy — a Harvey Wallbanger. Apologies for no ice, I forgot to refill the ice tray and put it in the ice box."

Both Val and Rich took healthy gulps of their beverages, smacking their lips together contemplating what they were tasting.

"Where did you learn to make those?"

"That tastes fantastic!"

Duncan sampled his own cocktail, smiling that his friends were enjoying it too.

"When I was stationed in Malta. I learnt a thing or two while in the warrant officer's Mess."

Rich took another large swig of the orange liquid.

"Have you got any others in your repertoire?"

"Oh, you know — one or two."

Unexpectedly, a car horn sounded twice outside. Nick poked his head through the gap in the drawn curtains, and saw a taxi in front of the house, the all too familiar clattery sound of its diesel engine echoed around the street.

"Ah! Our chariot awaits!"

The three friends rapidly downed their drinks, dashing outside to their ride. Duncan shimmied into the corner of the backseat alongside Val. As they drove into the city centre, she pointed various buildings and locations out to Rich that she found interesting and had featured within her life over the years. As she spoke, Nick suddenly felt her right hand on his knee, which slowly moved to his thigh and gently squeezed. Feeling incredibly awkward, and not desiring to cause a scene, the detective placed his hand on top of Val's. Gently and incredibly discreetly, he moved his friend's dainty dab into a position so it was no longer resting on his person, nor was his hand on her body.

Stepping out of the cab, Duncan whispered in Val's ear as Rich insisted on paying the taxi driver.

"You need to be careful."

"Why?"

"You damn well know why! If Rich had seen you doing that…"

"Sorry, Nick. Couldn't help myself. But you do look so delicious."

He frowned at her and shook his head in disbelief. Rich rejoined them as they made their way along an alley from a service yard into the shopping precinct, placing them a few yards away from a small glass tower, the entrance to the Locarno nightclub.

"Are we going for a swift half first?"

Rich eyed a nearby pub with an intrigued twinkle in his

eye, rubbing his hands together.

"Swift half?" Val turned her nose up at the idea. *"Remember, you're with a lady tonight, not on the lash with the lads."*

"Which lady where?"

Val swung her clutch bag at her partner, smiling at her fella's cheek at the same time.

"Richard Abbott!"

The couple embraced, laughing. Duncan was touched by how beautiful that was, a couple sharing banter and a laugh. He watched them with slightly envious eyes. The policeman wanted that in his life so badly. Someone he could share wonderful, quality time with, be romantic and soppy with, have cheeky banter with.

Situated inside the free-standing glass tower, the elevator rose up to second floor, whereby the doors opened onto a tidy enclosed bridge into the main building where the nightclub was. Rich took his attention off his lady for a moment.

"So you live on your own, Nick."

"Yeah, that's right."

"Have you got a girlfriend or are you divorced? An ex-wife on the fringes?"

At the moment Rich asked his polite 'getting to know you' questions, Val popped a mint into her mouth she found in her bag. The woman gulped in shock, and began to partially choke on the sweet. Both men, concerned at her situation, slapped her back to which she speedily recovered. Val's eyes watered, as she coughed.

"Thank you. I'm fine now."

After checking on the condition of his friend, Nick returned to Rich's questions somewhat awkwardly.

"Married? Er, no."

"Not met the right girl yet?"

Val now pulled a handkerchief from her small bag, and held it to her mouth as she laughed and laughed. Feigning she was coughing, Duncan could see she hoped she wasn't noticed. He had — and knew exactly why. He struggled to contain his own mirth.

"Let's get inside. I really need to unwind after the last few days."

Paying the admission charge and making their way into the club, Rich baulked at the fee.

"£1.25 per head to have a dance and queue at the bar to buy expensive drinks?"

"Hey, my treat! You'll like it in here. It's not normally that price. I think they've put it up for Easter."

"Humph! It'll keep the Riff-Raff out, no matter how good the band are!"

Finding a table on the balcony, the three had an excellent view of the entire club. Performing better than Duncan expected was a five-piece group knocking out cover versions of songs from Motown, the Beatles, to current Glam Rock.

"The stage revolves, you know."

Val pointed at the band, to which Rich gazed over his shoulder at the group now performing T Rex's hit *'Get It On'*.

"Really?"

"Yeah. Sometimes they'll be another band on the other side who'll play the exact same song as the one being performed front of house, just as the stage begins to turn. If you're too busy dancing or chatting, you may not even realise it has happened!"

Rich chuckled at the somewhat daft situation. As a waiter passed by, Nick managed to attract his attention, ordering a round of drinks.

"Really looks swish in here."

"Don't let the dress code fool you, Rich! That's mainly due to the public holiday. Last year Slade and Mott the Hoople played in here."

Rich gazed at Nick in open-mouthed wonder.

"We've nothing like this in Cheltenham. I'd have to go to Bristol for something similar."

Still in the Glam Rock genre, the band began performing a reasonable cover of David Bowie's song, *'Starman'*. Duncan's attention focused on the stage, as the singer sounded remarkably like Ziggy. Nick turned to Rich and Val, nodding.

"Now he's not half bad!"

"That reminds me, have you bought tickets to see him yet?" Val's excitement was clear. Rich butted into the conversation, highly excited.

"Bowie is playing here? When?"

"No, not here. His gig will be at the Theatre in June. Next time I'm passing I'll see if they've still got any tickets left."

After finishing their drinks, Val and Rich ventured down to the dancefloor, much to Rich's mock protests. Nick watched his friends attempt some rhythmic movements amongst the crowd. The dancefloor being so packed as music changed to a Beatles medley, it was near on impossible to dance properly. Swaying to the music in the direction the masses dictated was all that was feasible. Despite appearing awkward and somewhat ridiculous from Duncan's vantage, the sergeant had to admit it looked great fun.

As the group moved onto *'I Saw Her Standing There'*, he felt someone cheekily punch his bottom twice in quick succession. He knew it wasn't Val, as he could see her down below. Who on Earth could be that brazen? Slowly spinning around, he was met by a naughty grin and the friendly face of no other than Patricia Bayliss.

"Sergeant Duncan! Fancy a dance?"

Bumping into the Welsh barrister threw him slightly, as he didn't expect to see her tonight.

"Patricia! Lovely to see you!"

The lady threw her arms around the policeman, squeezing him tight. Nick reciprocated, happy to see his friend. He knew she was always warm towards him, but guessing the several gins she'd already sank amplified this. The odour of the spirit was overpowering the perfume she had chosen to wear that evening.

"Can I get you a drink?"

The brief answered his question with a stare that clearly said, *"Is the Pope Catholic?"* Duncan smirked back, as he managed to stop a different member of the waiting staff and place another order for a round.

Patricia stepped forward and took the detective by the hand, wolf-whistling as she gave him a visual once-over.

"My, my Nicholas. If I didn't know better, I'd say you're out 'On The Pull'!"

"I could say the same about you!"

The barrister was decked out in a fitted, deep blue crushed velvet off the shoulder number, which emphasised all of the Welsh lady's ample curves. Combined with matching heels and complimentary sheer black hosiery, you could say she was indeed dressed to kill.

"Don't be silly! No one is going to look twice at little old me."

"Really?"

Duncan raised his eyebrows, not believing that remotely. Right on cue, two men around the same age as the sergeant passed by, breaking their necks to give her the once over. Patricia tittered at the attention.

"Are you sure I can't whisk you away somewhere more secluded and private?"

The detective leaned forwards and spoke directly into her ear.

"Only if your real name is actually 'Patrick' and you've been dressing up in drag all these years."

Patricia dropped into a nearby seat and roared with laughter. Nick found his quip quite amusing as well, chuckling along for good measure. Maybe the alcoholic beverages he'd sank so far tonight had made him feel more 'comfortable' than normal too.

Unexpectedly, Nick felt another hand on his back touching him ever so gently. Duncan turned to find Val and Rich, taking a break from their physical exertions and eager for liquid refreshment. Their timing was impeccable, as the waiter returned with a tray containing the four drinks ordered. Picking up a drink, Duncan passed it to the barrister.

"Oh, pardon my manners!"

The off-duty policeman took a step back and spread his arms slightly in a grand gesture more akin to a TV gameshow host.

"This is Llanelli's finest, barrister Patricia Bayliss. We've worked alongside each other on more occasions than I care to admit. And this is my childhood friend Valerie Myers, this is her partner, Richard Abbott."

The three strangers smiled politely at one another, nodding a *'Hello'*. Picking up his drink, Nick took a healthy glug, while taking in the view of the dancing crowd and the stage once more. Just as Val had explained earlier, the stage began to slowly revolve. As the group played the Martha

Reeves song *'Dancing in The Street,'* the male singer began a strange duet with an unseen female voice. The stage continued to slowly turn, bringing a pretty long-haired blonde into view, singing in front of her own band. At a speed so fast it was yet to be given a measurement, Duncan's heart jumped several beats. He felt weak at the knees more so than any point in his life. For moving along the side of the dancefloor was Harvey. He was dressed immaculately, equally as sharp as Nick himself. Time froze for Nick as he watched. Dodging between other revellers moving to and fro attempting to dance, the brief made his way through the club with his relaxed, easy gait.

"Have you seen someone you know? You seem awfully distracted."

Val once again laid her hand on her friend's shoulder, scanning the masses below as to what, or more specifically who, had caught his attention.

"I thought I saw someone I know. That's all."

He flashed a flicker of a smile at her, trying to play the situation down. Val smirked back, her eyes telling the detective she knew he wasn't explaining everything. Duncan was too good a policeman not to notice this either. He couldn't help himself but try and see where Harvey was amongst the crowd. It seemed as though he had no choice but to do so. Something beyond his control was making him behave this way, and he was powerless to resist. Val leaned into the sergeant, speaking straight in to his ear.

"Your body language gives away what you're thinking and feeling. I hope he feels the same about you."

She gave him a peck on the cheek, and left him gazing out over the dancefloor.

Nick took another healthy swig of his drink, and tried to

see where Harvey had moved onto. After a few moments searching, he caught sight of him. Two other men had now stopped the barrister, from Duncan's vantage point it appeared they were exchanging banter. Harvey was trying to move away, but the two men appeared to not want to let him. One in particular began to poke and prod the brief in the chest. Becoming quite concerned, Nick leaned partially over the chest high banister in order to gain as good a view as possible. Harvey continued to back away from the confrontational men, but one persisted in the harassment. Duncan lost sight of the three of them as they moved to part of the club which he could not see from the balcony.

Worry and concern consumed the detective. Harvey was a placid, gentle, if a smidge timid man. The horrifying image of the encounter turning physical flashed through his mind. The solicitor would be near incapable of defending himself.

"I'll be back in a bit."

Duncan briskly darted past his three friends, down the stairs bouncing off other people trying to ascend, before forcing his way through the masses to where he last saw Harvey. The sergeant spun around on the spot, his eyes darting this way and that, but he could not see the brief anywhere. Maybe he'd left the club completely and was spending his evening elsewhere. Maybe he'd had enough of being picked on by those bullies, and gone home. Neither of these were the case, as he spotted Harvey heading towards the Gentlemen's toilets — followed a few moments later by the two men it was clear he was trying to avoid. Nick moved rapidly towards the public conveniences himself.

Upon entering the lavatories, the detective was met with the sight of the man who had been poking Harvey in the chest still verbally abusing him, with his co-hourt looking on.

"Why don't you just fuck off out of here! No one wants your sort here, Poof!"

The man prodded Harvey in the shoulder as hard as he could, the barrister only just kept his balance.

"See, you're such a Nancy you won't fight a real man!"

The thug continued to slap Harvey around the back of the head with so much venom, it was a miracle his head remained attached to his shoulders.

"Is there a problem here, lads?"

Nick had seen enough. He now feared for Harvey's wellbeing. He had to intervene. Upon realising it was Duncan who had appeared, the barrister's face lit up with joy. Witnessing his eyes fill with wonder and his huge involuntary smile first hand, the policeman's heart skipped a beat. Nick had never seen anyone in his whole life so pleased to see him.

"No, no problem," the aggressive bully began. *"At least not once Queer Boy here has slung his gay hook."*

The detective tried diplomacy to solve the situation. It might work.

"Lads, let's go have a drink. I'm sure we can sort out this misunderstanding."

Both of the bullies turned towards Duncan. Their body language clearly said they were in no mood for socialising. The on-looker, quieter of the two spoke.

"Why would we want to drink with him, a fucking cock sucker? And why would you want to stick up for it? Unless, you're one too!" He took a few steps towards the sergeant. *"Yeah! You're a faggot too! You are! You're a fuckin' shirt lifter!"*

The first thug decided to add his own four pence worth, while taking a large step towards Duncan, speaking in a cod 'camp' tone. *"Are you defending your boyfriend, Ducky?"*

After speaking, the thug unexpectedly leapt at Harvey, punching him in the stomach as he landed in front of him. This was followed by a meatier second as the barrister dropped to his knees. Taking that as carte blanche to begin, the other 'heavy' attempted to throw a quick combination of punches at Nick.

With impeccable reactions, the detective managed to bob and weave, leaning away to avoid any connection. As the thug attempted another attack, Duncan threw a series of rapid-fire punches to his abdomen, finishing with an upper cut to his jaw. The hooligan staggered backwards, losing his balance. Falling into an open toilet cubicle, he crashed down onto the porcelain lavatory, smashing the seat to pieces. Now lying motionless on the floor, he made no attempt to get back to his feet. Watching his friend take a beating, the other thug turned his attention from Harvey to Nick. Flying at him, he grabbed the detective in a neck-lock. The two men struggled, grappling and wrestling with one another.

"I'm not going to let no fuckin' poofter beat my mate up and get away with it!"

The policeman grabbed hold of the thug's arm, trying to move it enough so he could breathe easier. Finding this incredibly difficult, Duncan lifted him onto his back and leapt backwards into the wall. This had limited effect, as the bully hung on more intensely. Nick repeated the manoeuvre again, and again once more, throwing more of his bodyweight and strength into each jump as they slammed into the tiled wall. The thug lost most of his grip, partially winded.

Duncan caught Harvey staring at him wide-eyed and open-mouthed, as he fought the thug. Feeling the hooligan's grip ease, he took the initiative and elbowed the bully in the stomach. As the man recoiled winded, the detective stamped with all his might on his foot. Only, he connected with the guy's shin first, resulting in his own foot sliding down his leg and slamming onto the side of the thug's ankle. Short of breath and now in total agony, the hooligan released his hold. Nick spun around, planting a punch square on his attacker's nose. The bloody mess that instantly resulted on the guy's face proved how much force Duncan had put into his strike. Finally, the detective brought the squirmish to an end by kicking the bully full tilt in the genitals. As he collapsed to the floor, the once mouthy homophobe was now nothing more than a defenceless heap.

Nick crouched down next to where Harvey still was. *"Are you all right?"*

With huge eyes that clearly showed how in awe of the detective he was, Harvey threw his arms around Duncan in relief, squeezing him tight.

"Thank you."

Duncan wrapped his own arms around the brief. The heady scent of Harvey's aftershave was all consuming, as he buried his face into his neck. The sensation of holding him and being held by him was phenomenal. It felt like the most natural and normal thing to be doing, yet was like no other embrace he'd ever shared. It was beautiful. Nick swiftly learnt it wasn't only himself that had experienced something magical. As he leaned back on his haunches, he found he was holding Harvey's hands. The policeman gazed at the solicitor's slender, pianist-like digits next to his own, and watched in wonder as they began to caress his fingers. Nick wanted to melt into the floor.

The two men's eyes locked onto one another, each staring deep into the other's soul. Then, something truly amazing happened, as stunning as the sun rising every morning, as breath-taking taking as a Monet painting. Nick could see in Harvey that one elusive thing he'd been searching for all his life — that we all search for. He'd found *'The One'*. The detective didn't require his own well-honed sense of detection to deduce the barrister was experiencing the same.

Harvey threw himself forwards, wrapping his arms around Nick's neck and kissed him full on the mouth. And what a kiss! Duncan felt borderline over-whelmed at the intensity, but its addictive nature made sure he did not want it to ever end. He responded fully, clearly telling Harvey adored the smooch too. The brief changed stance, now holding Nick's face in his hands as he continued to lock lips with the policeman. It was the most passionate kiss the sergeant had ever had the good fortune to share. Just enough pressure applied to be seductive, yet not enough so it was tantalising. After what seemed like a blissful eternity the two men broke away, continuing to stare at the other breathlessly.

Duncan coughed twice, finding his voice.

"Wow! Where the hell did that come from?"

The solicitor's smile grew and grew as he gazed back at Nick, eyes huge in awe of what had just occurred. Opening his mouth to answer on the detective's question, Harvey was interrupted by something striking Nick around the back of the head at speed. The impact caused the policeman to fall forwards on top of the barrister, sending them both sprawling across the tiled floor.

The policeman rolled off the top of Harvey, rubbing the back of his head wincing in pain. The sergeant looked up to see where the blow had originated from, to be confronted with the sight of the first thug he had fought. Now recovered, the hooligan was holding the remnants of a broken toilet seat.

"I knew it! You're a fuckin' poofter too! You lot make me

sick!"

The thug swung his arm back to belt Duncan a second time. The detective instinctively held up an arm to deflect the impact away from his face and closed his eyes tight. Bracing himself, Nick prepared for the worst. A couple of moments later, a pronounced groan was heard throughout the room. Reopening one eye gingerly, the policeman witnessed the last thing he expected to see.

The thug dropped to his knees, before falling face first onto the floor next to Duncan. The toilet seat clattered onto the tiles, echoing noisily around the room. Now opening both eyes and sitting up, he was greeted with an even greater surprise. Something that sobered the sergeant up instantly, somebody he did not want to see in this situation. Standing over the crumpled heap of homophobic idiot, was no other than Detective Sergeant Sebastian St John. Nick's work colleague held the other half of the broken toilet seat, the look on his face seemed to debating whether he was going to need to use the improvised weapon again.

"Sebastian..."

Duncan addressed the other detective. St John placed the broken piece of Bakelite down, dusting his hands off.

"Yous twos get the fuck outta here!"

The Scotsman gestured towards the door, as he dragged the unconscious body of one of the Neanderthals back into the wrecked cubicle.

"Go on! Go!"

St John glared at the two men, snapping at them. Clambering to their feet as quickly as possible, Nick and Harvey darted out of the toilets, not stopping for the lift they ran down the stairs in the glass access tower and exited the club.

Darting along the precinct, Duncan led Harvey down a passage between the shops. Once clear of the main drag, the detective stopped to catch his breath. Glancing at Harvey, the barrister appeared to be not as fit as he seemed. But then, the mad dash over the last few minutes had led to them covering the best part of five to six hundred yards and down several flights of stairs.

"Are you OK?"

The brief stared back at him. Nick could see this was a rather rhetorical question. Harvey was shaken up, quite upset, and if Duncan didn't know better appeared as though he was on the verge of crying.

"Why are people like that, Nick?"

The policeman placed his hand on Harvey's neck and rubbed his thumb along his jaw-line.

"I used to get the same when I was younger. It's horrible."

"But no one would ever know you're gay! Look at you — the masculine, swashbuckling detective."

Duncan began to feel embarrassed at the comment. He never felt that way. Heaven knows how sub-consciously he exuded that sort of image.

"I guess I don't take any shit from anybody, about anything. I know what I am, and I'm far from ashamed of it. I have no issue with who I am, Society has. I'm an ordinary guy, just like my dad was, just like my brother is, just like you are."

The policeman's words struck a chord with Harvey. Nick knew such, as for the second time that evening Harvey kissed him. The solicitor started slowly, becoming more passionate, more sensual. Duncan responded, placing his hands on the brief's shoulders pulling him closer. Harvey murmured with delight.

"How do you do that?"

"Do what?"

"The way you kiss! I've never experienced anything like it! Ever!"

Harvey leaned forwards, took Nick's face in his hands once again, and kissed him once more. Pushed up against an advertising display case for a local sporting goods store, Duncan responded enthusiastically to the snog. He grabbed the brief on either side of his waist and pulled him closer. The kiss felt more amazing than earlier, as the two men could embrace properly. The sensation of the barrister pushing himself against him was exquisite. Harvey's touch was simply divine. The policeman held him in place, reluctant to let him go. He felt a wonderful tingle and intensity in his groin, as an erection began to grow and swell. However, this was denied reaching full potential as the 'clip-clop' of several women walking in heels echoed through the passage.

As the sound of people approaching grew closer, Nick and Harvey relinquished their hold on the other. Quickly, the sergeant reached into his inside pocket, retrieving his packet of Park Drive. Flicking the packet open, he speedily placed a cigarette into his own mouth and another into that of Harvey. The barrister recoiled, shocked. He didn't smoke. He took the tobacco from between his lips, somewhat disgusted. A few seconds later, a group of young women approached. Duncan began to rummage through his pockets, hoping to the casual observer it appeared he was searching for his lighter.

"Sorry Harvey. My lighter's in here somewhere. I swear I picked it up earlier…"

The young women passed by, all booze enhanced chat and giggly. A couple of them give Nick and Harvey a visual once over, one even winking at them. Duncan smiled back politely.

"What the hell did you do that for?"

"What?"

"Ram a disgusting cigarette into my mouth!"

"Well, it looks quite normal, two guys loitering in a dark passage on their own, trying to light their fags..."

Harvey gradually pulled a face that said that seemed fair and reasonable.

"Sadly, I think we're still some years away from people being comfortable with two blokes snogging each other's faces off." Nick winked at the brief, who returned with a saucy and cheeky smirk.

"Are you OK after those wankers kept hassling you?"

"Yeah, I'm fine. They were more physical than what I've encountered for some time."

Harvey smiled sheepishly at the policeman, taking his hand. *"Thank you for being my knight in shining armour."*

The solicitor gave him a peck on the cheek, and offered the detective the unlit cigarette back. *"No one has ever called me that before,"* Nick mentally glowed at the comment.

"Come back to mine."

Nick squeezed Harvey's hand, surprise spreading across the solicitor's face.

"Stay over? We haven't even had a date yet!"

The detective quickly corrected what he was implying, realising how forward his comment sounded.

"I meant, if you feel too upset to go home on your own."

"Er, I guess so."

They made their way through the passage, exiting onto a service yard behind the shops. Fortuitously, a black Austin cab had just arrived at the nearby rear entrance to the Hotel Leofric, dropping off a fare.

"Come on, quick!"

The two men sprinted to the taxi, climbing into the vehicle

before the driver had chance to argue. It was only once seated in the back, Nick suddenly remembered he didn't have the house to himself — Val and Rich were staying over.

"You'll be sleeping only on the sofa, I'm afraid."

Harvey gave the detective another glance that said that was obvious. Nick felt uneasy, once again considering he was coming across too eager to get him into bed. He peered out of the cab at the back of the hotel. Maybe he was behaving too hasty. He really liked Harvey, he didn't want to scare him away.

"I've got a better idea. The night's still young. Fancy a Brandy Alexander? I think Ray's Bar will still be open!"

The policeman shrugged an apology to the taxi driver, placing a fifty pence piece in his hand, and leapt out of the cab.

"Ray's Bar? I've never had the privilege. The regional legal practice's Christmas party was held in the ballroom last year."

"If Ray himself is on duty, we'll see if he'll put some Calvados into the cocktail, as to Metaxa!"

"Calvados? Are you trying to get me pissed, Sergeant?"

CHAPTER SEVEN
EASTER MONDAY
MONDAY APRIL 23rd 1973

Filling the kettle as silently as possible, Nick placed it upon the gas ring gently, and ignited the flame. The quiet of the kitchen was only marginally broken by the soft roar of the blue gas jet. He selected four mugs and dropped three teabags into a teapot. Leaning through the doorway and peering into the lounge, Duncan could make out in the stifled daylight a shape on the sofa. Underneath a blanket fast asleep lay Harvey. Nick watched the barrister as he was far away and dreaming. The policeman had achingly wanted to take him to bed last night, but it wasn't the right time. Circumstances within the Duncan des-res were against such a pleasurable excursion into something extremely naughty.

The detective became aware of someone in the doorway next to him. Glancing to his side, he found Val staring up at him, wearing a huge, over-size for her, men's dressing gown. Throwing her arms around him and giving her host a peck on the cheek, she stared at Harvey too. Val whispered into Nick's ear.

"You really are the total gent."

"Who? Me? How come?"

"You bring home someone who you obviously want to get into their pants, yet they spend the night on your sofa!"

Contrary to the self-confidence the sergeant normally exuded, he appeared rather awkward and shy.

"Well, it's kind of difficult to seize the moment when you've already asked friends to stay."

Val stroked the back of her friend's head tenderly.

"I can see how much you like him. I saw that last night in the club."

Duncan pulled a wry smile as he listened.

"I'm really impressed you didn't take advantage. Maybe snuggle up with down here..."

She pinched the policeman's bottom, catching him by surprise. Jumping slightly, he raised an eyebrow in her direction, akin to the new James Bond actor Roger Moore.

"A gentleman does not lower himself to such, Ma'am,"

"Oh, I'm sure you haven't behaved like a boy scout all of your life." Nick pulled a bemused face, and muttered under his breath.

"Plus, to give yourself to someone and be rebuffed is soul destroying."

"It's fine, Billy. You can stay at mine, tonight."

Duncan held up the warrant officer, taking his cap from his head before it fell to the ground. Tucking it under his arm, Nick hunted around in his trouser pockets with his spare hand for his keys. Finding them, he struggled unlocking the door while still supporting his inebriated friend.

"Dunks, I dunna wanna be any bother."

"It isn't any bother, silly."

The two men staggered their booze induced ballet into the small flat. Swaying like a ship on a heavy sea in a

242

storm, Duncan eventually made his way across the room and deposited Billy onto the sofa. As though practicing for a game of frisbee, he threw their caps onto the table.

"I think I've still got about half a bottle of grog in the kitchen."

One perk of being a Regulator, was being able to 'defer' the daily rum ration, Mid-day's Up Spirits. Duncan managed to persuade the bosun to bottle his, to be collected every couple of weeks. Nick had argued law enforcement required no distractions or working under the influence, so kept it for his downtime.

"Stand fast the Holy Ghost!"

The blonde-haired Geordie, Billy Lewis called out from his slumped and squiffy state, performing a cod salute. Tottering into the kitchen, Duncan found said bottle of rum in the final cupboard he searched. He repeated the same sequence trying to find two glasses. This proved even more arduous than finding the rum. Giving up, he removed his navy-blue mess jacket and draped it over the back of a chair, along with the cummerbund he was wearing.

It had been quite a Trafalgar Day, and being a Friday to boot — the start of the weekend — made it all the more special. Nick had been lucky this year — the rota had been kind to him giving him a shift that had ended mid-afternoon. He had been free to fully enjoy and join in with the celebrations, not having a repeat of previous years when he had to patrol around the base and nearby city — in fact most of Guz — seeking out those drunk and disorderly. It was much more fun being in the Petty Officer's Mess.

Tonight's celebrations at Guz though, were something

243

else. The Baron of Beef paraded by the young men in old-style naval uniform was a particular highlight. He was convinced one of the guys was giving him the eye, which tickled his ego. It seemed to be a night full of this. Nearly everywhere Nick glanced, another guy caught his attention. The guest of honour especially so — a Warrant Officer First Class attending his final function as a non-commissioned officer from the currently under refurbishment at Devonport, the aircraft carrier HMS Ark Royal. Nick was transfixed with the suave ginger-haired guy, as he led the toast.

Still, it was someone much closer to home was the main draw, one of his work colleagues — Billy. Well-travelled, with excellent taste, and as for that delicious North East accent... Billy had introduced him to a new drink that was fantastic. He tried to recall what the Geordie Master-At-Arms said it was. The more he tried to concentrate, the more the room span. Duncan grabbed the sink, steadying himself. Oh, yes! He remembered — Calvados. French apple or pear brandy or something. Perhaps mixing the spirit with the after-dinner port wasn't the best idea he'd ever had.

"Dunks! Where's that bevvie?"

Billy called from the living room, his thirst most likely starting to pique, Nick concluded. William Lewis' ability to drink like a fish was legendary around the base, and regularly used in competitive rivalry when ships visited. Leaning against the doorframe, Nick continued to sway. He offered the bottle of rum towards his guest like a waiter delivering an expensive bottle of claret to a diner. Now with his jacket taken off, wearing only a white shirt and bow tie, he fitted the bill perfectly.

"Nice one, Son."

Billy took the bottle from his host, removed the cork and greedily gulped away at its contents. Duncan flopped down on the sofa alongside his visitor, taking the bottle from the Geordie and took a hefty swig himself. Billy slumped against Nick, resting his head on his shoulder.

"Fancy going to the flicks tomorrow night? They're showing 'Sink The Bismarck!'. Have you seen it yet?"

Amongst the alcohol induced fog in his mind, with the man he found attractive snuggled up to his side, Duncan assumed this sounded like a date of sorts. He placed his arm around the blonde Master-At-Arms, pulling him closer.

"Er, no. I haven't Who's in it?"

Nick was so close to the Geordie, he could taste the distinctive fragrance of the Brylcream he used on his hair. This, combined with the Aqua Velva aftershave he wore and the rum vapours emanating from the open bottle, were quite hypnotic.

"I dunno, Bonnie Lad. I think some bloke who was ex-Navy."

"Humph! He didn't have to act too hard."

As he squeezed Billy yet closer, the Geordie inadvertently placed his hand on his host's knee. Duncan's arousal rocketed. Could his friend be interested in him? Billy leaned forward and reached for the bottle Nick was still holding. As he brushed past Duncan's face, Nick couldn't help himself. Filled with Dutch Courage, he lunged forwards, kissing Billy full on the lips. The blonde Warrant Officer recoiled immediately.

"What are you doing, Man?"

Duncan felt more embarrassed and awkward than ever before in his short life. Billy's reaction virtually sobering him up instantly.

"Er, just a kiss. I thought you might like one."

"Hey, I like you Dunks, but as a mate. Nothing more."

Nick wanted the ground to open up and swallow him whole. He felt completely devastated. He'd totally misjudged the situation and misread the signals he thought Billy was giving.

Thinking fast, he managed to somehow keep his composure. Perhaps he could play this misunderstanding down as merely a prank.

"I know that, Stupid! I was thinking for Pickle Night we could do something gormless, while in old-style uniform." Billy lifted the bottle of rum, taking a huge belt of the booze. He peered at Duncan, smiling broadly.

"I like your thinking, Warrant Officer Duncan. Imagine the Mess Secretary's face if we started holding hands and snog during the evening."

He laughed heartily, taking another swig of the rum. Nick smiled nervously, relieved a scene had been averted, but intrigued with Mr Lewis' idea.

A kettle began to whistle in the kitchen, increasing in intensity as the water came to a boil. Both young men stared into the kitchen. Duncan was the more confused and puzzled of the two, as he didn't remember placing the kettle on the stove. He staggered in there to investigate.

The sergeant dashed back into the kitchen, grabbed the screaming kettle and removed it from the gas.

"Are you OK, Nick? You don't seem yourself."

246

The detective seemed subdued, a little on edge too. He poured the steaming hot water into the teapot, and stirred the liquid watching it gradually become darker and darker.

"I got into a fight last night, defending Harvey. Two blokes were picking on him in the toilets, getting a bit too tasty with their fists. I fought them off."

"You did what?"

Nick glanced up at his friend and raised his eyebrows. It was only now he noticed the condition of his knuckles on his right hand — split and swollen. Val stepped forward, taking the policeman's injured hand. She caressed it tenderly.

"I'd hate to see how the other guy ended up!"

Duncan gave her a sheepish grin. Val shook her head in disbelief.

"I'd have expected you to be too old to enter into a bout of fisticuffs, Constable. Have you got any sticking plaster? You can't go to work like this."

"In the bathroom cabinet, I think."

She quickly nipped upstairs, returning to the kitchen as Nick finished pouring the tea. Taking his damaged dab, Val gently applied the flesh-coloured plaster.

"That's the least of my worries at the moment."

Val looked at Nick, confused.

"My work colleague, Sergeant Sebastian St John saved me. If he hadn't, I'd have taken one hell of a beating."

She gazed at her friend, hanging on his every word.

"There's a possibility he saw Harvey and me kissing in the toilets, after I fought off the thugs. One then went to attack me, but Sebastian stopped him."

Val pulled a rueful face, appearing to be thinking.

"Does this Sebastian know about your private life?"

"No. Nobody knows at work. I think my partner has inklings, but she hasn't said."

"Hmmm, I guess it has to be that way."

"Too bloody right! Imagine the palaver over a gay copper!" She stared at her feet and slowly shook her head.

"It shouldn't be this way. How does it affect your ability to be a policeman because of the gender of the person you share your bed with?"

"Exactly!"

Nick thumped the table with a clenched fist, his passion all too evident. The mugs of tea leapt a few inches into the air, along with Val.

All of a sudden, the two friends heard someone behind them yawn. Spinning around, they were met with the sight of the sleepy solicitor, Harvey. Wrapped in a blanket, he rubbed his eyes, squinting in the bright daylight.

"Are one of those mine?"

The brief pointed at the mugs of tea.

"Of course!"

Nick picked one of the drinks up, and offered it to his drowsy guest.

"Val, this is my friend and sometime nemesis in court, Harvey Wiseman."

Harvey pulled a face at the detective, as he reached out with his right hand, offering it to the lady.

"Harvey, this is my old childhood friend, Valerie Myers."
Nick's friends shook hands, smiling at one another. The policeman swiftly chugged down his own tea in two huge gulps.

"I've got to go. Duty calls. Can I ask a cheeky favour, Val?"

The woman eyed the sergeant suspiciously.

"What do you want this time, Constable?"

"If it's not too much trouble, can Rich and yourself give Harvey a lift home. I know it's rather cheeky, but if you could." Val rolled her eyes, while Harvey glanced at their host somewhat awkwardly.

"Yeah, we'll help. If that's what you'd like Harvey?"

"Oh, yes — thank you. I don't live that far away, only in Finham."

Nick embraced Val, whispering in her ear.

"Thank you. I'll keep you on my Christmas card list."

"Humph! I sodding well hope so!"

Releasing his friend, Duncan then gave the barrister a huge hug. Harvey squeezed the policeman tightly.

"Thanks again for being my hero last night."

Nick beamed a massive grin.

"I'll keep my cape in my car boot for next time."

Harvey squeezed him harder, and gave Duncan a peck on the cheek.

"I hate seeing people being picked on. Part of being a copper, I guess."

The two men released, allowing the detective to put his coat on. He kissed Val briefly, before reaching for Harvey and tenderly touching his face.

"We'll arrange something later in the week, eh?"

"Abso-bloody-lutely!"

The two men kissed, after which the policeman headed for the door. Looking back over his shoulder, he grinned and saluted his friends.

Duncan was actually putting a brave face on the entire situation, and didn't want to show his friends how worried he really was. It bothered him deeply St John had appeared last night. Nick had mixed emotions about his work colleague rescuing Harvey and himself. Obviously, he was pleased Sebastian had intervened, but extremely nervous over what he had seen. As he drove into the city centre along the deserted streets due to the public holiday, a sense of dread and the unexpected grew within him. If St John had seen Harvey and himself kissing, the Scotsman would have all the ammunition he needed to force him out of the Constabulary completely.

The Detective contemplated how intolerable life could become. He cursed his luck, knowing this could well be the end of his career. He'd found the man of his dreams, but potentially was about to lose his dream career. Dwelling on this was making the sergeant feel physically sick. He switched on the radio in an attempt to calm his nerves and take his mind off the situation.

As the radio clicked into life, the interior of the car was greeted by the back end of the news.

"It is estimated over, one hundred and fifty thousand people attended mass yesterday in St Peter's Square in the Vatican. Pope Paul VI gave the gathering, and the wider world, the Roman Catholic Church's Easter blessing.

Warwickshire Police have announced they will be holding a press conference later today as regards the recent unexplained deaths of three women in Coventry. The briefing will be led by Superintendent Frederick Franklin and Detective Chief Inspector Thomas Spencer.

In sport—" Nick turned the radio off. Football again! He sighed in disinterest. However, the news Police were holding a press conference meant how serious the situation was. Any murder is unacceptable, but to have three so rapidly was totally unheard of. Maybe this will assist with enquiries, but most likely result in a grilling by sections of the media over why the police hadn't done enough to protect these women, and why haven't they apprehended a suspect as yet. He didn't fancy being in the senior officer's position, as the whole matter was evolving so fast it was going to take a huge effort to get on top of.

As he parked at the station, the horrid feeling of foreboding returned as he gazed at the building. Nick wondered who St John might have already told. He knew he had to go inside, enter the office, but really did not want to. For the first time in as long as he could recall, he was afraid. Maybe a cigarette would help calm his nerves. Retrieving the packet from his inside pocket, he selected one of the Park Drive just as the lighter in the dashboard of the car popped out at reaching temperature. At least one thing worked correctly on his brother's car! He took several long draws on the tobacco, trying his utmost not to think of the worst.

There was a distinct possibility Sebastian only saw the hooligan about to attack him and nothing more, but Duncan's paranoia was getting the better of him. He began to panic. Nick felt his cantankerous colleague had seen everything. How matters stood between them, combined with his state of mental anxiety, the detective was convinced the Scotsman would do everything he could to tarnish his solid reputation. He was gravely concerned no one would see what a good, honest and fair policeman he was, only focusing on his private life.

Upon entering the office, Nick tried to appear as normal and nonchalant as possible. He was really having a terrible day — he now felt he was over-compensating trying to behave 'normal', which would in fact make him seem highly 'abnormal'. This was confirmed as he removed his coat and sat behind his desk.

"Are you all right? You look like you've got all the worries of the world on your shoulders."

The sergeant glanced up to see Cavanagh staring back at him, most concerned.

"I'm fine, Joan. Really."

Nick busied himself tidying his desk top, beginning to rummage through the drawers attached. He glanced up at the photograph of his father, mentally asking Dad for advice in how to steer through this situation. Duncan could tell his Scouse colleague was watching him, as he did nothing in particular with the stationary on the desk, but just move it about until he placed it back in the exact same place where he'd found it.

The detective's mind continually returned to the night before. During all his life, Nick had never been 'outted' as regards his sexuality, nor had he ever felt the need to 'come out' either. Heterosexual people never made a huge grand statement over they sleep with the opposite gender, so why should he have to 'declare' his preference? His private life was his own, it was as normal as the next person.

Making a cup of tea, he sipped at the pale brown liquid a few times as he made his way back to his desk. As he took his seat, Duncan became aware of someone approach, and perch themselves on the edge of the table. A hand gently rested on his shoulder. The fragrance of Charlie perfume filled his senses — he knew who instantly who it was.

"What's the matter, Nick? Yer acting proper west."

"Really, I'm O.K."

The constable leaned closer to Duncan. So close in fact,

to the casual observer she appeared to be thrusting her breasts bursting out of her fitted white blouse into the sergeant's face. Whispering, but trying not to raise her voice, the Liverpudlian continued.

"Nicholas Duncan, tell me what's wrong. I've worked with you now for close on two years, so I know when something is bothering you. It's all over yer grid."

The policeman sighed, placing his elbow on the desk top and resting his head in his hand.

"It's quite awkward."

"You can tell me anything, you know."

Nick still remained silent, but seemed as though he was trying to muster enough courage to explain.

"Is it yer Ma? Is she all right?"

"No, no. Mum's fine."

"What is it, then?"

Duncan swallowed hard, apprehension and worry written all too clearly on his face.

"I met someone last night in a club, and got into a fight defending them."

Cavanagh smirked, gripping Nick's shoulder.

"Is that all? You met a girl and got into a scrap? That must happen in every club in every town across the land!"

Nick sighed again, running his fingers through his hair.

"I met a man last night in a club, got into a fight defending him in the toilets, but one went to attack me when I was kissing him. St John stopped him, knocking him to the ground and saved me."

The sergeant glanced up at the constable, expecting to see her shocked and aghast. Instead, the Merseysider gave him an understanding and warm smile. She touched his face tenderly.

"I had a hunch you liked men rather than girls."

Duncan smiled back, placing his hand on top of hers. The scouser leaned forwards, placing her other hand on the other side of his face, kissing him on the forehead.

"Fuck me! I knew yous two were as thick as thieves, but didnae think yous were da close!"

Nick and Joan released one another, to find Sebastian removing his coat and taking his place behind his desk. Immediately, Duncan began tidying his own desk all over again. He deliberately avoided eye contact with the Scotsman, in fact ignored him completely. This wasn't lost upon St John, either.

"Wassa up with yous, Golden Bollocks? Cat got yer tongue?"

"Er, no. Just really busy. Like you should be, Scotland."

St John sneered at his colleague and turned his own attention to the paperwork laid out in front of him. *"Any moment now,"* Nick anticipated. *"Any moment he's going to say something."* He used his peripheral vision to watch Sebastian. *"He's just biding his time, waiting for the most embarrassing moment for his big reveal."* Duncan continued to over-think and dwell on his worst fear. He felt an overwhelming sense of nausea rising inside. Glancing up, he instantly made eye-contact with Cavanagh. As she gazed back at him, he saw the constable appeared equally as concerned as himself.

"Morning Each! Thank you for getting here prompt."

Spencer and Edwards breezed into the room, their faces more resembling a stock-broker who had lost millions.

"Inspector Edwards and myself have had a meeting with Superintendent Franklin this morning. Due to the gravity of

the situation, we will be joined by temporary staff from Birmingham and Leamington."

Some groaning went up from the back of the room, causing Spencer to stop his announcement and Edwards to interrupt.

"Oi! Oi! Get a bleedin' grip the lot of you!"

The chief Inspector began again. *"We're not insinuating you're not working hard enough, out of your depth or hit a brick wall. I know you're all doing your best, but more bodies on the ground will help you concentrate on the investigation, finding out the important details. You are still the prime detectives on the case."*

This appeared to plicate the disquiet, as the office calmed down.

"As some of you have no doubt already heard, there's a press conference later where the Super, Inspector Spencer and myself will speak with the media about where we're at. It goes without saying, if any of yourselves are approached by a journalist or reporter, please be polite and refer them to the DCI or myself."

"That would be the prime opportunity for Sebastian to tell the world about me," Duncan contemplated, taking nervous glances at the Scotsman.

"Sergeant Duncan…"

Spencer addressed the detective directly. Nick's heart sank so deep, he never realised it could drop to such a depth. Accompanying the near nausea, he was fighting, he was a whisker away from soiling himself as well.

"Yeah-Yeh-Yes, Sir."

Duncan was certain he was about to be summoned to the chief Inspector's office. Here it comes…

"Can you explain your hypothesis to the room about the three deceased women, please?"

To say Nick was flabbergasted, was a total understatement. He was speechless.

"Sergeant ...?"

The DCI prompted him again, all eyes in the room now on him. The detective coughed, appearing to clear his throat, but was actually stalling for time as he attempted to regain his composure.

"Er, yes. Ahem! Thank you, Sir. There are some similarities between the three murdered women, despite them being of differing ethnic backgrounds. Firstly, they're all around the same age. Secondly, they're all dark-haired with their hair styled near identically. Thirdly, they are all approximately the same height and build. Finally, they're all smokers."

Nick saw several of the other detectives in the room, including Cavanagh and St John nodding in agreement while scribbling down some notes as he spoke.

"So, it's fair to say the killer has a certain 'type' they go for."

Edwards stepped forward, holding a report at head-height.

"I've had chance to read thoroughly the post mortem report from Dr Tyler on Miss Wheng."

The inspector slapped the paperwork down onto the desk in front of him.

"The Doctor speculates she had been where she had been found for a few days, so it would appear Zhen was killed before Arosha Rana. Dr Tyler estimates most likely the night of Saturday April 14th or early hours Sunday 15th."

St John placed his hand in the air, to which the inspector

nodded he could speak. Nick's insides began to churn over and over once again. He wanted to throw up, he wanted to run away, he wanted to be anywhere but here right now. He couldn't take much more of this.

"Guv, wa dis Chinese lassie killed same way as da others?"

Duncan was so relieved. He wanted to melt onto the floor in a huge moist heap. Glancing upwards from a copy of the post mortem report he'd just been given, Nick made eye contact with Joan. It was extremely obvious she was worried about her colleague, as she sympathetically gazed at him.

A pronounced series of knocks echoed through the CID office, causing all gathered to stare in the direction of the interruption. Standing in the doorway was Rachel, rather timidly but determined to say something.

"Er, Sir..."

Spencer smiled at the WPC.

"Ahhh, Miss Ryce. How can we be of assistance?"

"Sir, there's a man here you asked to help with the investigation."

The DCI pulled a puzzled face, which quickly changed to one of realisation.

"Our translator, per chance?"

"Yes, Sir. A Skipper from Steelhouse Lane, Birmingham."
"Show him into Inspector Edwards' office, please, Rachel."

Edwards turned to his staff. *"Right, the DCI and myself will see what our translator can find out. The rest of you, scour the paperwork and statements we have — look out for anything out of the ordinary."*

This was the laborious, boring part of police work all coppers — Duncan included — found tedious. Checking and double-checking the leads they had just in case something had been missed or overlooked.

After what felt like an eternity had past, Rachel then reappeared escorting an academic of Chinese accent into Edwards' office. The detective team glanced at one another puzzled, as they saw the uniform sergeant swopping pieces of paper with the senior detectives and the newcomer. He watched out of the corner of his eye the four men in the inspector's office, as they took an age debating the contents of Zhen's handwriting.

"RACHEL!"

The inspector shouted loudly to gain the Liaison Officer's attention. So intensely, everyone in the office jumped in surprise. A fraction later, she sprinted across the office to the Guv'nor hanging out of his own office door.

"Yes, Sir…"

"Can you take our guests down to the canteen and find them a cup of barely bloody drinkable, please."

"Of course. If you'd like to follow me…"

The two translators followed the WPC, disappearing from view. Edwards attempted to sit down in his own chair, but leapt up as though he'd sat on something sharp. He dashed to the door, yet again leaning out into the main office.

"Rachel! Don't forget we need Doctor Li and Sergeant Peck to visit Zhen's student digs, translate her notes there."

The inspector turned his attention to his assembled detective team.

"Sebastian, Dermot — we have an address and a name. Go say hello, if you please."

"Guv."

St John and Ward seemed more than relieved to be getting

out of the office, exiting quickly.

"Right Peters and Lee, we've got that press conference shortly. But before I convince the media all is fine and dandy here, have we had any other developments?"

Duncan and Cavanagh assisted in collecting together Zhen's personal notes, returning them to the Incident Desk. The three detectives looked for anything new they hadn't seen before. *"There was one thing I noticed, Guv."*

Nick began to leaf through the Chinese student's pocket size appointment book, eventually stopping at a page in late March.

"Yeah, wasn't it the same day as the auditions for that musical?"

Cavanagh found the press cutting which Duncan had retrieved from her room.

"That's right!"

The sergeant found Arosha's diary. Flipping through to the same date, the three police officers saw a huge asterix marked on the page.

"And Arosha's name is on the audition list as well — here!" The Merseysider pointed to her name on the sheet. Edwards nodded.

"You two will need to go visit the theatre again. This time, ask that casting director questions specifically about the two women. See what they know."

"Yes, Guv."

"Have we any further leads on the vehicle seen leaving Coombe Abbey?"

The inspector shuffled paperwork, casually looking through other information, Duncan surmised, *"He's just waiting for something unusual to leap out at him — I'd do the same."*

"We definitely think it was an estate car, Guv. Not a van."

"How so?"

"The night watchman said he heard an ambulance siren on the Brinklow Road just after the vehicle departed. We've gotten in touch with the Ambulance Station, and managed to speak with the crew on duty that night. They say they did pass an estate car near the Abbey as they were on the way to a 'shout'. That was the only vehicle they saw that night."

"OK, crack on with which estate cars fit the description."

"Guv."

Edwards began to adjust his tie, checking his hair in the refection of a glass partition, smoothing it so his side-parting was even more pronounced than before.

"Right then boys and girls — showtime!"

The camera flash-bulbs popped at the most inopportune moment, causing the two senior police officer's eyes to water. Nick stood at the back of the conference room, not envying his colleagues in front of the assembled scrum of reporters.

"There's more here than I was expecting."

Cavanagh whispered under her breath, but was heard loud and clear by the two Detective Sergeants either side. Rachel peeped at the constable from around St John.

"This is my first time."

The three detectives only just managed to hold in their mirth as they heard the WPC.

"Yous never forget yer fust, Lassie."

Sebastian did little to make the situation regain its seriousness. Duncan tittered to himself, *"That's the funniest thing I've ever heard the Jock say."*

On his way to the podium, Edwards negotiated his way through the crowd. Performing a double-take, he changed direction and headed towards the ensemble of his staff. Nick saw the inspector point in his direction, making a bee-line for him. Duncan smiled pensively, his mind working over-time as to what the Guv'nor wanted to speak to him about. *"St John has told him something about last night,"* he believed. *"I just know it! Now I'm going to get my arse kicked by of all people my dad's best mate!"*

Albert approached the sergeant, placing his hand on his shoulder and gave it a friendly squeeze. Nick tried to appear *'casual'*, feeling anything but. He couldn't believe his life had come to this, being chopped down from the occupation he loved and lived for.

"Ahhh! My favourite people, and more specifically my favourite Scotsman!"

"Guv?"

"Any joy at that address in Coundon?"

"Nah! Nay answer. We tried several times, even asked da neighbours. No sign o' him all weekend, they said."

The inspector rubbed his chin in contemplation.

"Hmmm. Well, it is the Easter Bank Holiday weekend. Maybe he's gone away. Try again tomorrow morning first thing. Hopefully you'll catch him before he goes to work."

"Aye, Guv."

The in-built public address system thudded repeatedly several times, drawing everyone's attention to the front of the room. The group of detectives looked towards the front, where DCI Spencer was sitting next to the Superintendent. Spencer managed to catch Edwards' attention, gesturing to him to join them on the podium.

"*Must dash.*"

The inspector fought his way through the mass of bodies, taking his place next to the Super.

"*Ladies and Gentlemen, welcome to Little Park Street. Firstly, I'd like to introduce the panel here today. On my right is Detective Chief Inspector Thomas Spencer, on my left Detective Inspector Albert Edwards. Both are War veterans, having seen active service and are long-time respected members of the CID team here. My name is Superintendent Frederick Franklin.*"

The senior police officer took a hefty swig from a glass of water in front of him.

"*As you're all no doubt aware, over the last week three young women have been found deceased in highly unusual circumstances. The Constabulary has identified who these ladies are, and had the solemn and distasteful duty of notifying their families of the dreadful news. As the investigation is still on going at this time, we will not be releasing the identities of those who have perished, plus would ask the media to respect the privacy of all those involved and allow the detectives the time and space to find the perpetrator of these terrible crimes. I'll hand over to Chief Inspector Spencer, who can give more details of the case.*"

The DCI coughed a couple of times to clear his throat, and began. "*Thank you, Superintendent. I can confirm we currently have our squad of detectives looking into several strong lines of enquiry, which we feel will very soon lead us to the person responsible, and they will be brought to justice. Additionally, if any member of the public has information that may assist us with our enquiries, do not hesitate to come forward. All information is treated in the strictest confidence,*" taken most seriously. As the Superintendent has already said, the investigation is still 'live' and 'fluid', so many aspects we are not at liberty to discuss openly at this present time. However, we are open to answer any questions we can from yourselves."

Duncan leaned towards Cavanagh and whispered into her ear. "Which means they can effectively answer bugger all."

The scouser covered her mouth as she giggled.

"Some of the reporters will think we're having this briefing as a last resort, we're devoid of ideas of lines of enquiry."

Joan nodded as the sergeant softly spoke. Nick felt cold to the centre of his being, as a horrible scenario flashed through his mind. What if St John had tipped off one of the reporters with the tale of last night? It was entirely possible, not beyond the realms of probability. The sergeant shook his head in an exaggerated manner, trying to snap himself out of it. He was just being paranoid.

Superintendent Franklin took charge of the Q&A session, as the mass of journalists raised their hands. "Right, er, the auburn-haired lady front row."

"Thank you, Superintendent. Janet Larkin, Warwickshire Daily Post. Can you reassure young women across Coventry it's safe to enjoy a normal life, and not effectively quarantine themselves to their own homes?"

Edwards responded to this query. "I can whole-heartedly confirm, Miss Larkin, that the streets of Coventry are just as safe as they normally are. The general public should always exercise caution at all times, not only during times like these. There is no reason to panic, amend your lifestyle, or stop behaving and travelling in ways you usually do."

"Thank you, Inspector Edwards. Next a question from..." The reporters began to jostle and mutter as they raised their hands again.

"Er, the fellow in the third row, brown suit and black-framed spectacles."

"Thanks! Derek White, Coventry Evening Chronicle. Can you confirm these women who have been murdered are from ethnic minorities of the community?"

Nick exchanged anxious glances with his three colleagues. Everyone's face asked the same question — how the hell did the Press get hold of that fact? The chief Inspector spoke up.

"Mr White, as the Superintendent and myself have already clearly stated, we cannot reveal the identities of any of the women who have died. It potentially could jeopardise lines of enquiry we are currently exploring."

"Any further questions?"

More hands shot into the air.

"Erm, lady in front row wearing a paisley-patterned blouse."

"Thank you, Superintendent. Lucy Ferguson, BBC Radio Birmingham. Can you reveal how close the police are to arresting someone over these terrible crimes?"

The inspector removed his spectacles, and polished them briefly on his handkerchief, before returning them to his face.

"We have a couple of firm lines of enquiry, which we feel will prove successful."

"No, we haven't," Duncan thought to himself. *"We have no name yet, no motive, nothing, more's the pity."* Franklin pointed at another person in the crowd.

"You, Sir. Fellow in the burgundy jacket."

"Much obliged. Bryan Barrett, The National. With Coventry Police's resources being stretched to cover a triple murder enquiry, is the CID Department being as thorough as it could be?"

"Ouch!" Nick winced. *"There's no need for that!"* The comment also struck a nerve with Edwards.

"I can assure your colleagues and yourself, Mr Barrett, we have extra staff working with us from other locations across the county. No, nothing will be missed, ignored or taken for granted! I was pounding the beat around this City solving crime with the finest police officer I have had the pleasure to have served with, when all you were was a snotty nosed kid cacking your pants!"

Duncan was impressed with how the Guv'nor was defending the CID office, but he swelled with pride at the mention of his father. He knew the inspector came across as gruff and didn't suffer fools gladly, but he cared immensely about his work and detectives. Franklin stepped in, as the response from the inspector was somewhat heated.

"Thank you, Ladies and Gentlemen. That concludes today's press briefing. You can all collect handouts containing what we can inform you so far. Please do not hesitate to contact the press liaison if you have any further questions."

The three senior officers stood, beginning to leave the podium under a verbal bombardment from some of the media present. Duncan turned to Cavanagh, finding her doing her best to smother her laughter. This only tickled his own sense of humour further. Nick saw the scouser glance in St John's direction, finding the Scotsman behaving the same way.

"Snotty nosed kid cacking your pants!"

Nick barely repeated the Guv'nor's final remark, when he started tittering out loud. Hearing what he said, Sebastian began to chuckle along too.

"Dassa gonna sound grand on da Evening News!"

St John's comment did nothing to dispel the situation, as Joan and Rachel now began to giggle.

Back upstairs in the CID office, the four police officers had managed to supress their mirth. Edwards comments had been much required relief by Duncan, who now seemed a new man. The outburst by the inspector having cheered him up no end. Even seeing St John join in on the joke helped. As Nick sat at his desk, Edwards burst into the office. The Guv'nor's face was flushed, baring much exasperation. The senior detective paused, gazing at his team. Nick froze, staring back at the inspector, unsure of what to say or do. Remarkably, he could see in the corner of his eye, all the others were doing the same. A moment's silence passed, which felt more like a lifetime. Duncan broke the quiet, with a spluttery, stifled snigger.

"Oh, Piss Off— the lot of you!"

The inspector strode into his own office, slamming the door behind him.

As laughter echoed around the room, Nick picked up the phone and dialled Harvey's home number. The line clicked, fizzed, then connected. The dialling tone purred back at him repeatedly, but no answer. The sergeant picked up his pen, tapping it on the desk as he waited for Harvey to answer. The dialling tone continued its irritating, emotionless drone. Nick gave the continued ringing another minute, whereby he hung up. He pondered where he could be. Perhaps with his family? Perhaps involved in an emergency legal case? Possibly just out on a drive during the Bank Holiday. Duncan, still not entirely free of his paranoid clouded mood, began to contemplate his beau might be avoiding him. Maybe he'd over-done matters last night, kissing him in the passageway, those cocktails afterwards...

"Penny for your thoughts."

The Detective glanced up as he heard the familiar female melodic Merseyside tones greet his ears.

"Nothing important."

Duncan stared at the phone. Should he try Harvey again? He partially reached out for the receiver, but stopped thinking better of it.

"Nick, I don't think anyone will be at the theatre today, what with it being a Bank Holiday. Best we visit there tomorrow."

The Sergeant nodded in agreement.

"We best get over to the Swanswell, ask some questions."

"Er, that's a non-starter as well."

A puzzled look spread across Duncan's face. Cavanagh sighed, and continued.

"I've just found out they've been closed all of the Easter break. They've had their licence suspended for the holiday period, due to someone dealing pills there."

Nick shrugged his shoulders, spun around in his chair and grabbed his coat.

"Fancy that drink you've been twisting my arm about for an age?"

The Liverpudlian looked up from the shambles of paperwork littered across her desk, a smile spreading across her face rapidly.

"Yeah! Why not?"

The two friends left, Nick mentally in a much better place than when he'd arrived that morning. The sergeant turned to the constable, giving her a huge cheesy grin.

"You're paying though."

267

CHAPTER EIGHT
TUESDAY APRIL 24th 1973

"Mike One, Mike Zulu Two receiving, over."

Duncan rescued his portable radio from his young niece, hoping he could get away with his niece Katherine's broadcasted chatter as *'interference'* of the technological kind, as to *'mischievous child'* playing with something she shouldn't.

"Mike Zulu Two, could you report to Little Park Street immediately. Mike Victor One requires all staff on site, due to the circumstances. Over."

"Understood Mike One, Mike Zulu Two Out."

Nick instantly had a flash of paranoia. Was Spencer summoning him to the office to receive a dressing down over Sunday night? He wasn't due to start his shift till lunchtime, but it was quite common to be called in early when cases required extra attention. He did his best to push the prospect out of his mind. An idea struck him straight away, he wondered if Joan had been requested to come into the office early?

"Mum, can I use the phone, please? I need to make a quick call."

"Have you got to go, Love?"

The policeman turned around to find his mother looking concerned, having heard all that was broadcast through the pocket radio.

"Sorry, Mum. May I use the phone?"

Georgy nodded, to which her son stepped towards the small table where it was kept. He dialled Cavanagh's number. After several short purrs of the dialling tone, a female voice with a pronounced Ulster accent spoke.

"Hello..."

"Er, Hi Niamh. Is Joan there?"

"Yeah, she's around I'll just get her. Who's calling?"

"It's Nick from work."

"Ah, Hello Sarge. Didn't recognise your voice. I'll just get her."

"Thanks."

Duncan heard the muffled sound of someone shuffling away, some indecipherable speech in the background, followed by someone approaching the phone. An all too familiar Scouse voice spoke.

"Hello Sarge. Is everything all right?"

"Yes, fine. I was going to be a gracious gentleman, and offer you a lift to work. I'm only up the road at my Mum's at the moment. That is if you want to go into the office in the next ten minutes..."

"Oh, yeah! Thank you. Rachel phoned about half an hour ago, asking me to come in earlier than normal."

That was all Nick wanted to hear. He was just being paranoid after all. The sigh of relief he omitted was immense.

"Is everything OK, Nick?"

"Er, yeah. I'll be five minutes. See you in a bit."

"OK. See you shortly."

As the sergeant put the phone down, he was rugby-tackled around the knees by Katherine.

"Don't go, Uncle Nick! Tell us a story."

Katherine bounced up and down, reaching upwards to her uncle to be picked up. The detective lifted his niece up into his arms, only to find a split-second later Charlotte race out of the lounge and begin to demand same as her sister.

"Yeah! Tell us a story, Uncle Nick! Please!"

"Leave Uncle Nick alone, you two. He has to go to work."

Their grandmother attempted to assist, hopefully giving her son chance to escape their attention.

"Are you going to see your girlfriend? That lady who talks funny?"

Katherine began to interrogate her uncle, in the way only a child can. The queries still made Duncan feel uncomfortable.

"The lady who talks funny is my work friend. She's not my girlfriend, Katherine. I haven't got one."

"About time you did, if you ask me Nicholas."

The policeman rolled his eyes. When she made statements like that, he felt it would be years before he could fully open up and tell her the one thing he wanted.

"What time did Alex say he'd be back?"

Duncan tried to change the subject, plus was beginning to become impatient with his brother. He wanted his own car back. The dreadful experiences he'd been having with the Vanguard made him realise how blessed he was owning the Alvis.

"He said he'd be here by now, sweetheart. Maybe they've stopped at a pub for a bit of lunch on the way back..."

"Typical!"

"Uncle Nick! Tell us a story about Stirling! Tell us about his friends!"

Charlotte jumped up and down on the spot, pulling at Nick's trousers. Georgy picked her grand-daughter up, once again trying to ease the situation.

"How about I tell you a tale about Grandad? Tell you about the horses he worked with at the dairy."

"Yeah! Please! Story about a horse!"

"Mum, I've got to go." Nick lowered Katherine gently to the ground, giving her a peck on the cheek. *"Can you let Alex know I'll pop round his later? We can swop cars back then."*

Georgy nodded.

"Take care, Love. See you soon."

He leaned forwards, placing his arm around his mother and gave her a kiss.

"Bye, Uncle Nick!" Charlotte threw her little arms around the policeman's neck, squeezing him as tight as her small body would allow.

"See you soon, Shorty."

He also gave her a peck on the cheek, before heading towards his brother's car to have another fight with the contraption.

Fortunately for the Sergeant, he didn't have too far to drive. Cavanagh's shared home was only a few minutes away. Parking behind the policewoman's own vehicle, Duncan tooted the horn twice. Moments later, the Merseysider emerged from a nearby house attired in her usual smart and tidy style, with minimal make up applied, her hair drawn back in a pony tail. She approached the driver's door, gesturing for the sergeant to open the window.

"Shall I drive?"

"Please." As they joined the Ring Road, Nick noticed Joan appeared quieter and more subdued than normal

"Has the cat got your tongue?"

271

"Eh?"

"You're not as chatty as normal. I thought you'd be buzzing as Liverpool won the League yesterday."

"Oh, I suppose."

"Is everything OK? You know, I'm here for you, just as you're there for me."

Duncan placed his hand softly upon her shoulder. She sighed heavily.

"It's nothing I can't handle, but thanks anyway."

"Are you sure? If there's anything I can do to help, even if it's just lend a sympathetic ear."

Cavanagh once again went silent, concentrating on the traffic she was negotiating.

"It's Dermot."

Joan spoke in a manner that made Nick believe she could barely summon the enthusiasm to utter his name.

"Dermot? What has he done?"

"Nothing yet. He's just full of hot air."

"From what I've seen, I could've sworn Mr Ward was interested in Rachel!"

"Yeah, I've seen that too. But it's what he says to me when you're not around."

Nick recalled the other night at Coombe Abbey, when Dermot was breaking his neck to ogle Joan as she got changed.

"Are you interested in him?"

The constable huffed.

"He's a fine-looking guy, got the gift of the gab, but hardly makes a girl feel exclusive like."

Nick considered himself to be exclusive. He was certain he was. He couldn't believe what his eyes were showing him.

He stepped back behind the building he had just passed. The warrant officer removed his cap, and ran his other hand through his hair. How could Tony do it? How could he? After all he'd said and what they'd shared together.

Gingerly, Duncan peeped around the edge of the wall, to confirm what he had first seen. Yes, he hadn't imagined it. Tony Devereux, the man Nick had fallen for, couldn't get enough of, shared his bed with, contemplated he had a future with, was currently sitting in the passenger seat of a pre-War Humber Super Snipe staff car. That itself wasn't a problem and was quite ordinary. Duncan's issue was he was entwined with the driver, their arms wrapped around the other, hands wandering all over the other's body having a seriously good feel and grope. A full game of backseat bingo was about to commence.

It hurt Nick to the core. He felt betrayed and insulted to such a depth, he never would have believed it was possible to feel this devastated without experiencing it. But one thing above all else was cutting him to the centre of his being and beyond, more than anything else, more than anything he'd seen or experienced in his entire lifetime — Tony was currently snogging the face off 'Wren' Andrea Swan.

The warrant officer stepped back behind the wall again, taking several deep breaths. He wanted to curl up in a dark corner and cry his eyes out. At the same time, he wanted to run over to the car, pull Tony out, and punch him in the face repeatedly. Nick didn't want to look at the two of them again, but just could not help himself. For a man who was exceedingly adept in the bedroom as a homosexual, he was quite clearly also equally as

273

interested in the fairer sex. Devereux had undone Miss Swan's blouse and had thrust his hand inside as they smooched.

The warrant officer returned to his hiding place, heart pounding to such an extent he could hear his own pulse, nausea rising into the back of his mouth. *"I bet he's whispering all the things she wants to hear, just as he did with me."* Duncan began to crucify himself mentally. He felt such a fool, not just because he knew he'd been used, but taken for granted and exploited as well. He now knew Tony had gotten him into bed just for a shag. Wiping away tears, anger grew and grew within him. Not aimed at Lieutenant Devereux, at himself. He began to clench his hands into fists so tightly, it was a few moments before he realised he was beginning to crush his cap. *"What a complete twat I've been! How could I let myself get so sucked in?"* Nick continued to scold himself, until he heard a woman giggle.

Peering around the wall, he saw it was Andrea. *"Tony really has you wrapped around his little finger,"* the Master-At-Arms told himself. *"You're just another notch on the bedpost to that prick."* Devereux had removed his hand from the young woman's blouse, placing it lower down. Although Nick could not see exactly where, Andrea leapt and twitched occasionally, continuing to giggle. He couldn't watch any longer, and retreated again. The horn of the car tooted a couple of times randomly, Nick surmised the amorous twosome had caught the centre of the steering wheel unintentionally as they fumbled and mauled one another.

Beginning to regain his composure, Duncan started to

hatch an idea of how to let Tony know he wasn't going to be his doormat, not allow himself to be used by anyone. He took a few deep breaths, placed his cap firmly on his head, and straightened the millinery so the peak was 'square'.

Nonchalantly strolling from his hiding place, Duncan passed the car on the driver's side. Both Tony and Andrea were way too pre-occupied with sins of the flesh to notice him wander past. Turning abruptly on his heels, Nick strode to the driver's door. He slapped the roof of the Humber as hard as he could with his left hand, while opening the door as briskly as possible. The two love birds leapt out of their skins. The warrant officer leaned inside the old car, placing his face right next to that of the 'Wren'. He gestured to Tony's left hand somewhere up her skirt, her nude colour hosiery around her knees.

"He did similar to me last night, sweetheart. Heaven knows who it'll be tomorrow."

Not waiting for a response from either of the shocked pair, Duncan retreated out of the car, slamming the door shut as hard as he could. He wandered off at speed towards the warrant officer's Mess. A moment later, he heard a male voice shout after him which he recognised straight away.

"Is that a bit of jealousy, there?"

"Is that a bit of jealousy, there?"

"Piss Off!"

"Not even just a little bit?"

The Liverpudlian went silent again. Nick felt she now seemed to be deliberately avoiding eye-contact with him.

"He has that certain something women look for in a bloke."

"What's that, then?"

Duncan's curiosity increased ten-fold. He was interested to hear what she saw in Dermot. The detective constable wasn't Nick's cup of tea, even if he had been gay.

"Certain something..." he pondered to himself.

"He makes me feel special, Nick."

The sergeant understood this. He stroked the back of Cavanagh's head reassuringly. She turned to look at him, smiling.

"You'll find some guy one day who'll make you feel so fantastic, the likes of Dermot Ward will be a long, distant memory."

"I hope so."

The Scouser drove the last part of the journey through the city centre, eventually arriving at the station. Nick instantly saw the same as he had the other day outside the station — a dark blue Daimler saloon.

"I think I'm experiencing de-ja-vu."

"Eh? Come again?"

"Oh, sorry Joan. One day feels like the next recently."

The Detective gazed at the classy saloon car, still baffled why it was there. *"He's come back again. Why?"* This time, he kept his observations to himself. The brake lights of the Daimler flickered briefly, whereby it drove away. *"Strange..."* he still mulled in his head.

Entering the station and climbing the stairs, Duncan bumped into Rachel making her way downwards.

"Ahh! Rachel, can you do me a little favour, please."

"Yes, Skipper. Of course."

"Can you discreetly find out if anyone downstairs is making any enquiries about a known local criminal?"

"OK, who am I looking for?"

Nick stepped closer to the WPC, almost speaking to hear in a whisper.

"Find out if anyone is investigating into a William Perkins."

The liaison officer took out her notebook, and wrote down the name.

"William George Perkins, to be exact."

"OK, Skip."

"But keep it to yourself, please."

Rachel performed a cod Girl Guide / Boy Scout salute.

"Guides' honour, Mum's the word and all that! Could it be something to do with the murders of the three women?"

"I don't know. It might be."

"I'll be right back."

Cavanagh screwed her face up, as though she could smell something unpleasant at close quarters.

"William Perkins? That blert! Local gangland boss. Into extortion, protection rackets, money laundering, illegal gambling..."

"That's the Fella!"

"A Godfather wannabe."

"Yes..."

"Er, what's he to do with a triple murder investigation?"

"I don't know."

The detective constable appeared even more confused than before.

"He's not known for murdering young women..."

"No, it's not his bag. Having someone knee-capped, yes. Killing a young woman in her early twenties, no."

"So..."

"So what?"

"Why him? Why the secrecy?"

The sergeant was about to speak, but stopped as a group of the CID team pushed past them on the stairs heading for the office.

"Sarge."

"Morning Clive."

Nick returned the greeting, waiting till they were out of earshot before continuing his conversation.

"Twice now in the last few days we've arrived here, and parked on the street is his car."

"Are you sure it's his motor?"

"It's got a rather distinctive private number plate."

"Ahhh...that's why you asked Rachel to see if he's having his collar felt for anything."

Duncan flashed his colleague a look that said, *"Exactly!"*

The office door burst open, causing the two detectives to quickly spin around.

"Ahhh, Peters and Lee! If you don't mind getting your backsides in here, we can begin."

"Now that we're all here, updates on the situation." Edwards walked to the front of the office, standing next to the noticeboards clapping his hands together loudly.

"Right folks, uniform has conducted quite thorough house-to-house enquiries, and sadly they haven't come back with much as to the three murdered women. They've found one or two cases of domestic violence and a potential burglary suspect, but nothing they can't deal with for now. Sebastian, any joy on that address in Coundon?"

"None yesterday, Guv. I was gonna try again today."

278

"Well, what's keeping you?"

"Er... Guv."

Sebastian rose to his feet, nudging Dermot. The detective constable was occupied in a silent exchange with Cavanagh. Duncan could see she was initially ignoring him, but started to become more receptive to his advances. The Merseysider had gained a slight smirk, and appeared slightly flushed where her foundation hadn't been applied to the edges of her face consistently enough. St John prodded Ward again, who rose from his seat and began to follow the sergeant.

As he passed Joan, the detective constable dropped a small folded piece of paper on her desk. Cavanagh picked up the note, read its contents, and began to smile uncontrollably. She refolded the scrap, secreting it away in her handbag. Duncan flashed his eyebrows in a fruity manner at his female colleague, who's smirk grew even larger, before she 'mouthed' a guttural phrase more suited to the docks on the Mersey, than from the lips of a beautiful woman. Nick winked and chuckled.

Sebastian and Dermot began to make their way out of the office, colliding with Rachel as she darted inwards. Grabbing hold of the detective constable as she flew through the door, the pair spun around on the spot, before Ward released her and winked. Rachel smirked and simmered, something not lost on Nick. He glanced towards Cavanagh, but she was lost within the note Dermot had given her, re-reading it yet again.

"Fuck me! Have we now become an audition for 'Come Dancing'?" Edwards was far from impressed.

"Come on, yous!"

St John tugged at Dermot's elbow, to which the pair eventually left.

"Sorry, Sir."

Rachel meekly sloped to the rear of the office, trying to avoid the inspector's black glare.

"As I was saying, there's a fellow we want to speak with as regards Zhen Wheng. Hopefully Sergeant St John will find the man we want to speak with."

As Nick listened to the senior officer, he felt a piece of paper being slid into his hand as discreetly as possible. In his peripheral vision, he straight away recognised the brunette in the WPC uniform crouching down, skuttling away. The sergeant opened the note, *'Skipper, no one downstairs is currently investigating William Perkins. Sorry, Rachel.'* Duncan screwed the note up, and tossed it into the bin.

"We know where this chap lives due to the invaluable help the translators have provided. Upon his return from his jaunt to Coundon, Sebastian will have some useful information for us to work with."

A loud female cough echoed around the room, causing all gathered to stare at its source — Rachel.

"Miss Ryce, is there something you wish to share with us?"

"Er, yes Sir. I contacted the department store in the city centre where Wendy Kroy worked, about the maintenance guy who worked there she dated..."

"Have you gotten his address?"

"Er, yes I have."

The WPC leafed through her notebook.

"His name is Sean Naylor — he lives in Coundon."

If all eyes weren't on the liaison officer initially, they were now. Edwards moved to Rachel as though in a trance. He reached out, taking her notebook from her, reading the entry.

"Get to the radio control room immediately! Speak with St

John, tell him all of this! I want this guy brought in for questioning. Now!"

"Sir!"

Rachel dashed out of the office, quicker than ever before.

"Ladies and Gentlemen, I do believe we have our Prime Suspect."

The inspector turned towards the noticeboard, writing in block capitals the name *'Sean Naylor'*, drawing link-lines to all three women. Edwards stood and gazed at the board for a few moments.

"Oh, yes. The common reference of the theatre auditions. Duncan, Cavanagh, go have another nosey around. See if anyone there knows this Sean Naylor bloke as well."

"Guv."

Nick put his coat back on, making his way towards the door when Rachel burst back through again.

"Er, Inspector!"

"Rachel..."

"I meant to say, I took it on myself to go to the Swanswell Tavern before Easter."

She produced a box of matches carrying the pub's name from her pocket.

"You did what?"

"I went to the pub, Sir. Had a look around."

Edwards removed his spectacles, rubbing his face with his other hand.

"Would you care to explain why?"

"I, er, I thought it would help. Speed things up."

"Rachel, I admire your determination and eagerness to help, but please leave investigative work to established CID detectives."

The WPC stared at her shoes, not enjoying the dressing down. Duncan spoke up.

"Did you ask any questions, Rachel?"

"Only vague basic ones."

Quite exasperated, the Inspector chipped in.

"Such as..." *"I only asked did anyone know the murdered girls, was anyone aware of them."*

The Guv'nor wandered across to the corner of the office, shaking his head.

"Have I done something wrong, Skipper?"

"Not entirely. I just hope if the guy we're after uses the Swanswell, he wasn't in there when you were asking questions."

Edwards again had to add his own frustration.

"Or someone who knows him tips him off there was a policewoman asking questions! Interesting how he's not at his home address currently, isn't it?"

Rachel slumped down into a nearby chair, crest-fallen. Cavanagh placed her hands on her housemate's shoulders, trying to give some comfort.

"I... I'm sorry, Sir. I just... just wanted to help."

"You can by getting off your arse, get downstairs and radio St John! Go on!"

The senior detective gestured at the liaison officer with a teaspoon.

"Yes, Sir!"

Meekly, Rachel made haste and exited the office again.

Arriving outside the arc-deco theatre, Duncan once again noticed the David Bowie posters displayed, reminding him he needed to sort out tickets for the concert. The sergeant stepped from the car first, straight away giving the constable *'that look'.*

"*What?*"

"*You know what! No repeat of last time we visited, please.*" Joan rolled her eyes like a stroppy teenager.

"*Yes, Sergeant. Just don't have a repeat of the military mutual appreciation society, like?*"

He flashed a quick fake grin at her, before striding towards the stage door. Without bothering to knock, the policeman opened the door and strode inside.

Allowing his eyes to re-adjust to the twilight-like murk, Nick made his way along the passage. He could recall from memory where the manager's office was, wondering if Mr Sparkes would be available this morning. In the distance, sporadic piano-playing could be heard, the same stanza being repeatedly over and over again. As the acoustic music paused, a voice could also be heard sternly giving commands and instructions — at times being quite blunt and coarse.

"*What the hell is that?*"

Cavanagh voiced her bewilderment at what was gracing her ears.

"*I do believe we're about to burst into an audition. Can you tap dance?*"

The sergeant began to hoof around pretending to tap as the piano started once more, slapping his feet on the ground randomly, throwing his hands forwards at intervals. Rather than perform 'cod' tap, the detective's star-turn more resembled an inept Charleston.

"*You don't need to prove to me you have two left feet, Nick.*"

Joan chuckled, watching him continuing to execute

something, which in the most broad and liberal description of the word could be labelled *'dance'*. Possibly.

"Philistine! It takes years of practice to be this awful!"

The scouser pushed past Duncan, still giggling. Nick followed the detective constable, who herself was following the melody her superior was performing to.

After encountering several sharp twists in the bowels of the theatre, ascending a steep, wooden staircase, they found themselves stage-side. A group of young adults, predominantly women, were dancing in formation to the music. Both of the detectives jumped, startled as someone clapped their hands together loudly, shouting at the top of their voice.

"Stop! Stop! What have I told you shower? How hard can it be?"

Duncan and Cavanagh peeped out around the edge of the retracted curtain, to see Alison McLeod. Hands now on hips, she made an imposing figure at the front of the stage, with the position of her arms causing her shawl to billow out into a cape. With her copper-coloured hair, and purple dress, her persona was almost comic-book super hero-esque. The image of the Scooby-Doo character, Daphne Blake leapt into Nick's mind. In front of Alison were a troupe of young people, all around the same age of the three deceased women.

"If I explained this routine to a five-year-old, they'd understand! Honestly!"

Miss McLeod turned away from the dancers to face the empty seats where the audience would be, putting her hand to her forehead in exasperation. In the corner of his eye, Nick saw Joan politely wave in an extremely girly and simmering way. The detective tried to make out who the Merseysider had recognised amongst the gathering, glancing this way and that. He quickly saw who had caught Cavanagh's eye — Oliver Richmond. The tall, ape of a man was seated at an upright piano, smiling cheerfully as he fluttered his fingers in a childish wave.

"OK children, let's take it from the top. Once more with feeling, if you please!"

The choreographer barked her instructions, causing the troupe to hastily dash about the stage to predetermined places. The performers held far from ordinary poses, frozen to the spot awaiting something. A few moments passed, before a deliberate cough echoed across the stage from the front.

"Er, are we ready Oliver?"

Oliver was mentally somewhere else, as he 'mouthed' pleasantries with the detective constable. This wasn't lost on Nick, and noticed all too well by Alison as well.

"Oliver! Music please!"

The pianist snapped out of his bubble with a jolt, beginning the play the same tune yet again.

"And one, three, five, seven — one, three, five, seven..."

The choreographer counted time as the troupe begun their routine, moving between them with arms extended, slightly altering the pose and position of some. To Nick's non-performance art trained mind, this appeared to be bordering on molestation. Alison spun one pretty long-haired blonde around, her hands all over the leotard clad body of the young woman — before stopping dead as she caught sight of Duncan.

Clapping her hands together loudly, she brought the rehearsal to a halt.

"Thank you, boys and girls. Let's break for lunch!"

As Oliver stopped tickling the ivories, the ensemble

dispersed. The large woman slowly sauntered over to the two police officers.

"Hello Sergeant. Fancy seeing you again."

"Miss McLeod. Can we ask you a few things, if you're free for a short while?"

Alison peered down her nose at Cavanagh once again, barely able to bring herself to look at the constable.

"Yes, that shouldn't be a problem. How can I help you?"

Joan stepped forwards, withdrawing a copy of the audition list from her handbag.

"We've established two of the young women found dead recently — you might have heard about it in the news — attended an audition for your show."

McLeod appeared rather puzzled, leaning towards the constable to see the list with two names highlighted — Arosha Rana and Zhen Wheng.

"Do you remember them at all, Miss McLeod?"

Snatching the sheet of paper off Cavanagh, Alison appeared to be reading the names written upon it over and over again.

"How did you come by my audition list?"

Duncan was somewhat taken back.

"The theatre manager, Mr Sparkes allowed us access to a copy. As my colleague was saying, do you recall them?"

"Vaguely. I guess they weren't good enough to make the chorus line."

Cavanagh began to scribble into her notebook as McLeod spoke.

"Interesting coincidence two women who auditioned are now dead..."

The choreographer seemed to be thinking out loud, her

thoughts sounding quite chilling and macabre.

"I was thinking the very same."

The sergeant was far from impressed with her casual and blasé attitude to the circumstances.

"Were they friendly, like? Did they know each other?"

Joan continued with her line of questioning, which Nick could clearly see visibly irritated Alison.

"Constable, I can't say either way. I never paid any attention to them. After all, I'm trying to gather together performers worthy of appearing on stage, under my guidance. Just in case you hadn't noticed."

"Miss McLeod, any information we can gain which will lead us to apprehending the person or people responsible for these murders would be greatly appreciated. Just in case you hadn't noticed."

Duncan quickly intervened to quosh any ill-feelings.

"Alison, was there any reason in particular you did not select these young women?"

The lady in purple huffed. Reluctantly, she strolled over to the piano on the other side of the stage. The two detectives followed. McLeod picked up a folder from on top of the upright instrument, and began to leaf through it.

"I'm really busy, you know Sergeant. I'm already behind schedule. First night is looming uncomfortably close."

After a painfully long and somewhat unnecessary pause Nick felt, she withdrew a couple of sheets of paper.

"Oh, yes. Arosha. Copious enthusiasm, but arm and leg movements not smooth or refined enough."

Duncan glanced at Joan, nodding once and gestured at her notebook and pen in her hand.

"What about the Chinese girl, Zhen?"

"Zhen... er... Zhen...Oh, yes! Same as Arosha, enthusiastic — too enthusiastic, really. Too much energy. Stood out too much dancing in a troupe."

"Were either of the young ladies friendly with other people at the audition? Did they arrive with anyone else?"

"Like I've already said Sergeant, I wasn't paying attention. I was busy finding dancers for my musical."

"Have you heard of a man by the name of Sean Naylor?" Alison gave a blank, vacant gaze, gently shaking her head.

"No Sergeant. Should I?"

Again, Duncan noticed Joan had a silly smirk all over her face, making eyes at Oliver. The large man still sat at the piano, now slowly smoking a cigarette. He winked at the constable, smiling back at her.

"Joan..."

Nick caught his colleague's attention, flicking his eyebrows upwards once. She glanced at the sergeant awkwardly.

"Oh, sorry mate."

Oliver stood up, reached into his jeans pocket and retrieved a chrome cigarette case. *"That's a bit swish,"* Nick reflected. Oliver opened the case, offering it towards the detective. The policeman smiled appreciatively, taking a single cigarette.

"Thank you very much."

"Anytime. Always pleased to help the police."

The big man leaned towards Duncan, offering him a light from a corresponding chrome lighter. As he flicked the top open igniting a flame straight off, Nick took along, deep draw on the tobacco as it started to burn. He pulled a slight face as he exhaled, the flavour of the smoke was quite different to his own regular, favourite brand.

"They're American."

Duncan glanced at Oliver as he lit a cigarette for himself. Taking the tobacco from his lips, the sergeant gazed down at the thin, white stick between his finger and thumb. The brown filter had a gold stripe around it just before the white paper that encased the loose tobacco. Stamped on the paper close to the gold stripe on the filter in the company's own unique font was its manufacturer — Marlboro.

Oliver turned to Joan, offering her the open chrome cigarette case. The scouser shook her head with a polite smile.

"No, ta. I don't."

"I shouldn't, really. Need a reason to give up."

Once again, he winked at the constable.

"I don't need a reason!"

Alison took a cigarette uninvited from Oliver's case, lighting it herself. Nick watched her give Joan another incredibly black look, as the Merseysider shared silent sweet nothings with the pianist.

"Right, thank you both for your time and assistance. If anything else comes to mind as regards the two women, please don't hesitate to give us a call or pass a message on through Mr Sparkes."

Nick stepped forwards and shook Alison's hand. The choreographer nodded, a brief smile flashed across her face.

"Of course! You'll be the first to know, Detective."

Duncan began to walk back to where he had made his way onto the stage. If was only after half a dozen steps he realised Joan was not alongside him. Glancing back over his shoulder, he found the constable still batting her eyelashes at Oliver, giving him a soppy wave as she departed, and a hand gesture of a phone receiver placed next to her ear. Cavanagh became aware with a jolt her colleague was not just waiting for her, but watching her as well.

"What?"

Nick drove short distance across the city towards his own home from brother's house. It was such a joy to have Alice back, and lose that god-awful car belonging to his brother. He quickly lit a cigarette while waiting at a set of lights, mulling over the details of the day.

The elusive Sean Naylor had still not returned to his home for the second day running. He hoped that Rachel's improvised behaviour hadn't caused him to flee, as the Guv'nor had surmised. If he had, it would suggest strongly he's implicated more than anyone realised. However, Nick had to admit St John's idea of asking the local nosey parker-cum-parish warden, who fortuitously resided across the road, to contact the office the moment Naylor reappeared was a clever one. It saved leaving an unmarked car parked outside. Much less suspicious.

Looking around the Alvis, he quickly saw she was in desperate need of a wash, but the Alice's interior — especially the carpets — were absolutely awful. How could two people make so much mess in such a short space of time? Maybe the 'dirty weekend' Ellis and Alex had experienced had involved hiking boots more so than the bedroom. However, as he drove onto the elevated ring road that surrounded the city centre, his unfailing detective instincts piqued — he could see he was being followed.

Glancing in the rear-view mirror, the policeman made out the silhouette and illuminated headlights quite close together of a Mk II Jaguar. Duncan accelerated onto the dual-carriageway, watching behind him to establish if the Jag was attempting the same. It was. Racing past the exit for Pool Meadow bus station, and over the next traffic island at the end of the Foleshill Road, Nick made other road-users scatter or come to last ditch emergency stops to avoid certain collisions.

Peering again in the rear-view mirror, the Jaguar was still on his tail. The detective scoured his memory and thought hard — why would someone be so eager to follow him? Could it be something Alex had inadvertently done, and the aggrieved party recognising the Alvis? Passing the exit slip roads for the next two junctions, Alice was now exceeding the speed limit by some margin. For safety's sake, he flicked the switches on the dashboard activating the blue flashing lights on the front of the car and two-tone siren.

Coming off the ring road where it effectively ended at the section still under construction, Duncan threw the Alvis around an island — the route he wanted to take towards his home — and accelerated back onto the ring road in the direction he had just come from. The same shape filled his mirrors, the headlights burning away in the reflection he stared at. Attempting to re-join the dual-carriageway, Nick caught a clearer image of the car behind under the bright street lights. No wonder it could keep up as easily as it did, it was no Mk II Jag, it was a Daimler 250 V8! It's rippled chrome grill shone and glistened in the electric lighting. The Alvis' straight six was no match for the Daimler's engine.

Duncan threw his car up the exit ramp towards the Holyhead Road. Bearing off the island, the sergeant flicked the wheel to the right — deliberately crossing a red light, and bundled into Barras Lane. Seeing in his mirrors the chasing car was unable to follow becoming stuck at the traffic lights, Nick shot into the nearest side street. Driving around the back of a gas works, he swiftly grabbed the handbrake. He spun the wheel hard to right, sliding Alice around, instantly facing the opposite way. Coming to a dead stop, the policeman hastily leapt out of his car just as the Daimler appeared from around the corner.

The car had no option but come to an emergency stop, locking up its tyres and skidding a dozen yards or so. Nick strode at pace to the rear of the pursuing dark blue car, seized the chrome handle on the passenger door, and yanked it open. The detective reached inside, grabbing the person there by their coat lapels and wrenched them out. Duncan pinned them to the side of the car.

"William Perkins!"

The middle-aged man with salt and pepper hair coughed twice, reaching up and gently removed the policeman's hands from his coat.

"Good evening, Sergeant Duncan. I trust you're well."

Nick felt a hand grab his collar, glancing in that direction he found Perkins' driver-cum-heavy standing there.

"It's fine, George. Mr Duncan means no harm."

The driver took a step back, as the detective did same from his boss.

"Sorry Sergeant. Just doing my job."

"George Walsh! Are you still hanging around with this mafia wannabe?"

Duncan straightened his coat, turning his attention back to Perkins.

"What's got your knickers in a twist, Billy? I've seen you loitering outside the station."

"I just wanted to have a quiet chat Mr Duncan."

"As regards? Last time we spoke you were under investigation, then arrested, for your part in extorting money with menaces — a protection racket!"

"To which the charges were dropped, Sergeant. I was innocent."

A grin slowly spread across Billy's face.

"Yes, amazing what can happen when evidence that is circumstantial at best, is not collaborated by any witnesses, who miraculously decide not to talk."

Billy spread his arms wide, in a Christ-like pose.

"I'm a pillar of the local community, a native of this fair city born with nothing, now a very successful businessman."

"Just don't forget what happened to the Krays, Billy."

"I'm not a murderer, Mr Duncan. I'm a nightclub and casino owner."

"So were they!"

Billy's smirk grew even larger.

"This chat you so desperately want with me, why not just phone the office?"

Both Billy and George began to chuckle.

"An alleged gangster with a 'colourful' record contacting the Law off his own back..."

The crook shuffled nervously, placing his hands into his coat pockets.

"I've done some poking around of my own, Mr Duncan. And through my contacts there isn't anyone who has had reason, or would have reason, to have these women humped off."

Duncan nodded as he listened. He reached inside his coat, retrieving his cigarettes. Opening the left side of the packet, he offered it to Perkins, then Walsh. The gangsters took one each. By the time Nick had placed one of the Park Drive between his own lips, George had leaned around with an ornate lighter in his hand, firstly offering the flame to the policeman, followed by his employer. The detective nodded in appreciation.

"I've also put the word around to find out if its anyone we know, even on the fringes, who might be doing this."

Nick exhaled the vapours from his tobacco, speaking quickly. *"Billy, thanks for finding out what you have, and if you gain any further information, please pass it onto us. I don't want anyone or anybody taking matters into their own hands. We don't need any vigilantes, thank you."*

"Sergeant, what do you take me for?"

"I know your 'code', remember. No women, no kids."

The crime boss began to develop a disturbing, sinister grin which he was trying his utmost to supress.

"See what I mean. No 'street justice' please, Billy. Leave this one to the police."

"OK, Mr Duncan. As you wish."

The sergeant began to wander back to his own car, glancing back over his shoulder.

"I mean it, Billy. Leave it to us. We'll catch who did this and bring them to justice."

"Just make sure you do. That's all."

"Billy..."

The gangster stepped back into his Daimler, with George closing the door and strolling around to the driver's position like a proper chauffeur would.

"Good night, Sergeant."

Nick watched as the Daimler performed a three-point

turn, and vanished into the darkness.

Once back behind the wheel of his car, Duncan drove home. The detective pondered on what had just transpired. *"So, the local criminal fraternity are at a loss over who is responsible for these murders..."* he pondered. *"Intriguing..."* The realisation struck home they were looking for someone not on Police record. That would make the investigation doubly difficult for certain. The sergeant chuckled at the irony of the criminal underworld indirectly assisting the police. His mirth was cut short, as the reality dawned on him the Warwickshire Constabulary needed to find the murderer first before William Perkins and his mob.

It was a welcome relief walking into his house, switching on the lights and finding Stirling straight away rubbing his large furry mass against his legs. The plump tabby purred at his owner, pleased he had returned home. Extinguishing his cigarette in an ashtray, he fed the insistent, yet ravenous feline his slop.

Turning the TV on, and about to slump down in his favourite chair, the first thing he heard from the gogglebox made him wince. He'd dropped straight into an episode of the sit-com set in Liverpool, *The Liver Birds.* The comedic banter and inane comments made him think that's what it must be like to visit Joan's family. He wandered back into the kitchen to put the kettle on, finding Stirling had finished, and was now begging for more.

After giving him seconds of something that was masquerading as 'chicken in gravy', Duncan did manage to go flop into his single-seater Chesterfield armchair with a cuppa. As the sit-com finished, the *Nine O'Clock News* began. The detective wearily rose from his seat and changed channel on the TV. Greeted by the jolly-jangly piano-played theme tune of the snooker programme, *'Pot Black'*, he returned to his seat. It was either this, listening to depressing news about another strike on the cards in a factory somewhere, or come part way into a film that had already begun. Slurping on his cuppa, he watched the snooker. The warmth of the room, combined with the mental strain of the last few days, the drowsy policeman began to relax further. Tiredness crept up on him, and he began to doze.

Nick wasn't sure what woke him first — hearing the theme tune to *'The Old Grey Whistle Test'* or the phone ringing. Groggily, he got to his feet with much effort. Stirling had decided to sit on his owner's lap, and was highly reluctant to surrender his position. Standing bolt upright, Duncan had the helping hand of gravity. The tubby tabby clung onto the fabric of Nick's trousers — and a fair chunk of his flesh — until the Laws of Physics applied their unshakeable rules. Stirling dropped to the carpet, flicking his tail most displeased. Stumbling across the room towards the hall, the sergeant rubbed his legs in discomfort after being free of the feline's talon-esque claws. Reaching the phone, Nick lifted the receiver.

"Hello…"

"Sarge?"

A female voice with a thick Ulster accent snapped him out of his post-slumber fog.

"Yeah, who's that?"

"It's Niamh Maddox."

The detective's heart sank. Surely not another murder! Please, no! Not another young woman slain with all her life ahead of her.

"Hello Niamh. What's the matter?"

"It's Joan Cavanagh, Sarge."

"What about her?"

Duncan was all ears. Had something untoward happened to his colleague?

"She's turned up here at the station."

"I thought she was off duty tonight?"

"She is. Only she's turned up here. She's a little shaken and upset."

"Shaken and upset? What's happened?"

"From what Joan said, she was out on a date and it went wrong."

Horrible images passed through the policeman's mind. Scenarios he'd previously only seen in SOCO photography began to haunt him.

"Where is she now, Niamh?"

"In the canteen. I wrapped a blanket around her and gave her a cup of tea."

The WPC went silent for a moment.

"Er, Sarge...can I ask a favour?"

"What's that?"

"Can you come take Joan home, please. I'm on nights tonight, and can't get hold of our other housemate, Rachel Ryce."

"Oh, I know Rachel. Maybe she's out on a date or something."

"So, can you take her home for me?"

Nick was about to answer, but the Northern Irish WPC was quite obviously worried and didn't give him chance to reply.

"Please! If you don't mind."

The detective sighed, reaching for his coat from the end of the banister.

"OK, Niamh. I'll be ten minutes."

"Thanks, Sarge."

Driving back to Little Park Street, Duncan's imagination continued to work overtime. It performed back flip after back flip. He hoped nothing serious had befell his friend. In all his years as a policeman, Nick fortunately had never had something happen to anyone close to him. He was worried. Dashing through the darkness, he made the journey in barely five minutes and did not cease dashing until he burst through the canteen doors and saw the Scouse Detective with his own eyes. Hunched over a table, nursing a mug of tea with both hands, blanket still draped across her shoulders, Cavanagh looked a shadow of her usual brash, determined, super confident self. He sat next to her, placing an arm around her shoulders, pulling her into his partial embrace. He spoke softly.

"I'm not going to insult your intelligence asking are you all right — I can already see you're not. If you want to talk, I'm listening."

Joan sniffled, as though she was holding back tears she wanted to cry. After what seemed like an age, the Merseysider spoke.

"It's Dermot."

"What about him, Joan? Weren't you two were getting on?"

"We were. In a fashion."

"So, what's happened?"

The constable once again went silent, once again intently gazing deeply into her drink.

"He's a complete cunt!"

Duncan was a little taken back with the strength of the language his friend used. Before he had chance to speak, Joan began again.

"We went out on a date. All was going well, we went for a drink in the Three Tuns, I assumed we might move onto the pictures or maybe go grab something to eat."

Cavanagh painfully paused, as though a huge lump had become lodged in her throat.

"Can I get you another drink?"

"No, no — it's fine Nick."

She took a huge gulp of the mug of stone-cold tea.

"He...He started to come on strong before we left the pub. He said I was a prick tease, said I was gagging for it, I was leading all the men on in the office like."

"Well, I don't think you are."

The scouser sighed, placing her hand on top of Duncan's on her shoulder, smiling weakly at the sergeant. Duncan spun through his head, *"If that's all she's upset and offended about, she's more sensitive than I ever gave her credit for."*

"He touched me, Nick."

"Touched you? Where?"

Tears now did begin to flow down the Liverpudlian's face. To such an extent, it was clear to Duncan she'd been holding them back, but could no longer.

"We sat in a booth, so it was more private. He snuggled up to me, which was lovely, we started kissing and before I knew it, he had his hand up my skirt."

"Really?"

"Really up my skirt! I could feel his fingertips stroking the panty part of my tights between my legs."

Cavanagh buried her face in Nick's shoulder and began to sob.

"Disgusting pig!"

He began to squeeze her close. Only happening to glance downwards, he noticed she was wearing grey knee-high suede boots and a short black skirt. However, Nick was appalled to see the side-seam of the skirt was split. Duncan found it distasteful beyond words. In his head, he pictured Joan had thrashed her shapely legs about to such an extent in sheer panic and fighting Dermot off, the action had torn her clothing. He felt so angry his friend had suffered a sexual assault. Burying his face in her soft hair, Nick gave her a series of soft kisses on the top of her head.

"I'll sort him out when I see him! Dermot is not going to get away with this!"

"Just leave it, Nick. I'll deal with it."

The two detectives snuggled closer, holding the tender embrace for several minutes.

"Come on, let's get you home."

Cavanagh glanced at her friend, giving him a forced smile.

"Yeah, you're right. I can't sit here all night."

Wandering out of the station, Joan took Nick's hand and held it so tightly he began to believe her very existence depended upon the contact.

"See, I got my car back off my brother!"

The scouser chuckled politely, climbing into the passenger side of the Alvis. Pulling the door to, she leaned against the cold glass of the window, staring into space.

"Won't be long, Joan. I'll make you a decent cuppa, better than that dishwater they serve at the station."

"Nick, can you do me a favour?"

"Of course! What is it?"

The constable shuffled in her seat, on this occasion the slight flatulence sounds not instigating any humour at all.

"Er, if it's no trouble, and you don't mind, and if it's OK with you..."

"What is it, Joan?"

"Er, can I stay at yours tonight?"

Duncan turned to face his friend. He smiled tenderly and nodded.

"Ta, Nick. I really don't want to be on my own tonight." Cavanagh shuffled again in her seat, this time leaning against the sergeant and embracing his left arm, plus holding his hand. *"She really is in a bad way,"* Duncan rapidly concluded.

Once inside his home, the detective made that cup of tea he was boasting about. Joan sat on the edge of the sofa, sipping the brew. She let out a half-hearted chuckle.

"You're right. Your tea is much better than at the station."

"The bed in the spare room is still made up. That'll be comfier than sleeping on the sofa."

The constable flashed another meagre smile at her host, more out of politeness.

"Thank you. I... I don't mean to impose. It's just Niamh is on a night shift and heaven knows what time Rachel will be back. I didn't want to go back to an empty house."

Nick nodded. He understood.

"Are you sure you don't want me to have a word with Dermot, sort this out for you?"

"Nick, thanks all the same, but no. Last thing I want is you getting yourself into trouble wading in all John Wayne style, like you did Sunday night protecting Harvey!"

He couldn't help but stare straight at his right hand. He slightly caressed the flesh-colour sticking plaster that was still adhered across his knuckles.

"I'll deal with him myself. Best way to get back at these twats is to confront them."

The sergeant agreed, leaving the lounge and sprinting upstairs. Grabbing his button up pyjama top, he returned to Cavanagh.

"Here! Use this, if it makes you feel more comfortable."

"Thank you."

"Come on, best you get some sleep."

Joan nodded, following Nick upstairs.

Duncan had no idea what time it was, but it was still dark. All he knew there was movement in the room, and it had awoken him. Initially, the detective believed the disturbance was that big, daft pet cat of his, prowling about in the darkness as he did sometimes. He quickly knew the anomaly in the bedroom wasn't Stirling. It stubbed it's toe on the bedpost, and swore in fluent Scouse.

"Are you OK, Joan?"

"Can I get in there with you? Please...I'm cold."

Nick shuffled over to the right of his bed, flipping over the covers so she could climb in. Cavanagh slid under the sheet and eiderdown, reversing in so her back was towards him.

"Ta, Nick."

"What for?"

"Being so kind. Not everyone is."

He stroked her hair, kissing the back of her head.

"Nobody should have to endure being touched intimately, unless it's invited."

He felt her take his hand, and gently pull his arm around her, embracing her.

"Hold me."

The policeman spooned up behind her, sliding his arm around her. Joan fidgeted a few times, snuggling into Nick's front. The sergeant began to believe his friend was deliberately rubbing her bare behind into his groin. Repeatedly so. This motion, combined with all he could smell was his own aftershave on his pyjama top and not her perfume, caused an intense sensation inside him. As the flannelette fabric of the pyjama jacket dragged across his chest and snagged against the stubble on his chin, part of Nick's psyche no longer considered he was holding a beautiful woman, but reminded him in spades of when he used to cuddle up to Tony Devereux. The Naval Lieutenant only wore a pyjama jacket. He always had a bare behind he used to push into Nick's groin.

Hormones, saucy memories and sensation built up in Duncan's mind. The huge surge and rush he felt swept through his whole being, leading to only one thing — his penis began to become erect. The more Joan moved, the skin on her purt bottom rubbed his pyjama trousers, pulling the soft cloth around his genitals. This sent the detective wild. The thought only a flimsy piece of material was between his swollen member and the firm buttocks now pushing against it, only caused his hard on to swell and grow. *"Tony, you're such a tease,"* Nick fantasised. Much to his joy, Joan continued to grind against him. His erection grew firmer and larger, to which she responded grinding against gorged organ more so. Duncan pulled her closer to him, beginning to grind back. *"God, I so want to put that inside you,"* Nick spun through his head, imagining saying it to Tony. However, he'd done his usual. Joan replied to his breathless statement.

"I know you don't like girls, use your imagination like."

Images of Tony flashed before his mind's eye, how delicious his body felt, how he could keep staring at him naked for hours.

Completely unexpectedly, Nick felt a small hand reach around to the front of his pyjamas. With a deft touch that was exquisite, it reached through the gaping fly of the slumber-wear, pulling his rampant cock out. Duncan gasped as she gently stroked his shaft up and down, steadily masturbating him. Her technique was sublime. The sergeant felt her fidget about slightly, beginning to position herself against the tip of him. Pushing backwards, he slid inside her welcoming, moist slit. Nick knew she was enjoying the moment, as the constable bounced repeatedly, riding him as she slid up and down.

With the pyjama jacket once again in his face, images of being inside Tony filled his head, recalling the incredible euphoria that gave. Suddenly, Tony evaporated from his fantasy, to be replaced by someone else — Harvey. He imagined he was in bed with the solicitor, sharing something unbelievable and mind-blowing with him. He began to increase speed and rhythm, the feeling of well-being rising within him. Joan groaned and gasped, it being apparent she was in a much similar place herself. Nick couldn't contain himself much longer, grabbing her by the waist he pumped away into her deeper and more forcefully, increasing in intensity and speed. In reply, Cavanagh pushed back against him, internally holding and squeezing his tool tight. The fantasy of rolling naked around on the rug in front of his fire with Harvey filled his imagination. He couldn't hold back any longer, climaxing hard inside her, with the ferocity of a missile hitting its target. He shot hot cum into her, just as Joan came herself.

Pulse racing and heart pounding, he withdrew. Warm moisture slowly spilled from the two of them onto the sheets. Cavanagh rolled over, ripping the pyjama jacket off, and embraced Nick tightly. Duncan wrapped his arms around the woman, holding her equally as close. Joan found her voice first.

"Are you sure you're not straight?"

He didn't have chance to answer, as Joan planted her lips on his, the tip of her tongue pushing its way into his mouth searching for his.

CHAPTER NINE
WEDNESDAY APRIL 25th 1973

The teak-coloured door in front of him displayed the name and rank of the most senior policeman in the station, *'Superintendent Frederick Franklin'.* Nick nervously adjusted his tie in the hazy reflection visible in the varnished wood. Composing himself, he knocked the door twice.

"Come!"

Swallowing hard, Duncan grasped the door handle, pushing the door open. Entering the office, he found the superintendent was not at his desk. Dressed in full uniform with his ginger hair now showing flecks of grey, he was standing with his back to the door looking out of the window at the view across the city.

"You wanted to see me, Sir..."

The Superintendent glanced over his shoulder.

"Yes, Sergeant. Please take a seat."

The Detective sat down. After a long, drawn out painfully protracted silence, Franklin spun around on the spot, slapping a copy of a tabloid newspaper onto his desk. The headline on *'The National,'* one of those gutter press rags with a topless young woman on page three, made Nick want to fall into the nearest hole in the ground and remain there for the foreseeable — *"Meet Warwickshire's 'Bent' Copper!"* Alongside this, was a picture of himself smoking a cigarette.

To say Duncan was completely devastated was an understatement of biblical proportions. Tears began to well up in his eyes. He picked the newspaper up, and tried to read the article through the moisture increasing in intensity clouding his vision. What he could see of the text, it went into vulgar depth over his sexuality. *"How could this be? How is it possible they got hold of this information?"* He ran it over and over again in his head.

"Have you anything to say as regards this, Mr Duncan?" Franklin spoke calmly, but with intense sternness as he took his own seat at his desk. The detective's mouth was now so dry, he couldn't even swallow.

"Sir, it is the seventies now. Who I choose to sleep with, doesn't affect my job or how well I can be a policeman and a detective."

The Superintendent leaned back in his chair, placing both of his hands across his stomach, fingers entwined.

"That maybe so, but many of the population of this city are still getting over being bombed out of their homes by the Luftwaffe, let alone contemplate a homosexual copper! They won't accept it or find it remotely palatable. They'll consider you weird — a freak — how can you uphold the laws of the land, when you yourself are something that was illegal up to six years ago?"

Duncan gazed at his feet, trying to supress his urge to let the tears tumble. He feared the worst. It was the end of the job he loved, adored and lived for. Plus, Mum would find out in the worst way possible. He knew one of her neighbours would be breaking their neck to stuff the newspaper in her face, give her abuse and the *'How could you? How come you didn't know?'* angle. She didn't deserve or need that.

Unexpectedly, he felt a hand on his shoulder. *"I don't recall anyone else being in here when I walked in..."* he pondered. Duncan slowly turned, expecting to find the Guv'nor standing there. Instead, he got the shock of his life. He looked straight into the face not of Detective Inspector Albert Edwards, but a certain Police Sergeant Robert Duncan. His father.

Attired in the same wartime uniform he was dressed in within the photograph on Nick's desk, Bob Duncan was quite an imposing and intimidating sight.

"Dad!"

The Detective now began to cry, intensely so.

"Nicholas, I'm so disappointed in you. This brings shame not only on our family, but the Constabulary and the Navy as well!"

"But Dad..."

Duncan began to sob, breaking his heart the exact same way as he did at his father's funeral. Nick wiped his eyes, standing up in front of his dad. He reached out to embrace him, but was disturbed as the shrill sound of one of the telephones on the superintendent's desk started to ring. All three men stared at it intently.

Nick sat bolt upright in bed. He gasped for breath, not entirely sure where he was or what was happening. Had he just seen Dad? Was that meeting with the Super real? As he gained his bearings, it registered the phone was really ringing — he hadn't dreamt that part. As he went to get out of bed, he noticed the shape lying next to him and remembered the night before. What had he done? He felt disgusted with himself. He threw back the covers, and found at some point he'd lost his pyjama bottoms. Oh, there they are — a crumpled heap up the corner. The last thing he could recall was the young Scouse woman pinning him to the bed, rubbing her naked body all over his. Why had he let her? Why?

The phone continued to ring downstairs, showing no signs of relenting. Duncan grabbed his dressing gown, clambering into it as he flew downstairs. With one hand doing up the belt, he answered the call.

"Hello..."

"Golden Bollocks!"

Nick recognised immediately the blunt male voice with its thick Glaswegian accent.

"Morning Sebastian."

"Aye Laddie. Git yer sen oot o' yer fartsack, an git dressed. Anotha body has been found."

"Oh, for fuck's sake!"

The detective ran his hand through his hair. This was getting too much to take.

"Whereabouts?"

"Caludon Castle. An I've tried t' phone yer Scouse Sidekick, but she disnae answer. Pick her up on yer way."

"Yeah, see you shortly."

Duncan hung up the phone, darted into the kitchen to put the kettle on, before running full tilt back upstairs.

"Joan...Joan, wake up!"

The policeman shook the young woman several times, until she began to stir.

"Ummm, what's the matter?"

Cavanagh rubbed her eyes as she came to, yawning. Nick fully opened the curtains, allowing daylight to flood into the room. The Merseysider covered her eyes, wincing.

"Arrrggghhh! Nick! Can't you let a girl wake up gradually?"

Ripping the dressing gown off, he began rifling through a chest of drawers trying to find some clean underwear. As she became accustomed to the bright sunlight, and the view of her friend naked before her, the Scouse Constable smiled a cheeky smirk. Nick found a pair of pants, leaving the room at speed. He returned in the blink of an eye with some of Joan's clothes he had grabbed at random.

"Get dressed! St John just phoned. Another body has been found."

Joan sat bolt upright. The shocked look on her face was only off-set by the ample size and shape of her breasts. Completely ignoring this, Duncan threw her clothes at her. A skirt, a pair of tights and one solitary grey suede boot landed on the bed in front of her.

About twenty minutes later, the two detectives were heading across the city at speed to the crime scene. Cavanagh held two mugs of tea, as the sergeant pushed through traffic.

"I never knew Coventry had a castle."

"It hasn't any more. Caludon Castle is nothing more than a wall of medieval rubble. It's hardly Edinburgh or Windsor." Nick reached over to Joan, taking one of the drinks from her and proceeded to take a generous gulp of the contents.

"It's all right for you, Nick. You don't look like you're performing the Walk of Shame, still yet to return home after last night!"

While Joan had managed to do something with her hair, it was the remnants of last night's cosmetics she still wore that appeared questionable, and combined with her split skirt

Cavanagh was far from her usual on point best. Taking in his own reflection in the rear-mirror, he commented on his own lack lustre image.

"You think you've got issues — I haven't had chance to have a shave this morning!"

Joan laughed sarcastically.

"Well, you pull the rough look off perfectly. I've got no excuse."

"Just pull the collar of your jacket up. All of the guys will be paying more attention to your legs anyhow in those boots."

Cavanagh began to cover her face with her free hand.

"Oh, Bollocks! Dermot! I bet he's going to be here! He'll be proper snide!"

"He might. Stay close to me. You'll be fine."

Nick winked at the scouser. She smiled broadly in reply.

Heading eastbound out of the city, Duncan turned off the Ansty Road towards a small park area hidden behind a housing estate. Stepping out of the car, Nick could tell the constable now understood his comments about the 'castle'.

"It is a pile of sodding rubble!"

The Liverpudlian was clearly gobsmacked such was still given the title 'castle'. However, her reaction as regards someone's artistic licence and over-elaborate description paled into insignificance, as Nick nudged her and pointed to where a privacy screen had been hastily erected. It appeared to more resemble a tent that had been assembled half-heartedly by some inept boy scout. Stepping inside the screen, the two detectives found Edwards and St John.

"Guv, the newspapers are gonna love dis! Four women in Coventry now found dead."

"Hmmm, I know Sebastian."

"They'll over-react, really pester us! How are we gonna conduct a proper investigation now? They'll accuse us of not working fast enough!"

As the Scottish sergeant lamented the situation, Spencer stepped behind the partition straight into the conversation.

"Sergeant St John, I'll deal with the press, along with the Super — just get on with the case."

Duncan began to take a closer look at the deceased young woman. She was another brunette who was easy on the eye, although this time her hair was in a permed curly-style similar to T-Rex singer, Marc Bolan. Wearing a short leather jacket, beige short skirt matching colour boots, Nick imagined Joan or his sister-in-law Ellis wearing this ensemble.

Crouching down, he could already see her fingernails were perfectly manicured. Much care and attention had been given applying all of her cosmetics. Removing a pen from his inside pocket, the detective carefully moved her hair to one side to see her face. What struck Duncan straight away wasn't the make-up applied in the 'barely there' style, nor the discolouration of the skin from decomposing outside over a few days, but five o'clock shadow on the jaw and top lip.

"Has anyone examined this young woman's personal effects?"

Nick was incredibly curious. This woman wasn't all she seemed, in his opinion. Edwards opened his own notebook, flicking through till he found the page he was looking for.

"Er, this is one Sam Lambert, aged twenty-five, home address not that far from here in Binley."

The Inspector paused for a moment. *"Is something the matter, Nick?"*

The Sergeant began to compare the size and shape of his own hand, against that of the deceased.

"Joan, can you crouch down here for a second."

The constable obliged, tearing the seam on her skirt further. She cursed under her breath, trying her utmost to hold the material in place. Nick sniggered as he knew she was trying not to reveal the fact she was only wearing tights and nothing else, having gotten dressed in much haste. Duncan took her free hand, holding it next to that of the unfortunate Sam, and again placed his own alongside.

"Hmmm, just as I thought!"

Something made sense in the young sergeant's mind.

"Nick, what have you done to your hand?"

Edwards gestured at the skin-coloured plaster across his knuckles.

"Oh, nothing. I cut myself working on the car."

"Looks nasty."

The Inspector fell silent briefly, as though mulling something over.

"If I didn't know better, it looks like you've punched someone in the face. Several times, in fact."

Nick sheepishly looked at St John, who smiled a daft smirk.

"What have you noticed, Sarge?"

Cavanagh spoke up, bringing everyone back to the matter in hand.

"Guv, does the ID in her handbag say 'Samantha' or 'Samuel' upon it?"

"What are yer talking aboot, Golden Bollocks?"

Duncan put his hand up to silence the Scotsman. Flipping through his notebook, the Guv'nor had no answer. He stepped partially out around the privacy screen, speaking with a SOCO officer. Slowly he reappeared, a picture of bafflement. Edwards seemed to be struggling to grasp what he had been told.

"The ID in the handbag found with the body was a current driving licence, in the name of 'Samuel Henry Lambert'."

"Why wa a lassie be carrying a fella's licence? Maybe her boyfriend d' dis!"

All eyes turned towards Sebastian, as he began to ramble, thinking out loud.

"She's not carrying a man's driving licence, Columbo. She is a man!"

Nick began pointing out the differences between Joan's hand and that of the dead 'woman'.

"Look! Have you ever met a woman with this much stubble, more than I have right now…?" He gestured at the chin of the 'woman'. *"And it doesn't take a doctor to recognise the obvious…"*

With his pen, Duncan gently lifted the skirt to which Edwards and himself peered upwards.

"Nick! Have some respect, please!"

Cavanagh scolded her friend, visibly shocked over his behaviour. As the inspector and sergeant continued much to the constable's chagrin, the bulge in the crotch of the hosiery the detectives saw could only be made by one thing, something a female is born without.

"Now that's something I never expected to see looking up a lady's skirt!"

Edwards appeared to be a state beyond surprised with a fair portion of bewilderment added. He removed his hat and scratched his head.

"So we now have a murdered transvestite!"

Spencer removed his spectacles and shook his head in disbelief.

"A bloody good one too, by all accounts. Just look at the quality of the clothes and attention to detail with the make-up." The others nodded as Nick spoke.

"Does anyone know when Dr Tyler is due to arrive?"

Spencer spoke, enquiring as to the medic's whereabouts.

"There's an emergency at the Hospital, Tom. A big accident on the motorway, by all accounts. She's helping out."

The DCI nodded.

"Well, the needs of the living exceed those of the ones beyond help."

"So, he's a bufter then?"

All of the other detectives promptly turned towards St John.

"You what?"

No doubt still perturbed from Duncan lifting the skirt of the deceased, Cavanagh snapped at the other sergeant.

"He's obviously a Nancy boy. Wandering aboot in lassie's clothes…"

"Transvestites and crossdressers are mainly straight men, who feel the need to express a part of themselves they normally can't when dressed as a bloke. They are not gay!"

"Errrrh! Men in frocks! I mean, it's not right. As a joke on Telly when Danny La Rue does it, or that clown Dick Emery — fair enough. But a laddie doing dis kicks…" St John shook his head in disbelief.

"Hey, it's quite a turn on you know, a bloke in woman's clothes and underwear. You ought to try it tonight with your wife, like."

Joan gave him a wink and pouted her lips.

"Piss Off, yer whalloper!"

"Children, please!"

The Guv'nor spoke up, putting an end to the bickering.

"St John has a point. We have to keep all lines of enquiry open. Anything and everything."

Begrudgingly, the scouser slowly nodded at the inspector's words.

"Right folks, I'll see you back at the office. We've got initial details, SOCO will forward us the rest later."

The two inspectors wandered off together, with St John scampering after them. Nick could hear them discussing aspects of the four deaths as they made their way back to their own cars.

"Come on, Joan. Let's get you home so you can change and freshen up."

"Yeah, ta."

Sitting at his desk, Duncan read through the inventory of Sam Lambert's personal effects. There was nothing out of the ordinary, typical for a young woman in her twenties. But these were not the belongings of a young woman, leading the detective to pay more in-depth attention to the list. Almost at once, one item stood out. An address book-cum-diary.

"Guv, when will SOCO be finished with Sam Lambert's belongings?"

"Later this afternoon, with a bit of luck. Is there something of interest?"

"Yes. A pocket diary-appointment book."

"I'll take a butcher's when it arrives."

"And it says here he had a small, leather case containing

cigarettes, but does not say which brand."

"Hmmm, might be relevant."

The inspector went to enter his own office, but paused.

"Go find St John, Nick. Go with him to bring in that suspect, Sean Naylor. We've had a call off the neighbour — Naylor is home with his girlfriend."

"Guv."

Picking his coat up, Duncan shrugged his shoulders in a weird apology to Cavanagh. With her hair tied back in pony tail, fresh make-up and clean clothes, she bore a more professional appearance than earlier. The scouser smiled slightly, shaking her head, returning to the paperwork in front of her.

"Joan..."

She looked up from her desk.

"Yes, Sarge..."

"Can we have a word later? About last night..."

Cavanagh seemed rather awkward, repeatedly clicking her biro in her hand.

"Yeah, that's fine."

She gave a small smile, to which Nick patted her on the shoulder.

"Cilla Black!"

Both Duncan and Cavanagh turned to find Edwards leaning out of his office.

"Guv?"

"Go find Rachel, go visit Sam Lambert's residence. Due to the circumstances, the pair of you please be as delicate as you can."

"OK, Guv. Understood." Joan nodded, reaching for her own jacket and handbag.

Sliding into his coat, Duncan made his way through the building to the canteen. Sitting at a table was Sebastian and Dermot. As Nick closed in on the two seated detectives, he could hear the flannel and spiel they were exchanging. They boasted and bragged their proverbials off. Duncan glared at Dermot, but respected what Joan had said last night. Constable Ward glanced back at Nick with a puzzled look.

"*Scotland, the Guv'nor wants us to go collect this Naylor fellow.*"

"*Hassa, come back home?*"

"*Yeah. That nosey parker you found has been in touch. Our suspect has reappeared.*"

With a sick grin St John stood up, climbing into his own jacket. Dermot got to his feet as well.

"*OK, Sarge, let's go get him!*"

The detective constable placed his hand on St John's shoulder, turning him towards the door.

"*Er, Dermot could you please stay here. The Guv'nor wants Sergeant St John and myself to go get this guy.*"

Nick experienced some satisfaction in the disappointment and deflation Ward showed. Sitting down, he picked up one of the mugs on the table, beginning to nurse the dregs of the drink in cold comfort.

"*I'm just nipping to the loo, Sebastian. I'll see you outside.*" The Scotsman headed for the door and nodded, rummaging in his pockets.

Locking himself into one of the cubicles, Duncan sat down on the lid of the toilet. He put his head in his hands, pushing his fingers through his hair.

"*What the fuck happened last night? How the hell did I shag Joan?*"

Nick began to crucify himself mentally. This was turning out to be the worst week of his life. First, the fight in the Locarno toilets, St John rescuing Harvey and himself, followed by last night.

"If I can have sex with a woman so easily, maybe I'm actually bi-sexual. Am I really gay?"

"Am I really gay?"

"Well Nicholas, only you can really answer that question." Duncan held his cap in his hand, stroking the peak and stared at the Royal Navy emblem upon it.

"What I will say though, is please be fully aware of the legality of such a lifestyle. Many men have been incarcerated for such, some prescribed with psychiatric therapy much against their will."

Nick glanced at the chaplain, he knew he could confide in him and he would not be judged nor reported to their commanding officer either.

"Bish, I don't find women attractive sexually. I appreciate a beautiful lady, how she looks, how she might dress, how she walks, but no desire to kiss her or touch her."

"And what about your own gender, Nicholas?"

The warrant officer stared into space, unsure of what to say. He knew some straight men were severe homophobes, even believing all gay men are after anything in trousers. He hoped the chaplain in front of him, Leonard Downing, didn't think that way. At the moment, Mr Downing was more absorbed with dusting dandruff off the black epaulettes on his shoulders, emblazoned with the Cross entwined with an anchor.

"Yes Bish. I fancy men, but not all of them. Only a certain type."

Straight away, Tony leapt into his head. He liked the lean, athletic look. And dark hair, that reminded him of the American actor Tony Curtis. The chaplain swallowed quite obviously. Nick deliberated perhaps he was finding the conversation somewhat uncomfortable.

"How long have you felt like this? Being attracted to men, I mean."

"As long as I can remember. I did not wake up one morning and decide 'From now on, I'll be gay'. I know it's not easy to live life as a homosexual."

"Well, you've answered your own question. You know you're gay. And by the sounds of it quite proud you are." Duncan developed a daft smirk.

"I am, Bish. I've never been ashamed of who I am. I just wish Society would be equally as accepting."

Leonard patted Nick on the shoulder.

"Nicholas, we maybe in the sixties now and many things have changed, becoming quite ordinary. But sadly, for you and many people who feel the same as yourself, nothing really has. In time, I'm sure things will."

"I hope so, Bish. It's horrible having to keep part of yourself secret just to please those who are narrow-minded and don't approve."

"Many, many people can't accept or adapt to anything that isn't traditional and seen as 'normal'. Christ himself suffered such, at the hands of those who didn't understand or did not wish to."

The warrant officer gazed down at his highly polished shoes, his reflection stared back at him deflated and disheartened.

"But I am normal! I'm honest, I work hard, I even work to defend my country!"

"I understand that, but many see it as abnormal two men or two women can have an intimate relationship together."

"So that's my only crime — sleeping with someone of my own gender, and God forbid, falling in love with them?"

The Padre sighed.

"God would want you to fall in love with the right person, find your happiness."

"That's what I want too, Bish. I just find it difficult the Bible does not condone homosexuals, just straight people. 'Go forth and multiply', and all that. You know, 'Those that practice homosexuality will not inherit the Kingdom of God'. My best friend is a woman, I went to school with her, we grew up in the same area, I love her dearly. But I don't want anything physical with her."

"Well, your feelings are what they refer to as 'platonic'."

"Exactly! I want the whole package. To fall in love with someone who I fancy like mad too."

The chaplain smiled, chuckling.

"I think we all want that, Nicholas. And as for what the Bible says, your observations are true, However, there is strong evidence throughout the history of mankind homosexual relationships have always existed. Between the lines in some parts of the Bible, it can be interpreted so."

Duncan smirked to himself.

"I'm just going to carry on, Bish. I don't think people

like myself will ever be truly welcome, sadly. We're doing nothing wrong, we're behaving the same way as everyone, in the most natural way possible. What we get up to in the privacy of our own homes is no one else's business but mine and the man I'm with."

"I'd say you're doing nothing wrong at all. The Bible was written by men hundreds of years ago. Who are they to dictate being intimate with your lover is against the Law?"

Nick chuckled an ironic laugh.

"I think the permissive society needed to change things might never come. There was talk back home a few years ago, I did hear homosexuality would be decriminalised, but it didn't get too far for fear of a public backlash!"

"Well, take comfort in that! All we need is a change of Government and all sorts of matters begin to alter."

"We'll see, Bish. I'll heed your advice. I'll be mindful, careful."

"Nicholas, always be yourself. Never let go of that. By being true to yourself, follow what is in your heart, I'm sure God will lead you to happiness."

Duncan felt great comfort in the Padre's words. He was wonderfully understanding and sympathetic. If only the world had more people like him in it. Glancing down, he noticed the wedding ring he wore.

"Are you married, Bish?"

"Er, yes. I have been for a good twelve years now."

"Is your wife based here in Malta."

"Yes — Moira works here at St Angelo. Why do you ask?"

322

"You've got everything I desire. A long term, loving and supportive relationship, with someone you're attracted to." The chaplain nodded. Nick's words clearly rang true.

"You'll find that too, Nicholas — but please be careful. I don't want to be summoned to your court martial as a character witness."

"I will, Bish."

The warrant officer got to his feet, offering Leonard his hand. The Padre also stood, shaking Duncan's hand warmly.

"I know what I am. For better or worse, I'm gay."

"I'm gay!" Duncan muttered under his breath. Putting matters in perspective, he didn't find Joan sexy, although he could clearly see she was a good-looking woman. There was nothing about her that made him feel he wanted to take her to bed. Nick found he was turned on by a memory from the past of Tony, plus a fantasy of something he'd love to experience with Harvey. He realised nothing of what was buzzing around in his imagination was relating to any female, not just Cavanagh.

Catching up with St John in the car park, Nick caught the Scotsman taking a final couple of draws on his cigarette, before dropping it onto the tarmac and grinding it in with his foot to extinguish it.

"Ready, Golden Bollocks?"

"Yeah, let's get this done."

"We'll take ma motor. Yer mobile country house is fa too showy for an unmarked cop car."

"Beauty is in the eye of the beholder, and all that Sebastian." Nick gave his colleague a smarmy smirk.

"Besides, isn't it nicer to live life with a sense of style."

St John snorted sarcastically.

"Ever heard o' being inconspicuous?"

The Scottish Sergeant wandered towards a nearby Hillman Hunter, finished in a dreary grey. It was extremely inconspicuous. Nick thought Sebastian must have immense difficulty finding it when parking it. Climbing inside, Duncan's opinion of the car did not change, as he took in the sparce interior.

"I see no expense was spared in here when it was made."

"Piss Off! Good Scottish car, this. Ma Uncle works a' Linwood."

Duncan shook his head, chuckling. Sebastian's comment made it sound as though the main reason he owned the car was out of patriotism!

As they made their way out of the city centre, Nick began to notice the Scotsman held no indifference towards him, save for the usual irritating inane banter. *"Surely by now he'd be busting a gut to embarrass and humiliate me,"* he pondered. *"Only one way to find out…"* He swallowed hard, as his mouth went drier and drier.

"Thanks for the other night, Sebastian. It's great to have a mate who'll cover your back."

St John said nothing for a few moments, concentrating on driving.

"I'm nae gonna see a workmate have his heed caved in by some munter. Especially as yous just fought his bestie off."

"Yeah, they were picking on that barrister, Harvey Wiseman."

"Aye, I saw."

St John went quiet again, which only fuelled Duncan's anxiety further.

"I just wanted to say, I appreciate what you did."

"Nay worries. Juss next time, tell yer boyfriend t' be more careful wi' da company he keeps."

Nick couldn't help himself. He twisted in his seat in an instant to face the Scottish Detective.

"Boyfriend?"

"Aye, yer boyfriend. I saw yous twos cuddlin' anna winchin', juss before that jakey hit you."

Duncan didn't know what to say. His worst fears had been confirmed, but how come St John hadn't decided to tell anybody?

"What yous gets up to in yer life off duty is yer own business."

"Does seeing two men kissing bother you?"

Sebastian burst out laughing.

"Nahh! Means there's more women oot there fa us straight guys! Besides, ma kid sister is livin' with a lassie in Edinburgh. She's never said, but I know she's gay."

Not knowing what to say, Nick stared down at his feet. St John continued.

"Yer like men — big deal. I like women — big deal." Nick was astonished. He never in a million years expected the brash, lairy Scotsman to be this open-minded. He expected Sebastian to be as homophobic as they come, oozing with prejudice and intolerance. *"Just shows, you can never judge a book by its cover,"* he spun in his mind.

"Of all people, I never would've believed you'd be this liberal in your thinking."

"I donna care whose yer sleep wi', Golden Bollocks. As long as it's not ma wifey!"

"You can sleep easy that'll never happen."

Both men chuckled.

"Yous a good copper, Nick. That's all dat matters. But if yous make it to Inspector before us, I'll be seriously pissed off!"

This astonished Duncan as well. He'd never received any praise from St John in all the years he'd worked alongside him. A huge, broad smile spread across his face.

"Anna wipe da smirk off yer chops. It dunnae suit yer."

The two detectives glanced at one another, bursting out laughing.

Turning onto a housing estate after the Coventry Rugby Club ground, St John drove to the relevant address. Getting out of the car, the two policemen approached a house.

"Ready?"

Nick nodded to the Scotsman he was. With warrant card in one hand ready, Sebastian knocked the door firmly. After a brief silence, a lock reluctantly slid to and the heavy wooden door opened. A rather thick set young man in his early twenties poked his face into the opening, his mop of blonde hair slightly obscuring his vision.

"Hello..."

St John offered his open warrant card forwards.

"Detective Sergeant Sebastian St—"

The blonde lad vanished back inside the house in a flash, attempting to slam the door shut. St John wedged his foot in the door, then shoved it wide open as the young man vanished.

"Get round da back, quick!"

The Scottish sergeant dashed inside, while Duncan leapt over a small brick wall to the side of the front door and ran through the passage between the houses. Exiting back into the daylight, the detective sprinted to the end of the alley, turning hard left at the end. The old wooden back gate to the property flew open. Just as Nick approached, the chunky young man burst out of the garden, to which Duncan partially tripped him and gave him a shove for good measure. Not expecting the physical contact-cum-collision, he fell into the dirt.

Moments later, St John emerged out of the same back gate. He stood over the blonde-haired man, catching his breath. Stooping down, the Glaswegian grabbed him by the collar of his jumper, wrenching him back to his feet, before pinning him against a wall. Duncan found his own warrant card, stuffing it in the young man's face.

"Sean Naylor?"

"Yea...Yes!"

Naylor struggled to speak, trying to remove St John's hands pulled tight up against his chin.

"Detective Sergeant Nicholas Duncan, Warwickshire Police. The man strangling you is Detective Sergeant Sebastian St John."

"I can't breathe!"

Naylor continued to grasp at the hands holding him in place, struggling for breath.

"Haud yer wheesht! If yous hadnae ran, I wouldna be doing dis!"

"We want to have a little chat."

"Look, I can explain — about the stuff that's gone missing at work..."

Both detectives stared at the young man, then at each other. Both were completely baffled by his statement.

"What the fuck is going on, Sean?"

All three men turned at the sound of a female voice with a strong Chinese accent. Finding a black-haired twenty-something of Far Eastern origin — who resembled Zhen Wheng exactly. Nick had no idea how St John felt, but the stereotypical phrases of *'seeing a ghost'* and *'he couldn't believe his eyes'* didn't even scratch the surface. What he saw just did not compute.

"Jesus Fuckin' Christ!"

Duncan managed to find his voice and be more professional, after St John's blasphemy.

"Miss Wheng?"

"Yes. Is there a problem?"

Back at Little Park Street, St John escorted Sean to an interview room, while Duncan informed the Guv'nor of proceedings. Edwards removed his spectacles, placing them carefully on his desk. He rubbed his face with both hands.

"So, he admits to stealing goods from the shop, and his girlfriend is the spit of the dead girl we found in the rubbish at the Zoo!"

"Yes Guv. His house is full of stolen goods, St John said."

"What about the girl?"

"Cavanagh is speaking with her now. She claims to have the same surname as the deceased."

Right on cue, the Scouse Constable appeared in the open-door way, knocking the door twice out of courtesy.

"Ahhh! The very lady! Have you anything to share with us?" Edwards perked up at the sight of the junior detective.

"Yes, Guv. The young lady is Xiu Wheng, her ID confirms. She is the deceased's twin sister. They were both studying at the same University. The liaison officer is with her now, as we've informed her of the situation with her sister."

Nick thought out loud, something no one had considered

as yet.

"Could she be a suspect? Performed the murders with Naylor? Remember, we are looking for two people."

The Guv'nor rocked back in his chair, contemplating.

"Possibly. Find out her whereabouts for the last few weeks."

"She's just come back from a break with Naylor. They'd been up in Skeggy, like."

Duncan sniggered. *"Not Skeg-Vegas, Skegness!"*

"Yeah, the one and the same."

"Well, find out what you can. Like, is this seaside trip 'real' or B.S. And anything about this Sean Naylor. He'll be charged over his liberation of his employer's property, but he's also definitely a suspect."

Both Duncan and Cavanagh nodded as Edwards spoke.

"How did you and Rachel get on at the Sam Lambert visit?"

Joan stepped into the inspector's office, closing the door behind her.

"Rachel hasn't been in today, Guv. I took a stand-in FLO with me, WPC Rubeen Panesar."

Edwards and Duncan gave the Liverpudlian puzzled glances.

"Is she off sick?"

"She wasn't at home earlier when I went back. I assumed she was on duty."

The Inspector pulled his pondering face once again.

"Check with downstairs. Is she on leave today, or have they heard anything?"

"Guv."

"What did you find out visiting Sam Lambert's address?"

329

"Oh, yeah. No answer at the house, but the next-door neighbour gave us details of his girlfriend. And Ruby, the temporary liaison pointed out this — the young man does match the details of the missing persons' report we received early last week. Age, height, race, but not the wearing women's clothes bit."

"Interesting..."

Nick now began to ponder himself, rubbing his chin. Dramatically, the sergeant had a light bulb moment. He clicked his fingers, looking awfully pleased.

"We'll have contact details of the family who placed the misper report!"

"Very true, Nick. Get on it!"

The phone rang on Edwards' desk, interrupting him. The inspector picked it up.

"D.I Edwards. OK, thank you."

Returning the handset to its cradle, he addressed the two detectives.

"Looks like Naylor's duty solicitor has arrived. Nick, go interview him with Sebastian. Cilla, take this Rubeen with you and have a lengthy chat with the Chinese girl."

"OK Guv."

Duncan and Cavanagh spoke in unison and headed for the door. The sergeant paused, and turned towards the inspector.

"It's just occurred to me, Guv. Those photos we have of Zhen Wheng..."

"Yes, Nick..."

"Are they actually of Zhen, or Xiu?"

"Oh, yeah!" Cavanagh at once saw Duncan's point.

"And more to the point, who was actually murdered, and who did the killer think they were killing?"

"This is starting to give me a headache."

Edwards folded his arms on top of his head, the sergeant's words difficult for him to comprehend.

Finding some fresh interview scribe sheets. Duncan sprinted downstairs. St John was loitering near the custody suite, beginning to fill his own paperwork.

"Are yer ready, Golden Bollocks?"

"Yeah, let's see if our man with sticky fingers also has a taste for throttling women."

"Possibly. Did yer see size o' his dabs?"

"Yeah, like pit shovels. One swipe from them would tear your face off. Has he said much since we brought him in?"

"Nae much. Jus confirmed his name, address and straight away asked for a brief."

Duty Sergeant Rita Jones approached the two detectives, handing the Scotsman a typed sheet of paper.

"Sebastian, here's the inventory of the goods found in the Naylor residence."

"Ta muchly."

Both detectives scanned the list, which contained a fair cross-section of the items British Home Stores sold. Judging by the number of kettles and toasters Naylor had acquired, he must have had a 'fence' or 'outlet' to move them on.

"Would yous jus looka dat! An entire china dinner service!"

St John laughed. Nick chuckled too, seeing the silly side. That was until he caught a glimpse of something he did not expect.

In the corner of his eye, Duncan could see a man in a suit standing behind the uniformed sergeant. He suddenly realised who it was — he recognised the curly brown hair, the slight body frame, the suave just so suit. Slowly looking up from the list of stolen goods, he stared straight at Harvey. The two men gawped at one another, aghast. Duncan virtually froze to the spot.

"This is Sean Naylor's legal representative, the duty solicitor Harvey Wiseman from Bartholomew and Wiseman."

Nick could see Sebastian was now entering into a game of visual tennis, glancing at Harvey than him in turn.

"Jussa moment, Mr Wiseman."

"Certainly, Sergeant," Harvey replied politely.

St John pushed the other detective along the corridor, and into an empty side room. Quickly, he closed the door behind them.

"Nick, yer canna come into dis interview, wha wiv him on da other side o' table!"

Duncan began to regain his composure.

"Yeah, you're right."

He paced the room for a few moments, thinking fast.

"If I go in there, it'll potentially compromise any case we have against Naylor."

"Woz yer gonna do?"

"I don't know."

Nick continued to pace to-and-fro. Then, an idea leapt into his head.

"I'll tell the Guv'nor it would be good for Joan to be in with you, especially as Naylor is going to be charged for the stolen goods at the very least, and I can speak with the Chinese girl. Cavanagh has already spoke with her once. It'll throw both Naylor and his girlfriend having different detectives questioning them. We can hopefully glean if they are the killer, and accomplice we're after."

St John smiled too, nodding in agreement.

"*Gaun yersel! Ask the Guv. Hees should agree.*"

Duncan sprinted back upstairs to put his idea to the inspector, bursting into Edwards' office only to find him with the DCI. "*Guv, Sir, I have a suggestion...*"

All the detectives did establish was circumstantial at best. Once the interviews had been concluded, the team crowded around the incident desk skim-reading the transcripts.

"*Hmmm, nothing from Naylor looks conclusive at all,*" Spencer pondered.

"*No, Sir. He freely admits he knew Arosha Rana and Wendy Kroy, obviously Zhen Wheng, but claims to have never met or heard of Sam Lambert. Seems to be blagging when Wendy Kroy's name was mentioned. More to that than meets the eye. Possibly an ex, like?*" Cavanagh stated out loud what the others were quickly reading.

Duncan scanned over the interview minutes, keen to see for himself if there was anything that appeared unusual or note-worthy. In the corner of his eye, he caught sight of the acting FLO, a young Asian woman.

"*Come over here, Ruby. Take a look at this with the rest of us.*"

"*Thank you, Sir. But I'm not a detective — how can I help?*"

"*There's no need to be so formal. Call me 'Sarge' or 'Nick'.*" Edwards glanced up from the information in front of him, giving the WPC a welcoming smile.

"*The more the merrier, young lady. An extra pair of eyes is always useful. You might see something everyone else has missed.*"

The WPC stepped forward, beginning to read the transcripts herself.

"I didn't realise they let her sort onto the Force. Still, it keeps the natives happy I guess."

"Dermot! Shut your face! Ruby is a police officer exactly the same as you, same rank as you. If you've got a problem with her, take it up with me or the Guv'nor!"

The entire CID office fell silent as Duncan exploded. Ward sloped off out of the room, tail firmly between his legs.

"Sorry Ruby."

"It's all right, Sarge. Thank you."

"Nicholas, did you glean anything from the surviving Miss Wheng?" Spencer enquired as he cleaned out the thumb-size bowl at the end of his pipe.

"Yes, Sir. She's a student at the University of Warwick studying the same course as her twin. She said she met Naylor roughly eight months ago in a nightclub in the city centre, and does admit to selling on some of Naylor's stolen goods to students on campus."

"What about her sister?"

Duncan skim-read his own handwriting upon the transcript.

"Xiu says she hadn't seen her sister since the start of the Easter break, about twelve days ago. She's been staying at Naylor's address since."

"Can anyone collaborate this?"

"I guess the neighbour St John spoke with might help, plus speaking with the Warden at the Halls of Residence may well shed some light on her movements on campus."

"Let's keep an eye on this Sean Naylor and girlfriend. My gut feeling is we've found our killers."

Dermot breezed back into the office, carrying a large brown envelope like a trophy in front of him.

"Info and photos from SOCO about Sam Lambert."

Edwards took the package, removed the contents and spread them out over a nearby empty desk.

"Take a good look, Ladies and Germs."

The group of detectives browsed through the paperwork, which gave full details of how and where Sam's body was found, plus the condition he was in upon discovery. Duncan studied the photographs, searching for anything that did not immediately grab his attention at the crime scene earlier. Then, he saw it.

Quickly, Nick spun over to the noticeboard, removed the pic of Zhen with a mystery brunette. Returning to the new photos, he placed the pic from the notice board next to an image of Sam Lambert's face.

"I'd say these two are one and the same person!"

The other detectives rapidly formed a scrum around the two pictures.

"Fuck me! Golden Bollocks, yer right!"

"Are Naylor and Miss Wheng still in the building?" Spencer spoke more professionally, but above all poignantly.

"Xiu was let out the front after I'd finished interviewing her. Naylor may still be in the custody suite, as he was being charged."

"Well, quickly! Cilla, take Ruby downstairs pronto and see it you can find them!" Edwards became quite excitable and agitated as he spoke.

Cavanagh groaned. *"OK, Guv. Come on, Ruby."*

The scouser wandered off, muttering under her breath with the Indian Constable in tow.

"Right, the rest of you check for any other similarities." The inspector urged his team on, eager for more breakthroughs.

With Joan out of the room, Duncan decided to have a private word with the chief Inspector.

"Sir, there's a matter I feel you need to be made aware of."

Spencer gave the sergeant an intrigued gaze.

"And what might that be, Nicholas?"

Nick gently steered the senior detective away and out of earshot of the others.

"Sir, I just wanted you to know of something I learnt yesterday evening. There appears to be a situation between DC Dermot Ward and WDC Joan Cavanagh."

"Go on..."

"From what Joan has told me, they went out for a date, but it didn't end well. Dermot scared her coming on too heavy."

The DCI placed his pipe in his mouth unlit, pondering upon the words he was listening to.

"So, you're saying there could be some animosity between the two?"

"It's a possibility, Sir."

"Thank you for keeping me in the loop, Sergeant."

"I didn't want anything to jeopardise the investigation."

"Oh, I'm sure it won't come to that. I know you're close to WDC Cavanagh, as you work together frequently, so naturally you're worried about your friend. But this 'animosity' could just be a storm in a teacup, it could be something out of nothing. People do cry wolf when they're in a situation they don't want."

"I saw how upset she was afterwards, so whatever happened she did not take well."

Spencer removed his spectacles, and began to polish them with his handkerchief.

"Nicholas, in my experience of such a situation, it's nowhere near as bad as it seems."

"But Sir—"

The Chief Inspector raised his hand.

"I'll make a mental note of what you've told me, it won't be forgotten, but for now let's leave things be."

"Sir."

Nick was dis-satisfied with Spencer's response to the matter, to the point it left a nasty taste in his mouth. He assumed the DCI would take the matter more seriously. It was indicative of the senior officer's generation, problems women had, were dismissed or belittled.

The Chief Inspector returned to the group examining the SOCO paperwork, just as Joan and Ruby reappeared.

"Guv, they've gone. Naylor has been released on conditional bail. His brief made sure of that apparently, as it was his first offence."

Edwards stared in Cavanagh's direction, was about to speak but Spencer beat him to the punch.

"Let them stew overnight. We'll speak with them tomorrow. Put a car nearby to watch, though. I still feel Naylor hasn't told us everything, especially his personal relationship with Wendy Kroy."

"OK, Sir."

As Cavanagh returned to her own desk and went straight on the phone, Duncan began to check for any other links between the murdered people, as Edwards had asked. At random, he selected the audition manifest from the theatre. It took him a few moments to realise Ruby was alongside him, scanning the list as well.

"What are we looking for, Sir... er... Sarge?"

"Further links to each of the people who have been killed. The three dead women are on here, I'm just double-checking if Xiu Wheng and/or Sam Lambert is on here as well."

He gradually read through the list, when Ruby pointed out something she'd noticed.

"There! Surname 'Wheng'!"

Nick studied what she was pointing at.

"Well spotted, Ruby. But that's one of the deceased — Zhen Wheng."

"Oh..."

The young Indian woman was somewhat deflated. Duncan nudged her arm slightly.

"Keep looking, Ruby. It's highly unusual to find what you're after straight away."

The two police officers continued to scour the handwritten list. Nothing caught their attention. At least, not to the casual observer.

"Look, there!"

The Sergeant pointed at a name on the sheet of paper. Ruby read it out loud, slightly mystified.

"Mandy Lamb?"

"Yes! Think about it!"

Cavanagh repeated the name again.

"Mandy Lamb? What are you on about, Nick?"

"Sam Lambert was a transvestite as we know, but what about if he was a drag artist too. 'Mandy Lamb' may well be a stage name. 'Mandy' is a derivative of 'Samantha'. The

338

surname is quite obvious."

The group of detectives nodded as one. Duncan's reasoning made sense.

"I gets it, but a bit tenuous, Golden Bollocks."

St John pulled a bemused face, not entirely convinced.

"Thing is Scotland, some of the most tenuous reasons and assumptions turn out to be true."

"And here's another similarity / coincidence, call it what you will..."

Edwards drew everyone's attention to the manifest of Sam Lambert's personal effects.

"A box of matches, branded 'Swanswell Tavern'. I think we need to pay that pub a visit." The inspector stared straight at Duncan. *"Oh, those fags in Sam Lambert's belongings, Nick..."*

"Yes, Guv..."

"Chunghwa! Chinese! Same as the ones found in Zhen's personal effects."

"That confirms who's in that pic!"

The Guv'nor made some connection lines and markers on the noticeboard.

"But first, today's prizes for our lucky winners. St John, Ward — go to Sam Lambert's girlfriend's address and the address of the person or persons who made the misper report, find out what you can. Take Ruby with you. Duncan, Cavanagh — go back to the theatre, ask that casting director about Sam Lambert and Mandy Lamb. Afterwards, go to that pub."

The detectives nodded.

Cavanagh coughed in a manner to gain attention, as to clear her throat.

"Yes, Cilla..."

"Er, I think the Swanswell has had its licence suspended for a few days, so won't be open, Guv."

"Hmmm, well give it a try. Or some of you will be going back in the morning!"

"Guv."

"Alison McLeod is going to start to think you want to ask her out on a date at this rate. It'll be the third time we've spoken with her!"

Duncan shook his head and chuckled at Cavanagh's words, rummaging for his keys as he strolled across the car park.

"Nick! Sarge, can I have a word?"

The Detective glanced over his shoulder to find Dermot walking briskly to catch up. Duncan was still annoyed with the constable over his racist comments about Ruby.

"What's the matter, Dermot?"

Ward shuffled closer, reaching inside his jacket he retrieved an ageing and battered leather cigarette case. Opening the tobacco holder, he offered it to his superior. *"Perhaps a peace offering,"* Nick considered. Not one to refuse a smoke, he accepted.

"Mate, could you help me with my sergeant application. Remember, you said you would..."

Placing the tobacco between his lips, Dermot quickly did same, followed by producing a box of matches from a different pocket. Striking one, he cupped his hands as he offered Duncan first use of the flame. As Nick drew on his now ignited cigarette, he couldn't help but notice the branding on the matchbox — 'The Swanswell Tavern'.

"Yes, Dermot. When we're not quite so busy I'll give you

a few pointers and tips." It was then Duncan noticed the flavour of the tobacco. It was different to his own Park Drive but one he had tried recently. The aroma and taste were more than familiar. Gazing down at the cigarette between his fingers, he straight away saw the gold band around the brown filter. Rolling the cigarette within his fingertips, he knew what he was going to see, the American manufacturer's name printed just above the filter.

"One tip I will give you though, is keep remarks like those you made earlier to yourself."

"I was only saying it as I saw it, Nick."

"That's exactly the sort of thing you should keep to yourself, let alone think it at all! How do you expect to gain promotion if you're being derogatory and disrespectful to fellow officers?"

Ward took a couple of draws on his own cigarette, giving the sergeant a look that showed his defiance and belief in his out-dated views and opinions.

St John suddenly emerged out of the building, slapping the detective constable on the back.

"Are yer ready, Laddie?"

Dermot dropped his cigarette onto the tarmac, and rubbed it into the ground underneath his right foot.

"Yes, Sarge."

Duncan watched the two detectives walk towards Ward's car, a racing green Mk II Triumph 2500, and climb inside. Moments later, Ruby dashed out of the station, and clambered into the rear of Ward's pride and joy. They departed at speed in a cloud of burning rubber and noise. *"What a complete tit he is,"* Nick uttered to himself, as the constable was clearly showing off.

Taking a few steps towards his car, the sergeant suddenly noticed drops of oil on the tarmac. He glanced at Dermot's car as it vanished off into the city, noticing the small patch of oil it left as it had stood still. *"Hmmm..."* the detective began to ponder.

"What's the matter with that Gobshite?"

Cavanagh's potty-mouth snapped him out of his deliberating. *"He's really managed to piss her off,"* Nick thought to himself.

"Oh, nothing much. He wants me to help him with his application to become a sergeant."

Climbing into his car, Duncan started the engine. The eight-track player began broadcasting the contents of the cartridge that had been inserted into it — on this occasion The Everly Brothers. Ignoring the music, the constable continued.

"Sergeant? How he behaves and the bollocks he says, he'll be lucky to remain a detective!"

"He first tried for promotion the same time I applied."

"Sounds to me someone had a huge amount of common sense. I can't imagine that meff being any use as a sergeant. I bet he's the sort that would let having a position of authority go to his head!"

Duncan negotiated the traffic in the city centre, allowing Cavanagh to vent off her anger and frustration. *"Might prove to be therapeutic for her,"* he considered.

"Personally, I'm amazed he was considered suitable for CID! How the wanker ever made the grade to become a P.C is beyond me!"

Nick tried not to giggle, but nevertheless entirely agreed with the Merseysider.

Arriving outside the theatre once again, Duncan pulled a

copy of the picture of Sam Lambert with Zhen Wheng out of his pocket.

"Let's see if a photo can help jog people's memories and provide us with something we don't already know."

Joan nodded, as they both stepped out of the bronze Alvis. Gazing up at the side of the theatre, the sergeant was confronted again with the poster advertising the David Bowie concert.

"Oh, bollocks! I really need to sort those tickets out."

CHAPTER TEN
THURSDAY APRIL 26th 1973

It always appeared no one cared, or had bothered for an age. Nick dropped to his knees, beginning to pick the weeds and remove the debris that had blown onto his father's grave. Duncan took his handkerchief from his pocket, starting to polish the tombstone, giving extra attention to his dad's name. He stroked the gold inlayed letters on the anthracite-coloured marble that spelt out *'Robert John Duncan'*.

"I thought I'd find you here."

The detective gazed upwards at the sound of the voice he recognised instantly, finding Alex standing close by.

"He'd have been seventy today. We'd have had a huge party — he'd have hated it — we'd have taken him home to watch him open his presents, to which he'd moan we'd all spent too much and shouldn't have bothered. Then if someone had given him a box of those sweets he loved, he'd hide them in his Hi-Fi cabinet, and only ever let you have just one. And that was if you were really, really lucky!"

Alex crouched down next to his brother, placing a corsage of white lilies next to a collection of ivory roses. He placed his arm around the policeman.

"Weren't lilies Dad's favourite?"

"No, it was roses."

Nick leaned his head on his brother's shoulder. The two

men begun to chuckle.

"*I miss him so much, Alex.*"

"*Me too, mate. All the time.*"

"*Do you think he watches us?*"

"*I bloody well hope not! Do you want Dad at the end of the bed staring at you when you're having some sexy time?*"

The policeman screwed up his face at the mental image, laughing at the same time. Despite his older brother being a right royal pain in the derriere at the best of times, he never ceased to cheer him up.

Time seemed to stand still as the two brothers sat on the well-kept turf next to their father's resting place, an arm around each other's shoulders.

"*When you think of Dad, what's the first thing you think of?*"

"*I remember when we went on holiday to Great Yarmouth, and we all stayed in one of those basic static caravans.*"

Nick's face lit up at the memory.

"*Oh, yeah! It took a sodding age to get there in the Lea Francis. And remember that picnic in the dunes Mum took us all on, 'cause it was too breezy to sit on the open sand? Then in the middle of it, Dad chased us down onto the beach!*"

"*Yeah! I'd forgotten about that. Didn't Dad leap off quite a high dune, and 'bombed' into the soft sand below. He made a massive crater!*"

"*Yes, he did!*"

The policeman's eyes began to fill up with tears but not in sadness, in joy of the wonderful time he' had with his family as an adolescent. Nick realised it just wasn't him that was feeling a lump in his throat, he became aware Alex was somewhat sniffily as well.

"Come on, mate. Dad wouldn't want us sitting here like this."

Alex wiped his nose on his cuff.

"No, Nick. You're right."

Something caught the Sergeant's attention a few hundred yards away. In the corner of his eye, he was convinced he saw someone in the dark blue uniform of a copper. He turned briefly towards the person, and for a fraction of a second. could have sworn it was his father, smiling back at him. As he blinked, the person vanished. Nick rubbed his eyes, and began scanning the cemetery. There was no one there. He pondered should he tell his brother what he was certain he'd just seen. He thought better of it.

"Come on, Alex. Let's make a move."

Getting to his feet, he pulled his brother up from the grass. They wandered back to the church car park, a strange air of mixed emotions hanging over them both.

"Are you going round Mum's later?"

"Yeah, after I've taken the girls to Brownies."

"Fish and chips?"

"Oh, go on!"

The two brothers climbed into their respective cars, and went their separate ways.

Heading towards the city centre, the detective steered with one hand as he lit his cigarette. Taking a long, deep draw on the tobacco, he exhaled the vapours out of the open window. The nicotine hit eased his mental state. With the confusing progress of the multiple-murder enquires, wanting to tell his mother about himself, the aching he felt deep within himself about Dad, plus what happened in bed the other night with Joan he really didn't need any more stress in his life. Nick knew he had to get his head into the right place, he'd be expected to be on the ball. *"Sorry Dad, I'll toast you later when I'm with Mum."*

Duncan was aware of an uneasy feeling growing at the prospect of seeing Joan shortly. They'd had an awkward chat last night after they finished their duties, where they'd both been completely frank and honest with one another. Cavanagh had admitted she found him attractive, not just physically either. Nick had come clean as tactfully as possible but knew his words would have been really painful to hear. He did not feel or see her in the same light — just a friend, nothing more. They both admitted in many aspects they were perfect for each other. But who wants to be stuck in a platonic relationship, when the only time anything physical would happen was after too much alcohol at Christmas, birthdays and the occasional Royal Wedding? He thought she appeared to understand. The scouser knew he was homosexual, he had to uncomfortably explain he was thinking of men when he was inside her. It was one of those things that shouldn't happen. Duncan couldn't get the image out of his mind of how disappointed and deflated Cavanagh was.

"I caused that. How can I put it right?"

A short while later, Nick arrived at Little Park Street. Duncan flopped into the chair at his desk just as Edwards appeared to hold the daily briefing.

"Right Boys and Girls, let's have the latest — Sebastian?"

The Scotsman rummaged amongst the paperwork on his desk, eventually finding his notebook.

"Er, well wees visited da address of Sam Lambert's family. Turns oot, he lived wi' hees girlfriend at da place Cavanagh visited yesterday. He wenna missun da weekend befa Easter."

347

"How did his family take the circumstances he was found?"

From the doorway a male voice enquired. Without seeing the senior detective, everyone knew it was Chief Inspector Spencer.

"Hees parents' were shocked, very upset. Hees Dad didna wanna hear wha we had ter say. I left Ruby with them while I spoke with da girlfriend."

"Did she know anything, Sebastian?"

Spencer had now entered the office, now standing shoulder-to-shoulder with Edwards at the front.

"She said she knew Sam wore women's clothes, but as far as she was aware he never wena oot wearing them."

"She knew he dressed up?"

"Aye, tha's wha she said."

"I wonder how often he was venturing out dressed up?"

Nick pondered out loud, but could see by the reaction of others in the room nodding, it was a valid question.

"How about you, Mr Duncan — what have you found out?"

Spencer welcomed the sergeant to share his findings.

"Well, the theatre director — Alison McLeod — implies she has a rather vague recollection of 'Mandy Lamb', and can't be certain that's Sam / Mandy in the pic we showed her."

"Hmmm, I think I would've remembered her, or him."

"She said Guv, that she'd seen and met so many young women recently through the auditions, I quote 'One face merges in with the next'."

Spencer once again puffed away on his pipe with added vigour, more resembling an ocean liner at sea sailing full tilt.

"Seems reasonable. I pass so many different faces in

uniform within this building, I haven't a clue who is new and who's been on the Force for years."

Edwards chuckled a wry laugh.

"You'd better be on the ball with faces, Tom. I got word the people from the Chinese Embassy will be here later."

The Chief Inspector snorted, in a way that was clearly supressing a laugh.

"Don't you worry about that, Albert. The Super and myself will be meeting with the representatives."

"Right then ladies and germs, we've received the post mortem report for Sam Lambert."

Edwards held a file aloft.

"Dr Tyler's assistant, Dr Basra conducted the examination. He can confirm the cause of death to be exactly the same as the three other women. The family will officially identify his body later today. Also, looking through Sam Lambert's pocket diary found in his personal effects, he had marked the same day within it as the audition at the theatre. As you just heard from Sergeant Duncan, the casting director has confirmed he did attend — that we know. There's also a mysterious final entry, which we're looking into. Right, today's duties. Firstly, housekeeping — write up and add all new info to the incident desk, amend the noticeboard."

A groan was emitted by someone. Nick noticed the look on Dermot's face and his slovenly body language, and guessed it was him. He shook his head in disbelief.

"Secondly," the Inspector continued, *"Some people's morbid curiosity is obviously getting the better of them. We're receiving reports of members of the good old British public visiting the areas where we found the deceased. Bad news travels fast, so please be extra vigilant and on your guard."*

He took a drink from a mug the nearby Ruby was nursing. The Indian WPC looked on somewhat aghast at her beverage being pilfered.

"Thirdly, we need some of you to pay a few visits. Nick, go to Sean Naylor's home. Now he's had overnight to stew in his juices, give him a bit of a grilling about Sam Lambert. His girlfriend's sister knew him, so it's possible he did too."

"Guv."

Duncan acknowledged the inspector, gesturing at Cavanagh.

"Yes! Take Cilla Black with you, if you want her to hold your hand!"

"Oi!" The Liverpudlian scowled at both Duncan and the Guv'nor in turn.

"Sebastian, go to the Swanswell Tavern. Take some of the pictures of the dead girls — oh, and Sam Lambert — with you. See what you can find. Take Dermot with you."

Edwards had barely finished his request, when Detective Constable Ward burst with opposition.

"Go to a poofter's pub! Guv, please!"

"Is there a problem, Dermot?"

"Guv, do we have to?"

"Yes. I'm not asking you, I'm telling you. Is there an issue?"

"No, there isn't. But..."

"But what?"

"Can't Sergeant Duncan go instead? Sergeant St John has interviewed Naylor and I've spoken with his girlfriend."

The inspector paused for a second, contemplating Dermot's words.

"Hmmm, true. Yeah, go with that. St John, go to Naylor's

— be sure to scare the shit out of him, he might open up and blab if he's cornered. Nick, go to the pub. Take Joan with you."

"OK Guv."

Unintentionally, he caught Sebastian's gaze. He nodded briefly towards him, to which the Scotsman replied with a knowing wink.

As the detectives began to get to their feet, Edwards raised his voice to be heard over the hussle and bussle.

"People! Has anyone heard anything of Rachel?"

Ruby replied, having to raise her own voice as well.

"No Sir. She didn't turn in. I think someone said she might still be off sick."

The senior detective nodded.

"Miss Panesar, could you follow me, please. I'll need your liaison expertise when the Chinese party arrive."

Spencer beckoned the WPC to follow him, to which she obliged, scampering along in the DCI's wake.

Nick leaned towards Joan, whispering in her ear.

"Have you heard anything of Rachel?"

"Nah, nothing. I heard Niamh come home this morning, but seen nothing of Rach."

Duncan still found this rather odd. A dedicated and eager young policewoman who seemed to live for her job doesn't turn in for her shift. That was baffling. But as he recalled, Cavanagh did say last night when they spoke after resolving their own situation, Rachel's grandmother was in ill health. Nick contemplated if his Mum's health took a turn for the worse, work would be the last thing on his mind. That's where she was.

"Have you ever been in here, Nick?"

"Oi! Just because I'm gay doesn't mean I'll stereotypically frequent a gay pub!"

"Soz I spoke!"

Duncan parked his Alvis around the back of the Swanswell Tavern, as a dray lorry unloaded its boozy cargo into the cellar of the public house. The huge truck took up most of the confined car park, with little space for anything else.

"Actually, yes. I have been in here a few times for the occasional sherbet."

Cavanagh burst out laughing.

"I have too. A few times with Niamh."

"Careful! They'll think you two are an item!"

"Bollocks!"

"And for a change, could you please refrain from chatting up the blokes we're questioning."

The Scouser reacted such, Nick was absolutely certain she was in no mood for daft banter.

"I fuckin' well do not!"

"Er, Oliver Richmond, every time we visit the theatre."

Joan's hostility ceased.

"Well, we get on. And I think he's quite cute, like."

"No shit, Sherlock! I reckon you have a soft spot for Mr Oliver!"

Cavanagh began to blush.

"Shut yer face! I bet you feel the same when you see that solicitor."

The Sergeant grinned broadly. She was absolutely right. Joan gave him a smarmy smirk and got out of the car.

Strolling around to the front of the pub, the two detectives found the main door firmly locked. However, music could clearly be heard inside, someone crucifying the Supremes' song *'Baby Love'*.

"Let's try round the back. There was that dray lorry delivering."

Making their way past the truck, parked in a manner it seemed to have *'landed'* where it was, the police officers walked straight into the landlord of the Swanswell. Wilton Anderson stared at the two detectives intently, particularly Duncan. He even fluttered his eye-lashes and smirked at the sergeant.

"What do you want now?"

"Can we come in please, Will? Hopefully you can help us with a few things."

Anderson eyed Duncan and Cavanagh with the height of irritation, his attitude gradually changing.

"You'd best come inside, then."

Squeezing past the open cellar hatch and dray lorry crew depositing their delivery, they followed Will into the pub. The publican had a dainty, somewhat effeminate gait, dressed in rich purple and deep pink satin shirt and fitted flares. Nick was of the feeling if his trousers were any more fitted around his old man and backside, he'd be arresting him for gross indecency.

"If this visit is about the twats dealing pills and poppers in here, that's been dealt with."

"Glad to hear it."

The interior of the pub had the all too familiar fragrance only a public house could possess — stale beer, old tobacco smoke and sour smell of stagnant vomit. Here, he could see the origin of all the racket. A drag act going through their paces. The singer was now attempting Dusty Springfield's famous hit, *'I*

Only Want To be With You'.

"For fuck's sake, Barry. Put some balls into it!"

Will gestured at the singer, who paused from singing momentarily to give the landlord a two-fingered 'V' salute. Sitting down at a table away from the small stage area, the detectives joined the host.

"I'm not here to talk about the drug bust the other month, I'm here to talk about those people who were killed recently."

Cavanagh reached into her handbag, withdrawing a selection of photos of the deceased. Will picked them up, looking through them.

"This is Detective Constable Joan Cavanagh, Will. Joan, this is Wilton Anderson, landlord of this dive."

"Oi! Cheeky fecker!"

Nick winked at the publican.

"We believe they all may have frequented here, as they were carrying branded boxes of matches from this pub."

The landlord returned the pictures to the table, spreading them out.

"You know, you two are the second pair of coppers to ask me that very question this week."

Nick and Joan exchanged confused glances.

"Second pair of coppers? So you've already been visited by the police about this?"

"Yeah, well I guess so."

Duncan was finding this whole thing unnerving, rapidly becoming agitated at the situation.

"Guess so? Who were they, Will?"

The sergeant knew Rachel had already visited the pub, but who was this mysterious other 'copper'?

"They came in a few nights ago. A grumpy looking cooze

in a suit, mid-thirties, with a brunette who had massive jugs."

"Go on..."

"She was asking the same as yourselves, had we seen the murdered women or knew them."

Cavanagh quickly placed her notebook on the sticky table top, scribbling into it furiously.

"Did she give a name? Or show a warrant card?"

"He showed his ID, Detective Constable or something. Oh, what was her name? Er, erm Wise...er, no...Rise...nah, oh dear. Hang on! Oh, yeah — Reece. No, er...Yeah, Rice — that's it! Oh, hang on—"

The two detectives gazed at each other with a sudden sense of realisation.

"The thing is, she returned the following night."

"Rachel came back?"

Nick was beyond astonished. None of what the publican was saying made any sense at all.

"Yeah, but on her own, not with the suit. She was chatting to different people, but took an age with a tall guy with curly hair."

"Do you know him?"

"No, not at all. But she left with him."

Duncan continued to nod as Will spoke, but froze at his last comment. Joan almost dropped her pen, recovering to catch it at the last second.

"You seem extremely certain. Were you watching her all night? They could've just been on a date."

"Are you sure you don't know him?"

Both detectives bounded questions at their host. Will was taken back by their verbal bombardment, sliding back in his seat.

"Whoa! Whoa! No, I wasn't watching her. I couldn't take my eyes off the guy — he was gorgeous!"

"Could you clear up a few queries please, Will?"

"If I can."

"Do you know any of the deceased people at all?"

The Sergeant pushed the photographs on the table each a little closer to their flamboyant host. Will huffed and puffed, giving the images the once over yet again.

"Nah! Not regulars, as far as I know."

Nick noticed his Scouse colleague didn't appear to be satisfied with the response they were receiving.

"So the names Arosha Rana, Wendy Kroy, Zhen Wheng and Sam Lambert don't ring any bells, like?"

"No, never heard of them."

Another dead end. Or maybe not. Duncan quickly considered an idea.

"What about the name 'Mandy Lamb'?"

The landlord's face brightened briefly, but a fraction later changed to shock and horror.

"Mandy? No! She was one of the favourite singers in here. Superb Nancy Sinatra tribute act."

Cavanagh tapped the pic of Sam Lambert with Zhen Wheng. Will put both of his hands to his mouth, becoming increasingly upset.

"Oh my God! I barely recognised her with dark hair. She was strawberry blonde as Nancy."

Something suddenly dawned in Duncan's mind, as a penny dropped.

"The Nancy Sinatra? That was Mandy, I mean Sam? Wow!"

"You heard her... er... him sing in here, Nick?"

"Yeah. Must be about six months ago."

Nick picked up the image of Sam and Zhen, taking a few strides towards the stage. Abruptly, he stopped. Holding the photo shoulder high, he smiled broadly.

"Joan, come take a butchers' at this."

The Constable did as she was asked.

"It's in here! They took the photo here!"

"Will, I don't suppose you have security cameras installed?"

"Humph! How much money do you think I have? Besides, what would I need them for?"

Anderson shrugged his shoulders at the Sergeant.

Making their way back to Duncan's car, the detectives found the dray lorry had finished its delivery and departed.

"Small world, eh Nick?"

"Indeed. All of the deceased with connections indirectly to this pub."

"Thing is Joan, we have no proof they bought the branded matches here. They could've been given to them, or they may have even found them."

Nick had barely driven two yards out of the car park, when Cavanagh erupted.

"Stop the car, Nick! Stop!"

Duncan brought Alice to an emergency stop, to which the Merseysider leapt out of the car. He stared into the rear-view mirror, watching her running back towards the pub. Turning the engine off, he dashed after her.

"Joan, what's wrong?"

Darting back towards the Tavern, the policeman came to an abrupt halt. The constable was standing still, as though in a trace. Gently, he placed his hand on her shoulder.

"Are you all right?"

"Nick, I think that's Rachel's car."

He gazed towards the corner of the car park that had been obscured by the delivery truck. Parked all on its own was a Triumph Herald Convertible.

"That scruffy thing?"

"Yeah, I swear that's Rachel's."

Duncan wandered over to the car. Wrapping his handkerchief around his right hand, he tried the driver's door — locked. Peering inside, he couldn't see anything out of the ordinary.

"It's a fairly common car. Are you sure it belongs to her?"

"I think it is. I'm certain it is."

"If it is her car, why has she left it here?"

Joan shook her head in disbelief, as she peered into the car from the other side.

Arriving back at Little Park Street, Nick was taken back by how quickly Joan sprinted into the station, and straight to the CID office. By the time he had caught up with her, the constable had found Edwards by the Incident Desk, informing him of what she thought was Rachel's car.

"You two, follow me downstairs. Let's find out about Miss Ryce."

Edwards addressed the uniformed sergeant on duty, Rita Jones.

"Hello Rita, I wonder if you can help?"

"Wot yer are, Cocker! Wot do yer need to know?"

The three detectives glanced at one another as the dispatch sergeant spoke in her thick Black Country speech.

"Our FLO, WPC Rachel Ryce, she hasn't been on duty for the last couple of days. I was wondering if you've heard

anything."

Rita consulted the log on her Incident Desk.

"Nah, she hasn't turned in — again! Doesn't say here why she's off. She's pool-ley I'd say."

Cavanagh began to show severe signs of concern and worry.

"Sarge, she's my housemate. I'd have seen her at home if she was ill."

"Didn't you say her Gran might be sick, Joan?"

"I think she would've told Niamh or me, if she'd gone to see her. Or at least told the control desk."

"Rita, is there a patrol car over that neck of the woods that could check the house?"

"Maybe, Cock." The uniformed sergeant turned to the young detective. *"Where do you live, sweetheart?"*

"Foleshill, edge of Radford."

Joan pointed to the exact street on a map on the wall over the control desk.

"I'll sort it, Duck."

Rita moved over to the radio, slipping the headset on.

"Guv..." Duncan attempted to grab the inspector's attention.

"Yes, Nick..."

The Detective Sergeant gestured with his head to the corridor. Edwards obliged.

"Guv, something you need to know. Before we spotted what we think is Rachel's car at the Swanswell, we spoke with the landlord. He said Rachel had gone back to the pub to ask further questions for a second time."

"What?"

To say the senior detective was incandescent with rage

didn't even scratch the surface.

"And the first time she went there, the landlord said she'd arrived with a guy in a suit who showed a Detective Constable's warrant card."

Nick seriously believed Edwards' eyes were going to burst out of his face, and smash through his spectacles.

"Are you thinking the same as myself, Nick?"

"The guy in the suit?"

"Yes!"

Both detectives spoke at the same time.

"Dermot!"

"Guv, they're sending a car around to my house, but I don't think she's there."

The Inspector re-entered the control room, ignoring Cavanagh's comment.

"Rita, could you find the whereabouts of—"

A red telephone on the desk began to ring excessively loudly, with a bright light on the control desk flashing in time to the phone pulsing. Rita picked it up swiftly.

"Warwickshire Police, Little Park Street."

Seeing the desk sergeant busy, the inspector turned to his detectives.

"I want to see Dermot immediately. If he's been acting off his own back with Rachel, I want to know why."

"He's asked me a couple of times to assist him with his sergeant application. Maybe he's trying to find out some crucial piece of information to impress."

"Well, he's fucked that up well and truly! But what about Rachel?"

"Rach wanted to become a CID detective like me," Cavanagh added.

Edwards raised his eyebrows.

"Really? I know she's desperate to impress, but there are better ways. I've enough on my plate with St John and His Nibs here bickering like teenagers every opportunity they get!"

Duncan gave the Guv'nor a sheepish glance.

"Albert..."

The Inspector gazed over his shoulder, finding Rita in the doorway. The Desk Sergeant had pure horror on her face, worsening by the second.

"Are you all right, Rita?"

"You're not going to believe this, Cock. Another body has been found."

Nick heard the words, but they didn't actually register. He thought he heard the Desk Sergeant say another body had just been found. No, not possible. Not again. They had four to deal with, give the deceased the respect they fully deserved by catching their killer. There wasn't another. He'd misheard Rita.

His worst fears had been confirmed. Both the Guv'nor and Joan were gobsmacked. Duncan managed to find his voice, as both his colleagues froze to the spot.

"Wherebouts, Rita?"

"War Memorial Park, Kenilworth Road side."

The lady from the Black Country had barely finished speaking, when Nick felt the inspector's hand between his shoulder blades, shoving him along the corridor. In the corner of his eye, he could see Edwards had done same to the Scouse Constable.

"Rita, inform DCI Spencer of events. Tell him were on our way."

The Guv'nor bellowed over his shoulder as he began to

pick up speed moving towards the exit with his two detectives.

"Wot yer are, Cocker!"

"And SOCO. phone Leek Wootton too!"

"Righty-o! But Albert, there's something else..."

None of the three plain clothes officers heard her reply, as they sprinted out across the car park to Duncan's car.

Moments later, Alice blasted out of Little Park Street and across the city centre, siren blaring and blue lights flashing. Nick drove the wheels off his car, driving in a style more suited to an ambulance trying to get a dying patient to hospital faster than fast. Arriving at the entrance to the park, the Alvis came to a flying stop just as uniformed constables were beginning to cordon off the access road.

"I can't get my head around why she would return to that pub the following night."

"Me neither, Guv."

"Does this mean Naylor is in the clear, like Guv?"

"Not necessarily. Sam Lambert died before the others. This could be the same."

Walking briskly through the cordon, they could see another small area taped off around a thick patch of undergrowth, an impromptu privacy screen already erected.

"Maybe she went back to speak with someone again, clarify something?"

Joan still pondered over her house-mates behaviour.

"Maybe she just had a date."

Duncan added another angle, which Edwards appeared to think was feasible, but pulled a puzzled face.

"Hang on — a date with a gay bar? I didn't know she's like that!"

"Guv, I don't think Rachel is. Remember what Joan said

362

the other day? Many straight women go to gay bars as they aren't hassled by blokes just trying to get into their knickers. Intriguingly, some straight men go there to meet straight women who are 'serious', not only after a bit of 'How's Your Father'."

The experienced detective exhibited a more intense level of bafflement that ever before. Cavanagh nodded in agreement. Edwards rolled his eyes and shook his head in disbelief.

"I've seen and heard many things since I've been a copper, but never that before."

As the three detectives approached the small area shielded from view, Duncan noticed something that he hadn't initially. All of the uniformed officers were wandering around pre-occupied, their faces not wanting to accept or believe something. Others were in obvious shock.

"Something has happened. Look at uniform."

The Scouse Constable approached a WPC she knew.

"Terri, what's the matter? What's happened?"

"Joan, it's awful."

The uniformed constable burst into tears. Holding her hand to her mouth, she dashed towards the outer cordon sobbing. The detectives watched their colleague depart, even more confused as to what was happening. Reaching the privacy screen, they stepped around it. No one expected to see what they found, not in their weirdest, worst nightmares.

"Oh My God!"

Cavanagh began to cry uncontrollably.

"Jesus Fuckin' Christ!"

Duncan didn't know what else to say. He'd seen some disturbing sights in his law enforcement career, but never this.

Nor had the inspector.

"I wasn't expecting that!"

Lying on her side, wearing some of her best clothes, face made up perfectly, was WPC Rachel Ryce.

"Maybe she was on a date, after all."

Nick said the first thing that came into his head, but all the comment did was fuel Joan's hysteria further.

"Her eyes! Her eyes are still open! Close them, Nick!"

The Merseysider shoved Duncan forwards, before completely pushing him out the way and began to crouch down herself. However, she was preventing from doing so by the inspector, who seized hold of the young detective.

"Leave her, Cilla. SOCO need to examine the scene first."

The Sergeant knelt down on the soft earth, having a quick visual examination. Taking his pen from his inside pocket, he carefully turned back the turtle neck on her tight fitted jumper slightly. At once, he could see severe bruising on her neck and throat.

"Same cause of death as the others, I'd say."

Now a complete jabbering wreck, Cavanagh move away from what she was seeing.

"Sorry — I... I can't do this."

Ducking around the privacy screen, the Scouse Detective vanished.

"Nick, go follow her — make sure she's all right."

Duncan nodded.

Nick darted after his colleague. Walking briskly, Cavanagh was using a now hastily taped off improvised pathway.

"Joan, wait up!"

The Liverpudlian slowed down. Upon facing her, he saw

tears streaming down her face, her mascara now nothing more than dark grey streaks down her cheeks. He wrapped a protective arm around her, pulling her close. Hearing someone walking in their direction, the sergeant was pleased to see it was a WPC he knew.

"Glenda, could you take Joan for a cup of tea back at the station. She's in shock and needs some comfort right now."

"Certainly Sarge."

The sergeant stepped back around the privacy screen, finding the inspector gingerly opening Rachel's handbag using his handkerchief.

"Just a moment. I'm trying to find out if she was carrying her notebook and hopefully wrote something down that will be useful."

Holding the small pleather bag open without depositing any fingerprints, Edwards gestured for Duncan to reach inside and retrieve what they wanted. Wrapping his own hanky around his hand, Nick carefully slid inside the bag and lifted out the notebook. Now free of the handbag, Edwards now laid his handkerchief on the ground, for which the sergeant gently placed the notebook upon.

"What was the last thing she wrote?"

With much difficulty using only the tip of his pen, Nick managed to leaf through the handwritten pages following the inspector's request. Duncan saw notes she'd scribbled when with him the last few days, but the last few pages related to something he didn't know.

"Guv, looks like she made some notes during or after visiting the Swanswell."

Edwards twisted his neck to read the WPC's handwriting. The younger detective began to dictate.

"Many students, one or two knew Zhen question mark."

The two detectives glanced at one another, unsure of what to make of that. Duncan continued.

"Cliental very friendly, not just gay men, men in drag too, comfortable chatting to each other."

"Well, it takes allsorts."

"Then her final entry is just plain odd."

"Odd?"

"Yes, Guv. Look…"

The two detectives stared at the writing on the tiny page trying to comprehend what it meant.

"7.30, O."

"What the hell is that supposed to mean?"

"Maybe it's incomplete, she never finished what she was writing."

Before Edwards and Duncan had chance to discuss their theories further, Dr Tyler stepped around the privacy screen followed by one of the SOCO officers.

"We meet again, Detectives."

The Doctor solemnly greeted her colleagues.

"Sadly Jocelyn, this has cranked up the anti several notches."

Tyler gazed at the two policemen somewhat puzzled, as she placed her large brown leather bag on the ground.

"We've lost one of our own."

Edwards gestured towards Rachel.

"She's a WPC? Oh my God! I'm so sorry. I…I didn't know. I was only told it was another murdered young woman."

"This is Rachel Ryce. Our Family Liaison Officer."

The Doctor placed a hand over her mouth in shock.

"Excuse me, Sir." The SOCO officer moved around

Rachel, taking pictures from as many different angles as possible.

"*I didn't know her, but what a waste.*"

Tyler shook her head as she spoke.

"*She would've made a fine detective. So much potential.*"

Edwards nodded as Duncan made his hypothesis.

"*I need a radio. What's St John's whereabouts? Dermot is with him.*"

"*What are you thinking, Guv? Hopefully not the same as me.*"

"*I think I am. It makes me feel sick and angry. I need to see Dermot. Now.*"

The Guv'nor and Nick stepped out from behind the screen. Edwards collared the first uniform constable he happened across, relieving him of his personal radio. Duncan could see his superior was more fiercely determined than ever before.

"*Mike One, this is Mike Victor Two. Over.*"

Almost straight away, control replied.

"*Mike One receiving. Go ahead, Albert. Over.*"

"*What's the whereabouts of Mike Zulu Three, Rita? Over.*" After a slight pause, a response.

"*Mike Zulu Three currently enroute back to Little Park Street. Over.*"

"*Thanks, Rita. Mike Victor Two Out.*"

The Inspector gestured to the sergeant.

"*Let's get back to the station pronto. We need to have a chat with Mr Ward, with the DCI present.*"

On the way back to the station, Duncan couldn't help but notice Edwards was more subdued and introspective than ever before, in all the time he'd known him. The Guv'nor stared forwards as the Alvis sped back into the city centre, his face a picture of utmost seriousness, mixed with disbelief.

"I really hope I'm wrong about this, Nick. Just when you think you've seen it all, something happens to remind you, no you haven't."

"I think we need to keep an open mind, Guv. Hear what Dermot has to say first."

"Humph! I've only ever dealt with a bent copper once before. If he's starting to act 'rogue', that's the start of the slippery slope."

The sergeant nodded in agreement.

"That was Eric Collins, wasn't it?"

Edwards' face darkened at the mention of the name.

"I treated him the same way your dad treated me, better in fact. I foolishly believed he'd replace me as department Inspector eventually. The biggest irony is, you caught him and have now got his job!"

Something didn't make sense in Duncan's mind. Every time they obtained a serious lead about William Perkins, it would go 'cold' or prove mysteriously incorrect. On a couple of occasions, completely wrong to such an extent, it was embarrassing. Perkins always appeared to be a couple of steps ahead of them. Nick's own sense of detection told him the gangster was being tipped off, somehow. The Detective Constable developed an idea. It would prove if his hunch was right.

"It's really good of you to give me a lift, Nick."

Edwards climbed into the front passenger seat of Duncan's Standard Ten.

"What's your Riley in the garage for, Guv?"

"Only a few minor repairs to get it through its M.O.T."

The Constable raised his eyebrows, glancing around the interior of his own pride and joy. The inspector chuckled.

"Don't knock her, Nick. You've got her into fine fettle for her age."

"Flew through her last M.O.T — not even a minor!"

Edwards whistled. He was impressed.

Out of the station emerged one of the CID team, Detective Sergeant Eric Collins. The middle-aged man wandered over to his own car, a barely year-old Mk III Humber Sceptre.

"Speaking of new cars, nice piece of kit Eric has bought himself."

"Hmmm, remains to be seen how he affords it."

Sliding into the custard yellow motor, he flicked what was left of his cigarette across the car park from the driver's window, and heading into the city. Duncan started his car, and began to follow Collins at a distance.

"What are you up to, Nick? My house is the other way."

"Sorry, Guv. I've got this hunch about Eric, if you'll indulge me for a short while."

"Indulge you? Eric is a trusted, long-time detective, he's been showing you the ropes of CID since you transferred over from uniform."

The young detective went silent, concentrating as to where the Sergeant had driven off to in the darkness. Nick was in luck — he made out his car in the distance departing towards Gosford Street.

"If you're wrong Sunny Jim, you're going to owe Eric one hell of an apology."

"I know."

Reaching the junction with the ring road, Duncan saw the Humber turn towards Hillfields.

"Do you know where Eric lives, Guv?"

"Holbrooks, if my memory serves me correctly. Look Nick, what the hell is this all about?"

"Well, he's not heading home, is he?"

"For Christ Sake, he could be visiting friends, going for a drink with his mates, picking his kids up, anything!" Keeping his distance as he followed, Nick lost sight of Eric as the Sergeant turned off the road they were on.

"He's gone down one of these side streets — why?"

"Nick, this is getting ridiculous! We're all entitled to a private life outside work."

Gently edging past the Binley Oak pub, Duncan could see no tail lights of any vehicle, let alone the Humber he was trying to find. Nick pushed the throttle into the carpet, causing the Standard to fly along the road. He braked hard just before the next junction, passing the street slow enough he could view along the road. At the top end of the short throughfare lined either side with Victorian terraced houses, was the Coventry City Football Club stadium, Highfield Road. Severely out of place compared with the surrounding buildings, the rear of the West Stand towered over the nearby residential area. More specifically, the constable caught sight of two cars parked next to one another, lights still on. Performing a near emergency stop, Nick immediately reversed the car back. Switching the lights off, he turned into the side street and crawled gently along.

"What the fuck are you hoping to see, Sherlock?"

Duncan knew he was starting to try the patience of his superior.

"That, Guv!"

The Constable pointed at what was happening in front of them. The Humber Sceptre belonging to Collins was parked next to a dark-coloured Mk II Jaguar, which could be — as Duncan and Edwards edged closer — clearly distinguished as a Daimler due to the chrome work on the boot lid. Standing between the cars were two men chatting — one was obviously Eric — the other man the Guv'nor recognised instantly.

"William Perkins!"

Nick brought his car to a stop, parking at the end of a row of vehicles already there. The detectives watched the two men continue to talk, quite animatedly at times, before Perkins reached inside his coat.

"Oh, no! Please, not that!"

Edwards began to panic, but there was no need. The gangster pulled an envelope from his coat, bulging to such an extent its contents were nearly bursting out. Perkins handed this to the detective, to which Collins briefly leafed through what was inside, before he secreted it away inside his own coat. The two men shook hands, and climbed back into their respective cars.

"That's why we're getting nowhere trying to prosecute the bastard!"

The Guv'nor was incandescent with rage. The Daimler turned around, and sped away into the night.

Without being prompted, Duncan gunned the engine of his little car, turned the headlights onto full beam, and launched forwards. Collins had begun to gently turn his car around, when he had to brake hard as Nick's Standard emerged out of the darkness, going nose-to-nose with the Humber. The constable leapt out of his motor, jumped across the car bonnets, reaching the driver's door of Collins' vehicle. Wrenching it open, Duncan leaned inside and removed the ignition key.

"Nick, what the fuck are you doing?"

The Sergeant sprung out of his car, squaring up to the younger man. Duncan grabbed him by his coat lapels, pinning him to the side of his car.

"Detective Sergeant Eric Vincent Collins, I am arresting you for corruption and bribery while being an active police officer and detective of one of Her Majesty's Constabularies. You do not have to say anything, but it may harm your defence if you do not mention when questioned something which you later rely on in court. Anything you do say may be given in evidence."

Nick read his superior his rights through gritted teeth, trying his utmost not to lose his cool.

"Eh? Fuck Off! Who do you think you are, coming across all Billy Big Bollocks?"

Collins snatched hold of the hands thrust under his chin, roughly pushing them away from his person. Surprising Eric further, Edwards appeared next to Duncan. He reached straight inside the Sergeant's coat, finding the envelope with its excessive sum, pulling it into full view.

"And I suppose you merely asked William Perkins for a loan as you couldn't make it to the bank before closing time?"

Collins' shock and surprise compounded with his speechless stance. If this wasn't the look of someone caught red-handed, a rabbit frozen in car headlights if you will, Nick didn't know what was.

"*Of all the people...*" Duncan shook his head in disbelief and anger.

Duncan shook his head in dismay at the memory. Having someone who can't do their job properly is one thing, but a crooked copper was another. He too hoped Dermot wasn't going to be another to add to the list of shame — or worse.

Nick followed the Guv'nor into the station building, heading straight for his office. Sat behind Edwards' desk in his chair was Cavanagh, a blanket around her shoulders, a mug of steaming hot 'something' in her hands. Trying her utmost to be of some comfort, Ruby gently rubbed the constable's shoulders. Joan's make up had now ran down her face to such an extent, it made the Liverpudlian resemble a lame Alice Cooper impersonator. The Sergeant was snapped out of any amusement as to his colleague's appearance, as she began to sob and sob, breaking her heart. The Inspector crouched down next to her.

"Joan, I know this is absolutely horrible for you right now — it is for all of us — but I just wanted to say two things."

Nick heard Edwards speak so tenderly. The only time before he'd heard him talk this way before was to his Mum at Dad's funeral.

"Firstly, this is the horrid side of our job. I hate it. I want to tell you it'll never happen again, but I can't."

"Why Rach, Guv? Why?"

The Scouser cried and cried. Nick had watched his mother cry with a broken soul as his father's coffin was lowered into the ground, crying what seemed an endless flood of tears no one could stop the tide of. Just like that day, he felt helpless observing his friend do the same.

"I promise I'll find who did this and find out why. The other thing I wanted to say, is I'm sure Rachel wouldn't want you to be like this. I know she was like your sister, and you're going to miss her terribly — we all will."

Cavanagh threw her arms around the senior detective's neck, snuffling into his shoulder. Edwards put his arms around the constable, holding her close.

"There there. We all feel the same, Joan."

Releasing the Guv'nor, she began to dry her eyes on the cuff of her jumper sleeve. Duncan stepped forwards, offering her his handkerchief. She flashed the weakest of smiles in thanks, taking the cloth from him.

"Guv, can you promise me one thing?"

Between huge sniffles and gasps, Joan gradually started to regain her composure.

"I'll do my best, Cilla."

Cavanagh chuckled slightly at her nickname, still drying her eyes on the hanky. Nick looked on as she turned the white fabric black.

"Let me help find her killer — keep me on the case. Please."

Edwards pulled a face that clearly said he wasn't sure if that was a good idea.

"We'll talk about it tomorrow, eh? You get yourself off home and get some rest."

The Merseysider nodded, still wiping her face.

Movement in the main office caught Nick's attention. Over his shoulder, he saw St John and Dermot return, making themselves at home at their desks with their lunch.

"Guv!"

Duncan gestured with his head towards what he had just seen. Becoming rapidly aware of what the Sergeant was referring to, Edwards stood with a renewed sense of purpose. Nick saw the fire in his eyes, an aura around him he'd never noticed before.

"Christ! I'd hate to get on the wrong side of him!" he thought inwardly. Removing his jacket, he strode to the door with increased purpose.

"Nick, with me."

Duncan did as he was requested, following the Inspector. The Guv'nor moved into the main office like a heavyweight boxer walking to the ring for a title bout.

"Dermot! If you'd like to accompany me…"

Detective Constable Ward was confused.

"OK Guv, Where to?"

With a mouthful of sandwich, he went to put his coat back on.

"The Chief Inspector's office — Now!"

Edwards placed an arm around the junior detective, frog-marching him straight into the DCI's private room. Nick followed, glancing over his shoulder at a bemused looking St John.

"We'll explain shortly."

The door slammed shut behind them, causing Spencer to look up with a jolt from his paperwork.

"What's the matter, Albert?"

"Sit!"

The Guv'nor pushed Dermot into the seat in front of the Chief Inspector's desk.

"I think we've got a case of foul play, Tom."

"What?"

"Sunny Jim here, at the very least, has been acting rogue."

Spencer got to his feet, placing his pipe in the ashtray on his desk.

"Is this true, Mr Ward?"

"Sir, I've done nothing wrong—"

Edwards flew at the constable, pushing his face right into his.

"Wrong? I've got you at the Swanswell Tavern a few nights ago with Rachel, and now we find her dead in some bushes!"

"Oh My God! The girl found today, that's Miss Ryce?"

Spencer was visibly disturbed by the news, slowly returning to his seat. Duncan spoke.

"I'm sorry to inform you Sir, but the body found earlier today is WPC Rachel Ryce. The Guv'nor, WDC Cavanagh and myself positively identified her."

"I'd like to know your whereabouts outside work for the last couple of weeks, Mr Ward."

"Yes Guv — all right, all right. I went to the pub with Rachel. I thought it was a date, bit of a strange place to go, a poofter's bar. It was her idea."

"Really?"

The DCI now began to become as agitated as Edwards.

"Yes Sir, it was! Once we got there, she was more interested in asking random people questions about the murdered girls, scribbling away into her notebook."

"And it never entered your pretty little fuckin' head to inform us of this? Duncan told me you'd like to be considered for promotion. Really?"

The Guv'nor was absolutely fuming. The severity of his demeanour had reached such, whatever day of the week it was, if Edwards told you it was Wednesday — it was Wednesday.

"Someone amongst my detectives has also been leaking information to the press for whatever reason they see fit!"

"I wasn't me, Guv! Honest!"

"I'm not saying it was, Mr Ward. But it's interesting how Derek White at the Coventry Evening Chronicle knows more than he should. And that's a very nice and shiny Triumph 2500 you're now driving around in. Wish I could afford one on my Inspector's salary!"

"Mr Ward, your notebook please."

Spencer reached out his hand, to which the constable retrieved the piece of stationary from his inside pocket and gave it to the chief Inspector.

"And your warrant card, please."

The DCI repeated his request, but on this occasion, Dermot appeared he couldn't believe what he'd just been asked. With extreme reluctance, he found the small leather wallet containing his police identification, and handed it over.

"I didn't say anything, as I didn't want to get Rachel into any bother. She's a nice girl, very keen, a good copper."

The Inspector went nose-to-nose with the constable.

"She's now dead!"

Edwards backed off, giving Spencer chance to speak.

"Detective Constable Dermot Ward, you are hereby suspended from active duty forthwith, on the grounds of gross mis-conduct. You will now go with Detective Inspector Edwards and myself to an interview room, and account for the time periods the inspector has mentioned. After which, you are required to leave the station. An investigation will be

conducted into your behaviour and the events that have occurred. You have the right to speak with your union representative and / or your commanding officer but no other member of the Warwickshire Constabulary. Do I make myself clear?"

"Yes Sir, but...but it's not my fault. I'm sorry for not speaking up about Rachel, but I've done nothing else wrong! Please..."

Inadvertently, Ward made eye contact with Duncan.

"Dermot, I don't think you fully realise what the Guv'nor wants to know — you're now a suspect yourself."

Nick chuckled to himself, "That's Karma. Considering how you treat women, you've got what you deserve. Especially due to how upset you made Joan the other night." One of the most horrified expressions Duncan had ever seen spread across Ward's face, as the sudden realisation of the severity of the situation dawned. Edwards turned to the sergeant.

"Nick, take Joan home please. She's in no fit state to do anything today. Tell her to take tomorrow off too, if she wants."

"OK Guv."

"I'll make Sebastian aware of all of this, he can assist SOCO at Rachel's place, as we'll need to see if there is anything useful there."

Duncan nodded, leaving the chief Inspector's office to find Cavanagh.

It took Nick sometime to coax Joan out of the station and into his car. He could tell she didn't want to go home. The constable was more reluctant to do so than the other night. As he drove from Little Park Street towards Cavanagh's residence, she once again snuggled up to him, embracing his left arm.

Arriving outside her house, the sight of the building caused the scouser to enter into a flood of tears once again. In the street, Duncan recognised St John's drab car and the front door, ajar.

"It's just hit home she's gone. She won't ever be doing this again, coming back here."

"Would you like me to come inside with you?"

The Merseysider nodded.

Wandering into the dwelling, Joan headed straight upstairs, Nick presumed to her own room. He saw her fighting further tears, which were not aided as St John loomed out from one of the other bedrooms.

"We'll be as quick as we can, Lassie." The Scotsman tried to reassure the constable.

"Joan..."

A female Belfast accent spoke behind Duncan, to which Niamh Maddox pushed past, embracing the Scouser. The two young women sobbed and cried. Neither seemed to be finding any real comfort in the other.

"Would either of you two like a cup of tea?"

Nick felt that might help, with the shock the two constables were enduring.

"Aye, if yer dunna mind. Two sugars."

Duncan scowled at Sebastian, as he announced his request.

"I'm sorry Niamh, I...I can't stay here!"

Cavanagh dashed into her room. The Irish Constable displayed even more shock and upset than before.

"Sebastian, can you take Niamh downstairs and make us all a drink, please?"

"Why me, Laddie?"

Nick pulled a face at his colleague, gesturing with eyes to

where Joan had vanished.

"Oh, aye. Yeah, aye. Let's put the kettle on, eh?" St John ushered the Irish WPC down the stairs.

Duncan knocked the bedroom door gently, slowly entering into the room. Cavanagh was sitting on the edge of her bed, staring out of the window into the distance at nothing in particular. Tears continued to roll down her cheeks. He sat down next to her, taking one of her hands.

"I have a suggestion."

The Liverpudlian turned towards her friend, wiping the most recent tears from her face she'd shed.

"How about you pack a few things, come stay at mine tonight — in the spare room!"

Joan glanced at him with a daft smirk.

"Yeah, the spare room. Let's have no repeat of the other night."

The Sergeant nodded.

"I've enough to deal with losing my housemate, let alone having some of the most tender and beautiful sex I've ever had, but with a bloke who's gay!"

The pair giggled at the ridiculousness of her statement.

"Come on, you. Pop your toothbrush and some clean knickers in a bag, and let's go see if St John has figured out how to use the kettle."

Joan giggled slightly, wiping her nose on her cuff as she sniffled. Duncan's face lit up, as he had another idea.

"Hey, do you fancy fish and chips for tea?"

Nick unwrapped his tea, trying his utmost not to burn his finger tips on the hot contents.

"Does anybody want any bread and butter?" Georgy

asked everyone, departing towards the kitchen.

"Yes please, Mum!"

Alex was having more luck opening his fish and chips. Either that, or he had asbestos lined hands.

"Not for me, thanks Georgy."

Ellis was already tucking into her meal, the steam emanating off the battered fish not deterring her in the slightest.

"How about you, Love?"

"Yes please, Mrs Duncan. If it's not too much trouble."

Georgy patted Joan on the shoulder, disappearing out of the room.

"Sorry to hear about your friend, Joan. That's horrible."

Ellis expressed her condolences. Cavanagh smiled politely.

"Thank you. It's still a huge, massive shock. It doesn't feel real. I still think I'll get home, and she'll be there. Making her usual mess in the kitchen, finding pieces of her uniform scattered around the lounge..." Joan stopped.

To everyone it was clear feelings were extremely raw, as a huge lump became lodged in her throat. Alex leaned across and took Scouser's hand.

"I'm not going to lie to you, it never goes away." Nick saw his brother gaze at him, to which they both glanced at the picture of their father on the mantelpiece. *"But one thing I do promise you, everyday gets a little bit easier."*

Cavanagh smiled back at the older Duncan. *"Thank you, Alex."*

Nick was still struggling with own meal. He'd almost managed to separate his piece of battered fish from the wrapping paper, when the one thing he didn't want to happen did — the batter coating split away from the seafood it encased, with a fair portion remaining adhered to the paper.

"Oh, shit!"

Georgy wandered back into the lounge, just at her younger son's sweary outburst.

"Language, Nicholas! Especially at the dinner table, and in front of ladies!"

The policeman began to sulk somewhat.

"Sorry, Mum. I always lose most of the batter from my fish."

He continued to pick at the offending piece of fried flour, it coming away in small flakes.

"Where are the girls this evening?"

Joan asked a more normal question, possibly trying to be as ordinary, everyday as she could under the circumstances Nick contemplated.

"They're at their Brownies meeting. There'll most likely be another task they have to do, in order to earn yet another badge."

The Constable smiled softly.

"I remember that. Going to Brownies and Girl Guides. I went straight from Guides into the police. Funny how the path your life takes you can seem so exciting, so much fun, but contains so much unknown and unexpected danger."

All at the table went silent at Joan's words. Everyone thought them from time-to-time, but who really deliberated on such? Life really is so short, who knows what tomorrow will bring. Rachel didn't the morning she awoke the day she was murdered. She didn't think, *'Today is going to be my last.'* After running this through his head, Nick had an epiphany. Do it now. Tell Mum. Now!

"Mum…"

"Yes, sweetheart…"

Mrs Duncan sedately picked at her tea, sprinkling a little more vinegar onto her chips.

"I've got something I want to tell you."

Georgy glanced at her son, somewhat puzzled.

"Mum, I've wanted to tell you this for a long time now, and I'm sorry if it upsets you or makes you see me differently, but it's who I am."

The older lady leaned forward, taking her son's hand.

"Nicholas! Nothing you could ever say or do would change my opinion of you."

"Mum, you don't understand—"

"Really, nothing can be that serious or terrible you feel this worked up over, surely."

"Mum, I'm gay!"

She stared at Nick, slightly shocked. Struggling for something to say, she managed two words.

"You're gay?"

"Yes, Mum. I'm a homosexual. A poofter. A fairy. A shirt-lifter. A Nancy boy. A faggot. I'm 'bent'."

It went so silent in the room, it was possible to hear the soft tick of the clock on the mantlepiece quite clearly. Ellis, Joan and Alex glanced at one another in turn, not sure as what to say or how Georgy was going to react. Mrs Duncan let go of her son's hand, returning to eating her fish and chips. Nick didn't know if her reaction was favourable or not. He watched as she dipped a chip into a splodge of tomato ketchup, savouring its flavour as she chewed. The policeman felt like he wanted to throw up, his pulse now echoing in his ears, drowning out the tick of the clock in the room.

"So you don't like women?"

Duncan's heart pounded to such an extent he began to believe it was going to leap out of his chest and perform a dance on the table. *"She can't handle it. I knew it! She's taken it badly. I knew I shouldn't have said anything."* Nick tortured himself mentally as the stony silence continued.

"No, Mum. I don't like women that way."

Georgy finished chewing on a piece of fish, beginning to place a few chips onto a slice of buttered bread.

"Well, you best get yourself a boyfriend then."

Nick let out a huge sigh of relief, leaned over and embraced his mother.

"Just do what makes you happy, Nick. As long as you're not hurting anyone, that's all that matters."

Releasing his mother, the policeman became aware of everyone else staring at him, smiling. Rather than being self-conscious, Nick began to smirk.

"What's the matter with you lot? Haven't you seen a gay bloke hug his mother before?"

They all giggled, even Cavanagh in her state. The detective smiled back at his colleague, seeing his actions had actually cheered her up no end. Joan took his hand, entwining her fingers with his.

"I'm made up for ya, Nick. That must've taken so much courage."

His smile became a grin. He winked at the Scouser.

"Hey, remember what St John calls me? I'm Golden Bollocks!"

Joan now laughed out loud. Georgy didn't.

"Language, Nicholas!"

CHAPTER ELEVEN
FRIDAY APRIL 27th 1973

Stirling awoke Nick climbing onto the bed, then on top of him, and began to 'pad' with his paws.

"You need to go on a diet, Sunshine," he addressed the cat. It felt like he was being ran over.

"Mmmmm, speak for yourself!"

Duncan froze as he heard a female Scouse voice answer. He suddenly released it wasn't just Stirling sitting on him that was giving him a restricted sensation, a slender arm inside a purple satin pyjama sleeve was around him. The owner of said arm and pyjamas was lying directly behind him.

"Joan, what are you doing in here?"

"I was cold. Anyhow, I kept my pyjamas on."

"Good!"

Nick began to sit up, forcing Stirling to jump out of the way.

"Anyhow Nicholas Duncan, don't flatter yourself. You weren't that good a shag!"

The Sergeant stared at Cavanagh open-mouthed in astonishment to which she winked, gave him a peck on the cheek, and leapt out of bed. Joan picked Stirling up, draping him across her shoulder in a fireman's lift.

"Come on, you. Let's find you some breakfast."

She wandered off downstairs, Duncan called after her.

"A cup of tea wouldn't go a miss!"

Cavanagh shouted back.

"Make your own! Who the fuck do you think I am — your mother or something?"

"Charming!"

Nick giggled to himself, beginning to smile broadly. Joan seemed to be close to her normal feisty, no-nonsense self. He wouldn't have her any other way.

"Are you sure you're ready to go into work? Remember, the Guv'nor said you could take a few days off if you want."
Duncan reminded the constable of how the situation stood, as he negotiated Friday morning rush hour traffic.

"No, I want to go to work. I want to help catch Rachel's killer. I won't be able to do that stuck at home feeling sorry for myself."

Nick could hear the determination in her voice. The broken, tearful delicate girl he saw yesterday had evaporated, now evolved into the hard, tough woman who sat next to him. Duncan turned the radio on, catching the news.

"Speculation is rife the Watergate scandal in the United States goes right to the very top, to the President himself Richard Nixon. Police arrested burglars in the Democratic Political Party Headquarters in June of last year, with investigative journalists finding they were financed by the Republican Party to find information about strategy in a future Presidential campaign.

Here in Britain, thousands of workers across various sectors are expected to go on strike next week over the Government's fiscal policy to control inflation. Prime Minister Edward Heath's cabinet have introduced a wage cap, whereby earnings for all employed workers will not exceed a certain level.

Another conflict the Government is involved within is the Cod War with Iceland. The dispute over fishing rights in the North Atlantic Ocean near the Scandinavian country continues. Recently, the Icelandic Parliament has requested assistance from the United Nations, NATO and even the American Government, as Royal Navy vessels have begun escorting the British trawler fleet.

In local news, Warwickshire Police are in the midst of a major investigation, following the mysterious deaths of five people over the last couple of weeks."

Nick quickly pushed the cartridge of the 8-track into the player, whereby the interior of the car was filled with Roy Orbison's hit single, *'Only The Lonely'*. *"Hopefully this'll distract Joan from where the news bullet-in was heading,"* Duncan speculated. As the song began, the Merseysider rolled her eyes and emitted a long sigh.

"I can't believe a guy so in touch with modern life, listens to such awful music!"

"Oi! I saw the Elvis LP's amongst your record collection!"

"Well, it's his hips..." Cavanagh smirked.

"I know."

The Sergeant smirked back, giving his friend the sauciest of winks.

Arriving at Little Park Street, the two detectives stepped out of Nick's car the same moment Edwards climbed out of his Riley.

"How are you this morning, Young Lady?"

The Detective Constable gave the Guv'nor an indifferent gaze.

"Could be better, Guv. But bawling my eyes out isn't going to find Rachel's killer, is it?"

The Inspector smiled at her sympathetically.

"I'm happy for you to remain on the case Miss, but I'm concerned your emotions may well get the better of you. And cloud your judgement."

"It won't, Guv."

Duncan could clearly see Edwards wasn't so sure.

"I tell you what, you shadow His Lordship. I know he'll treat you accordingly under the circumstances, and will help if you're finding it all too much."

The Liverpudlian smiled slightly. *"OK Guv, I understand."* The senior detective strode off into the station building.

"So, I've got to babysit you now?"

"Piss Off! Just give me chance to assist, Nick — that's all."

"I think the Guv'nor is just worried you've been emotionally compromised."

Joan nodded.

"And you're not in the right mental state to be a policewoman and detective."

"I am, Nick. I promise if I can't cope, I'll drop off the case, or if you feel I'm not up to it, I'll step down."

"You'll be fine."

The two detective's attention was drawn to the entrance of the station, as someone shouted at them. Leaning half out of the doors, they could see Edwards waving at them erratically with his trilby.

"You two, get your backsides over to the Swanswell. I've just heard SOCO are going to be there within the hour to

retrieve Rachel's car. See what you can find out, what you notice — anything."

"OK Guv."

The Sergeant glanced at the Constable.

"Sure you want to do this?"

The Merseysider nodded.

The police tow truck blocked most of the road as it reversed through the restricted opening to the pub car park. Nick's attention was on the Triumph. Unlocking the driver's door with his hand wrapped in his trusty hanky, he peered inside. The Herald had that unique fragrance all older cars seemed to have — cheap vinyl seats that had gotten too hot in the summer weather, and damp carpets that never truly dry out. Rachel's car also being a convertible had the odour of an old tent, from its canvas folding roof.

"Sorry, Sarge. You can't go in there just yet." Frank gestured with his trusty Leica he needed to take some pictures.

"Oh, of course."

The SOCO officer began snapping away from every feasible angle. Cavanagh loitered around the car, peering around from behind Nick.

"It doesn't seem any different from the last time she gave me a lift last week."

"Sarge..." Frank attempted to grab Duncan's attention.

"Could you carefully open the boot for me? I want to get a few photos of the contents and where they are before they get shaken about when on the lorry."

"Sure!"

Once again with handkerchief wrapped around his hand, he grasped the chrome handle and pulled the boot lid open.

The police officers straight away saw a pile of clothing. More specifically, a WPC uniform with Rachel's collar number on its epaulettes.

"I take it she got changed in a hurry!" Frank set his camera up upon a tripod, repeatedly shooting pictures.

The sergeant swiftly spoke up.

"Part of the uniform is missing."

Joan and Frank stared at the mass of clothes, unable to establish what Duncan had seen — or not, as in this case.

"Tunic, skirt, blouse, shoes, cravat…"

"So what's missing?" Frank was mystified as well.

"Ah, I've got it — her hat!"

"No, Frank. Not that. She would've kept her bowler in her locker at the station. There's no hosiery — where are her black tights?"

"Maybe she didn't change them went she went out, Nick."

Duncan contemplated this for a moment. He was sure when they found the WPC in the bushes yesterday, she was wearing American Tan ones. He'd have to check when they got back to the office.

"The scally! That's my bag!"

The Detective Constable pointed to a tan leather handbag in the boot. She smiled ironically, shaking her head.

Unexpectedly, a male voice with a slight camp lilt began shouting across the car park.

"Will you lot fuckin' hurry up and Piss Off! You'll be putting my punters off!"

Over their shoulders, the three police officers saw the Swanswell landlord, Wilton Anderson approach purposefully. Will trotted across towards them, but caught the edge of his Cuban heels on the ground and stumbled. The magazines and newspapers he was carrying scattered across the tarmac.

"Oh, fuckin' hell!"

Nick and Joan retrieved the glossy publications, mostly lifestyle and music publications.

However, one of the magazines was actually a thick envelope branded by a national pharmacy chain, containing colour photographs. Some of the images slid out, were picked up on the breeze and began a new, unexpected journey. Cavanagh showed a quick pair of heels, chasing after the pictures, catching them before they blew under a nearby fence and into a small lake-cum-pool attached to a neighbouring public park. Innocently, she started to glance through the images.

"When were these taken, Will?"

The Liverpudlian became extremely interested in them.

"Oh, a few weeks ago, now. Why do you ask?"

"In a couple of them I can see Arosha Rana and Wendy Kroy!"

Duncan was flabberghasted at hearing what his colleague announced. Reaching over, the sergeant took the pictures from Joan to see for himself.

"With Sam Lambert!"

Nick pointed at the crossdresser, to which Will frowned at the detective.

"Apologies, Mandy Lamb."

Behind them, the engine of Rachel's Triumph started at the third time of asking. They watched as Frank reversed the convertible car onto the recovery truck. Something grabbed hold of the sergeant's attention in the background of one of the photos. And again, in one of the others. Nick snatched the spectacles that were on Will's head, trying to use them as an improvised magnifying glass.

"Joan, look at this!"

Duncan pointed at the person he had recognised.

"Fuckin' Hell! Alison McLeod!"

"Will, do you know her?"

Taking his spectacles back off the Detective, Will gave him a disapproving look, and examined the photograph himself.

"Oh, her? No, not really. She comes in from time-to-time."

Duncan and Cavanagh inspected some of the other pictures further. It was clear Alison was talking to someone. The mystery person was unfortunately obscured by a pillar inside the pub, or had their back to the camera.

"I'd love to know who that is."

"You know who that is…"

Will began to explain, glancing at the two detectives. Both returned his gaze, hanging on his every word.

"That's the bloke your friend left here with the other night. Mmmm, such a scrummy looking boy."

The Sergeant strained and tried, but as much as he wanted to, he couldn't make out the man's face.

"Can we borrow these? I'll return them as soon as I can."

"Yeah — sure. But you owe me one."

The publican winked at Nick, with a cheeky grin. The sergeant smiled back politely, while Joan rolled her eyes.

Back at Little Park Street, the two detectives caught up with Rachel's car. Housed inside an ample garage, SOCO were meticulously going over the Herald.

"Have you found anything, Frank?"

"Nothing as yet, mate. Fingerprints on the exterior door handles unusable, as degraded too much in the damp weather the last few nights. Inside obviously found Miss Ryce's prints on the driver's controls, but a few of unknown origin on internal door handles and on the dashboard."

"Er, Frank a couple of those may well be mine, as she gave me a lift last week like."

The SOCO officer nodded.

"Is there anything else of note you've found?"

"Cigarette butts — dog ends."

Frank leaned inside the car, and slid the ashtray in the centre of the dashboard open. Inside were three spent cigarette ends, all the same brand. The gold stripe around the brown filter tip was instantly recognisable to the sergeant.

"Marlboro Longhorn," both Frank and Nick announced in unison.

"Hang on, Rachel didn't smoke! I should know, sharing a house with her!"

Quickly, the sergeant developed an idea.

"Frank, is it possible to lift prints off cigarette filter tips?"

The SOCO officer deliberated for a few moments, beginning to nod his head.

"Yeah, I think we might be able to. They've been kept dry and out of the weather. They shouldn't have degraded."

"Thanks! Hopefully we'll find a match on the system."

Nick and Joan left Frank to his work, heading back for the office.

"My only concern about finding prints, is we find a usable set and they belong to someone not known to us."

As Cavanagh nodded, a grave darkness spread across her face.

Upstairs in the CID office, Nick updated the information on the noticeboard and incident desk. It was a mystery why Rachel had parked her car at the pub. The logical thinking behind it, was she most likely met someone on a date or was meeting friends. However, his gut feeling was she had returned there to undertake some further enquiries off her own back. Duncan glanced over at Joan, who seemed surprisingly cheerful on the phone to someone. He turned his attention back to the information before him.

"Are we all up to date like, Nick?"

"As well as can be. From what St John found out yesterday speaking with Sean Naylor again, the young man is adamant he does not know Sam Lambert or Mandy Lamb. He has come clean about Wendy Kroy — she is his ex-girlfriend. They were effectively working as a 'team' at the shop, syphoning goods out of the stores, claiming they were either damaged or faulty."

"What about his whereabouts for the dates in question?"

The Sergeant could glean from Cavanagh's constant queries she was eager to make the case progress.

"His explanations are vague at best. No concrete alibis. He's definitely still a suspect."

Nick looked at the Scouser, somewhat concerned. He couldn't tell if this was all too much for his friend, or did she have the bit firmly between her teeth, continuing to catch the killer for Rachel.

"Are you sure you're all right with all of this? Coming into work?"

"Oh, yeah. I want to be here. I want to help."

"You don't have to, you know."

He took her hand, giving it a comforting squeeze.

"I know. Please don't worry, I'm fine. Besides, I'm seeing a friend later. That'll cheer me up."

"Who's that? Do I know them?"

Cavanagh went quiet, smiling awkwardly.

"Oh, it's a bloke!"

"Yes, it's a male friend, Detective Duncan!"

Nick leaned towards his friend, whispering in her ear.

"I've got a date too!"

"Ooo! Now let me see, who could that be with?"

Joan pulled a deliberate over-dramatic thoughtful face, placing her index finger on her chin.

"Wouldn't you rather spend sometime at home, after, you know..."

The Constable screwed her pretty little face up, shaking her head.

"Nah! That's going to just make me feel worse. And I'm sure Rachel wouldn't want me to mope about feeling sorry for myself."

Duncan nodded enthusiastically in agreement. He felt Rachel would want that as well, wherever she was now.

"What have we got, Peoples?" Edwards emerged from his own office, glancing around the noticeboard.

"Well, there's St John's report from his visit to see Naylor yesterday."

Nick began to point out the new information he had on the Incident Desk.

"Oh, yes. I read that earlier. He's still very much Prime Suspect in the chief Inspector's opinion. Especially as having no real alibi for his whereabouts."

"Haven't we got enough to charge him, Guv? Surely something will stick."

"Sorry Cilla. The Director of Public Prosecutions would throw it out, insufficient evidence."

Cavanagh's face echoed the disappointment she felt inside.

Abruptly, the office door burst open and in strode St John with Ruby in tow. He held aloft a report which Duncan recognised straight off — post mortem.

"Here yous is — the latest from Dr Tyler."

Nick watched Joan carefully, expecting her strong façade to crumble, but credit to the Liverpudlian, it did not. Cavanagh was one of the first of the detective team to browse through Dr Tyler's findings.

"Well, that confirms what we already suspected, Rachel was murdered the same way as the others."

"Guv, when we collected Rachel's car from the Swanswell, we happened on a few photographs of interest."

Duncan spread them across a desk for all to see. He pointed at several of them in turn.

"Arosha Rana, Wendy Kroy, Zhen Wheng and Sam Lambert."

"So, it's a possibility all of them knew each other."

"Yes, Guv."

Edwards, St John and Ruby studied the images intensely.

"Such a crying shame, all of these young people having their lives cut short."

Ruby shook her head in disbelief at the waste of life.

"However, the one thing I've spotted is…"

Nick pointed at someone in the background of the two images.

"Alison McLeod, the theatre choreographer."

The Inspector picked up the photos, giving them his full

attention.

"Could just be one of those things. We're all free to visit whichever pub we like, when we like."

Duncan became crest-fallen at the Guv'nor's words. He really believed it might be something.

"But then again Nick, it could be useful. Maybe she saw something that could help us."

Cavanagh groaned.

"Are you all right, Cilla?"

"Yes, Guv. Fine. Just yet another visit to the theatre now on the cards."

Edwards patted her on the shoulder rather patronisingly.

"It would appear so."

The office door burst open once again, this time signalling the arrival of Chief Inspector Spencer.

"Morning Each! What's the state of play?"

"Morning Sir," the group of detectives returned the DCI's greeting.

"Morning Tom. Well, still no further forward. Naylor claims he was elsewhere on the dates the deceased were killed, but has no real alibi."

Spencer nodded as he listened.

"Well, at least that's something to work with. The media are hounding us for further details, including some of the international press. The Super and myself will issue a statement to them on the steps outside of the station this afternoon."

"Sir, will we be announcing it was a police officer found murdered yesterday?"

"No, Miss Cavanagh. Not at the moment. Imagine the response from the general public? They'd think if we can't even

protect ourselves, how can we protect them?"

Joan nodded she understood. Nick watched her approach the noticeboard, gazing at the photo of Rachel. It was the 'stock' image they held of all officers, attired in full uniform. Rachel appeared so happy and full of glee in the picture, smiling broadly at the camera.

"Also, Albert, Rachel's family will be coming in. Could you speak with them, please?"

Edwards pulled a face that clearly said he'd rather not, but knew he had to.

"All right Tom. I'll see them downstairs in one of the nicer interview rooms."

"Very good! Might be a good idea to take the FLO with you." Spencer gestured to Ruby. The WPC smiled, nodding.

"OK Sir."

"Guv, Sir, may I come along too?"

Cavanagh spoke up, exceedingly eager to be included. Edwards sighed slightly, smiling at the Scouse Detective softly.

"Joan, maybe it would be better if you see Rachel's folks at home. I'm sure your other housemate could do with the moral support right now, as well."

The Merseysider flashed a brief smile, nodding her head.

"Nick, could you take Miss Cavanagh home, please."

Joan seemed shocked.

"What about speaking with Alison McLeod again, Guv?"

The Guv'nor chuckled.

"I thought you were sick of the sight of her! They'll be no harm in Sebastian visiting her to ask a few questions."

Duncan picked up his coat with a deflated look, gesturing Cavanagh towards the door.

"I've never been in here before."

Joan gazed out of the window of the Bridge Restaurant, over-looking the grassy public square of Broadgate in the centre of the city. Buses painted maroon and cream came and went, parking around the edge of the square that was Broadgate. Nick scanned the scene too. The Lady Godiva statue in the middle of the well-kept lawn needed a thorough wash in his opinion. The most famous woman who originated from Coventry sat naked on her horse, riding side-saddle covered in bird-droppings.

"Yeah, it's quite nice. My Mum always used to bring me here when I was down in the dumps as a child."

From her vantage point, Cavanagh watched the shoppers come-and-go, moving from store-to-store at the top of the Precinct.

"I used to love watch the traffic circulate the grassy island. The cars and buses seem so small from up here, like toys."

"Did she really ride naked through the streets of the city, like?"

"Who?"

"Her on the horse."

"Legend has it, yes she did. As a bet with her husband the Earl of Leofric. If she did, he said he'd lower taxes or the rent for the people of Coventry, I can't remember which exactly."

"I dread to think what she would have had to have done if she lost the bet!"

Duncan nearly choked on his milky coffee, as he laughed at the same time as he took a large swig out of the glass cup. Snatching a linen napkin from the table, he mopped the beige froth from his nostrils. Glancing up, he caught the Constable trying her best to supress much hilarity behind her hands placed over her own mouth. It was good to see her laugh. There was an infectious electricity that danced in her eyes when she did, that made you want to join in too.

"So, who's this bloke you're out on a date with tonight?" Joan picked up her teaspoon, and stirred her drink. A daft smirk gradually spread across her face, like the second hand on a clock steadily sweeping around.

"You don't know him. But he's really nice."

"Is he better looking than me?"

Joan laughed out loud now. So much so, other diners gazed over at her wondering what all the fuss was about.

"That's not that difficult, really."

"Why you cheeky…"

Duncan threw his napkin at her, to which she threw it straight back.

"Where's he taking you? Hopefully not just a local working men's club for bingo and the offal raffle."

Cavanagh tittered further, receiving more disapproving looks from nearby tables.

"No, were going to the Old Hall over in Keresley for a drink."

"Oooo! Hark at you, very swish. I haven't been there in ages."

The Detective became aware of someone standing next to him. Glancing upwards, he found one of the waitresses loitering.

"Er, I'm sorry, Sir, but we've had a few complaints about the noise and rowdy behaviour. If you don't mind, could you and your wife keep it down a bit, please. It's disturbing the

other diners. I don't want to have to call the police or anything."

Unable to help himself, Nick reached inside his jacket, and withdrew his warrant card. Flicking it open, he thrust it towards the young woman.

"We are the police!"

The waitress sculked away, tail firmly between her legs. Joan giggled even more.

"I think you enjoyed that!"

"Too bleeding right! Drink up, I'll take you home so you can shave your moustache off for tonight—"

Duncan hadn't even finished his sentence, when a cloth napkin hit him in the face.

Nick returned to the office around an hour later, avoiding the scrum of reporters and photographers on the street hassling the Super and DCI. With the room effectively to himself, he browsed through the information they'd collected, gazing at the noticeboard repeatedly to follow the chain of information and how the five people were linked in different ways. He knew the answer was here, amongst all of this plethora of data, somewhere hiding within the items recovered and photographs borrowed. If he concentrated enough, put the pieces of this conundrum together, he'd find the killer.

Losing a colleague had hit home hard, and while he'd tried to comfort Joan as she lived with Rachel, no copper ever wants to see one of their own, fall.

"I thought yous had gone home, Golden Bollocks."

Nick looked up to see St John enter the room.

"No, not yet Sebastian. I wanted to see if there's anything I've missed. How did you get on at the theatre?"

"She wasnae there."

"Alison wasn't there?"

Duncan's sharp sense of observation piqued, as he noticed the cigarette Sebastian was savouring. St John began to become uneasy, as his colleague stared at him.

"Wassa matter, Nick?"

"That cigarette you're smoking — it's a Marlboro Longhorn. Where did you get it?"

The Scotsman held the tobacco between his fingers, staring at it.

"Where did you get it, Sebastian? You normally smoke Woodbines. I've worked with you long enough to know they're your favourite brand."

"Jesus! Whadda yer questioning me fa?"

"Sorry."

Nick toned down his enthusiasm by several notches.

"I've found cigarette butts of that brand at some of the crime scenes."

"Oh, aye I see. Not many folk smoke these."

St John took repeated fast tokes on the cigarette, after which he stubbed it out in the ashtray on his desk.

"That huge laddie at da theatre gave it me."

Duncan paused, running what Sebastian was saying through his head. "Huge laddie…" It dawned on him who the Scotsman was referring to.

"You've met Oliver Richmond, I presume."

"Aye, built like a bus. I wudna wanna meet him up a wynd on a dark night! He said the lassie wudnae be back till Monday."

Nick began to consider this, waiting till Monday for some extra information that could prove crucial.

"Can't we get a contact address or phone number off the theatre manager? He seemed quite helpful when I met him."

"I'll try again in the morning. He might be there."

The Scottish Sergeant opened a drawer in his desk, producing a packet of Woodbines. St John selected one for himself, and offered the packet to Duncan. He took one, watching Sebastian take a lighter from his pocket and light his cigarette before offering it to him. Nick noticed Sebastian's hands, he couldn't help but not do so. They were quite grubby considering all he'd done was drove to the theatre and back.

"Wass wrong with yous now?"

"Oh, sorry Sebastian. I was puzzled by the muck all over your hands."

Holding the Woodbine firmly between his lips, the Glaswegian turned his hands over this way and that.

"Soz, Mutha! I was only helping that Big oaf with his daft, old van. He could barely hold the front end up as he tried to put some oil in the engine!"

"Sorry, mate."

Duncan sighed. Placing the Woodbine on the edge of another ashtray, he rubbed his hands over his face, and began massaging his eyes.

"I think the last couple of weeks are catching up on me."

"Go home, Nick. Get changed, go out, get pissed."

Duncan chuckled.

"Yeah, I might just do that."

He slid into his coat, quickly tidying up his desk. On Cavanagh's desk, he noticed she'd left her notebook and pocket diary. *"She really must be away with the fairies to have forgotten them. Luckily, she won't need them again till the morning,"* he reflected to himself.

"See you in the morning, Sebastian."
"Aye, get yer sen outta here!"

Nick stood in front of the mirror affixed to his wardrobe door, taking in the refection of himself wearing just a white shirt, and his underwear. He sang along to the music echoing through the house. Buddy Holly hic-cupped his way through *'Rave On'*, with vocal assistance from the detective himself. The only dilemma he faced tonight was what to wear. 'Smart' went without saying, but not too 'smart'. There wasn't need for the 'killer' suit. Opening the wardrobe, he selected something more subtle. Easing himself into a tailored ensemble, he went to select a matching tie, but stopped. No. Not a tie tonight. That would take just enough off the image not to be fully formal, but still sharp enough not to look out of place in a cocktail bar. Re-attaching his Polerouter, he perused his aftershave collection, before selecting his favourite and usual fragrance. Checking himself out in the mirror one final time, he was happy with what he could see.

Barely making it half way down the stairs, there were a series of knocks at the door. Nick hurdled the remaining steps to reach the door in one single bound. He couldn't open the front door fast enough.

"Hello Stranger!"

Harvey smiled as Nick greeted him, giving his host a wolf whistle as he gave him the once over.

"Hark at you!"

As the barrister stepped into the hall, Duncan couldn't contain himself, grabbing Harvey pulling him close.

"Why Sergeant, it's so sudden!"
"Shut up and give us a kiss!"

The two men embraced, locking lips and smooched. Harvey threw his arms around Nick's neck, beginning to run his fingers through his hair. Duncan responded, slowly moving his hands from the solicitor's waist, inside his jacket and up his back, hauling him yet closer. Their tryst became more intimate and sensual. Surprising the policeman, Harvey forcibly pulled Nick's jacket open and pushed it over his upper arms partially disabling him. The barrister proceeded to push the detective against the wall, nearly knocking the life-size print of Buddy Holly off the wall. They kissed each other as though it had been years since they had last performed the action. Catching his breath as Harvey paused during his passionate attack, Nick managed to speak.

"How about we have that date before we end up naked on the rug in front of the fire?"

Each stared into the other's eyes breathlessly, the air crackling with sexual static.

"Yes Nicholas, good idea."

Duncan re-adjusted his jacket after his partial de-bagging.

"I never realised you went to boarding school..."

The solicitor chuckled.

"Er, yes I did, actually. How did you know that?"

Nick fluffed the lapels of his jacket several times, winking at his guest. Harvey smirked.

"Right, shall we venture to our place of choice?"

"Oooo! Yes, please! Do Daimler's have a signature drink, like Ruy's Bar at the Leofric?"

Gazing into the face height mirror next to the front door, the policeman made certain his hair was just so.

"To be completely honest, I haven't a clue. It's just opened. They may only allow hotel residents in for now."

"Well, we can always go back to the Leofric if that's the case." The solicitor gave him a satisfied smirk.

"Come on, Sergeant. I'll drive."

"Why, don't you want me plying you with strong alcoholic beverages or something, Mr Wiseman?"

"That would be fantastic Nick, but a) I'm driving, b) I've got that legal shin-dig tomorrow, and c) ..."

Harvey took a step towards his beau, placing his hands upon Duncan's shoulders, he whispered into the detective's ear.

"You don't need to get me squiffy to get me into bed."

Nick threw his arms around the barrister, planting a smacker on his lips. So intense was the kiss, Duncan was expecting his beau was going to collapse or tumble, as he could feel the solicitor go all weak at the knees momentarily. Harvey sighed in pleasure.

"Shall we go on this date, before we do end up on that rug?" The detective chuckled, nodding.

"Yeah. We'd best."

A few moments later, the two men were heading into the city centre, Harvey's swish Humber Imperial effortlessly gliding along the road.

"I could get used to this."

Nick made himself comfortable in the leather-clad front passenger seat.

"You'll be the first Detective Sergeant in the history of British Policing to be chauffeur driven."

Duncan tittered at the ridiculousness of the suggestion.

"You know, I can't decide which is more luxurious — this Humber or my Alvis."

Harvey pulling a face that said he'd struggle to find an

answer to that himself.

"So how's work, Sergeant?"

Nick sighed.

"Do we have to talk 'shop', Harvey?"

The barrister giggled as he drove along. Duncan couldn't keep his eyes off the solicitor, and it appeared Harvey felt the same. The two men gazed at one another, smiling.

"Harvey! Look out!"

As they exited the ring road behind the Pool Meadow Bus Station, the brief abruptly performed a severe emergency stop to prevent a certain collision. So harsh was Harvey's braking, it stalled the engine. The big Humber skidded to a halt, throwing Duncan forwards into the walnut veneered dashboard. The solicitor hit the horn, as the offending vehicle that caused him to stop so harshly vanished up onto the elevated ring road and into the night.

"What a complete tool!"

Harvey started to curse the other driver, before turning to Nick.

"Are you all right?"

"Yeah, I'm fine. Good reflexes you have there, well done!"

"I'm sorry. It was that prat in the Triumph Herald estate who thinks he owns the road."

The policeman rubbed his left shoulder. Groaning slightly.

"That wasn't a Triumph Herald estate, Harvey. It was a Triumph Courier van."

The pain in Duncan's shoulder vanished faster than how it had appeared in the first place. The sergeant froze momentarily, as he had an epiphany. Everything in the case, the information they had collected, everything fell into place. He knew who was responsible. It all made sense. Nick reached over to Harvey, giving him a huge kiss full on the mouth.

"I know who's done it!"

"Done what?"

"The murders. I know who's responsible."

"Really? Just now, just like that."

"It's really hard to explain..."

A car behind them blasted its horn, eager for them to move.

"I've got to get back to the station. Right now."

"Seriously?"

"Yes. Quickly, Harvey. Please!"

The solicitor sighed heavily, restarted the engine and drove the short distance to Little Park Street.

Arriving at the station, Nick was out of the car, into the building and up the stairs, before the barrister had chance to apply the handbrake and turn the engine off. Once in the CID office, Duncan began to rummage through paperwork on the Incident Desk. He heard the door creak on its spring-loaded hinge and close softly. A man's methodical footsteps strolled in his direction.

"Nick, what's going on? How come you say you know who's behind all of these murders?"

The Detective did not respond, as he continued to search for what he was looking for. Then, he found it.

"This statement was made by the nightwatchman at Coombe Abbey. He saw an estate car leave the park the night Wendy Kroy's body was dumped in the children's play area. He said he saw the reflection of an estate car in the side of a parked coach. He wasn't sure of the make or model, although he did recall seeing the side window full of something inside, same colour as the car."

"I don't follow, Nick. How's that relevant?"

Rapidly, Duncan raced across the office to a bookcase, retrieved a thick, bound encyclopaedic-style publication. He slammed it down on a desk, beginning to leaf through. Finding the desired page, he stopped.

"Here! The Triumph Herald Estate, manufactured from 1961 to 1971."

Harvey studied the images and details of the car, still full of bafflement and confusion. The sergeant leafed through to another page in the book, showing a near identical vehicle.

"The Triumph Courier Van, manufactured from 1962 to 1966. Spot the difference?"

The brief examined the different images for a few moments.

"They're identical, except for the van has its side rear windows filled in."

"Exactly! Most people would not really notice any difference, like you didn't earlier when that van cut you up. An ambulance crew saw a car near the scene that night — a car! Not a van. In the dark, a Triumph Courier looks like a Herald Estate!"

Nick read the nightwatchman's statement again.

"He even said the estate car leaving had its number plate in the middle of the rear, and pointy tail lights. Look at the pictures!"

Duncan pointed at the page within the book. Harvey nodded.

"And I know who owns a Triumph Courier, a certain Oliver Richmond who works at the theatre."

"So would he have had chance to come into contact with the deceased?"

"Yes! Definitely! Well, except one. However, Alison McLeod has some weird sort of friendship with Richmond, and she can be placed at the Swanswell Tavern where one of the victim's cars were found. So it's possible they operate as a pair. It would've needed two people to put Wendy Kroy's body in that small tunnel."

Nick pointed at the photographs on the noticeboard.

"Nice pic of my client there — Sean Naylor."

Duncan gave Harvey a glance that clearly said that doesn't matter at the moment. He quickly found the photos he had borrowed off Wilton Anderson, showing them to the solicitor.

"There! That's this Alison McLeod I mentioned."

Suddenly, the Detective noticed something in the picture he hadn't before. Dashing over to his own desk, he delved through the drawers, finding a magnifying glass.

"Well, bugger me! If it isn't the man in question himself!"

In the reflection of one of the mirrors behind the bar, the detective could make out Oliver Richmond.

"Several of the deceased had branded boxes of matches on them from this pub, plus the fifth victim was seen leaving with him! That puts everyone in the same place! Plus, Alison and Oliver smoke the same brand of cigarettes — we have found butt ends at several of the deposit scenes."

The solicitor nodded, listening to what the policeman was explaining.

"Nick, it's all quite incriminating what you're saying, but from a legal angle it's all circumstantial at best. The Director of Public Prosecutions will throw it out. You're going to need something much more substantial."

"It's Richmond! I know it, Harvey. He's chatting these women up, then murdering them. A drag artist in one case, but *perhaps that's why he was killed."*

"He's accosting young women? Hardly original modus operandi."

From out of nowhere, Duncan had the most terrible feeling wash over him, soaking right through into his core. It showed visually too.

"Are you all right? You look like you've seen a ghost."

"I've just thought of something awful. Please, let me be wrong this time."

Nick started to pace around the office, putting his head in his hands.

"What?"

"My partner, Joan Cavanagh, she was extremely receptive of Richmond's advances when we visited the theatre several times through our enquiries."

"Oh, yeah! I know Joan, she was questioning my client, Sean Naylor the other day. Has she met up with this Oliver yet?"

"Well, I know she's seeing a male friend tonight, but she was rather cagey and reluctant to tell me any more."

"So maybe it isn't Richmond she's meeting tonight. You're worrying over nothing."

Duncan cast his mind back to when they visited the theatre on Tuesday.

The big man leaned towards Duncan, offering him a light from a chrome lighter. As he flicked the top open igniting a flame straight off, Nick took along, deep draw on the tobacco as it started to burn. He pulled a slight face as he exhaled, the flavour of the smoke was quite different to his own regular, favourite brand.

411

"They're American."

Duncan glanced at Oliver as he lit a cigarette for himself. Taking the tobacco from his lips, the sergeant gazed down at the thin, white stick between his finger and thumb. The brown filter had a gold stripe around it just before the white paper that encased the loose tobacco. Stamped on the paper close to the gold stripe on the filter in the company's own unique font was its manufacturer — Marlboro.

Oliver turned to Joan, offering her the open chrome cigarette case. The scouser shook her head with a polite smile.

"No, ta. I don't."

"I shouldn't, really. Need a reason to give up."

Once again, he winked at the constable.

"I don't need a reason!"

Alison took a cigarette uninvited from Oliver's case, lighting it herself. Nick watched her give Joan an incredibly black look, as the Merseysider shared silent sweet nothings with the pianist.

"Right, thank you both for your time and assistance. If anything else comes to mind as regards the two women, please don't hesitate to give us a call or pass a message on through Mr Sparkes."

Nick stepped forward and shook Alison's hand. The choreographer nodded, a brief smile flashed across her face.

"Of course! You'll be the first to know, Detective."

Duncan began to walk back to where he had made his way onto the stage. If was only after half a dozen steps he realised Joan was not alongside him. Glancing back over his shoulder, he found the constable still batting her eyelashes at Oliver, giving him a soppy wave as she departed, and a hand gesture of a phone receiver placed next to her ear. Cavanagh became aware with a jolt the sergeant was not just waiting for her, but watching her as well.

"What?"

Nick suddenly noticed Joan's notebook and pocket diary on her desk. He leapt across the office, his mental state of panic quite clear as he knocked chairs out of his way. Seizing the diary, he clumsily leafed through to today's page. He read what he saw out loud.

"7.30, O."

Harvey looked equally as puzzled as Duncan.

"What's that meant to mean?"

Once again, the policeman ignored the question aimed at him, continuing along his train of thought.

"I've seen that somewhere before."

"What? That sort of reminder?"

"Yeah! Now where was it?"

The Detective sprinted back over to the Incident Desk, beginning to scour through the personal diaries of some of the deceased.

"There! Sam Lambert put the same in his diary — '7.30, O'."

"Now, that is a coincidence!"

"Sure is — huge."

Glancing up at the noticeboard, Duncan noticed a photo of the personal effects of Rachel, laid out in a tidy row. Her notebook having been left open at its final entry.

"Look! There it is again — the same note! I tell you Harvey, it's Richmond!"

"I hate to piddle on your bonfire, but it's still circumstantial at best."

"I've got this really nasty feeling about Joan — she's in danger."

Picking up her diary up again, he read the entry again and again, contemplating.

"Of course, The Old Hall!"

"What about it? An over-priced restaurant and so-so cocktail bar in Keresley."

"She was going there on a date with this mystery bloke. She's on a date with him! I know it!"

"Well, the question is, were they meeting there at 7.30, or was he picking her up at 7.30?"

He pulled back his left cuff and read the time on his Polerouter. It said it was just after 9pm.

"Come on! Hopefully we're not too late. We've got to find her. I've already lost one colleague this week."

"Eh? A copper has died?"

Duncan leaned towards the noticeboard, stabbing the image of Rachel in full uniform with his index finger.

"Oh My God! I never knew! I'm so sorry, Nick."

"Yeah, there's a media blackout. No one outside the station or Rachel's family knows we've lost one of our own."

The solicitor put his hands over his mouth in distress and shock. Nick watched as he stared at the photograph of Rachel.

"Come on, we need to find Joan!"

The Detective pulled Harvey out of the office, down the stairs, and outside into the car park.

"Keys! I'll drive. Please…"

The brief tossed them to the policeman, who jumped behind the wheel of the Humber and fired up the engine. Harvey had barely climbed into his own car, before Nick had them under way, traversing the city. Duncan once again proved he was no slouch behind the wheel.

"Crikey, Nick! I don't think she's ever been driven this way before!"

Duncan maintained his focus on the road ahead.

"Can't this thing go any faster?"

Beginning to become quite concerned, Harvey buckled his seat belt up. The brief gazed out at the scenery streaking past, negotiating traffic islands with scant regard for the Highway Code, jumping several red lights as though they didn't exist. Seconds later, the policeman flicked the steering wheel into the Old Hall car park. The large motor slid to a halt across the gravel surface, as Nick hit the brakes with more purpose than ever before. The dust cloud he'd caused was still airborne when he leapt from the car, and began briskly walking around all of the parked vehicles.

Seeing what he thought was the van rocking to and fro, he dashed over. But he'd fallen foul of the exact thing Harvey had — it was a Herald Estate with courting couple inside who he'd now disturbed. Waving a meek apology as the occupants swore at the him, the Detective moved on.

"Can you see a Triumph Courier van?"

Harvey joined in with the search, strolling this way and that.

"No, Nick. Not one of those."

Duncan cantered around the amassed cars again. *"Maybe they've arrived in Cavanagh's car,"* he considered. The image of Rachel's Triumph convertible parked all alone at the

Swanswell burst into his mind.

"Harvey! Look out for a scarlet Singer Chamois. They might be in Joan's car."

The barrister nodded, walking around the car park once more. Reluctantly, the policeman had to concede defeat — neither of the vehicles they were seeking were here.

Back inside the Humber, Duncan stared into space. He felt he had failed. Furious with himself, he fought back tears. Heaven knows what could be happening to her, and when she needed help, he was nowhere to be found. He continued to torture himself. Harvey placed his hand on Nick's shoulder, squeezing slightly, trying to comfort him.

"Nick, we've done all we can."

He sighed, bowed his head in dejection. Starting the engine, he carefully turned the big car around, edging back towards the road.

"I'll never forgive myself if something has happened to her. I should've seen these connections days ago, before Rachel was killed in fact!"

Switching the headlights onto full beam as he began to turn back towards the city centre, something caught Duncan's attention on the road. Braking hard again, he jumped out, and crouched in front of the Humber examining the tarmac.

"Nick, what's the matter now? We've done all we can. I'm sorry if that's hard to accept." The barrister wandered to the policeman's side, crouching down next to him. *"Let's go back to mine. We'll order a takeaway, get a half decent bottle of wine, have a quiet night in."*

Yet again, the detective was mentally elsewhere.

"That Triumph has been here. See these oil spots on the road?"

Harvey sighed again.

"Mate, hundreds of cars leak oil. That's extremely tenuous at best to link it to this Oliver Richmond fellow."

The solicitor hooked his hand under Duncan's arm, attempting to get him to return to the car.

"There were oil drips and a trail on the road at the scene of the first woman we found, some on the road outside the theatre where Richmond parked his van…"

Nick then recalled what St John had said earlier that afternoon in the office.

"Wass wrong with yous now?"

"Oh, sorry Sebastian. I was puzzled by the muck all over your hands."

Holding the Woodbine firmly between his lips, the Glaswegian turned his hands over this way and that.

"Soz, Mutha! I was only helping that Big oaf with his daft, old van. He could barely hold the front end up as he tried to put some oil in the engine!"

Duncan stood up, and began to walk away from the restaurant.

"Look, Harvey! The trail heads away from the city towards Corley!"

The brief could see the splatter on the dry tarmac, but appeared puzzled as to which direction it came, and which way it went to.

"How do you know the vehicle in question hasn't arrived from Corley, then departed towards the city?"

Nick smiled.

"Basic physics. Liquid forms a certain pattern on the ground when expelled from a moving source, thus it's direction

and speed can be determined."

Harvey didn't quite understand this — the expression on his face clearly stating this.

"I'll explain it in more depth another time. But for now, we need to follow those drips."

Driving along the country lane at a speed brisk enough to make progress, but steadily sufficient as to not lose sight of the oil splatter, the two men headed towards Corley. The Humber's bright headlights picked out the shiny droplets, leading them the way onwards. Passing the Horse & Jockey pub, several other road users caught up with them, quickly over-taking. The trail abruptly formed a small puddle, before embarking into a smaller side road.

"I guess he had to wait there, giving way to traffic."

Harvey nodded.

Continuing along, they passed through a thicker, wooded area. The tree canopy made it easier for the car's headlights to make out the trail. The tree cover opened, where the moonlight lit up a T junction where the oil splatter bore right. As Duncan began to steer in that direction, he brought the Humber to a dead stop and killed the lights.

"What have you done that for?"

"Look!"

Nick pointed at what could be seen through the hedge and undergrowth — two stationary cars, both with their lights on.

"That could be anything, Nick."

"Hmmm, I've got a weird feeling it might be 'something'..."

The detective edged the car around the junction, and found exactly what he'd been searching for since he'd left the station — a Triumph Courier van. However, boxing the light commercial vehicle in up against a hedge, was a white Hillman Minx convertible. The driver's door of the white car flew open, to which out stepped a thick-set woman with shoulder length dark hair. As Nick and Harvey slowly rolled closer, the woman strode to the passenger door of the Triumph with much purpose. She wrenched the door open and proceeded to dive inside, grabbing hold of the passenger sitting there. Both men glanced at one another in amazement.

"I think someone has been caught with their pants around their ankles!"

Harvey chuckled, as the van rocked side-to-side due to the struggle obviously happening inside.

"Hang on, I recognise that Hillman! That's Alison McLeod's car! That was parked outside the theatre next to that van."

Duncan had barely finished speaking, when the driver's door of the van opened. A tall, large man forced his way between the van and the hedge it was against, running to the passenger side.

"That's Oliver Richmond!"

Nick couldn't contain himself any longer. He leapt out of the Humber and ran towards the van. As he got closer, he could see Oliver trying to pull Alison away from the individual inside the van.

"Alistair! Leave me alone! I want you as a friend, nothing more! Leave me and this girl alone!"

"Alistair? Odd..." Duncan contemplated. Oliver and Alison continued to struggle as the detective closed in.

"You'll see, Ollie — just like the others!"

The woman swung a punch at the large man, which connected with the side of his jaw. The blow sent Oliver crashing against the side of the van, smashing his head against the bodywork, to which he dropped to the ground in a heap. Alison returned her attention to the interior of the van. Immediately, a young woman could be heard screaming from inside. The vehicle continued to rock and bounce side-to-side.

Reaching the large woman, Nick grabbed hold of her, trying to pull her back out. She lashed out with a leg clad in a knee-height boot, the block heel winding the policeman as it caught him in the ribs. Realising more severe force was necessary, Duncan punched her as hard as he could repeatedly in the kidneys. Recoiling with the impact, Alison stood up.

"I told you Ollie, this will—"

She froze briefly, upon seeing the detective before her, with her precious Ollie unconscious on the road. Glancing quickly into the van Nick saw to his horror the one thing he didn't want to — in a crumpled heap gasping for breath was Joan. She had indeed been on a date with Richmond. The scouser pulled away at her clothes around her neck, trying to make her breathing easier. The constable stared at the sergeant with such a pleased and grateful air, it touched Duncan to centre of his being.

Seizing the initiative, Alison threw her hands around Nick's throat before he had chance to fight her off. She pinned him against the roof of the van, continuing to squeeze and maul his throat. Instinctively, the detective grabbed at the large hands attempting to prise them off. He instantly understood now how those other five people died. They stood no chance, Alison's hands contained so much power and strength. Duncan squirmed, coughed and gasped. He was gradually losing consciousness. He attempted a couple of punches at her head, but his strength was rapidly vanishing. He tried yet again to

420

pull the woman's hands from his neck, but she just squeezed even tighter.

Someone appeared out of the darkness and leapt on Alison's back, trying to pull her off the policeman. Keeping Nick pinned down, she took one hand off him, and swung an elbow at the person behind her. As it connected with the face of the individual, Duncan heard Harvey recoil in agony — the solicitor had tried to rescue his friend. In the corner of his eye, Nick could see the brief had dropped to his knees in pain, to which Alison returned both hands to him.

Duncan ventured to swing a right hook at her, but he found he had no real energy left to exert such a task. His fist barely lifting from his side.

"Sorry Detective, but you shouldn't stick your nose in where it's not needed."

Pathetically, he tried to throw one final punch, but his hand slid into the pocket of his overcoat.

In this most unlikely of circumstances, Duncan's fingertips found in his pocket what he'd been searching for in what felt like an absolute age — his chrome Zippo cigarette lighter. An idea leapt into his straight away. He clutched the metal lighter, and withdrew it from his pocket. Flicking open the top, he spun the strike wheel. A bright yellow flame erupted, illuminating the darkness. The policeman could see it in the corner of his eye. It caught Alison's attention as well, she slightly released her grip on him.

Nick took this as a cue, it could well be the distraction that could save his life — he pushed the lighter into her face. Alison baulked, releasing her hold of the detective. He continued to push the lighter at her, to which without warning her hair ignited. It caught fire. Within seconds, all of the fringe and entire headband were up in flames. Screaming in terror, she began to pat herself vigorously to extinguish the fire. Proving unsuccessful, she grabbed her hair at the back of her head, removing it in one piece and threw it onto the ground. It was a wig!

As Duncan stood up rubbing his throat, he gazed at her stamping the small blaze out. *"So that's why Richmond called her 'Alistair'!"* As his breathing began to return to normal, the sergeant could clearly see 'Alison' was actually 'Alistair' — a man, a crossdresser, another transvestite! *"No wonder 'she' had so much strength in that grip!"*

As Nick stood up straight, Alistair returned his attention to the detective. Before the crossdresser had chance to try anything, Duncan lashed out at him, landing a roundhouse series of punches to the face, followed by a hefty blow to the stomach. Alistair dropped to his knees in agony. Completely winded, the detective hit him one last time with a huge upper cut, putting Alistair on his back and knocking him out cold. He shook his right hand instantaneously after landing the final blow, tucking it under his left arm. It felt like an explosion had torn through his fist, sending a bolt of lightning up his arm. Nick shouted out in distress. It hurt so much, more than when he was being strangled a few moments ago. He took several deep breaths, fighting the rising nausea it caused.

"Nick, are you all right?"

Cavanagh climbed out of the van, gasping and croaking for breath, barely able to speak, still clasping at her throat.

"Yeah, I'm fine. I think I've just broken my hand."

The policeman unexpectedly felt a hand take his damaged fist.

"I think you've broken a couple of your knuckles."

Harvey gently stroked Duncan's smashed up digits. Nick could see in the moonlight the solicitor was not free from injury himself, as he suffered a blooded nose and a split top lip.

"That'll be a bit of a talking point at your legal benefit dinner tomorrow!"

He reached out, gently caressing Harvey's face.

"Hmmm, tell me about it!"

Duncan glanced in turn at his two friends, and chuckled.

"I would've liked you two to have met under better circumstances, and I know you've both already met briefly in a professional capacity the other day, but Harvey — this is my partner, Detective Constable Joan Cavanagh. Joan — this is Harvey Wiseman, my partner."

Harvey beamed at the introduction, getting carried away stroking Nick's hand.

"Oow! Careful!"

"Sorry."

Nick began to rummage in a couple of his pockets with his left hand.

"Are you looking for your fags?"

Joan croaked and scraped.

"No, these."

The Sergeant held aloft a pair of steel handcuffs.

"Do you always carry those with you?"

The barrister gestured appalled at the restraints.

"Only on first date."

Nick winked at Harvey in the near darkness.

"Help me cuff these two to the car. We best get uniform here and an ambulance."

As Duncan hooked the handcuffs through the chrome

423

door handle, he happened to glance inside the Hillman. He noticed what initially appeared to be four scrunched up black rags in the centre console, next to the gearstick. They looked like the type of thing a driver would use to wipe condensation off the windscreen, but there was something not right about them. Reaching over and selecting one, Nick found they weren't rags at all, they were ladies' black tights.

"The bastard! He was keeping trophies!"

EPILOGUE
WHITSUNDAY
SUNDAY MAY 27th 1973

Despite it being a warm, late Spring day, there was a pronounced chill inside the cavernous cathedral. The occasion did not help. While it was to give thanks, the congregation's mood was sombre and reflective.

"Let us give thanks for having these remarkable people touch our lives, enriching our time here on Earth for the better. Their value, worth and kindness will never be forgotten."

The Bishop of Coventry's words echoed around the interior of the vast building, as he addressed all from his lectern. Nick glanced around those gathered, noticing the mix of grieving relatives, national and local politicians, Police, press and general public. He had heard Her Majesty and the Chinese Embassy had sent representatives as well. He eyed the TV cameras at the sides of the mass pensively.

The Detective scanned down the order of service he held between his fingers of his right hand, still in the cast that was fitted to his fist several weeks ago. Large pictures of the five people who had been murdered around Easter were placed in front of the altar. They showed them cheerful and enjoying life, not a care in the world.

"Quite a cute guy."

Harvey whispered to Nick, pointing at the image of Sam

Lambert on the order of service.

"Amazing voice too. Such a waste of potential."

The solicitor took the itinerary off the sergeant, gently squeezing his fingers that protruded from the cast. The two men gazed at each other and smiled.

"You look gorgeous in that uniform."

"Really?"

Nick gave himself the once over. Wearing full dark blue dress uniform, Police Sergeant regalia on his sleeves, a Naval C.G.M ribbon over his heart and his cap on his lap, he surmised he didn't look too shabby. It had taken forever to make the buttons on the front of the tunic shine like they did, all the more difficult with his right hand partially incapacitated. And as for the chrome numbers on his epaulettes showing his collar number, luckily Cavanagh obliged.

"You know you look hot. I'd do you."

Harvey winked at his partner, to which Duncan replied with a saucy smirk.

The Sergeant started to feel a hand trying to take his left one. Glancing down, he saw the manicured fingertips with baby pink nail polish slide between his fingers, and squeezed his hand slightly. As he looked up, he gazed straight at Joan. The Constable's face was a picture of sadness. It was clear she was fighting the urge to cry as well. Nick smiled at her, squeezing her hand a few times in reassurance.

"And now ladies and gentleman, distinguished guests, a few words from Superintendent Frederick Franklin to bring this service to a close."

The congregation applauded politely as his Excellency left the stand, to be replaced by the senior policeman.

"Thank you, ladies and gentlemen. May I first echo the

words of His Excellency, the Bishop of Coventry. We should celebrate those we have lost, not mourn them being taken from us. I wasn't blessed in meeting any of the five people we remember today, but from the number of you attending this memorial service, I can see they were held dear, loved and meant the world to each of you. I'd rather be talking to you under more jovial and pleasant circumstances, and wish something of a more cheerful nature had led to the World's press descending upon the city. I'd like to pay special thanks to my detective team who found and apprehended the perpetrators of these horrible events, who were attacked and injured themselves in the process."

Nick and Joan glanced at one another. He couldn't help but stare at Cavanagh's neck. A white, sterile dressing was clearly visible under the collar of her blouse, behind her Sillitoe tartan cravat. He suddenly became aware of the Scouse Detective gazing at his right hand encased in its plaster cast, his fingers still entwined with Harvey's.

"Those responsible now arrested, will face the full might of our justice system. These people have no place in Society, and they will be made an example of. Unfortunately, those lost will never be coming home, but they will never be forgotten. On behalf of everyone, thank you for attending."

A huge, prolonged round of applause ensued. Unable to join in normally, Nick slapped his left hand onto his thigh, much to Harvey and Joan's amusement.

The Bank Holiday weekend weather had been kind on this occasion, as the congregation emptied out of the cathedral onto St Michael's Avenue, the walkway that separated the old and new cathedrals. People gathered together to chat, the air and atmosphere of the day starting to brighten and lift. Well, almost…

"WDC Cavanagh…"

"Guv?"

"Next time you're required to wear full dress regulation uniform, I want to see you in official constabulary footwear!"

Nick, Harvey and Sebastian glanced down at Joan's feet. She was wearing the correct uniform of a WPC, complete with bowler hat, her hair even styled into a bun on the back of her head. But it was clear Edwards had an issue with her choice of shoes — black patent heels.

"Yes, Guv."

Cavanagh rolled her eyes, not enjoying another flea in her ear. Duncan stifled his laughter, trying to hide his grin behind his plaster cast encased hand.

"I doubt it very much if you pounded the beat around the docks on the Mersey wearing those!"

"No, Guv."

Nick eventually had to turn away. He didn't want Joan to catch him giggling.

Straight away he caught sight of Patricia Bayliss a couple of dozen yards away or so. The Welsh barrister smiled at Nick, pointing at Harvey and elaborately 'mouthing' his name. Duncan beamed a huge grin back, nodded repeatedly and gave an odd thumbs up with his plaster-encased hand. Patricia smiled back, screwing her face up into a 'Awww, lovely' expression, blowing Nick a kiss. The sergeant reciprocated, but was spotted by St John.

"Blowing a kiss to your boyfriend, Golden Bollocks?"

Nick and Harvey exchanged a few nervous glances before Duncan retorted, speaking in an unnaturally camp voice.

"It was meant for you, Darling," to which Nick blew him a kiss with his injured right hand. *"The way you look in that uniform..."*

"Fuck Off, smart arse! Yous will be frustrated at da moment, unable to use yer right hand!"

"Oh, Sebastian! Fancy coming around to help?"

"Piss Off!"

St John ran his finger around his shirt collar, his discomfort at wearing the dress uniform quite clear for all to see.

"I canna stand dis monkey suit. I was glad to see the back of it after doing the beat back home in Paisley."

Cavanagh chuckled at the Scottish sergeant's whinging, then leaned towards Nick and closely examined the white medal bar with navy blue edges on his chest.

"What have you got that for?"

"A medal the Navy gave me. I'll tell you the story sometime."

Smiling, Nick surveyed the rest of the crowd. He watched the super smoozing with the Lord Mayor and Home Secretary, chuckling at how false and forced their body language was. They all appeared they wanted to be elsewhere, rather than the conversation they were trapped within. Then something — or more correctly someone — caught Duncan's eye. A man attired in a police uniform, which obviously was an extremely common sight at that exact moment, but this man stood out. His uniform was wrong — it didn't fit in with all the other modern constabulary staff. He suddenly became aware the uniform was out of date, it was wartime. The man stared directly at Nick with a huge beaming grin. He then realised who it was. In wide-eyed, open-mouthed wonder he stared straight at his father.

"Dad!"

The Detective pushed through the crowd, trying to get to him. Duncan momentarily lost sight of his parent, as other people moved about obscuring his view. A moment later, he caught sight of the Police Sergeant again.

"Dad, hang on!"

This time Bob Duncan turned, stared straight as his son, winked and saluted him with two fingers from over his right eye — the same salute he himself gave people. Sergeant Duncan Senior began to wander away, as Nick pushed and forced his way through the scrum to get to him. Once again, he lost sight of his father, stuck within the crowd.

"Dad! Wait for me!"

Nick called after his father yet again as he scrambled between the mass of people, but by the time he reached where he last saw him, no one was there. The Detective Sergeant spun around on the spot, extremely puzzled and confused. Had he just imagined seeing his father? Surely, he had, hadn't he...?

"Sergeant Duncan?"

A male voice snapped Nick out of his quandry. Peering over his shoulder, he saw an Indian Sikh gentleman approaching him, waving. Instantly, he recognised Baljinder Rana.

"Sergeant..." Bal hailed the policeman again.

"Mr Rana..."

Bal extended his right hand towards the detective, to which Nick automatically offered his own — encased within its plaster cast! The two men locked finger tips and performed a weird 'hand-shake'. Both chuckled at the ridiculous nature of the physical greeting.

"How long have you got to wear that?" Mr Rana gestured at the cast.

"Oh, only for another week or so. Makes tying my shoe laces a bit of a sod, but I get by."

Bal smiled and laughed.

"I'd just like to say, on behalf of my family and my community, thank you."

"What for, Sir?"

"You kept your promise. You told me you would catch those who took Arosha from us. You have."

"I was only doing my job, Mr Rana."

"Please, it's more than that Sergeant. If this City had more police officers like yourself, it would be a much safer place."

Nick blushed, uncontrollably so.

"I wouldn't go as far as that. I'm just one member of a team. Everyone involved should receive your praise and gratitude."

"You're modest, Mr Duncan. If you'll indulge me, why did they do these things? Why did they kill my Arosha and the other people?"

"It'll become public in the trial in a few months' time anyhow."

Nick paused for a moment, seeing that Bal wished him to continue.

"Not condoning any crime, but these murders were text book crimes of passion. The man Arosha started dating had an ex-partner who wouldn't let him go. They became jealous to such an extent, they would kill."

Mr Rana listened, absorbing what the detective said.

"Thank you, Sergeant. Once again, thanks for all you do."

"Oh, I'll be around. There's plenty to do. Everyday."

NICHOLAS DUNCAN WILL RETURN IN
'NOT FADE AWAY'

Printed in Great Britain
by Amazon

11212642R00253